Threads

Nell Gavin

ISBN 0-7414-0916-X

Published by:

INFINITY
PUBLISHING.COM

Infinity Publishing.com
519 West Lancaster Avenue
Haverford, PA 19041-1413
Info@buybooksontheweb.com
www.buybooksontheweb.com
Toll-free (877) BUY BOOK
Local Phone (610) 520-2500
Fax (610) 519-0261

Printed in the United States of America

Printed on Recycled Paper

Published January, 2002

Acknowledgements

Many thanks to
Dona Carter, Leslie Mort and Gary Leverence
for their support, inspiration
and encouragement.

Also thanks to "Lady Gryph"
for her assistance with dialog.

Most especially,
I would like to dedicate this book
to Patrick, Matthew and Peter.

Foreward

by Nell Gavin, 2001

One of the more surprising aspects of researching a book about Anne Boleyn is discovering the manner in which each reference disagrees with every other reference on some point or another. There is scant verifiable information on her—there is much more speculation—and various biographies take different views on what the same scant information reveals about her. The perspective on some events switches radically again when you read a third book. So, those who have read one of Anne's biographies but not the others, and who question some point or another may find the reference in another book.

I preferred some versions of Anne's story to others. While I read several references and used facts from all of them, I preferred and relied most heavily on the information in "The Six Wives of Henry VIII," by Alison Weir.

I also rejected a good deal of the information credited to Eustace Chapuys, Spanish ambassador during the reign of Henry VIII. His reports to Spain (their content is quoted or referred to in all of the biographies) were filled with condemning propaganda about Anne that probably contained some truth. However, it was most likely largely distorted or untrue because the things Anne is credited with doing (her extensive charities, her defense of free-thinkers and religious heretics, and her courage in submitting to death in order to defend her daughter's crown) are not in sync with the she-devil Chapuys described. Later, he made similar remarks about the were not supported by statements from other witnesses, or even by logic. Unfortunately for Anne Boleyn, it was ill advised for anyone to speak well of her after her death, so much of her history is comprised of the Chapuys reports with little rebuttal from friendlier factions.

When I massaged viewpoints and conclusions out of frustrated necessity, I felt less as though I were manipulating history than striking a plausible compromise between facts that amount to "good guesses" on the part of a number of scholars. Nevertheless, there are a few instances when I knowingly adjusted the timing of an event or rearranged the characters. At these times, I gave greater weight to the plot. But for the most part, the facts are as accurate as I know to make them (given the divergence of opinion), except for Anne's childhood and all of her private thoughts, which remain open to conjecture.

In *"Threads"*, the Anne I offer to you is the one I kept seeing in each of her biographies, whatever facts they presented or how those facts colored her, the Anne who was always described as an "enigma". I think that term applies to anyone who has a difficult personality, but whose character is essentially good.

Most importantly, *"Threads"* is a fantasy. It is not, nor is it intended to be, an historical reference.

Prologue

London

Year of our Lord 1536

I could not see the crowd any longer. Were it not for the sound of an occasional involuntary cough, I might have thought myself alone and dreaming. In the midst of this unnatural stillness, I could sense the thousands of unsympathetic eyes I knew were fixed upon me. I could neither hide from them, nor could I stop myself from visualizing the faces and the stares.

Suddenly, startlingly, a bird flapped its wings and took flight. I imagined all faces were turned toward the sky and all eyes were now fixed upon the bird. For that one moment, all in attendance would have forgotten me and would allow me to quietly slip away before they even noticed I had left them. That fanciful imagery and a final prayer were all the comfort I could give myself.

A voice with a heavy French accent shouted: "Where is my sword?"

Then, in one instant, a hand reached for mine, and a voice gently said "Come," and I followed. Disoriented yet aware, I looked down and saw the crowd, its taste for blood satisfied by the day's entertainment. I thought, "Wait," and saw Henry in my mind and in a flash I was with him for one last moment. He was mounted for the hunt, surrounded by huntsmen and hounds, awaiting the sound of gunshots that would announce my passing. They rang out as I watched and he inwardly flinched, outwardly revealing no emotion at all. He would now race to Jane, would make her his wife in only 10 days' time, and would never speak my name aloud again.

I looked at him and thought, "*Why?*" like a wail, a keening, and could see he was disturbed, though determined not to be. Denying.

I knew he could sense me. It was in his thoughts, and I could read them as if they were spoken aloud. He was agitated and fearful. "*Damn* you, Henry," I thought. He heard me in his mind, and thought he was mad.

Then I turned away from him one final time and floated toward the light and toward memory. Like a rustling, I felt him reach toward me then catch himself. Like a whisper, I heard him say to me, "Damn *you*," but the words were not spoken except in his thoughts, and they carried no conviction in the face of his anxiety.

I sensed there were tears, but his face was stone and tears would not be shed. He would restrain them and hold them within like a cancer, and they would change him and the lives he touched from this day forward. He would never face what he had done. He would do it again and again as if to trivialize the sin. By feeling less next time he could prove it was not sin, for did he not feel righteous? If it were not right, would he not feel shame?

I know this because I know how Henry could twist logic to suit his ends. He could speak for God Himself, he believed, based solely on what he knew to be truth within his heart. He was my husband and I know him to his soul. He was often mistaken.

And so, many more lives would be lost by his decree. It would torment him till the end and he would be guilty, defiant, dictatorial, irrational and dangerous, never realizing that much of it was the denial of grief and conscience. It would be a sad end for a man who, oddly, wanted very much to be a good one.

With concern that was habit more than heartfelt, I absently thought, "He should cry," then left him.

Good-bye.

PART 1

The Memories

Chapter 1

I still have my immortal soul. I had thought myself shorn of it when I first lay with Henry. My love for him now feels as if it were comprised of greater parts misfortune than sin though, and it seems to me that I will not be dashed into a fiery Hell because of it. It seems, in fact, as though I might find peace.

For a while, I do. Peace: The healing time until being prodded to action—a short stop on my way. I linger there as long as I am allowed, but there is business to attend to, and so I move along.

Elsewhere, beyond that, there is to be no time for peace. There is to be time only for memories, and these soon became all-encompassing. I see each moment of my past existence as a surgeon examines a cadaver organ by organ, and I am horrified, then confused, then satisfied by turns.

Death is not as I had expected from hours, months, and years of religious instruction, nor is it the dark and frightening place of lore. There are neither harps nor terrifying images. I sprout neither wings nor horns. It is not as I had imagined, nor is it as I had feared. Yet it is what I had known it to be, deep within me, like words I had once memorized long ago, but forgot till now when I am awakening from a lifetime of unconsciousness.

The first memories that come to me are of my life, the life just past. From birth to death they pass in a rush, but are unblurred as if time is compressed. I see the entire span of my life without recriminations, but also without rationalizations. There is no escape from the things I had done, no opportunity to right wrongs or explain things away, or even to look in another direction to avoid seeing. My thoughts and actions lay before me harsh and real.

I then go back again and watch myself from infancy, more slowly and lingeringly. I examine the relationships within my family. I follow the course of my music. I watch my educational and spiritual development and my emotional decline. Like separate threads all crazily woven into the whole, I see my friends and then my enemies, and myself in tangled interaction with them all.

I see my courtship with Henry, a fairy tale. I watch us marry in the cold of January, in joyful secret, then I see the most loving of unions besmirched and defiled and twisted into a nightmare from which I could not awaken. I spend the largest part of my time examining my relationship with Henry, for it was Henry who ultimately defined my life. It was always Henry who brought out the worst of my failings and weaknesses. Ultimately, it was Henry who ordered my death.

He cannot freshly harm me here, and for that I am grateful, but the harm he previously inflicted reverberates and grows. There is nothing to heal it but time. Even here, there is no other cure for heartbreak. I wish that death were a magical cure for all that ailed my spirit in life; it is one more thing I expected and found false. I arrive with the same baggage I carried with me in life. There is nowhere to lay it down here either, no more than a woman with child can lay aside her babe before its birth, for it is within me. I am as I was, just not encumbered with flesh.

I expected the pain to leave and find it has not. It will not go.

I hear words as if they were music on the air. I sense but cannot see the source of them. They float around me like physical beings of vibrant form, and color, and substance. Sometimes they strike me like clamorous blows. Sometimes they whisper comfort and encouragement. Sometimes they weep with me. At times, they even laugh. The intent of the words appears to be to drum some truth into me as I watch myself in a situation where I failed to heed them. They change according to the scene I am examining.

My companion does not identify . . . herself? The Voice seems more female than male, although gender does not exist in this realm. She merely calls herself my "mentor", or "teacher", seeming almost as a mother would.

She scolds and nurtures like a mother.

The Voice, and the words, describe an ideal toward which I am striving so that I might compare myself to this and view my progress. Jesus Christ is the example with which I am most comfortable, and is therefore referred to most frequently, but is not the only one. There are others for me to measure myself against: Moses, Abraham, Krishna, Buddha, Muhammad, as well as nameless other souls who have reached understanding.

"Compare myself to Jesus Christ?" I wonder. I had done that in life, and had thought myself humble until now, when my Judgment Day (if that is what this is) has come. I am raw with humility.

But still.

I cannot recall anyone in my life who was Christ-like, or Buddha-like, if you will. I have never met a person such as that. Does that not make the assignment unreasonable? Are we not all incapable of success? Is it not merely something to lamely strive for without expectation of reaching the goal because *no one can*? Are the words of Jesus Christ (or Buddha, or Abraham . . .) not simply scripture bandied about by the devout, believed in theory but rejected in action?

I would stand at the gates of heaven and argue, Henry once shouted to me in a rage. And so, in a way (are these the gates of Heaven after all? I cannot say for certain.) I do.

Henry knows me very well indeed.

Just as I saw my life in rapid passing, I now see scenes that show a servant who was crippled and in pain, and yet was always kind and high spirited. We ran to her with our little aches and disappointments and sought her comfort, heedless of the pain she was suffering while she soothed ours. She neither preached Scripture, nor was she particularly pious or prayerful, although she wore a small iron cross on a leather strap around her neck and took her place with the other servants in the chapel during Mass.

I see her seated on a three-legged stool in the kitchen by the door, shelling peas into a large wooden bowl. Her walking stick is propped against the wall behind her. I see her wipe her brow, for the fire is lit and hot, and I see her laugh.

She always laughed, and knew how to make everyone around her laugh as well, and knew how to speak to us so that we might feel ashamed of ourselves when we misbehaved without ever thinking she loved us less. We took her for granted until her death, when a lonely gap remained where her bright voice once was. We left the walking stick in its now permanent place against the wall, and never removed it or allowed it to be used again.

I discounted the value and the contributions of the servant because she was not of my class, and therefore not of as much worth as I.

"There is none of more worth than any other," I hear. The Voice tells me that the servant has far surpassed me, and that I should look to her example for guidance.

I am further reminded of her child, a strange-eyed girl who spoke thick of tongue and could not learn. She was said to look like a Mongol, and had a graceless, slow and heavy gait. The other children ridiculed and teased her, and the adults slapped and scolded her for her clumsiness and stupidity. Her smile was as bright as her mother's despite this, and she loved her tormentors with a heart-breaking stubbornness. She hugged them, and brought them flowers and little presents, then wordlessly died one night in her sleep, leaving the rest to ponder their cruelty.

I am grateful that I was not among those who were cruel. I am grateful that I returned her hugs. I felt such pity toward her.

"There are many whom we pity who in fact should pity us."

I had felt deserving of pity in the last years of my life. I even was willing to change places with the likes of Ruth, and be an idiot servant girl in order to let someone else be queen. It seems to me, though, that the Voice is referring to something other than the treatment I received from Henry, and my fall at the very end.

"We are all on the same road, some ahead of us and some

behind. We do not always recognize ourselves as being among those who are struggling farther back, and misunderstand, scorn, and even persecute the ones who move ahead of us. History is littered with such as these: eccentrics, geniuses or unwavering idealists being among the most noticeable. These change the world almost by force, though the change most often does not take place during their own time, they are so far ahead of it and therefore so rarely understood.

"The less noticeable shine a light with simple good-natured long-suffering, and they shine that light for us despite our impatience, ingratitude or scorn. There is always a beacon shining if we look for it and open our hearts. We will each be a beacon ourselves, one day. It is just up ahead of us in the very direction we all are traveling. Those who follow behind us need our wisdom, for the ones who shine now will leave at the end of the road, and it will be left to us to be the light."

One of these "lights" was our gnarled and crippled servant Rose, who shelled our peas, and whom we kept out of charity. She did nothing more than slow and flawed handwork, and often could not leave her bed at all from illness or pain. She created troublesome expenditures and excessive inconvenience in nursing her back to health each time she took to her bed. If she was well enough to work, we were sometimes impatient that she took such tedious trouble to perform her tasks, and that her twisted hands could only deliver sorry results. Yet when she died, even Mother wept and retired to her room. We recalled that she never complained, was always eager to be of service, and when we no longer had her, we all found her contributions to have had great value and missed them. An emptiness remained in place of love we had never noticed, nor realized we needed.

I mourned that I had taken it for granted, and mourned for myself that I should have to continue through life without it. I did nothing to earn it. In fact, with the contempt the upper classes are taught to feel toward the lower, I presumed it was my due and the source of it, Rose, not worth much. I awakened to her worth only upon her death.

There was no pettiness, or criticism, or sarcasm or wickedness in

Rose. She had no selfishness or ill-intent. She seemed almost to have lived the life Jesus taught, and I only see this now with being shown. Yet all who should have recognized godliness overlooked her. She was too meek to draw notice, and her position was too lowly.

Her physical limitations, idiot child, and station in life were not a punishment for her, the Voice explains, but were designed by her own heart so that she might be an example for the rest of us. She endured her trials out of generosity and love. Her daughter did the same.

"Only a large soul, far advanced, can give so much just so that others might see more clearly. Such is a means of allowing the rest of us to place our own grievances in their proper perspective, and of showing us how much even the weakest among us is capable of giving. We can see, or not see. The choice is ours."

I feel suddenly sad for her, that her efforts were not appreciated and rewarded while she lived.

The lecture pauses, and the Voice aims a personal comment toward me.

"Adulation is transitory. Is it not?"

I agree, feeling a wave of pain. Adulation most certainly is transitory.

"Then it hardly matters whether or not Rose received adulation or acknowledgment during her lifetime. It is not those on earth whom we need to impress. They are often misguided in their assessment of worth. Yet there are souls, like Rose, who show them what is worthwhile and through this, some people see and grow."

I interject: "But if it is not seen, what worth has it? The point of it is lost. Did she waste her effort on us?"

"Do you feel it was wasted? Your mother did not."

I do not know the "mother" the Voice seems to be referring to. The mother I remember could not be touched by the likes of Rose, or by any other thing. Her heart was ice. Upon hearing of Rose's death, she did not weep for long. Yet she did weep . . .

The Voice continues.

"It is like written music. Its beauty exists whether or not we choose to play it, or choose to listen. If we choose not to see, the choice and the loss are both our own. What we should see is that there is none among us with nothing to give, and that giving is our purpose. At the same time we should respect and show gratitude toward those who are giving themselves so that we might understand this."

I grow small with understanding. I realize with surprise and then shame that I am one of those who did not recognize herself as struggling farther back.

A far yawning distance stretches before me on the road. I brace myself, not knowing yet if the balance of my life will allow me to move forward, or if I slipped even farther behind.

I cannot demand a better position or order someone to move me closer to the front. I have no power over this except to slowly edge my way forward with painful effort, like everyone else. It is vexing, for I expect crowds to make way for me. I am not accustomed to viewing servants as my betters.

Then I feel shame at my expectation of special treatment. One of my daydreams in life, toward the end of it, had been that I should be like one of the faces in the crowds who knelt and bowed—and sometimes stared and pointed as I passed —any one of them; it mattered not. Remembering, I feel a sense of anticipation for I am now their equal. Relinquishing my expectations is a small price to pay, to finally be one of them. I am pleased.

I am well-pleased, and eager to get to work. I even feel a sense of pride in my position on the road, for there is a swell of souls that surrounds me here, and only a narrow trickle of souls toward the front. I want to be among the masses, unwashed, if need be. I want to be a face in the crowd, unrecognized. I want no special treatment and no special acknowledgment—I have had enough of that, and it grew sour within me.

I am anxious to proceed.

Chapter 2

I now reacquaint myself with The Law, which is only in essence the same as I was taught. It is more stern and forgiving, more fair and unyielding than I had thought in life. I cannot buy it off with rituals and tithings and outward displays of piety. I cannot fool it with secrecy, self-delusion, or excuses. It does not require approval by my peers and church leaders. It has no respect for position, wealth and power; it rather views these as detriments than advantages. It is as Jesus said, but not as my teachers interpreted His words.

The Commandment of The Law says: "Do unto others as you would have them do unto you."

It means this. It means me.

I am here to learn where I failed and where I succeeded. Then I will return to try again, to see if I can overcome my faults and repay my mistakes. It will take many attempts because the human soul must be forced into improving. It is stubborn and self-absorbed, and resistant to disruption of its habits and beliefs both in life, and here, beyond it. It does not go to Heavenly Glory without a fight, and it travels a long hard road to get there. I have yet a long hard road to travel. I will not return to Peace yet, or even soon. I have much to face, and many strengths to develop first.

My purpose, at this stage, is to remember. From this strange and uncomfortable vantage point, I view myself more closely than I care to, my eyes pried open as it were, my face held firm so I am forced to watch. With each memory, the Voice reminds me of The Law and how I measured up to it in that instance. I know I am forgiven. I also know I am not complete. I am forgiven for having had to borrow—we all borrow through our sins; it is expected and is a step in the process of growth. However there is no escaping payment. I pay for what I take, and am paid for what I give. It is as simple as that. I see where I paid in this last life, what I earned and where I took.

The borrowing brings me incredible sorrow, more than I ever would have thought.

I will be held harshly accountable for seemingly minor things, forgiven for things I had thought unforgivable, rewarded in instances I had thought I would be punished, and shown the error of ways I thought were right and good. I will pay, but not for things I had expected. I also will receive ample reward for small thoughtless, seemingly unimportant acts of kindness and love, and I see there had been many. Each moment counts in the final tally, which will shape my future as it did my past. I am to work toward compiling the tally myself, from the beginning of that life to that last moment when I knelt blindfolded before my executioner and an eager crowd.

One works here at self-assessment until successfully completing the job, then takes the tally and uses it like currency toward the next existence on earth. The tally determines destiny, good or bad, upon one's return there. This destiny, so called, seems frivolously unfair and incomprehensible only in the realm of forgetfulness that we call "life" where the steps leading to seeming injustice are hidden. Here, it is the Word and it is the Wisdom, and I am in the midst of this, understanding and ashamed, attempting to heal from a past and prepare for a future I have created for myself.

The Law is a stern one, but fair to the smallest molecule. I see that it is fair. I see also that I have woven my own tapestry thread by thread from the beginning of time, and have no one to blame but myself for the pattern and the outcome. I would prefer to have woven somewhat differently, in many ways. Regret is easy. It is so much harder to be good when one is flesh, existing in a state of forgetfulness, influenced and seduced by so many things. The most seductive sin, I suppose, is passing judgment on others, and the next must be the acting out of one's anger when one has the power to hurt the ones who wound us. I was guilty of both things.

One is so much better off without power. It is something I will henceforth avoid by choice. It is harder not to pass judgment, or to restrain the temptation toward vindictiveness. One can always find the means to feel superior to someone else no matter what one's circumstances, and can easily feel justified in punishing enemies. So, I am caught again, as I have been caught many times in the past, and I will pay.

For now, I spend this period between lives in reflection and analysis and the setting of goals so that I can begin saving toward the day when the debts come due. In terms of time, I do not know how long the process of analysis takes. There is no time, here in the Memories, or rather, time does not move at the same pace or in the same measurable direction as it does on the physical plane. I believe many years have passed when I first see my life fly past me and find it was a matter of moments. I think mere hours have passed since I arrived only to find it was years. It would be startling were I not absorbed in my task and guided by a presence that reassures me.

I turn back to my life and I watch.

PART 2

Two Pegs Above Mutton

1501—1532

Chapter 1

Like a shadow from the first, there was Henry, spoken of frequently in our household, reverently, as much a fixture in my life in the beginning as in the end. I heard references to him and his father the King and his brother, the heir to the throne, from my earliest days. Names that meant nothing to me were to weave themselves inextricably into my life, first as a backdrop and then as my life's primary focus.

I see my home, the very home in which I first heard Henry's name. How odd it is, the manner in which perceptions change from a distance. There were times when I found this place to be insufferably dull, isolated and provincial. I chafed with boredom and impatience, anxious to be rid of it and on my way to more exciting places and events, rarely missing it, or not missing it at all when I was away. Even thinking of it as "home" seems odd, as I lived in a number of places during my life and spent considerably more time away than I ever spent here. Yet home is what this is, and I now equate the structure and the grounds with the very word "beauty".

This home—my home—was a tiny castle in Kent called Hever, built within two concentric moats, surrounded by rolling grassy fields and thick groves of trees. Ducks glided down the outer moat, which appeared upon first glance to be a stream, and sheep grazed on shallow slopes nearby. I endured pain and loss, perhaps equal to that which I felt in other places, yet can only envision the sky above Hever as blue, the clouds as white and wispy, the air as sweet, and the flowers blooming in the meadow as if it were springtime.

My father had inherited the little castle which, while outwardly very pretty, was several hundred years old and could not possibly serve us comfortably as a home without significant improvements. So, within the castle walls and attached to the tiny castle, he had built for us a large house with three adjoining wings of three floors each. Within it, the hallways joined one another at right angles forming a square that surrounded a little inner courtyard with the castle at the forefront. On the face of it, you approached a cold, walled-in fortress when you rode up the drive, but as soon as you passed through the gates and entered the courtyard, you were surrounded by charming, vine-covered walls that displayed glinting, diamond-paned windows and architecture in the modern Tudor style. On first sight, you knew you were entering a world that was safe and warm and cheerful. It was within this world that I grew.

The courtyard led to the kitchen, so its walls were lined with barrels of kitchen goods. Within these walls were hunting dogs, servant boys struggling with water buckets or bushels of meal, scullery maids exchanging glances with horse hands, several scratching, soon-to-be-killed-and-roasted chickens, and the head housekeeper scolding all of them for being underfoot, or slow, or inattentive.

The courtyard was a very jolly place. There were whiffs of wood smoke, cooking smells of fish or game, and the heady, delicious aroma of freshly harvested herbs. There were laughs and shouts, grunts from men carrying heavy loads of goods, and the sound of voices singing. I sometimes watched these scenes from the diamond-paned windows in the hallway above, and sometimes wandered down, as a child, to immerse myself in the bustle and the company. I was not supposed to be there, mingling with the underlings, in everybody's way, but if I kept myself very quiet and stayed small in a corner or behind a barrel, I was often unnoticed and forgotten, and thus was allowed to remain. This rarely lasted long. In a short time I would speak up in order to comment on or question something I saw, or would join someone in song and betray myself, then be scolded out of my hiding place, guilty and uncovered, usually pulled back inside by my nurse.

The family did not enter by way of the kitchen as the help did, but instead we made our way up a winding stone staircase just inside the castle gate. Inside the house were wood-paneled walls, elegant tapestries, and sumptuous furnishings lovingly polished by servants. Most of the rooms were forbidden to my siblings and me when we were small, and our early lives were spent in the narrow confines of playrooms and nurseries on the second floor.

My own room, located in a far corner, was only large enough to contain my bed. Mary's room, of course, was larger, she being the eldest, and George's room the largest of all (even though he was the youngest) since he was the male heir. As a female, and a middle child of very limited worth, I was provided with only the tiniest of drafty, leftover spaces, and a window too high to look out until I was grown. However, my room had the advantage of providing me with a spiral stone staircase in one corner that allowed me convenient access and ready escape to the floor below if I heard someone unwelcome approaching from the hall. For this last reason, I considered myself a very fortunate little girl indeed, and my position an enviable one.

In later years, I would be required to move myself to another room, as it would be too difficult for the household to keep me locked inside a room with a second entrance. This action became necessary in order to prevent me from trying to run away to Hal, whom Henry would one day decide I should not wed. The move was, from my parents' perspective, a success. From mine, the larger prison with the pleasant view and just one entrance was very cold comfort indeed.

But I leap forward too quickly. Patience has never been one of my strengths.

Within this house, I see my family, first my mother, stern, distant, coldly well bred and proper. Then I see my sharp-tongued, quick-witted and shrewd brother George, and my sister Mary, pretty and sensuous, personable yet self-serving, always matter-of-fact—except when her heart was involved.

I see Father, only rarely there, the changeable one, jovial and harsh by turns. He was a man who dominated any room and all its occupants with his commanding voice and his presence, and who answered only to his wife, and to the King. Father was driven by, and hence drove his family with his forceful ambitions, his greed and his vanity, pushing us ever onward to seek out and to achieve position even higher than he himself had been able to grasp. And so, I obediently did. I focused on ambition and personal gain, just as I was expected to, to please him.

I see, of course, myself interspersed with the rest, viewed now as I have never seen myself before. I am worse, and better than I had known myself to be.

My upbringing fostered petulance and superiority. My tendency toward self-absorption, natural to all infants, was nurtured and encouraged, and my "needs", so called, were heeded by servants who sprang to action at the sound of my tiny voice. I learned I had a right to this, and believed that I did. I knew myself to be superior, and knew that I should never want—even for one moment's time—for anything I could obtain through someone else's efforts, and by my own command.

My superiority stopped with the Tudor family, of course, and with various levels of nobility that were higher than my family's. There were those with whom I was forced to be humble. Innate superiority was also of no use in impressing my parents. Compared to them, I was inferior, and (they sometimes reminded me) barely worthy, for I had been born with a deformity that shamed them, and caused me endless embarrassment.

I had what was called a "sixth finger" on my hand. It was merely a growth more than a true finger, but was difficult for me to accept with equanimity, as one should accept such things. This was particularly true since I had dark hair and skin, unlike my prettier sister. I was physically not what my parents would have wished, and temperamentally not inclined to the quiet meekness they demanded of their female offspring. I continually fought against being a disappointment to them.

I developed a habit of carefully crossing two of my fingers to disguise the deformity. I camouflaged the hand with over-long sleeves and graceful gestures, but was still to be reminded of it. It was one of the first things mentioned when I was described to anyone and, I find, always shall be. "The mark of the devil," some said, although my parents scoffed and laughed at such unenlightened attitudes and told me not to heed them. I sometimes thought of it, though. It is hard to be a child and hear one is marked by the devil when one wants only to be good, but finds it difficult to be good sometimes. My willful moments made me fearful of Hell, once they had passed and I was set upon to examine them.

I never quite lost the anxiety that all I did and all that happened to me was a manifestation of being marked. It was from my disfigurement that my ambition to be a nun first took root to prove, perhaps, that if I strove, I could transcend the devil and be as worthy of God as others. Later, I felt driven to read my Bible and pray for hours each day, never feeling quite certain I had prayed enough, always feeling that I had a bigger obstacle than others to overcome.

My sister Mary was the obedient one, at least in the presence of parents or nurses. She knew how to smile meekly, and to agree, and to make pretty promises. She knew how to lie sweetly, and to weep piteously. Whippings were rare for her, and rewards were common, but I was not jealous of this. I wished only to be as loved and as lovable as she. She was one more reminder that I was wanting, and I could not blame her for that. The fault lay with me for I was flawed at birth, and felt this must be a reflection of my soul.

Unlike Mary, I was too honest, and too forthright to deceive those who had authority over me. It was against my nature to withhold secrets, and it was within my nature to vocalize my observations, so I took most of the whippings while Mary watched, exasperated by my "Stupidity. 'Tis pure stupidity to tell them that, Nan. Just smile and nod, then hold thy tongue and they will never know nor care, so long as thou dost *appear* to be compliant and obedient." I could not do that, even smarting from the latest punishment. I would obey as much as a child is able, but I could not stop myself from babbling about some thing or another that I should have known would make tempers flare. I could not restrain myself from bursting with descriptions of the garden in the rain, when I clearly should not have ventured out and could only have done so by stealth, or from commenting on the sweets I had stolen from the kitchen, forgetting how I had come by them.

My indiscretions also cost servants and my siblings some peace of mind, for I prattled on about everything I saw. Their displeasure and anger and, on occasion, their punishments, cost me moments of the sincerest, most devastating shame, yet still my tongue wagged, for I had not the power to stop it in spite of the cost to myself or to them.

Despite my physical and temperamental failings, my parents dearly loved me. I learn this with amazement for, while my father's affection was preoccupied and dismissive, I see it was strong, and my mother, the mother with the heart of ice, appears to have felt toward me a love of surprising depth. It is amazing because I never knew they felt love at all. I cannot even formulate a question, yet I am in need of reassurance that what I see is truth, for I am inclined to disbelieve.

Where in the heart of the mother who pursed her lips at me, or inside the father who used me and abandoned me at my death was there love? It was not visible. I am certain of that.

I am reassured the love was there, or they would never have tolerated my temperament and nature to such a degree in that time and place. Had they loved me less, they would have cruelly beaten me into submission, as they had been taught to do. Instead, my parents even allowed me some say in decisions that concerned me. They were, by comparison to others in our time and against their better judgment, remarkably lenient and indulgent toward me.

One has to step back sometimes, and having done so, I marvel that I missed what I could not see at the time.

I made my parents laugh, and amused them with stories and songs, and assaulted them with endless effusive displays of affection even in the face of their own detachment. My tongue was never still, and my eyes were always darting about and crinkling over some small joy. I could not help loving them with boundless energy, and that kind of love is a flattering thing. They first pitied me, and then I made them laugh, which is the surest way for a child to carve room for herself in a parent's heart. I now find I gave them more pleasure than they ever allowed me to see. I wished with all my heart that they could love me as much as the others, and in truth, they did. Yet I was never certain of their love, and never felt worthy of it.

Would I have been different had I known?

I would think of my parents when I accepted Henry's hand, and feel I had finally succeeded in making them proud of me. That belief gave me joy almost equal to the joy I felt in being loved by Henry. It is a moment I would freeze in time, for it was by far my happiest, and a moment for which I paid most dearly.

It was a moment my mother and father did not wish for me or for themselves, knowing Henry. They did not fully share my joy, yet still, I thought they must. I thought I was giving them a gift.

Chapter 2

When we were children, our cuddles came from nurses and servants, as did the swats that landed on our bottoms. Our parents were careful not to spoil us with kisses and affection, as it was commonly thought that such parental weakness brought harm to a child's character. They maintained in the spirit and popular wisdom of the times that children must be brought up sternly, distanced from their parents whom they revered and respected, rather than openly loved. They wanted what was best for each of us, and the widely held belief was that cold harshness and parental distance were best. They settled for criticism, parsimonious praise and material gifts as a means of expressing themselves and their love for us.

Father and Mother (or "Sir" and "Madame", as we publicly addressed them) were godlike creatures who came when we misbehaved, and administered verbal instructions to the nurses on how to handle us. Then they retreated, leaving the care and handling of the three of us to others. However in secrecy, the nurses disobeyed orders that they should distance themselves from us as well, so they held and snuggled and nurtured us without our parents ever suspecting. It was the scoldings Mother and Father saw, never the hugs.

I was too boisterous for a girl, tumbling down the stairway with my brother George, while our shrieks rang out in the hall. I often hurled myself into cartwheels, even attempting flips behind garden hedges, tearing my skirt on thorns and having to account for it later. "Pure wickedness," I was told with clucks and fiery glances. "A lady doth not fling her skirts to the breeze with her limbs in full view of God and man! Thou art tempting Satan! Such sinful immodesty!"

From the moment I toddled upright, I was drilled for hours in walking like a proper lady, and so I walked as a proper lady walks. "A lady doth not gallop; she doth glide. Head erect, chin proud, small steps—*small* ones, Mistress Anne. Move only the lower portion of thy limbs as much as thou mayest. Mother of God! *Heed* me, thou wicked girl. Straighten thy back. Arms bent up at the elbow lest the blood move to thy hands and make them as pink as the hands of a kitchen maid. Up! Up and *stay* up!" The words were punctuated with smacks from a wicked long switch. Two steps out of view of anyone, however, I broke into a giggle and a giddy run.

I liked games that called for movement and running. I also liked games of pretend, and played the beautiful maiden while George harassed me as a fearsome dragon or a highway robber. When Mary joined our play, she would insist upon being the beautiful maiden herself, and my role became that of the handsome prince who would save her. George was ever the villain, for he loved to roar and make noises to frighten us into scrambling out of the nursery and into the hall. I would cast magic spells on him to make him die upon the floor where he would twitch and moan in gleefully dramatic agony. Always, the nurses would scurry toward us scolding and upset that Father or Mother should hear us outside the boundaries of our playrooms. We slid down the banisters, and ran from room to room to escape them, hiding in wardrobes or under bedsteads in dusty, muffled concealment while they called to us and threatened us in dangerous tones. Once found, we were separated and spanked, or punished with isolation, or denied treats or, in particularly bad instances, turned over to Father whose punishment was more severe.

If he was at home and not traveling in service to the King, Father always came with his whip when I misbehaved or threw fits of temper, lifted my skirts and thrashed me.

I see Father now, sweeping into the room with iron fury, larger than life, made larger by rage, voice booming, eyes coldly examining me upon his approach. As he draws ever closer, I grow ever smaller, weeping, contrite and terrified, too frightened even to beg for mercy knowing I would receive none from my father or his whip.

Frequently berated for "wickedness" and "willfulness", I routinely confessed myself to be "wicked and willful" when I asked forgiveness from the priest. There, admittedly, were episodes of violent emotion if I did not get my way. I believed from my upbringing that I should have my way, and so I demanded it. However, mine was frequently less a display of will than of volatile temperament, and my demands often less self-centered than a manifestation of strained nerves. I grew ill-tempered when excitement or pressure stretched me past a very tenuous endurance.

I was forced to test that endurance daily. Both our parents and the nurses made it clear that none of us was ever to draw attention in public. They warned and forbade us, but the strong desire to appear in control and to please was within me as well, so I obliged. I was aware of always being watched and assessed. Each time we ventured out, I was expected to be silent and to behave with impeccable decorum. I wanted approval, so no one could ever find fault with me when it was necessary for me to behave, and I would always hold the excitement of the outing within me until I was once again safe in my home. There I would explode into a tantrum as my only means of releasing my feelings, and fall exhausted into sleep.

Emotion affected me to the extreme and would result in my becoming feverishly agitated. When I was happy, I would be overcome by a happiness that always seemed to be far happier than that which others felt, and hence unseemly. Then my emotional reserves became entirely spent on this emotion and I would violently snap, collapse into tears, and fling myself until I was drained.

Grief was always over-felt and even more exhausting than happiness. I could feel it for days or weeks with no decrease in intensity. The dismissal of a servant, the departure of a favorite visitor, the death of a robin I had unsuccessfully attempted to nurse, or—God forbid—the death of one of my little dogs, each had the effect of leaving me prostrate and hysterical while I mourned and missed them. I was inconsolable at such times, and refused any pleasures.

Impatience and exasperation with me prompted whippings that sometimes had the effect of taking my mind off the grief and placing it elsewhere. For this reason, my parents viewed these as necessary and beneficial. Each time a tragedy struck, I was called aside and whipped. I grew up expecting to be rightly punished for misfortune.

It is difficult for an adult to make the distinction between will and emotional upset. It is even more difficult for a child. The reason for my tantrums was of little interest beyond the fact that they occurred and must stop. I should have control over my behavior, yet I felt possessed by the Devil himself when the hysteria overcame me. I cringed with shame and remorse at the passing of each episode, and accepted the whippings with a sense that I had failed.

Always, I sensed the difference between others and myself in the power of my emotions, and felt ashamed that I was less calm than Mary, and less able than George to view matters with level-headedness. It was so difficult for me. I was too easily carried away and wished to hide this, for expression of feelings always drew frowns or gasps, and was generally viewed as something base and common, as well as inappropriate. I prayed often that God might make me good.

I never learned to feel less intensely. I knew not how to change it. I never learned to control the hysteria either, except by degree. However, knowing that one simply does *not* express emotion, I was able to repress my feelings in public with such a force of will that I appeared cold. I could not cry or shout or misbehave before outsiders; I had too much pride and was too aware of my station and of the inevitable fury I would incur to ever indulge in such antics. In public, I was a perfect little girl. I was a credit to my parents. Inside, I was churning with emotion, and was always on the verge of erupting.

The little girl grew into a woman, and did not change so very much.

It should not be thought that I spent my entire childhood in fits of hysteria or subsequent punishment. In truth, the household considered me the "sunny" child and, though I did not know this, it was I, not Mary, who was the favorite of the nurses and the servants. I was gregarious and precocious. It was I who was first to give hugs and kisses, and who grew wildly ecstatic over the return of a nurse from her visit home, or at the birth of a servant's child. I knew the family histories and medical complaints of all of them, brought treats to the babies, and kept company with the old ones and sick ones as they lay abed, prattling as ever to all who would listen. In return, they loved me as their own, despite the scoldings I cost them when I blurted out some truth they wanted hidden.

I did not distance myself from underlings, except when I wanted them to serve me. I knew proper protocol, and the servants expected it of me when they were on duty. I could be quite demanding and cold if I was ill or hungry or feeling bad-tempered. Otherwise I merely ordered them about with self-centered impatience and expectations that were sometimes selfish and unreasonable.

Even so, I was not as bad as most in my station. I fully knew our servants were beneath me, but I *loved* them. They were my world, and as much my family as Mary and George. When I was ill tempered or spoke harshly, they forgave me and served me with parental patience and good-humor. I grew up expecting to be forgiven my moods. I grew up expecting to be understood.

I was never to entirely disabuse myself of the illusion that all servants, and later my ladies, loved me as I loved them because of the servants I had in my earliest years. Toward the end, virtually none except Emma was a friend, yet I thought them so, and spoke too much or spoke to them harshly expecting, once more, to be forgiven.

Aye, but then, I could never hold my tongue. I never could, poor wicked wench.

Mary and I were close as children, and remained so, even as years pulled our interests in different directions. I concentrated on music while Mary liked to paint; I chose the Church, and Mary chose young men. We maintained our intimacy up to the time Henry came between us and forever strained our relationship. While still children, though, we whispered and plotted, and planned our grand lives, and slept in the same bed (I could not endure to spend the night alone, and crept down the hall and into Mary's room), hugging each other during cold nights. Mary told stories of the great man she would marry and the grand house she would have, whereas I fantasized myself into sainthood and told stories of that. We made up frightening tales about the things to be found in the woods, or the fantastic magical spells cast by an old beggar woman we often passed in our carriage when we went out for air, then went to sleep pressed close for warmth.

George sometimes crawled into bed with us until he grew too large and proud to be with his sisters. Our nurses slept soundly, and they were country women raised three or more to a bed themselves, so even if they woke and checked in on us, they did not mind or waken George to send him back to bed alone. He feared the darkness and liked the company. He would weep, if forced to leave on those nights when the very villains he often pretended to be himself were lurking in his wardrobe or hovering outside his window. He outgrew the need by the age of six or seven, and would look fierce if anyone mentioned that he had once scurried into bed with his sisters from fear and need of comfort. When I think of us though, I think of us that way: three little poppets nestled sleeping and intertwined while the nurse snored softly in a nearby room. That sweet time swiftly passed for us.

It was George to whom I turned as we neared ages 9 and 11, and Mary, at 12, was less interested in childish play. We chased one another while Mary looked up from her needlework with patronizing boredom or conversed in soft-spoken, well-mannered phrases with the older women in the household. George was a companion as wicked as I, and as prone to mischief. We often recruited Emma, a servant's child, to join us in devilish pursuits that led us upstairs and down, inside and out, with nurses threatening us from all directions. Without Mary's restraining influence, the number of whippings for each of us increased.

I missed George's companionship, when he went away to school and I left home to live on the Continent. When I came back, he was a man, and I was a woman, and he was concentrating on his career and his fortune at court. We had much to say at first, and the intimacy was still evident, but we had lives apart from the family now, and found our opinions had diverged over those years. George was very serious and intense about his future and his prospects. I was more flighty and carefree, content to attend feasts and masques, and to chatter among the women at court about the women who were not present in the room. We each experienced exasperation in the company of the other, and heard word of each other mainly through George's wife, who carried messages back and forth between us.

Meticulously well-informed, George was opinionated about the subject of politics and liked to discuss it at length, whereas I had no opinions except to comment on the personalities involved, what they wore and whom they had bedded. At first, I politely extricated myself from his conversations when they turned to current events. Later, I sought him out and grilled him endlessly, not only for information concerning that which was taking place now, but all things that had led up to it, and his speculations as to where an event might lead. The result was a huge surprise to both of us: I had a head for it, and a mind sharper than that with which I had thus far been credited. George viewed me differently afterwards, and spoke to me with more respect and less condescension. Over the course of several months, it lessened his habitual annoyance with me somewhat, but alas, did not erase it entirely. His wife still formed our strongest link to each other.

I spent a good portion of my time in George's company after my duties required that I obtain a better grasp of politics within and outside the court. He assisted me with an understanding I had previously neglected to develop, and his coaching spared me some embarrassment. In pursuit of the goal of educating me for my duties as Henry's wife, we spent many hours together before and after I wed, giving neither Henry nor anyone else cause to believe we were engaging in unnatural acts. Henry once caught me affectionately kissing George's cheek, and at the time had smiled. He had also smiled at the stories I told him about our sleeping all to a bed as small children.

From those two things (and from fanciful suggestions from George's by-then-unhappy-and-embittered wife, whose comments Henry had encouraged) Henry concocted his charge of incest.

✠

I pause here at the thought. I feel outrage strongly enough to kill. I whirl into a frenzy of anger while words come to me, calming me, soothing me, attempting to reason with me as I reel about in pain and affront.

I move ahead too quickly, I am told. Fury keeps me picking at a sore I would be wiser to leave alone. There is much time here, to dwell on anger, but it serves no purpose. I must stay with the task at hand.

"Calm yourself. Calm yourself . . . "

In time I do, and I move forward.

✠

During the years we were growing up, Henry VII died and was succeeded by his son Arthur, who took Katherine of Aragon as his bride. Arthur, a weak sort, died soon afterward leaving a wife and a throne he had not lived long enough to claim. His younger brother Henry laid claim to both. That Henry should ascend the throne was never questioned. That he should also claim a woman as part of the inheritance was looked upon by some in askance.

When Henry was 14, his father made him publicly declare the arrangement of his marriage to Katherine was not of his choosing in order to shame the Spanish crown over some passing political peevishness, but in fact, the marriage *was* of his choosing. On first sight Henry, at age 10, had wanted Katherine and would stop at nothing to have her. From his perspective, the death of his brother was a convenience that confirmed what he knew to be true: God intended for her to be his wife.

Others stated that God did not approve of marriage to a brother's spouse, but Henry was adamant and his father certainly had no objection. Spain and England had both had gone to some trouble to marry Katherine to the British crown. At the same time, Spain's queen, Isabella, was dying and anxious for her daughter Katherine to be settled. Rome proved the hardest to convince, but Henry pressured his father who manipulated the stakes so that all involved would approve.

Katherine, who was never asked how she felt about any of it, suffered through the haggling like a head of beef at auction, then went to Henry, finally, as his wife.

Henry dearly loved Katherine, and was clearly born to be king despite his position as second son and his early expectation of entering the Church. My family talked of nothing but Henry for months, even years, it seems. He was such a fine, strong king and we were so proud to be his subjects. His well-known feelings for Katherine fueled Mary's and my adolescent fantasies and yearnings for romantic love. To a young girl, he was the perfect king and she, the perfect queen.

Katherine, the fairy tale princess from Spain, intrigued me. For a time, I developed a preference for anyone or anything of Spanish origin, fixing a mantilla upon my head and posing before the looking glass, insinuating myself into friendships with Spanish visitors, practicing Spanish dances on my harp or lute. I referred to Katherine by her Spanish name, "Catalina", and reverently rolled the word over my tongue, sometimes in a whisper to myself, like a love poem or a song.

I developed so strong a reversal of those feelings, as years passed, that my distaste will transcend that lifetime. I have grown to so thoroughly dislike the country and the people and the language and the music and the history that the word "Spanish" equates itself in my mind with "hellish".

Had Katherine been Danish, I would have detested the Danes.

Then, however, I was proud that my dark hair and complexion were like that of my queen. Our great king had chosen a dark bride rather than a golden one, and he adored her. For the first time in my life, I was not ashamed to be dark and for that, I fervently loved her.

Mary was frivolous with her intellect, as was I, and liked to daydream, sketching landscapes from the window. Developed early and eagerly interested in young men, she often sat in a reverie of love toward one gentleman or another, and sometimes spoke of being attracted to the King. Most young ladies were, when Henry first entered his manhood. Mary talked of tossing him roses and of having him bow to her from the jousting field like a romantic figure from the days of the Crusades. Then she flitted on to the next young man who caught her fancy and dreamed of him instead. She planned for a handsome knight to fetch her away someday, and worship and adore her. In the meantime, anyone of good name would do, and in the absence of a young man of good name, a masque or a festival would suffice.

Through the years, I would be her confidant and her friend, applauding her for attentions paid by an eligible suitor (or later, amorous kings) and wiping her tears when he would disappoint her. I hid as much as I could all the details from Mother, and Mary did the same for me. It was always best that Mother know less rather than more, and she knew only as much as we were jointly incapable of withholding from her.

At this I see Mother's face, and even here I stiffen from resentment and anxiety. The mother I reflect upon was not soft. I always picture her in the dim light of the sitting room in the evening, always in a restrained and muted glow, not in sunlight or surrounded by garden flowers as some fondly recall their mothers. I see her, handsome and slender, appearing taller than she was, standing very straight and proper and inflexible, issuing quiet orders that were to be obeyed promptly and without question. I think of her and still feel I have to strive to be better and am close to failure, for her requirements were high and unforgiving.

Mother was a "presence" at Hever, which had seemingly been built, not to be occupied, so much as to provide a backdrop for her. Within it we were all merely satellites circling her. This included my father whom one would have thought was the more powerful figure of the two because of his gender and his success at court. This was not the case. Mother had the better bloodline and the sharper tongue. It was always Mother who had the final say.

Father's family was more recently come to wealth and power and was more conscious of them than Mother. She assumed they were her due and never questioned it but ever felt she was due more by right of superior birth and superior personal attributes. Father, by contrast, knew they were things one fought for with wit and energy. He enjoyed using them for the purpose of being seen and acknowledged as someone of importance. Mother simply *knew* she was someone of importance. All who met her knew this also.

Mother frightened me more than did Father. My mood turned dark in the face of her disapproval, sometimes spiraling into despair, whereas Father's whip merely gave me pain that passed within hours. I could always be certain why Father was issuing a beating: my own behavior was the cause of it.

With Mother, my failures were less defined. She had little patience with persons who fell short. One delivered what she expected and no tolerant understanding would be forthcoming if the end product was not as she had demanded. With Mother, I had to guess, sometimes, what "falling short" entailed. I too often discovered what it meant with unpleasant surprise.

She often seemed disapproving without saying how or why I had failed her, so I tried to make her expectations solid and substantial in order that I might understand and meet them. I strove for perfect manners, and perfect curtseys, and perfect gestures, and perfect accents, and perfect posture, and perfect dance steps and perfect ways that things could be *done.* I wanted to please her so much that any small failing caused me embarrassment as intense as death. There was a hopelessness in that. She was looking for a perfect way for me to *be* and I was imperfect. Yet I remained possessed by the need to make her proud of me. I turned my resentment in upon myself and increased her disappointment in me by adding my own. My mother's expectations tainted the image I had of myself and I always fell short. I always fell short.

Ironically, there was a tenderness to her character that she did not ever show, and which I did not suspect. She kept Rose and her idiot child, who contributed nothing in the way of tangible servitude and often needed care themselves.

"They have nowhere else to go," she would coldly snap when asked. "I would not risk Hell by turning them out to beg or starve."

Her servants ate clean and wholesome food, received the same medical treatment as the family, lived in comfortable quarters and had no unreasonable tasks demanded of them. They were given generous Christmas baskets, then were secretly slipped pouches of coins when they came to Mother and privately wept about ailing parents or a sickly brother. When questioned about missing coins, Mother would face my father with narrowed eyes and insist that he miscounted. It happened frequently but he would not risk challenging her. It was only the servants (and my father) who knew this side of her, for she hid her compassion and publicly denied her charitable actions (if they were uncovered) were anything more than irksome duty. It was Mother who drew from the servants the passionate loyalty they felt toward all of us. It is only now that I know this.

She also had a tenderness with regard to marriage. It was she who allowed me to remain unwed for as long as I did, searching for a man I could love. She had loved my father, and had married beneath her to be with him. To my knowledge she did not regret the decision even though it meant sacrificing some of her own position and lowering the prospects for her children. They would not force me into a loveless marriage as so many parents did, she vowed, though not to me. Time passed and Mother made earnest efforts to marry me off, but she heard my objections to her choices, and left me unwed and unpressured. In the meantime she simply spoke untruthfully about my age and waited, for she believed in true love. I took my time in the search because I believed in true love as well.

Their intention being to secure me a husband of some small worthiness, although their expectations were grim given my defects of appearance and my hand, my parents spared no effort or expense toward my education and my acquisition of "charm". I had considerable charm to begin with, if one could call a babbling tongue and a shameless desire for attention "charm", so they intended to enhance what they considered to be my only hope. That "hope" included my being taught—and actually learning—what *not* to say, and when, and to whom. That most important lesson went unlearned.

At age 11, I was sent to the Netherlands where I became a ward of Margaret, Archduchess of Austria, and where I was tutored beside the children of European royals. My father had served the Archduchess in an official capacity as diplomat, and through this had become friendly with her. In appreciation, she extended him an invitation to send his daughter to her. This unique opportunity was to have gone to the elder child, Mary, but Father viewed me as the one in greater need of any advantage. He also judged me to be the brighter of the two of us, and therefore the one most apt to bring credit to the family name. So he sent me, the second daughter, in her stead.

It was here that my musical training began, in a place where the greatest musicians of the day were gathered. Ah! The blessed chance that led me to that place! For two years I resided among the angels, listening to music that these beings had smuggled from heaven to earth and which transported me to a state of shivering ecstasy. My fingers ached to reproduce it, and my determination to be one of them was fixed for a lifetime.

Then, my father called me home because the political situation had become uncertain, and because another opportunity had presented itself.

It was the general wisdom of the time that charm and manners should be acquired in France, at court. Our opportunity came when Henry's younger sister, Mary Tudor, was sent to France to marry its king, Louis XII. My father was rising at court, and had made himself useful to King Henry on several occasions. His efforts and position entitled him to make arrangements for my sister and me to go as part of Mary Tudor's entourage, and so we and a number of other young ladies of rank sailed across the Channel with her.

The crossing proved dangerous. It was ill-timed and the weather was fierce. The fear that we might sink was very real, and that fate was only nearly missed. England's finest young ladies heaved and vomited and writhed in the most exhausting distress. Prayers for death were spoken aloud, and although mine were among them, I thought I must already have died and gone to Hell and was suffering punishment for a grievous sin.

The Princess was carried off the ship, for she had no strength to walk. The rest of us straggled behind with matted hair and soiled gowns, drifting like pale waifs onto dry land, supporting each other and mutely following as we were instructed, our stomach muscles still reflexing as if the firm dry ground was pitching waves. We were days away from a state of physical comfort. Some of us were years away from fear of travel by sea. Most of us viewed France, the unwelcoming gray land beneath the overcast winter sky, with distaste.

I, myself, cast one long, lonesome look back across the Channel toward a home I had only barely touched again after two years, and missed.

Mary Tudor's wedded "bliss" (or rather lack, thereof) was to last only a few months. The royal husband to whom she had unwillingly gone was an old man who died conveniently soon after the ceremony. Before going to him, she had bargained with Henry, agreeing to marry only upon the condition that she be allowed to choose her own husband after she was widowed which, she hoped, would not take so very long. She already had a lover in mind, a commoner, and she was determined to marry him. It was only through this bargain that such a marriage was even remotely feasible, scandalous as it was.

Henry intended to keep his end of the bargain (with hopeful plans to persuade her against it if he could possibly manage it). He was a meticulously honorable man in his way. I give him that. Not many a king would have given weight to a manipulative promise he made to a mere woman when so much was at stake. The royal princess in a marriageable state was of the highest value to him in political negotiations. Most would have simply ordered her to marry, sold her off and been done with it. Yet he gave her permission to marry the man she loved because he was a man of honor and had given his word, and because her tears had torn at his heart.

King Louis of France had not planned to support a score of English ladies, nor did it please him to do so, so he ordered most of our gaunt, unhappy party back on a ship to England immediately upon our arrival. Mary and I, however, remained. Then, after his death, the princess was married once again (in secret in the event Henry changed his mind and withdrew his approval; Henry howled with outrage upon learning of the elopement, and of and his sister's distrust and betrayal), this time with joy both during the ceremony and in the years to come. She returned to England with the rest of the young ladies who had made the journey with her.

However, Mary and I were *still* to remain in France. It was an "honor" we were told, bestowed upon us because of the invaluable service of our father to Henry. We became full-fledged members of the French court.

On the one hand, I was spared the Channel crossing. On the other, I disliked France, and had done so from the day I stepped stinking and wretched off the ship and set my shaky foot upon her soil. I would eventually grow to love it there, but my initial reaction was dismay and despair.

From that first day when we were installed at the palace, our guardians "protected" us from the reality of life in the French court with strict rules, endless religious tomes and moral lectures. These teachings were markedly different from the behavior I observed among the French courtiers.

The people at court were shrill, catty and innately boorish beneath their sophisticated social polish, treating young English ladies as bumpkins, or as sexual toys. We were sometimes the butt of humor we did not understand, which made the men laugh and the women glare at us, and were sometimes groped or followed by courtiers who found the stalking of us great sport.

This worsened with the death of Louis and the coronation of Francis I, for this new king took part in the sport himself and led much of the misbehavior.

For me, it was a frightening place among people strange to me, seemingly all wild people following the example of a wild and decadent king. It became a living hell when I was caught in the hunt. I wanted nothing more than to go home. I ached with it. I often thought of England at night and wept, for years, but I adapted over time as I was young and had no choice in the matter. My hints in frequent letters went ignored.

Under the strict religious teachings I absorbed with great drama, heartfelt emotion and romantic intent, I may well have become a nun, except for the rapes. I did not speak of them, but carried a scar on my neck where the miserable jackal cut me with his knife as I fought. When I whispered to someone the name of the man who had caused the wound, she made the need for secrecy clear to me and all who tended me. Hence, news of it went no further. The very few who knew the truth explained that I was abed with a fever, not a wound, then sharply warned me to cover my neck. I received a "gift" of an unfashionable wide choker necklace, and orders to wear it. I wanted no one to know, and willingly complied.

I henceforth took to wearing high collars or wide bands of cloth or metal around my neck to hide the scar and to deflect questions about its source. When asked, I said I had a mole I wished to cover. History has kept my secret for me, although the mole has since grown to "large" and "disfiguring" (It is ever irksome to hear about yourself as relayed by persons who do not know, or whose intentions are to discredit you). In time the scar faded, but I still wore the neckbands because I still saw the scar there, large and red, even after others could not see it there at all.

He came back several times and had me. In a matter of weeks I lost the solidity of my religious faith, for where was God? I still held tight to the vestiges of belief, particularly as they pertained to Hell, and read the Bible with a driving desperation, pulling apart the words in an effort to find evidence that my soul was not entirely lost. However, I had no further desire to become a nun, even had the damage been reversible and I been made physically whole again. Now despoiled and no longer worthy of God, I concentrated on the art of making engaging conversation in two languages, and of becoming attractive to men. If one is not a nun, one must become a wife, and my focus turned from the one ambition to the other.

Still, for years I saw the scenes during sleepless nights, replaying the attacks and imagining myself fighting harder and killing him. I twisted the bedclothes and gritted my teeth. My blood surged with fury and murderous thoughts and my soul writhed with hatred and vengeance. With all my other failings, I now had to suffer guilt for having allowed a man to be with me in that way, and for fantasizing his manhood painfully severed and removed. I did not confess these thoughts to a priest as I might have once. I knew without asking for forgiveness that neither the priest nor God would forgive me, for the man in question was one over whom I would surely burn in Hell.

I hated my own impotence most of all. I had had no choice for a number of reasons, his knife among them. However, the sin—in my mind—was my own. He called me horrible names and told me the fault was entirely mine, and I believed him because I did not know otherwise, and because a man such as he can only speak the truth. He beat me about the face, and always had the tip of his knife at my throat. Still, I should have stopped him. I should have been able to run. I should not have been tempting to him, somehow.

I fully expected harsh punishment for these events and my thoughts about them and, throughout my life, I dreaded facing Judgment. I find instead that I am not to be punished at all. Here I find that the murderous thoughts were not sinful; they were born of trauma and pain, and were a natural progression of healing. I did not nurture them, nor did I act upon them. I did the best I could, and that is all that is ever asked. The act itself was indeed a severely punishable sin but the sin, I am reassured, had never been mine just as Mary had always known. Not mine . . . I wish I had believed it in life.

The horror ceased for me when I had my first menses. He chose that time to come to me, lifted my skirts, saw, and twisted his face with contempt and disgust. He left me unharmed and turned instead to a little maid of 10 years, never forcing me again. Still he touched me for the rest of my life, and his actions led me down a path to my death.

Ah, but he might have killed me sooner. He would, in a sense, be my killer either way.

Except for those who were present the first time, only Mary knew about my "visitor". Our parents did not know, for action on their part, even had they dared take action, would have had serious repercussions. They received no word of it from my hosts, and neither Mary nor I was eager to enlighten them. There was the obvious shame. I had a strong desire to protect myself from the judgment and scrutiny of others, and from the fury my mother would have aimed toward me for letting it happen.

Ill-fortune carries with it a stench and leaves a wide berth around its victims. Understandably, considering the undeniable stench of rape, there was little sympathy forthcoming from the small knot of ladies who had tended me after the first one. A woman who was raped deserved no sympathy, for it was still fornication in the eyes of God, and the victim's fault not the man's. Men could not be severely faulted, for they were not built to withstand temptations of the flesh, as women were. Far worse were raped children, who were an abomination for having tempted God-fearing men into performing beastly acts. The women viewed me as sent by the devil. My deformed finger did not soften the sincerity of their conviction.

Their inclination was to distance themselves and to be cold and sharp toward me. I had caught the eye of a man they secretly knew had unspeakable tastes and needed no act of seduction to tempt him into performing unnatural acts with a child. However, they had to take sides. Even had they felt inclined to pity me, they preferred to side with the influential and the powerful against the weak, for it was more advantageous to their ambitions. Sympathy toward me would demand self-examination and the questioning of their values, with the discomfort that brings. Their hearts were not large enough to withstand that kind of scrutiny.

They conveniently forgot the circumstances in a very short time, and sternly viewed me as a teller of tales and a seducer of priests. They convinced themselves this was true, for to believe otherwise would require action on their part—or guilt if they took no action—and risk to themselves. Rather than suffer a conflict of conscience versus self-promotion and advancement in court, they reported me as a troublemaker and revoked a good deal of the little freedom I had. In the meantime, they smiled and curtseyed and simpered before my attacker, made his way clear for other attacks, and averted their eyes when he prowled the halls.

There were a few outcasts like me among the young ladies of the court, and our numbers grew. I did not know the reason for it, then. Our chaperones gave very generalized explanations for why we were unacceptable socially, or else amplified our minor infractions. They discouraged unblemished young ladies from associating with us lest we prove a bad influence, though their true motive, hidden even from themselves, was to prevent us from confiding to the other young ladies on the subject of the rapist.

The outcasts did not have the desire to seek solace among each other, for none knew the others had experienced the same outrage. We feared that our own stench would grow through association with those who were also ostracized, so we suffered in isolation, stripped not only of our virtue, our God and our faith, but of our friends and our trust. We each struggled to regain acceptance from the majority by rejecting each other. We each thought we were the only one.

Only Mary tended me afterwards each time, and made excuses for my having to remain bedridden until the injuries healed. Mary was, as always, very careful about appearances in front of our chaperones. In public she disassociated herself from me and spoke to me coldly, but in private she did as she pleased. I was extremely fortunate to have had her, for there were others with no one at all. One of these eventually took her own life.

Mary was more knowledgeable than I in matters of men and women. She had taken pains to learn all she could and did not think I was at fault.

"The scurvy, bloody serpent," she spat each time I came to her, shaking and bleeding, four times in all. "The bloody pig," she swore. "'Tis not thy sin, dearest. He will burn for it."

"'Tis blasphemy to speak so, about a man of the cloth," I whispered through chattering teeth. "He is chosen by God."

"I think *not,*" Mary hissed. "He doth perform the devil's work in God's name is all. Thou hast been ofttimes warned of such as he." She pressed a cold cloth into my hand and told me to lift my skirts and apply it to myself. I did and winced. "In sooth, he is the devil himself in disguise," she continued. "How better for the devil to hide himself, than as a proclaimed man of God? Methinks there is no better strategy."

Touched again by the devil, I knew not what to think about the state of my immortal soul. I knew I must be careful to preserve what little I had left in preparation for the time when I was to face God's judgment. I was well and truly frightened.

"'Tis *not thy sin*, Nan," Mary snapped through tight lips. "Give it not another thought." Then she leaned over and tightly held me for a long moment. We both started to weep.

Despite the sorrow my situation brought her, Mary happily adapted to the lifestyle in France. She was not averse to the gropings and stalkings, and had learned to piously slip past our chaperones and meet with young men in the far chambers. It became her favorite diversion, and she did this while retaining a reputation of chastity in the early years. I did not know for certain if she was chaste, for she did not offer details, nor did I ask or want to know. Either way, she appeared to be chaste, and for a time I believed her to be so. She ever had the ability to wear Virtue like a cape, just as she had as a child, until the cape became too tattered to cover her and she landed, quite publicly, in the bed of King Francis himself. At that point, I could not help but know.

As for myself, I made the best of things and passed my days. When, in the very earliest months, the old King Louis had died and Mary Tudor had prepared for her return to England, I thought I saw an escape and a reprieve, but found my father's earnest efforts and appointment as Ambassador had chained me for years to come. I was tolerated by the persons in the French court for his sake and for the sake of my sister who, as ever, had charmed all within her circle. I even had official position there, grudgingly given to me for diplomatic reasons and with great show, but without sincere good wishes.

Eventually the circle of women all died or left, or lost influence without the support of the ones who were gone, and my social position became sound. I was drawn into the society around me by earnest friendship from some who did not know I should be spurned, and had no one to tell them so. Furthermore, my sexual experience would have had no bearing on their opinion of me, and a rape such as mine would have been greeted with a shrug. With the coronation of Francis I, the court overnight became like a brothel where virtually all participated and few condemned.

It was in France that I learned to make a man keep his distance.

It was in that environment of lascivious pleasures that I first learned to respond to men with sudden, quicksilver escapes, and where I first issued the charming and teasing refusals that later drove Henry to near-madness. Through the years, and in the midst of constant assaults against my virtue, I feared and hated the sex act too much to succumb willingly. Lest I be called upon to participate unwillingly, I took the greatest pains to never walk the halls alone.

Throughout, I made the time endurable by counting days, and while in France learned much that later proved useful in making me a polished and educated lady of the court. I hurled myself into my music, and practiced as if possessed by demons. I had the greatest admiration for the mannerisms and styles of the French and adopted them fully, learning fluent French and potent feminine wiles. From the experience I learned to be as charming as the French, and more charming than most women in the English court. It was my duty to learn these things, and I was ever the dutiful child.

My parents were not displeased with my progress when I returned to them in 1522 grown, educated, more attractive than they had hoped, and impressively honed. I was inwardly battered as well. It settled in the corners of my mouth, and when I was not being watched, in my eyes.

✠

At this, my memories search even further back, and I see that this life just past was not the first. Somewhere within me I must have always known this, for these ancient memories are as familiar to me as Henry's face. They play a part in the work I am performing now. I must sort out my entire history to understand the tapestry I have woven and to prepare for the work ahead.

How I came to be Anne is a lengthy story that does not bear telling. Some things, however, seem more important than others and I see these first.

In France, there was considerable importance placed upon the ability of a woman to attract a man. I learned the lessons easily. On viewing this, I suddenly see myself in Egypt three millennia before, a common prostitute. I was already knowledgeable in the art of luring men so I effortlessly absorbed the lessons taught in France, and even surpassed them. From this combined background I became a woman who seemed to possess great beauty, though I had very little. Poetry and songs were written for and about me. Men swarmed about me, then stuttered and blushed in my presence. I had countless compliments, yet some knew I was plain. *I* knew I was plain. Henry, however, did not. He thought I was of astonishing beauty, always, and through him, I almost believed it myself.

I see an injury to my husband forced me to the streets. He could no longer earn a living to feed us and our children, and would not go out and beg. I went out and begged in his place, and found that men were not often willing to give me alms without something in return. I was young and comely, and the offers came frequently. Less frequently came the pittances I earned from pleading for food for my babies.

One day out of weariness and desperation, I accepted an offer and pocketed the payment. I did it again, and then again. The alternative was starvation. Sometimes a choice is as simple as that. In England one became a wife or a nun. In Egypt, one became a wife or a whore and if the husband was shiftless or crippled or dead, one could live as both. Choices were limited.

In Egypt, I developed a cynical, bawdy wit, and came to enjoy raucous gatherings of many people. I learned to play music for the first time in order to entertain my customers, and I learned to flirt. I came away with a defiant, stubborn resolve to accept no gifts of any kind from men for, hating the life and having put it past me, I was too proud to go back, and so viewed gifts from men, no matter how innocent, as an insult. I also learned to be ashamed, and to feel myself less valuable than others, and to question my own worth. Lastly and most importantly, I developed a vicious tongue.

I missed a lesson in Egypt. There was much I might have gained from that life, and the most important lesson was to not judge others for their choices or circumstances. I moved on to the next life and failed the test. Having rid my own self of the stigma of the working girl, I chose to place myself above and separate from women who were moving through that same experience. I also judged those who either committed adultery or were accused of it. I chose to be superior and to scorn them, and would usually be in the midst of the crowd of stone-throwers when more "virtuous" women attacked those who were less so.

Throughout three subsequent lives, I was tested. Each time, I had the choice to forgive or to judge and each time the debt accumulated. As the devoutly religious wife of a village leader in the last of these three lifetimes, I encouraged my husband to prosecute and punish women for their sexual indiscretions. I argued that their actions were against the will of God. It was also against local law, in that place, that women be unchaste. I leapt upon each accusation I heard, and saw that guilt was proven on the basis of suspicion and hearsay as much as on fact.

During that particular lifetime, and in that place, it was written that adulterers be cast out with stones and forced from the village. The punishments I urged were more severe and, safe in my position of power and righteousness, I created extreme public humiliation, embarrassment, distress, ruined families and ruined lives for several women.

For one woman, the punishment was death. She was guilty but this does not matter. What matters is what I felt in my heart as I watched her die. I felt vicious self-satisfaction, feeling I had pleased God and proven my own greater worth.

If administering lawful punishment is ever sinful, it is one's heart more than one's actions that make it so. The sin comes from finding pleasure in issuing the sentence, or from doling out punishment beyond the law because it pleases one to do so. Punishment is a solemn duty. It is not an amusement, or a triumph, or a means to stake out personal vengeance, and yet I had made it so.

I should have had more tolerance, not less, and was to be taught the lesson once more, as Anne. If I failed to learn it that time, I would be shown again in increasingly more difficult circumstances until I finally came to understand that I must show mercy toward everyone, including those who indulge in behavior that prompts my disapproval. I may not pass judgment even if I believe God is in concurrence with me.

"Judge not that ye not be judged," are the words I hear now.

"For with what judgment ye judge, ye shall be judged and with what measure ye mete, it shall be measured to you again."

My personal feelings, I am reminded sharply, are of no consequence in the final judgment, which is God's alone, and I do not speak for Him. Imposing my disapproval onto others succeeds only in bringing it back upon myself. Invoking His name as I do so is blasphemy.

In this manner, I wove my own death and the events that preceded it.

I see that I already knew Henry in Egypt.

There are snippets of sights and sounds forcing themselves into my thoughts, and in these I see that I have been tied to Henry since far beyond Egypt . . . since beyond memory. I cannot find the beginning of it.

He is always there.

There he is most recently, a crying child, a small boy and I am dying—his mother—and he wails in terror when I pass, shaking me to force sight into my open eyes. Who will take care of me? Where do I go? Screams that make me shudder with grief for him echo in my thoughts. I did not mean to abandon the child, yet he has been seared and scarred by my abandonment. I see the scars I left in him.

Mercifully, I was sent to retrieve him soon afterward as the Black Plague spread and made a victim of him as well, unfed, uncared for and alone amid corpses and chaos. Ah, yes of course, I know of this now. It is so much a part of me, how could I forget? How could I not have recognized that terrified child in Henry? His love for me was not, at first, the love of a man for a woman. It was the desperate need of an ill and orphaned little boy for his mother, and I did not see that in my forgetfulness. I see it now. He pursued me and obsessed over me as only a lost child could or would. I see it all.

The memories move me back through time. I see us performing together for an audience, scooping up coins and bowing to the applause.

Earlier, we are tied in marriage to each other's siblings, unhappily forced apart although we feel a violent attraction.

Further back, our most recent roles are reversed. I am his

mistress, minor royalty, and he is my servant—a slave—and this amuses me. Still remembering his "place" and mine from that previous lifetime, remembering me as "Mother" later on and as an equal partner in a number of other lives, he found it difficult, as Henry VIII, to understand that I was now beneath him and not worthy of a king. He also found it difficult to silence me, or to patronize me, or to ignore me when I spoke. I found it just as hard to hold my tongue or to lower myself before him or any of the others, in spite of my inferior lineage and their unquestionable power. He could not make me mind him, poor Henry.

I see humor in it all, and for a second want to share it with him. Only Henry would laugh as well, or at least the Henry I knew in the beginning. I miss him. Even in my anger and hatred, I miss "that" Henry.

I see so much.

Beyond that, I see we are tested more rigorously. There are marriages where one or the other is infirm, and the healthy partner assumes the role of caretaker. There are lives where we are sworn enemies due to tribal loyalties. There are lives that place us in destitution, squalor and anger, and lives where we each cannot stomach the other because of some grievance or another. When we hate each other, we hate with strong passion. It comes, I see, and it goes. I see also that, even in the worst of these situations, we have still chosen to be together, and always manage to find a way to bring it about. We have a stronger need to be together, even fighting and hating, than we have to be at peace, apart.

We always meet somehow, and sometimes clash, but we are always drawn.

We are not drawn by preference. Hatred and love are interchangeable cousins, and each of these has carved an impression on our souls. In the carving we became bound, and with each successive life, the bond grows stronger. What we can never do is avoid or ignore each other for, in being bound we can choose to postpone our pairings, or we can separate after meeting once we have handled our business, but we cannot choose to never meet. There will always be circumstances that place us in each other's path, accidental meetings, coincidental events. We will almost always inhabit a place upon the earth when the other is also there, just as we always have.

We marry in most of these recollections. We are usually married. Sometimes he is my parent or I am his. Sometimes we are siblings. Sometimes we are each the opposite gender, sometimes we are the same gender, but our usual bond is that of marriage. He is my soul mate. There are such things, and he is mine. There are bonds stronger than death or marriage vows, and we are bound in such a way. I would rather not hear this or know it, but the knowledge comes to me, and I resign myself to it unhappily. I once would have felt great joy.

Thus far, we have always forgiven and moved passed it. We will not be together again, I find, until I can forgive him once more, and he in turn can learn to control his fearsome temper. To meet before then would bring further damage to us both.

"Is he not damned?" I ask hotly and with a small amount of hope. "I should think I would have no reason to meet him again at all."

The Voice speaks again: "He deserves your forgiveness."

I am very, very angry. I do not want to forgive. I cannot forgive, just as I cannot stop loving him. I am changed because of his cruelty and need to heal if I am ever to forgive. I must forgive because it is Law and I am as bound to the Law as anyone, but I will require lifetimes away from him before I am ready, and it seems a hard task.

In the meantime, I want never to see that life again or think of that place and time or be reminded, and yet I must because the memories crowd inside me. It is what I must do. I vow that when I finish, I will place it all behind me, and never ever look back again. England is a dark and haunted place to me, and the era when I lived one that will have no appeal even after I reappear on earth and forget the reason I recoil.

Time passes, how much I cannot say, and I am still here, forced to watch and examine. It is a long and painful process.

Chapter 3

All three of us had exceptional minds and a quick grasp of most concepts, but as females, Mary and I were first painstakingly tutored as proper ladies of a certain station, then dismissed as having thoughts of no consequence. We were taught that God had created us for no reason other than to breed and serve men, and we accepted it as one accepts the world one is born to. My thoughts, however, begged for release. My tongue was a quiver, and each opinion I held was an eager arrow in search of its target.

I grew to have a mischievous preference for discourse with men, who were often taken aback by forceful attitudes daintily packaged in an attractive woman. I had beautiful eyes and smiled teasingly when I spoke to them, feigning maiden modesty between verbal jousts. I was mercurial and had a charming wit. I flattered, then teasingly insulted by turns, now smiling impishly, now lowering my eyes and blushing. Most of what I said was lost with the cocking of one of my eyebrows, and the man would press closer, changing the subject to my eyes. I had eyes that lit up with playfulness. There are men who cannot resist a tease.

However, there were men—and of course, women—who were immune to me and actually heard the words. These words were often purposely scandalous and inflammatory, and only sometimes a reflection of my true feelings because I loved to argue and test my wits, and because I enjoyed tweaking the pompous, just a little.

It was Emma's influence, I suppose.

Once I was under Henry's protection, I said exactly what I wished to say. Prior to that, I sometimes spoke wickedly in private or succumbed to the temptation to engage in verbal battling, but most often I maintained a sense of place, and sought to please everyone I met. This changed when I became his mistress, and worsened when I was his wife. At times I felt irritable from the pressures imposed upon me and no longer bothered with self-restraint. At other times, I simply liked to play Devil's Advocate. I tossed explosive comments about religion and politics into a discussion just to see how they would land and to see the reactions of the people involved. I was particularly irksome in this respect when speaking to those whom I disliked, and with these, I often took sides or expressed opinions simply to infuriate. It was a very, very risky and costly amusement.

Even more costly was my penchant for gossip, and for unkind observations. I was not alone in this. I associated solely with idle ladies and courtiers whose main source of diversion was a generalized verbal viciousness toward their absent peers. Clothing, mannerisms, intelligence, rank, love partners, appearance and weaknesses all were subject to critique and contempt. I took an active part in the sport. Cruel comments I made in private grew to be public declarations once my opinions earned greater interest and respect. Words I spoke were universally heard, even when I spoke them thoughtlessly, intended them to merely be witty, or was provoked by a momentary personal irritation that had more to do with mood than real displeasure.

It does not please people to hear secondhand that which they were not intended to hear about themselves.

It does not please me to be reminded that this "harmless" amusement costs a hefty toll in the borrowing, and that the punishment for unkind words and scornful laughter against another is every bit as severe as for striking that person with murderous blows.

"It is not what goes into a man's mouth that defileth him . . ."

It is what comes out. I have spoken and laughed myself into a tangled net of harsh punishment. It is not the first time I have done so.

Henry himself was an incorrigible gossip, having to know all that went on with everyone, digging and prodding me for stories that might amuse him. He also applauded my verbal games because he loved a mental challenge. The more provoking the observation, the more amused he became (provided the subject was not critical of himself). I willingly accepted his encouragement, and thus placed myself in danger more times than I knew. It escaped me that some men viewed me with a seething resentment and would seek to punish me for besting them with my wits. There were others, men and women alike, whom I had infuriated that sought repayment. All of these bristled at my audacity, knowing I was taking advantage of a situation where they could not respond to me and risk the King's displeasure. Still others found me amusing, and I suppose I thought they all did as a result. One sees one's tactical errors clearly from this vantage point. I should never have underestimated the evil that can spring from bruised pride and wagging tongues.

But, again, I jump ahead.

Upon our return from France, Mary married, had a daughter she most properly named for the queen, and was installed at court as lady in waiting. After a span of time, Henry noticed her and chose her. Mary went to him with little self-examination or concern, either for her spouse or Henry's.

Mary was pretty and charming and eagerly sought him physically, all qualities Henry preferred in a mistress. He was well-pleased by her company for a time. However, Mary was vocal about her love for him and made demands, and often burst into tears over real or imagined omissions in the sincerity of his attentions.

Henry did not love her, and viewed her need for him as cumbersome. When she found herself with child, he saw no further use for her, and sent her back to her husband who would keep her and the infant in a household at a distance from court. As if to make a point about the line she had attempted to cross in his affections, and because of his convenient doubts of the child's actual parentage, (even though he had Henry's red hair), Henry never acknowledged her child as he had Bessie Blount's.

While Mary was still Henry's mistress, I was sent to court myself. I watched the scenes unfold, then ached for Mary who seemed broken by the King's abandonment. I heard the talk at court, and all the clucking remarks about her behavior. How could the young lady be foolish enough to imagine that a king would want her for love? She might have learned from Bessie Blount, who had retained the King's attention for quite some time, that love was not his interest and was not to be expected. He had a wife, Katherine, who fully owned his love. He did not want love from a silly girl. That "silly girl" had a husband, which made her behavior even less to be endured. Henry wanted a playful but sensible woman who tended to his needs and then retreated, satisfied with money and gifts and, if necessary, a respectable arrangement of marriage to someone else.

I remembered those comments and felt pain for Mary that she had earned such pitying contempt. I prayed I would never look like such a fool.

I let her weep and shout out her anger and betrayal and her hurt to me. I gave her what comfort I could, and counseled her, not knowing how. Mary's pain was real, and my heart truly broke for her. I hid the talk and the sneers from her, and was angered at Henry even knowing, as I did, that he could not have done things differently. The blame for such foolishness was Mary's alone, for in truth she had been foolish, but Henry's coldness angered me nonetheless.

Life was not as we had planned, when we were children. For Mary, it turned out to be tolerable. Her husband eventually died, and she then fell in love with a soldier. She had no wealth, but was blissfully wed, and was quite content with her lot, particularly after seeing the dangers she had escaped by not winning Henry's love. She outlived all of us, and had a fair life, overall. She was deserving of it.

Chapter 4

From my first breath, I was taught duty and honor. Raised to be petulant and demanding, I was also trained to fear God, and to love those whom I served, and to serve them loyally. I served Queen Katherine, and I loved her. Having finally met the fairy tale princess, I found her to be tedious and self-righteous and inclined toward vicious, secret vengeance while always maintaining a façade of sanctimonious piety. However, I loved her still. It was my duty, and a nearly lifelong habit. I suffered through her company, not admitting to myself that her company was insufferable to me, so proud was I to be in her circle. I overlooked her shortcomings and the boredom I felt in her presence, and tenaciously felt love toward her because she was my Queen and it was my duty to love her.

The hatred I came to feel for her was as strong as the love, and Henry the cause of it. Beneath it all, I wished her no harm. I never did. I only spoke so out of anger and hurt, and never acted upon the words—or meant them. Throughout everything, all of it, I had a childish desire for her to love me, but knew not how to make it come about. And so I hated and punished her because she had spurned me, and because I wished to hurt her, and I could. I neither screamed for her blood at any time, nor encouraged Henry to kill her. There was no subterfuge and secret plotting. There was no poison, nor talk of poisoning as her supporters vehemently accused. I did not hide my hurt and anger behind a veil, or act upon it in secret. I hated her openly for all to see, and bespoke a hatred even stronger than the strong one I felt.

I also loved Henry. I had fallen in love with him as a child when I had seen him, tall, handsome, young and glittering at the festival following his coronation, while I stood in the shadows with the other children. He was already a man, 18 years old, enormously tall, with red-gold hair and broad shoulders. Most strikingly, he had an air of vibrancy and energy, and a very infectious laugh. He turned and saw me for a moment—I thought he did—and my heart skipped. He became the man against whom I always compared the others. I saw Henry often in my daydreams through the years, even after he grew thick about the middle and lost the appeal of his youth. After becoming one of Katherine's ladies, I hated the disloyalty toward her I knew my daydreams signified, and often considered them a crime against God, thinking in that way about a man who was married to the woman I served. I feared punishment. I forced myself away from the daydreams as much as I could. However, the love was already there when Henry first decided he would have me, and had been for many years. It was my secret, and no one guessed.

I felt painful jealousy, when Henry chose Mary as his mistress. Too proud to show it, I pretended I found Henry's company to be tedious, and his person to be unappealing. I paid him only the barest compliments and attention when he appeared in the music room, and grew increasingly solicitous of Katherine in whose eyes I could see a shadow of reproach when she spoke to me. Already. Even then—even when it was my sister, not I, who held his interest.

Perhaps it was my haughty disdain that fascinated Henry after I first caught his eye. He expected attention from women, and indifference preyed at his pride. More likely it was my singing voice and my skill on the lute, for I was an impressive musician. Henry earnestly aspired to be one himself, as music was his very greatest passion. However, he gave no indication of an interest in me, even after he had discarded Mary and I continued from loyalty toward her to snub him as much as I dared.

For a time, he seemed not to notice that I was snubbing him. That chafed me. I increased my attentions toward other men when he was present, and watched Henry from the corner of my eye.

Even after I met Hal, I viewed Henry's acknowledgment of my attractiveness as a prize to be won. It was a secret wish of mine that he find me as appealing as he had Mary. It was only partly competitiveness. A part of me had always felt impatience toward him for looking right through me when I was beside my sister. It was *I* whom he should see. I knew not why I thought so, but it was a sense deep within me, that Henry should recognize and acknowledge me. I brushed these thoughts away as imagination and confessed them as pride to a priest, yet watched him still for signs that he had noticed me, expecting it. Waiting.

Vanity, infatuation and a little too much mead overcame conscience and resolve one evening when I saw my opportunity to steal Henry's attention for a moment. Finding myself near to the King at a court dance, I coyly looked across at him and caught his eye with an expression I now know to be that of an Egyptian prostitute. I tempered it with English modesty so as not to be crass, but the look still was one universally understood by men. I looked at him in this way for just a split second before my mouth twisted into a half smile, and then a full grin that even exposed my teeth (which one tried never to expose).

Having grinned so improperly (Henry thought: "delightfully"), I turned away from Henry to face my partner. We circled in opposite directions, men on the outside, women within, and the two circles stopped. Henry had elbowed and manipulated his position so he could be across from me. I curtseyed, and looked up at him shyly, lowering my eyes with blank, well-bred English innocence, then darted him a quick glance, the prostitute, prompting Henry to throw back his head and laugh.

"Bewitching Mistress," he whispered as he took my hand and led me around the circle. "When might we see more of you?"

In a dangerous breech of decorum, but with mead-blunted senses and the somehow certain knowledge that I would not anger him, I blinked at Henry three times maintaining well-bred English innocence. In a low, shocked tone of voice I asked, "More? Of me? Your Highness, I show you as much as I would allow *any* man to see of me. I fear I dare not show you more and still retain my reputation. Please do not ask again, Your Grace." I gave him the stern frown of a humorless tutor then, laughing, I broke away for the start of the next movement and danced away with someone else.

He followed me in the circle with his new partner, then leaned over and whispered "Impudent!"

I cocked my head feigning a failure to understand his meaning, and whispered back playfully: "Quite so! Your Grace most certainly is impudent!" Then I twinkled and dimpled at him to soften the insult and danced away with my glance meeting his a few seconds longer than necessary. For the first time of many, his eyes followed me and the sensation was electrifying. It is a heady feeling, being noticed by a king. It is thrilling to be noticed by a man you have always secretly loved.

It was a game. I was compulsively flirtatious, another legacy from Egypt, and often toyed with men in that way (while keeping them always at arm's length). I did not really want Henry at that time; I simply wanted him to notice me. Having succeeded, I was ready to return to my comfortable obscurity and occasionally flirt with him when the situation presented itself. I had no desire to bed him, for I was promised to Hal Percy. This infatuation for Henry was a totally separate thing from the love I felt for Hal, and was being played out in my imagination rather than in my heart. I did not know there was a deep well of real love beneath the surface. I was merely giving a gift to a dark, plain young girl who once parted her lips in awe over a glance from a handsome man. That is how I saw it.

That is not how Henry saw it.

Eyes followed his, always, and rested upon me. Within minutes, everyone knew whom the King now viewed with interest and, even then, tongues began to wag. The speculation would die down when nothing came of it, and I would think my life could go on as I had planned, but Henry would not forget me. It would just be some while before he would take action. He would spend the ensuing months watching me, thoroughly assessing the situation, and putting all the pieces into place while I unwittingly prepared for my life with Hal.

The first indication that a harmless flirtation had proven harmful occurred when Hal Percy asked for permission to marry me and Cardinal Wolsey refused him following instructions from the King. The reason given was that a woman of my lower status was not suitable for a man of Hal's position. There was also the matter of a marriage arranged for him when Hal was a child, and this marriage was now to be forced upon him, much against his will and most bitterly against mine. No worse misfortune could have befallen us. We were wondrously paired, and should have lived a long and contented life together. We both grieved, as we had chosen each other for love.

I blamed Henry for this, and resented him deeply. I grew silent and melancholy. I slept and cried and stared at the ceiling. I withdrew for many months to home at Hever, and stayed there nursing my spirit and my grudge until my mother prodded me back to court. She was alarmed by the length of time I could maintain that level of despondency, and was anxious over the time I was wasting.

During my absence from court, the King began appearing at our door for this or that—some minor business or another—and would request that Mistress Anne be present. It grew quickly into a situation of unmanageable difficulty for me. At first merely stubborn and angry over my broken marriage plans, I eventually found my emotions complicated by our growing familiarity. I found myself fighting with my conscience as I grew ever more flattered, then interested in Henry's appearances, and ever more interested in charming him. My love for Hal forbidden, I found I had an outlet for it elsewhere, in Henry. There were fewer and fewer days when I thought of nothing but Hal and my grief. There were more and more when I knew exactly how long it had been since the King had last visited, and when he was likely to come again.

I am stubborn though, as I said, and feared God and Katherine as much as I loved Henry. I also knew the pain it would cause my sister, whose heart Henry had broken when he had fancied then discarded her. He had also (unproven rumor had it) "fancied" and discarded my mother once, before turning with interest toward me. Part of me found his attentions to be insulting and frivolous, and I snapped (out of his hearing) that I feared with his insatiable appetite for Boleyns, he would next take an interest in my brother George when he had tired of me, or else one of the sheep in the Boleyn pastures.

I would not, I said in private to Emma, be chosen only two pegs above mutton.

"Then, by my troth, if thou dost insist upon declining him, we must hide George and ready a sheep!" Emma had replied with mock urgency. "After he satisfies one appetite, we can roast the little darling to satisfy another, and so please him twice yet still spare thee."

Another part of me wanted him, but this I did not confess to anyone. I perhaps might not have been so adamant about denying him otherwise. In the act of turning him away, I saw myself as fighting demons in both my spirit and my heart, and I drew upon my usual forceful will to do it. Had I not felt so deeply, I might have gone to him with a shrug.

From a personal standpoint, I was reluctant to embark on a relationship with Henry because I had a deep fear of losing myself in him, as I had lost myself in Hal. I was familiar with his tactics, and could look forward to his pushing my infant and me away, as he had done with Mary, or pushing me onto someone who owed him a favor, as he had done with Bessie Blount. He was looking for a new wife, it was rumored, but I had no illusions that he would find one in me. I was too proud to bed him with those expectations, and still too angry about Hal whom I had, since our handfasting ceremony, viewed as my husband.

I was too afraid of what Henry would do to my heart. I had now experienced a broken heart and was not strong enough to suffer another.

There were also the moments—these came with frequency—when I would think of him as king and feel as if I had climbed to a great height. The view of the ground from this crest left me frozen with terror. I suffered just that feeling in my stomach, when I thought of Henry as more king than man. Once he knew me, he would uncover my unworthiness and spurn me, because all that attracted him was on the surface, I believed. I could combat my discomfort and fears of disappointing him only by tormenting him with mild tauntings to keep him at bay, and to make him more man than king.

Back in court, I wanted Katherine to know my loyalty was with her. I made great show of this, and I was sincere. She has never thanked me.

I turned Henry away, tactfully but firmly, again and again for all these reasons.

For doing this, I was called a "whore". I could not please them. They would have me be a whore no matter what I did or did not do, simply because Henry loved me. Had I lain with him the first night and been discarded in the morning, they would have not have objected to me at all and oddly, would not have used the word "whore". The court was roundly promiscuous and my behavior would not have been questioned, for their own behavior was far, far worse. I had never heard the word used for Bessie Blount, his longtime mistress. It was rare to hear the word used with any of his lovers (although Henry had used the word with Mary, to my anger and indignation). To be selected by Henry was an honor, and was treated as one. Others had never prompted these furious protests as I did, when the issue was love and not purely sex. The more I tried to prove my modesty, the faster came the judgments.

My refusal to bed Henry, who had never before been refused, prompted accusations of manipulation. I was withholding my favors until his desire reached the point where I had him enslaved. "They" knew this with absolute certainty.

I did not want a slave, and it still infuriates me, for I was not manipulative! That was Katherine's forte, not mine. I was too honest. These were accusations based on jealousy, or prompted by anger over loss of favor. Many personal ambitions were tied to the crown of Queen Katherine, and Henry's love for me threatened them.

People also project onto other people what they themselves feel in similar circumstances. I was surrounded by grasping, ambitious rabble who presumed I was of their ilk. What you hear of me is more a reflection of the speaker than the woman spoken of, especially with regard to my motives. No one can speak for another's heart. Certainly no one ever spoke with accuracy for mine!

Who could have predicted what would happen? Surely not I. I merely wanted Henry to leave me in peace! Could no one see? Even history has failed to recognize my impossible situation. Even after I had recovered from the loss of a marriage that would not only have been advantageous, but to a man I deeply loved, after my dear Hal married someone else, I still had to deal with the issues of duty and responsibility. I would not hurt or betray people I loved by becoming King Henry's mistress, though he repeatedly begged. I would not disappoint God and lose my tattered immortal soul by encouraging the interest of a married man.

For months, years, I did everything I could to dissuade him, finally even saying we would have to marry before he could have me. Exasperation prompted that demand for marriage, and I was not sincere. How could he have taken me seriously? Who—with sense—would make that demand of a *married king*? Even a king rumored to be looking for a new wife. What insignificant lady of the court would seriously demand that a married king discard his queen for her, except as an act of desperation concocted by a pair of giddy women amid shrieks of laughter? A marriage of my own choice was my aim. It was not a decision I wanted to entrust to Henry when his interest in me had dimmed. I would never find a husband under the glare of his attentions and I was nearer 30 than 20, to my mother's continued dismay. I would soon be too old for a match even half as agreeable as the one I had lost, were one even to be found at all. So, straight-faced but inwardly laughing, watching so I could be certain to have his expression right when I relayed the tale to the others, I pretended to have impossibly high expectations, so he would turn me away with disbelief and contempt.

I intended it to be the final episode in a story a very small knot of ladies had been enjoying for many months. The picture I had in my mind, and the role I was preparing to act out for the ladies, was of Henry growing apoplectic over my insolence. I imagined him ordering me out of his life as he had Mary, who had only asked for his love. With impish anticipation, I practiced Henry's bug-eyed fury in the looking glass in preparation for the telling of my final chapter.

I had gotten very good at mocking poor lovesick Henry, and loved to tell a tale for an audience. I was not above orchestrating the scenes and the players for the sake of the tale, which is what I was doing with Henry in this instance. I was creating a funny ending to a long story. I do not like to say, "That's all it was," for laughing at Henry's deep felt love was a despicable act of cruelty. But I was not, as everyone insisted, coldly and calculatingly using him to advance my position. I am innocent of that.

He agreed to my terms. He humbly agreed to my outrageous terms, and my heart broke for him, right then and there. Tears of shame sprang to the corners of my eyes when Henry took my hand and gently kissed it.

"As thou dost wish," he had said softly. "I am thy servant, and if that is what pleaseth thee, that is what I must do. I shall set to work on it immediately."

I had never dreamed he cared that much for me—not really. His words of love had meant nothing to me, as I thought it was a game to him. I was out of his reach and, if caught, would become the object of his contempt. We were playing chase, like children, nothing more than that.

One did not disrupt one's life and a country's entire political and religious foundation over a game of chase. It was the first moment when I truly knew it was no game to Henry. I did not understand until that moment. I swear upon the blood of Christ I did not understand, or I would never have tried to provoke him with a demand for marriage. I would have agreed to become his mistress very early on, and remained so, had I known the extent to which his feelings could take him and the havoc they could bring to all. It was, however, too late for that the moment Henry agreed to take me as his wife.

The hurt and betrayal I would inflict upon those whom I was serving or protecting were nothing compared to what I was doing to Henry. His feelings for me would not, or could not, be undone by my turning away and his disappointment would exceed even God's. I knew it must. I had been making sport of his sincerity, while he was offering more than I could even fathom at the time, resolving to discard his wife, his daughter's claim to the throne and his God. For me. He had broken my heart with pity for him already, and I did not yet know in entirety the sacrifices he could make for me.

"Oh, no, Sire!" I had said, frantic. "I truly was not serious . . . I cannot ask it of you . . . no, no *please* . . . "

Henry turned to me in alarm.

"*No*?" He whispered faintly with a terrible pain in his eyes, "What dost thou mean, 'no'?" Then louder, hurt and accusing: "Thou art taunting me again. I beg thee—"

"Please, I only meant—" I only meant what? To make sport of him? To laugh? I was entrapped by my own cruel foolishness and frightfully poor judgment. I could never speak aloud my original intention in making the demand. I silently prayed that my friends would know better than to mention it lest Henry find out how cruelly I had laughed at him. I could not bear for him to know. I would henceforth have to endure the embarrassing accusations and criticism rather than confess. I would henceforth be known as a woman with incredible vanity and nerve, and shameless grasping ambition, but that was easier than watching Henry understand the truth.

He covered his face with his hands. I thought he might weep.

"Oh, Your Grace. I spoke out of turn. That is all I meant. Oh truly I cannot ask it of you. I will be your mistress. That is all I want from you, nothing more. Oh please . . . "

I was, at first, aghast, but later turned the prospect of being Henry's wife and queen around and around in my mind. Not only would it quiet my critics, I predicted, but it might suit me as well. Most certainly, it would please my parents, I thought. As time went on, I felt more and more that it would suit me. And then, I felt I would die if I could not have it. I truly felt as if I must be a queen or die. It had taken root in my mind, much as the thought of a male heir had taken root in Henry's.

In the end we were wed. It would have been best had I cut out my tongue before suggesting marriage. It would have been best had I died before accepting the title of queen. I think there is nothing in life I would wish for less, than to be a queen. It is a vanity and an encumbrance I wish for not at all.

What started as a jest turned most shockingly monstrous.

Some time after the time we first discussed marriage in 1526, I was stricken by the "sweating sickness" and hovered near death for days. The impact this had on Henry as he waited a safe distance from infection cannot be described. He could not come to me. He could not risk death; he had to survive to rule. So he waited, hearing word of dozens and dozens who died (including my sister Mary's husband) as the sickness swept through London, sending prayer upon prayer heavenward for my recovery. He could not lose me, he swore. God help him, he could not.

God heard Henry's prayers over the prayers of those who wished me dead, and so I managed to survive.

The illness had an impact on me as well. I could no longer pretend to Henry that I did not love him. I had nearly died without telling him so. That seemed to me the greatest sin of my entire life, and one that must be rectified. From that point onward, my letters to him and my speech grew warmer and fonder.

Yet I refused to be his mistress for four years more. In my heart, I was still bound by my vows to Katherine, even though our enmity was far-progressed by then. There was a nagging shame in the midst of my anger and it made me hesitate, even as I was anxious to take what Henry offered me. I was also adamant that I would not be discarded as my sister had, and was persistent in reminding Henry of this. I would not be a great fool. I would have it all, or Henry would have nothing.

Despite my insistent virtue, I had finally tucked Hal away in a far corner of my soul and had turned the full focus of my affections on Henry.

Henry was gentle and charming and funny. I was still teasing, but now took some pains to encourage him, for I truly wanted to be with him. Even had the discussion of marriage not taken place, my illness would had forced me to face him—and myself—with the truth about my feelings for him.

I had come to deeply care for him, and to feel a kind of

connection with him. He somehow knew me better than anyone but Hal ever had, catching me constantly off guard with his insight, and what he knew, he loved. This discovery, that Henry knew me well and loved me still, quieted my initial fear that he would scorn me. I marveled at his love as if it were a miracle.

His eyes were pulling me, and I was drawn by his physical presence into imagining what it would be like to lay with him, and to wish it. I began to imagine more and more and to wish it strongly enough to know that I would not be turning him away for long. I was growing weak, then found myself growing stronger in my resolve to see my imaginings come to pass. I thought of God, and prayed for His forgiveness. I knew I would have to sin, and soon.

Finally, it was time. Years into our relationship, after years of effort on Henry's part to marry me, when we had finally reached the point where it seemed the marriage could really take place, it was finally time. I had no plan, nor did I know how to say the words, but I could no longer wait. More importantly, I began to fear that Henry could no longer wait. I felt I had pushed him as far as he could endure.

I worried and rehearsed before Henry's arrival, then nearly fainted from nerves when he appeared and I had to face him, knowing as I did what I was planning to suggest.

Henry usually arrived unannounced, creating havoc and internal discord within the house. Cooks fretted and scowled and shoved boys off to the storehouse for provisions, servants snapped at one another and raced to ready rooms, Mother wrung her hands and pressed her temples, and Father privately muttered complaints about the expense of feeding the King's robust appetite, and that of all his party.

In a short time following his initial visits, acknowledging their frequency, my parents permanently relinquished their own room to Henry and found another, thus ensuring that the finest bedroom in the house was always kept ready for him. Each time Henry came, he brought with him his own very large lock, and had it bolted to the door of this bedroom before he had barely set foot in the house. It, of course, would never have occurred to him that anyone might feel inconvenienced by his presence, or his demands.

I was always whisked into my room where my hair was hurriedly arranged and my gown examined carefully, while Father entertained the King with conversation. On the occasion of this visit, I spent these moments deciding "Yes" or "No" and vacillated once again. I decided to let the evening progress on its own, and choose my course before the end of it.

It was necessary for me to warn my mother in advance that I might be joining Henry in his room. This brightened her up considerably, and went far toward the curing of her head pains. She was transformed into a woman bustling and eager, delighted that I had finally decided to settle the matter. I could now place myself in a position to reap more substantial material rewards from the friendship than the baubles and dresses I had first cringingly come to accept and was now accumulating with indifferent expectation. Never mind that Henry had sent her other daughter away from him tearful and distraught. Mother was counting coins, imagining recognition for my father and brother, and wealth, status and favor for us all. My brother was looking at a position of more responsibility, and at acres of land. My father speculated on the titles he could earn through my horizontal efforts as he had through Mary's and perhaps, though I had no proof, through my mother's. There was a festive mood in our household with each member thinking of his fortune and his ambitions. Meanwhile Mary remained silent miles away, her heart and thoughts closed off to me. I thought of her more than I did the others. I thought of Katherine.

I wanted none of Henry's gifts. I wanted no payment for this. I only wanted Henry.

On that evening when he came to visit, he began to tell a story to amuse me. In the telling, he mimicked members of the court with a comical precision that delighted me. Standing before me, he acted out the roles of the players until I began to laugh far more than was considered seemly. At one point, I squealed and hugged myself, and pressed my chest into my thighs, while tears rained down upon my cheeks. I collapsed with helpless, heaving laughter, and nearly slipped off my chair and onto the floor. Henry reached out and caught me seconds before I would have fallen, limp. He did it in a way that suggested he was not embarrassed by my behavior, in fact, he seemed genuinely delighted that he could so entertain me. He resumed his comical soliloquy, glancing at me from the corner of his eye as I delicately covered my mouth with my hand to disguise my hiccups. He then sent me into a fit of giggles by raising an eyebrow and frowning with each dainty "Hic". His eyes were twinkling with pleasure even as he frowned.

My mother found excuses to enter the room and deliver surreptitiously reproving glances and faint shakings of her head, and even fainter grimaces and hissed warnings. She then exited until the next eruption of mirth. I could barely see her through the tears and when I could, I laughed harder. Meeting Henry's eyes as my mother disapprovingly swept out I could not stop laughing, nor could he.

My gleeful outbursts, rather than offending Henry, spurred him on to further demonstrations. He clapped when I timidly contributed one of my own and, emboldened by this, I joined him. We created imaginary, ridiculous conversations between courtiers: a host of familiar characters swearing undying love to the persons they hated most; one of Katherine's somber and black-garbed ladies cornering a handsome young man on the stairs; an intellectual, flagrantly effeminate nobleman wooing an illiterate horsehand. Each successive play was more outrageous than the last. We gasped for air, we were laughing so hard, and Henry, still laughing, picked me up and pulled me squealing and giggling onto his lap. He had never before ventured that kind of familiarity.

Hearing my loud laughing protests, my mother approached with a shocked frown, saw, froze, then turned quickly away and disappeared with a look that suggested she would not return.

"Had I but known she would do that," Henry whispered, "I would have clutched thee to me far sooner." And then reverting to pompous formality he boomed: "We shall take note of the strategy!" He threw me into yet another fit of giggles.

Quieting down, still chuckling, Henry touched my chin to bring my face toward his and looked in my eyes. "My lady, I do love thee," he said quietly. "I will love thee ever more. Knowest thou this?"

I knew he did, and I knew he would.

"Aye," I whispered, "As will I love thee." I twisted around and took his face in my hands and smiled at him, lightly stroking his beard with one finger. I could feel a catch in his breath.

"Dost thou? Speak again," he said in a whisper, his mouth close to my ear.

I laughed. I had learned from Mary's mistakes, and would not demean myself before him with plaintive, desperate proclamations of strong emotion, though I felt emotion strongly.

"*Dost* thou?" he insisted more loudly, laughing back at me in all but his eyes.

"It is late," I said, climbing from his lap. He pulled me back, and shook me by the shoulders gently. I laughed still, avoiding his eyes.

"Answer!"

I sighed and rolled my eyes with feigned weariness. I yawned.

"Cruel thing!" Henry said reproachfully, letting me go.

I stood before him and said " Your Grace." He looked at me for a moment then turned away in disgust. "Henry. Look at me." It was the first time I called him "Henry" though later, as we grew more intimate, he would ask me to call him "Rex".

He did not comment on my familiar use of his Christian name, or seem to notice. He was pouting. He turned his head to avoid me as I moved around him, and crossed his arms over his chest. He looked ever so like a small boy.

I moved closer. Henry's pout filled me with amusement. It seemed the time to confess. I could pull back once again if needed, to maintain his interest. That tactic, I noticed (as had everyone else) was effective with him. I placed my hand on his shoulder and he did not move away.

"I love thee," I said. "I have always loved thee. Even from the first. Even when I turned from thee." I ran my finger up his cheek. "I love thee immeasurably." My voice had become a soft caress.

Henry stiffened in preparation for the teasing blow that was sure to follow such a pronouncement and turned to me with narrowed eyes.

"Without measure, dear Henry." I said more firmly. "Truly." I touched his hair, briefly grazing his ear with my finger causing him to jump involuntarily.

He reluctantly turned to me, and saw I was not teasing. He hesitated for a moment in order to absorb this, then reached for my hand and lifted it to his lips. He said nothing, but looked at me with a child's guileless expression of hope while he considered what my words had meant.

I spoke again with a constricted throat.

"I love thee only. I thank thee for thy patience, and for thine efforts to have me." I slipped back on his lap, and wrapped my arms around his neck. Pressing my lips to his ear I whispered "I wouldst that I could stay with thee this night." I grew embarrassed and warm at having said such a thing, and at the feelings that welled up in me as I did. I blushed and pressed my eyes closed. Once again, I was looking down onto rocks from a vast height.

"I may stay the night then?" He asked in a high voice, with a catch in his throat, stiff, not looking at me or moving. "With thee?"

"Aye," I whispered, my head whirling at the thought, and my body tensing with anticipation and old fears. "If it pleaseth thee."

It did. Henry found the suggestion quite suitable to his wishes.

There were routines to be followed: dressers to undress us, bedclothes to be turned, nightshirts to be worn. Dozens of persons attended to the preparations, or witnessed them. The inevitable Act itself was no doubt clearly overheard by those who had bribed Henry's guards, and now stood with ears pressed up against the door. It was short-lived; Henry had been denied far too long.

I knew this would be duly noted by the servants in the hall.

I lay there, inexperienced but for violent rape, and thought of the wonder of it. He had touched me, and I had felt warmth and love and pleasure. More than that, I felt close to Henry as I never had with anyone before, even more, I feared, than Hal. I was in love with him beyond hope. I knew that now.

Hesitantly, he asked if it had been as I had expected.

"No," I answered. His face fell until I continued. "I expected pain, and revulsion, for that is all I knew." I stopped myself, panicking. I had spoken too much. I changed the direction of my speech and said, "I knew not that I could love a man so—" I leaned over and cupped his face in my hands. "I will love thee ever more. I am your Anne."

And ever will be. Here, in the Memories, I know that.

He looked prepared to weep for just a moment, before controlling himself with a laugh. He was a feeling man, always. I held him and laughed as well. We fell silent, and absently touched fingertips, laying side by side.

And then he tried again.

I smiled and felt a rush of tenderness toward him. Eyes locked in his, the smile disappeared and my hands reached up to embrace him, and, still looking into his eyes, unblinking and unfocused, I felt him enter me then the push! and we both whispered "ahh" into each other's lips and held tight. We murmured our love to each other, and smiled, and touched each others faces and nuzzled each others' ears. It was a pleasant thing for a while, a much longer while this time, and then slowly it became a very focused pleasant thing. I moaned softly.

"Father in heaven," I whispered. "I feel quite strange . . . " then a gasping pause. "Oh *Go-od!*"

I fully had Henry's attention now. He nuzzled me and asked, "Does it feel good, my precious? Is it good?" I could sense his chest expanding with excitement, because he was able to please me.

I was to find he worried much and often about his abilities. I was to find these worries would one day come to haunt me.

"Aye," I whispered while my head lolled. "Aye, 'tis quite good." I blindly reached for his face and touched his forehead and cheek lightly. "I do love thee. Oh God I do love thee."

He shuddered at the words, struggling hard to be deserving.

I felt my body take control of me in ways I had never before experienced. My limbs encircled his waist, and my pelvis whipped up to meet his, pushing frantically in rhythm.

His excitement grew. He found pleasure in speaking aloud the unspeakable, and whispered it to me. Wicked speech. Foul speech. I felt my desire grow frantic.

I whimpered and moaned and twisted. The large, heavy bed

creaked and slammed, while the wooden canopy shuddered dangerously above us, and the drapes that hung from it swung back and forth.

Nothing mattered except that I loved him and needed him. I was spiraling into some sort of queer darkness that Henry had made for me, where every one of my nerve endings demanded that he keep going.

My frantic declarations of love were nearly a shout. Henry's eyes were crazed as he thrust faster and harder. Mine rolled back in my head as I felt a tingling shoot all throughout me. My head pitched back, and my pelvis shuddered and I grunted an animal grunt, ashamed but unable to stop the sound, and then I groaned *very* loudly and *very* long.

I heard muffled, quickly silenced tittering in the hall.

Henry's sounds joined mine. He was dripping sweat, pressed close, nuzzling me, trying to speak of love in gasping, broken breaths. I clutched at his back with my fingers and held, then released and let my arms fall to my sides. I emitted one soft "Oh God" and one truly heartfelt "I do love thee!" then a last dying moan. The sensation receded, and I was normal again. Not normal. Better.

Following just a few seconds behind me, face contorted, Henry moaned as if in agony then collapsed on top of me, kissing all the parts of my face. His eyes were shining. He lay there happy and exhausted until his gasping breaths returned to normal. Then he rolled over onto his side and pushed his hands across his face to catch the perspiration.

The sounds I had made, and words I had spoken and heard with such eagerness, suddenly seemed very shocking and unseemly, now that the urgency had passed. I thought of the ears against the door, and then of the fact that this was King Henry VIII, ruler of all England. Having just coupled with the man, I remembered the King. I went numb for a moment from the shame.

"God's blood." I buried my face in the crook of his arm. "I can never look at thee again." I felt I was speaking the truth.

"Nor I thee," he answered amiably. "We have most shamelessly disgraced ourselves."

"This was unspeakable humiliation. I cannot bear it," I murmured into his arm, dying a slow painful death of intense and total embarrassment. Why could I never be calm? How could I have allowed myself to behave in that manner with the King?

"A reprehensible display. I thoroughly agree and am most ashamed of myself." He tickled me under the arm and leaned over to kiss me. "Most ashamed indeed."

"No! Turn away. I cannot look at thee!" I pulled away sharply. This was far worse than an unbridled laugh. My mother, were she among those pressed to the door, would be dying, by now, a most horrible death. I knew Mother would never stoop so low as to listen to her daughter's lovemaking. I had no doubt though, that she had someone planted there whose report could kill her later . . .

"Then I shall have to take thee from behind, to spare thee the sight of me." He nodded agreeably and said "Hmm. Next time. Indeed I shall."

I sat up, looking away, attempting dignity. "I will be quieter next time."

"You will be louder, next time. I will see to it." He pinched my buttock.

"I could not *be* louder," I argued, covering my face.

"Thou *couldst* be louder, and very much *more* so. I found thine involvement to be weak and unspirited. I expect hearty yodeling from my women, and all throughout. Not just at the end. I shall have to train thee. Starting . . . " He thought about it and shook his head contentedly. "Soon. Not now."

He pulled me down and I buried my face in his side. I stole a peek at him and saw him staring at the ceiling with a very peculiar, very happy smile on his face and knew I had pleased him much, in large part because he had so obviously pleased *me*. That softened my embarrassment, as had his teasing. Yodeling indeed, I thought, inwardly rolling my eyes. I felt the pumping of his good strong heart and loved him.

"By your leave, my dearest love, doth . . . doth the Queen moan?" I whispered impulsively, knowing it to be a dangerous question, but faintly hoping for reassurance that I had not behaved with uncommon boorishness. I took such liberties with Henry, and he allowed me to.

Henry stiffened and looked at me sharply, then relaxed and tried to hide a smile. "Katherine? Moan?" He started to say something, then imagined it in his mind and stopped to laugh till tears formed. He reached around me and hugged me close to his chest. "Katherine *prayed*," he said. "In Spanish. It sounded as if it were for a male child, but I suspect instead that, in her heart, it was for me to be quickly done. I *know* it was. Certainly, prayers for a male child were never heard. Prayers for me to be done were most assuredly answered."

He grew silent for a moment, then sighed and looked at the ceiling with an expression of sadness, replaced in seconds by one of impatient displeasure. I was surprised by his confession, which came to me in a soft, distant voice with his eyes still fixed upon the ceiling.

"She lay there passionately praying, while I hammered away with passion of another sort like a dutiful *fool* of a husband and never, my dear Anna, never *ever* moaned. I could not get her attention." His voice drifted off faintly and he was still and silent, staring.

Then he roused himself and turned to kiss my head. "I shall never be able to perform the act again without a cacophony of moaning. In truth, I shall not." He nuzzled my ear and murmured, "I shall insist upon it always. Remember that."

I smiled.

"And furthermore, I should like to request of thee never make love to God, when I am with thee."

"There is but small danger of that," I assured him.

"And now *I* have a question," Henry said softly.

"Yes?"

"I was not the first . . . I could tell as much earlier tonight."

I was silent.

"Was it Henry Percy?"

I shook my head.

"Who then?"

I could not tell him the name. He knew the man, who was now in Rome. We, to some degree, required his assistance in proving Henry's marriage to Katherine false in the eyes of the Church. I had a needling concern that he would remember me and thwart the process. I would not start a battle over a beast with a persistent hunger for little girls, and further destroy Henry's chances of bringing us together. Henry would not believe me anyway. Yet the rest he had to know. I pulled the velvet band from my neck and showed him the scar, now small and barely visible. It was, perhaps, too small to satisfy Henry.

"I was forced, sire. Many years ago, when I first arrived in France. I was a child. I have not been with a man before or since, till thee." The anxiety rose to my cheeks. "Thou wilt not tell anyone? I beg of thee no."

"How do we know you tell the truth?"

How indeed? This question would one day be asked of me again, in less indulgent circumstances with the rapes and the scar never mentioned.

I stiffened and my heart pounded when it occurred to me that the question was presented to me with the more polite and distant "you", rather than the affectionate "thou".

More frighteningly, he had referred to himself with the royal "we".

"Henry, I have loved thee since I was a child. Yet I denied even thee, for years, and thou art a king and the most agreeable man I have known, and were relentless. Consider that an ordinary man would be forced to wait for me at least as long. Consider that no ordinary man would wait, as thou hast, and would leave."

I thought of Hal. He was also no ordinary man. I hoped Henry knew this.

"I speak the truth."

Henry thought about it for a moment, silently.

"I cannot take it back, Henry. It was forced from me. But, in truth, had I not been forced, I would be a nun. Thou wouldst not have me now." I dimpled and flashed him a naughty grin, attempting to cover up a small fear that rose in my heart. "I would be making love to God."

Henry did not laugh as I had hoped he would. The small fear grew.

"You will not tell me who?" he asked.

"No," I whispered.

He lay pensively staring at the ceiling for a very long moment, then smiled.

"It matters not," he said. "I am in love."

For now, the matter was resolved.

The world knew about us within hours, and predicted it would last only hours longer now that Henry had discovered, finally, that I was equipped no differently from other women. People nodded sagely or shook their heads. All of England knew Henry's only interest in me had been physical; my only advantage had been in denying him, and now Henry had me. I was not a beauty and did not have royal blood. I brought him no political advantage. It was only sex, and Henry had been sated.

Poor stupid whore, they said. Poor dimwitted thing. Soon, and she would be off, they said, and good riddance to bad rubbish.

Yet I stayed. Henry moved me into his apartments, took me with him everywhere I could possibly be taken, and wrote to me daily, when I could not come along—sometimes *twice* daily. Henry could not abide writing letters, but would write letters to me twice each day.

Katherine was sent away.

"Next week," they said. "He is tiring of her."

And yet, I stayed.

I would have been called upon to stay with him still, had I bedded Henry in the beginning. He would have followed me still, if I had held out longer. It was not purely sex, although we both found sex to be utterly necessary, and it was not infatuation. I did not have Henry "bewitched". We were truly and forever in love with each other and wanted only to marry, and be together, and live our lives.

That is all.

'That is all,' I say. And here I laugh.

Once we had tasted each other, we were insatiable. I wandered the court with heavy, drowsy eyelids, always aroused, always thinking of him, always wanting my limbs to be wrapped around his waist, experiencing that moment in coupling when anguish gives way to release. I thought of it endlessly, making distracted conversation and preferring no conversation at all, except with him.

He watched after me wherever I went, his eyelids as heavy as mine. His touch was electric, and he touched me as often as he could, sometimes under a table, sometimes with seeming unconsciousness, although I knew it was purposeful. We could go no more than a few hours without excusing ourselves and meeting in some corner where I would tear at his codpiece, and he would lift my skirts, lean me over a table or chair or against a wall, quickly take me then return to his business. We took the risk because of need, and because his chambers were too far. We were scandalous, and there was nothing we could do. We needed relief throughout the day, and all through the night.

I was to say, "There is urgent business—," and then I was to name the empty room where he would meet me. I interrupted meetings of historic importance to pull Henry away. Few people were amused by this except for Henry and me, and they all knew (or I presumed they did). Foreign diplomats would shift irritably, kings and queens would be halted in mid-sentence, bishops would humorlessly wait. Then Henry would return with some small thing or another askew where it had not been fastened or adjusted properly, and the meeting would resume where it had left off. I would be at his side to attend for the remainder, with or without the approval of his guests. No one mentioned his short absences within his hearing and mine, but they were watched with amazement and disapproval, and perhaps a little envy, by everyone.

We did not live in isolation. We did not speak to each other, or embrace each other, or quarrel in isolation. From the first moment we were intimate, the time we spent coupling was measured and the outcome remarked upon. It is difficult to maintain harmony in such circumstances, difficult to accept that one is being watched by all for signs of monthly bleeding, or for sickness that portends an infant, and to know there are those who would wish both you and the infant dead. It is difficult to love a man no one would have you love, and difficult to know that powerful advisors are cautioning him against you. It is most difficult to be hated when one only seeks to please.

Every word I spoke henceforth was heeded, and repeated, and changed either in its tone, or its intent. My sense of humor had always leaned toward irony. I suddenly saw my ironic comments taken literally—oftentimes with the exact opposite of my intended meaning—and found myself judged by these, and my entire character reshaped in the eyes of all who did not know me, and some who did. My mistakes were announced everywhere, and continue to be retold and embellished throughout history, through all time. I was forgiven for none of them, and with each retelling my ill-temper or my bad judgment, or my "vicious scheming" grew worse.

As for "history", or rather that accumulation of hearsay commonly thought to be the true representation of the past, I have some knowledge of it here. I do not recognize the woman they call "Anne Boleyn" either in her temperament or in some of her actions. I certainly do not recognize the motives, thoughts and intentions attributed to her. The historic "Anne" is not much loved, whereas I was loved much, and might have been for the span of my normal life, had I not "demanded" Henry marry me.

That one misspoken, insincere demand was the beginning of a period of humiliation and soul-crushing loneliness that continued through the entire remainder of my life, even during those times when I had unprecedented honor and tribute bestowed upon me. It caused me anxiety, and took a sharp toll upon my temperament. This created an even greater backwash of anger and disapproval from those who were on the receiving end of my moods until there were far more who wished me harm than not. In retrospect, they had good reason: I became a shrew.

Henry's love had a very high price.

Chapter 5

Henry wanted a woman who could challenge him, to whom he could talk, and with whom winning an argument was a true triumph. He wanted an equal partner. He did not feel himself henpecked—not at first. He felt exhilarated by the parrying between us, and proud that I had intelligence enough to force him to think as he defended his position when we disagreed.

We liked to argue. Henry liked *me* to argue. It made his eyes shine when we disagreed, and made him cross when I sat silent, or calmly reasoned with him as Katherine had. He would bait me endlessly to get a reaction from me, and would sulk if he could not.

"Good God, woman!" he would bellow. "Hast thou no ears? Hearest thou not what I just said? By Jove, I *know* she has a *tongue*!" He said this drolly, affectionately.

Once in answer to that, I stuck out my tongue at him and made a face. He broke into a smile, then grew fierce again as he resumed his pursuit of a disagreement. I was obliged to join him lest he grow truly ill-tempered.

"By my troth, you speak gibberish," I would often say with mock condescension. "Speak sense and I will happily give thee my response." Then I would assail him with the reasons his logic was faulty. He would pace back and forth as he rationalized his position and I would sometimes concede, sometimes not. As he spoke, he often looked at me for approval. Was I coming around to his thinking? When he sometimes saw that I had not, he would change the direction of his logic to be more in line with mine, and would then take credit for having "convinced" me.

As suddenly as the argument had begun it would be over, and Henry would be purring into my ear. Those who spread their comments throughout the court never mentioned the purring, or the smiles, or the personalities involved. What they observed was that our relationship was "volatile" and "fraught with conflict".

Henry would be irksome or tired and would snap at me, and across England it was said that he was preparing to forsake me. He had a terrible temper, and was prone to rages. I was not afraid, and sometimes shouted back. This meant only that he felt sure enough of me to show his anger, and I felt sure enough of him to stand in his path. In normal conversations, once Henry grew less uncertain of me, we would snap and parry and quarrel in perfectly good temper. We could not do this without witnesses, and editorials, and interpretations of what he meant and what I had done to provoke him. He could not accept a playful verbal jab from me without raised eyebrows and the word "henpecked" being whispered. These observations would get back to me and, from nerves and strain and anger over being hated and misunderstood, I subtly grew shrill.

I was poorly suited to the notoriety. I was bred for a life as nobility, not royalty. There is a difference, reflected in my lifelong inability to handle pressure. Daily I faced situations I had grown up never expecting, nor wanting, nor been taught to face. I was high-strung and nervous by nature, and suffered from a shortage of confidence originating in my appearance and my hand, and in my mother's habit of finding me lacking. My level of confidence lessened further, when public examination of my family history revealed me to be inferior, then sunk even lower when it became a common topic of discussion that I had no appealing attributes to attract any man, much less a king.

One cannot successfully face an enemy while one is questioning one's own worth, and presuming the enemy is worth more.

I suppose I was fair game, but I did not have the inner strength to maintain my poise in the face of it all. There are dangers in court and in politics, and I was only safe as long as Henry loved me. Public opinion might sway him. He was daily advised to cast me off. I grew frightened and depressed for, as I had feared, I had lost myself and my heart once again. I pressed Henry for safety nets, first a marriage and then a coronation. He gave me both, and neither saved me in the end.

I began to sense it would not end well for me. I could not fight the world forever. I had nothing to cling to but Henry's love for me. Even the smallest sign that I might lose it made me frantic and ill-tempered toward those who could not answer back to me.

At the very basis of my insecurity was the knowledge that Henry had a wife whom all but Henry—and Henry's God—considered to be his true wife and his queen. While I had to make a public show of support for Henry's position that his marriage was false, I also secretly considered Katherine to be his true wife, and I acknowledged her as queen.

I was consumed by guilt and discomfort over my own more tenuous position. I was the most-loved woman, but I was still the "other" woman. I was a threat to the country and the wellbeing of Katherine, whose subjects loved her greatly. I was of childbearing age and so threatened their beloved daughter and her claim to the throne, should I produce a male infant. Few of my countrymen viewed me with sympathy or came to my defense, and perhaps my position was indefensible. I would have happily avoided being in that position at all.

Sudden silences fell over groups of people, when I approached, and unkind remarks were carelessly flung in my hearing. Few ever knew this; I hid it well by holding my head up and feigning cold indifference, but I was sensitive, and words or snubs stung me like nettles. I grew more and more withdrawn as time passed, and grew more cold and demanding in my public demeanor. I developed a habit of displaying a haughtiness of manner to hide my trembling lip and palpitating heart, for I was too proud to show that they could reach my feelings and hurt me there.

I perhaps focused more on the snubs and sneers of the English subjects outside the palace and the Spanish faction within, than I did on the sudden race among the others to win my favor. Some sensed the wind now blowing in favor of Anne Boleyn would continue for some time to come, while others insisted their careers were safer if they showed more loyalty to Katherine. There was no possible way for a lady of the court to overthrow a queen, they said. Common sense told them my days were numbered.

I was fully aware of the choices being made, and was stabbed to the heart by some who chose to side against me.

Once again, as in my childhood, my public image did not reflect my behavior in private. When I felt hurt, my petulance took hold and I turned childlike. I stopped reasoning as an adult, and knew only that someone must take away the pain. I did not know how to endure, or to fight. They do not teach "endurance" in the French or English courts. Since I was female, fighting political battles was a lesson I had never heard discussed by my tutors or at my parents' knees. I had learned Latin and music and sewing. I knew how to handle lazy or thieving servants, and to run a household. I was skilled at directing my maid servant in arranging my hair. I was taught to speak fluent French, and to interpret conversations at court, and I knew what colors were most flattering when selecting fabric for a gown. I was not brave and strong under siege, and knew not how to be. I had no examples except for Mary, and she had handled her crisis with Henry by breaking Mother's Venetian crystal (retaining enough presence of mind, I cannot resist observing, to break Mother's rather than her own) and crying for weeks. When distressed, I could not measure my actions as Katherine could, nor weigh my words with care, and it is here that one can pinpoint exactly where my downfall originated. I became a child under stress.

For the love of God, I swear I did not want to break up Henry's marriage. However, once spoken aloud the thought of marriage to me had germinated in Henry's mind, as did thoughts of a legitimate male heir.

I was powerless to stop him, and concentrated instead on chiding him to speed up the process. Once we were married, people would stop being mean to me, for I would be his wife, not his whore. I was obsessed with this. I wanted everyone to stop being mean. The talk and the accusations, the rumors and the vicious comments all tore at me. It wounded me that the masses of people all throughout England knew my name and hated me. I could not leave the palace walls without hearing them scream insults and tauntingly shout my name as I hid within my carriage, hands pressed over my ears and eyes shut tight. It humiliated me that I was being called a whore when I had worked so very hard to retain my respectability and God's eternal grace.

In private quarters, away from prying eyes, I would "retire from nerves" and succumb to hysterics.

"Make it stop!" I would demand of Henry, over and over again. I screamed and cried until my face swelled, agonizing over another list of hurts and insults I had accumulated since the last bout of tears. I mourned losses of friendship, and shuddered with pain from each successive broken trust and unflattering rumor. Henry would sit helplessly, holding me, thinking of what he might do, soothing me as well as he could while I clung to him sobbing.

I sometimes threatened Henry by saying I would leave him because I could not endure the strain. During those episodes, the terrified little orphan would surface and begin to weep and plead with me. My heart would break, and I would comfort him and promise him no, I would not leave. I could not anyway, except by death. I can truthfully say that, had he been stripped of his riches and his crown and been banished in shame to an island of rocks, I would have followed him there. I would have had no choice. I was tied to the man like a dog.

People do not understand simple love.

One after another, good friends were turning coldly polite.

Others were feigning friendship they had never thought to cultivate before. I knew not whether I was being used for my influence or to provide them with gossip or both, and knew not which of them to trust. Lies were being spoken as truths, and were carried throughout the palace and beyond. I could not be certain who was the source of them. I made guesses, sometimes incorrectly, and alienated some who had done no harm out of suspicion that they had. I grew closer to, and confided in some who were, in fact, the source of the lies, not suspecting.

As anyone else, I wanted to be liked, and loved, and understood. Instead, I was England's most detested female villain. Nothing would change that, except perhaps a marriage. If I were married and legally under Henry's protection, they would have to stop attacking me, and so I pushed, and Henry pushed, and Katherine and her supporters pushed back with tenacious, bitter strength.

In the end, the Roman Catholic Church in England would be replaced by the Church of England with Henry at the head of it, Katherine would be disgraced and exiled, Henry's daughter Mary would be declared a bastard and I would become Henry's second wife.

Through all this, Henry fought like the devil for me. He was so proud of me. He elevated my status to ridiculous heights, often pulling me into roles for which I was not suited, and he listened to me when I spoke on matters of state (I chose my position from conversations with my brother George) giving far more weight to my opinions than they deserved. He defended me, and rewarded those who would show respect while punishing my critics. He gave me more power than I wanted or was capable of handling, and the manifestations of that power were heavily influenced by my insecurity, hurt and anger. I learned that power could be used to spite people. I learned that power could silence and punish.

It is here that I get into trouble. Here in the Memories, my shame comes not from love for Henry, but from misuse of power. I find my punishments will come from spiteful acts made possible by the large power Henry foisted on me, and even from the small power each person has to make others feel loved or unlovable. I misused the small power as well, most often with my tongue.

Ironically, it is my love for Henry that will soften that punishment. I will gain for having tried for so long to protect his wife and my family, and will be forgiven in large part for succumbing to him because my intent was not selfish, nor was it frivolous. It might have been punishable under other circumstances, but these are considered, and weighing largely in my favor were my conscious efforts and reluctance to bring anyone pain. Also considered was my strength against the strain of loving him without holding him; I held out for just as long as I could and still be human in the face of his persistence and my need of him. Given greatest weight was the force of pure love that in the end caused me to bring harm to so many people. The love far outweighed any ill-intent toward anyone.

Love in any form is salvation to the soul, I learn, and when punishment is meted out one's capacity for love is taken into account. I will be punished less severely than I would, had I gone to Henry and sought power solely from ambition rather than tempered the ambition with duty and love. My misuse of it was the sad result of a situation I proved too weak to handle. In this it matters little what people said about my motives. God was taking notes.

✠

Elizabeth I, the Virgin Queen, was conceived on a table amid muffled grunts and moans, and furtive, rushed gropings, while Cardinal Wolsey waited for Henry to complete some Urgent Business in the library. She was there inside of me when I smoothed my gown, and tenderly straightened Henry's robes and sent him back to Wolsey with kisses and titillating promises. She joined us that evening when I made good on my promises, and left Henry seemingly without bones or muscles or will to do anything but breathe. It is odd that she would never herself know the sort of pleasure she had such intimate involvement in, when she first came to be. I find that odd, and sad. I have always felt sorry for Elizabeth.

✠

Trying not to wake Henry, I was on the floor, hovered over a chamber pot, retching. He heard the sound, and was immediately awake, grinning, watching me. He was speechless with joy. He would have a son! He climbed from the bed and squatted beside me, and gently wiped the perspiration from my brow. I heaved and vomited, to Henry's unending delight. He was thoroughly charmed. I smiled at him weakly, then heaved again. He clapped his hands together and kissed the top of my head.

"It could be bad pork," I chided him, somewhat recovered.

"Yes, it could," he answered beaming.

"Or a distressed intestine."

"Or that. It could indeed be that."

"Or I could be with child. Dost thou not even *consider* it might be a *child*?" I snapped at him playfully, smiling.

He had stood up, and was filling a goblet with water to hand to me. He also dampened a cloth with which to wipe my face, and was turning to me with an expression of stern importance, although his eyes were twinkling.

"With child? No, I had not given thought to that, but I will certainly consider the possibility when I have time. Right now I am too busy to think about an infant. Matters of grave importance and all that. I am an important man."

"Thou art in thy night shirt, speaking to a woman whose head is in a chamber pot."

"As I explained, I am a very important man. It is an important nightshirt, she is an important woman whose head I love most dearly, and–"

I finished with him, knowing how he would end the sentence "—and it is a *very* important chamber pot." He laughed, delighted at how well I knew him now. He gave me a look of such tenderness I still shiver to think of it. I accepted the water, and drank carefully lest it sicken me further as Henry gently pressed the cloth to my cheeks. He then set both the cloth and the goblet upon the floor beside me.

He helped me to my feet, and lifted me gently to the bed where he sat down and held me in his lap. He buried his face in my hair and was silent, holding me.

"I love thee, Rex," I said simply.

"I love thee, Anna," he answered, then drifted again into silence.

When I turned to look at him, his face was raised to the ceiling and two tears glistened in the corners of his eyes.

Henry always knew how to break my heart with love for him.

PART 3

Roses and Rain

1522—1523

Chapter 1

While I was still in France, negotiations were taking place to betroth me to an Irishman named James Butler, although I was not advised of this at the time. When I returned home and discovered the plan, I made attempts to learn more about James and his family—and grew increasingly resistant to the match. They were distant kin to me, and were holding some property Father wanted returned to the family. He would not have wasted Mary, his eldest, on a match like this, but found it suitable for me.

The Butler family was violent and capricious, and furthermore, his father expected young James to return to Ireland with me in tow. I had no desire to live my days far from home in the midst of a notoriously bloodthirsty Irish clan, and I said so.

The stalling of negotiations saved me. Things said, and actions taken by the Butlers over time forced a wedge of doubt into my mother's thoughts. These doubts were reinforced by my own complaints and arguments. Finally my wheedling, and the certain knowledge that I had found my true love, convinced Mother to persuade my father to halt the plans entirely. We all now looked to another man to wed me.

During my first years at court, I could not resist flirting, but I had never known what it was to be in love, except for wild infatuations I often felt toward various handsome men I had known throughout my life. Infatuation died instantaneously, more often than not, once I engaged them in conversation and found them to be boring or silly or stupid. Meanwhile, I whirled through court like a modest temptress, treating the act of searching for a husband as a dance in which partners were changed with each round of a song, and none was fair enough to keep.

I was an irrepressible flirt, but I was not heartless. I focused my art upon those men with whom the act of flirting was a game, and the object of one's attention just a momentary distraction. Court was filled with such as these, and a mating dance was played out in jest several hundred times each day between courtiers and ladies. We were very adept at declaring eternal love and admiration toward each other in passing, knowing it was meaningless and presuming it was harmless. We had little to think about but love, and gossip, and the increase of our fortunes, and in flattering those who might enhance them. Most flirtations were motivated by the last.

I did not bait men who had feelings for me that I could not return, nor did I encourage them by responding in kind to their sincere declarations.

Neither did I torment those whose feelings I could wound with my flightiness and teasing. Hal was such a one, wearing his heart very firmly on his sleeve so that feminine wiles were really quite cruel and took unfair advantage. I could not bring myself to practice them upon him. He was too sweet and gentle, and he brought out in me something tender and solicitous. I had attempted to tease him once before I knew him well, but swallowed my words in the next sentence when Hal shot me a lost look, blushed and grew silent. I never had the heart to tease him again, and each time I saw him my voice grew soft and gentle.

I soon found blushes working their way to my cheeks when he looked at me. My eyes were ever darting about for sight of him, and I slipped into a sulk if I somehow missed his appearances.

Henry, or "Hal" Percy was a page for Cardinal Wolsey, a regular at court, and a favorite of all. He had a somewhat eccentric appearance—very pleasant to me, but of the sort that begged for closer study. Was he handsome? Or was he ugly? His hair was pale, as was his complexion—the one seemed almost to blend into the other—yet a face that should have had no life (since it appeared to have no blood) contained two eyes that burned like coals upon a bed of ice. They flashed with intelligence and energy of thought, and gave no doubt as to the liveliness contained therein.

Hal was sought after by a number of ladies (or their mothers) with an eye for his titles and his prospects. Gossip made me aware of him early as a very eligible gentleman, and my lineage made me fear that he was a prize beyond my reach. He had no shortage of opportunity among the ladies, for along with his enviable social position he had no shortage of charm. Yet he was shy with women, despite his seeming confidence and efforts to be in their company.

He had no difficulty in flirting with ladies who were spoken for or who were older and past his interest, and he did this shamelessly as if he were an actor on a stage. At the same time, unmarried young ladies (and their mothers) were often disappointed by dull responses and abrupt departures by a frozen and fleeing Hal, who sought refuge in groups of back-slapping men. He had nothing to fear, but was ever fearful of a pretty face as if he were in danger of rebuke or rejection. No amount of reassurance seemed to cure him of this.

I presumed his reticence came from an old break in his nose, which was left somewhat flattened and misshapen. My deformed hand gave me ample compassion for Hal's discomfort and, while the other ladies increased their encouragement, I had the unwitting insight to decrease mine and make no gestures beyond those that were mannerly and friendly. In the process, I made him less frightened of me, and more interested.

Quips and quick repartee were common among courtiers. Hal initiated most of it. If puns were flung about, Hal was most assuredly in the midst of the verbal missiles, whipping a play on words into a limerick or poem in moments, to my, and everyone else's, delight. He saw humor in everything, and had a way of conveying it that drew people to him irresistibly. He had the quickest, most amusing wit of any man I had ever met, and a way of making the simplest events of life seem fantastic and hysterical. When Hal was in the room I would laugh continuously, for his mind was sharp and astute, and he had a habit of viewing things from a perspective even more cock-eyed than my own.

He was as amusing as one of the jesters, and was able to fling remarks at them so quickly that the jesters themselves sometimes stopped, speechless, and laughed at Hal. He once stood up and joined them during a feast, causing the room to explode with mirth throughout the show, and afterward took his seat to heated applause and a good deal of back-slapping from both the jesters and the audience. Wiping his eyes, the King joked that should Hal's fortunes take a turn, he could count upon a grand career among the court fools. Then Henry "crowned" him with a fool's cap, and gave him a gift of a silver goblet, and seated him at his own table for the duration of the feast. Hal pleased Henry as much as the rest of us, for Henry ever loved a sharp wit and a clever tongue.

He was adored by all. "Lord Percy!" everyone would shout when he entered. "Join us!" His presence alone had the effect of relaxing taut faces and diffusing a charged atmosphere. He never knew this about himself, for he had no means of comparing that which occurred before and after he arrived, and no way of seeing people as they were when he was not present. His view of the world was sometimes naive, and always forgiving. He could not see the dangers that were present for those of us not quite as personally blessed as he, and saw goodness in everyone, for that is all people ever showed him.

He was a sensitive man, and somewhat of an "artist". He dabbled in poetry and music, and was otherwise as useless a man as any who had ever been born to too much wealth and position. As one might expect of someone with heightened good intent, he could easily be brought to grief by any reproof, and would hang his head, suffering guilt of excessive proportions over having disappointed or offended for the smallest transgression. As full of wit and good humor as he was, he took feelings very seriously, and was an easy target for some who liked to bedevil his conscience, for he would always take the bait. There were a few who would scold him over things he had not done just to see his look of remorse, but even they did not do this cruelly. One could not tease Hal without lowering one's eyes from shame. He was one whom I (and everyone else) was most careful not to wound.

I had seen him at court and had always felt an attraction as I could never resist a man with wit. Hal's wit bespoke of a very impressive intelligence, and I also could not resist a man with a clever mind. His physical attributes were of little concern to me once he met those two criteria, but I was pleased by his face and figure as well. I would never have noticed him, had he not satisfied my parents' requirements of wealth and position, and he most certainly was not wanting in that regard. But it was his mind that I most loved. I found him to be as irresistible as everyone else did, and made every attempt to be within earshot of him, if not within his circle.

Hal was not one whom I could ensnare with tricks or lure with wiles. I was forced to wait and simply "be" while praying he found what I was to be enough for him.

My interest was returned. He had long seemed smitten with me from a distance but, being Hal, could not approach me with the flowery words and courting gestures he found came so effortlessly to him when he was with the older ladies. His wit failed him when he was facing me. Rather, he would stand and look in my direction, his body tense with every emotion eloquently projected from his posture and his eyes, and wait for a sign that he could speak to me. I gave him many, but he would wrinkle his brow into a helpless frown, which was Hal's best attempt at appearing self-contained and busy with important thoughts, then turn quickly away to speak to someone else. That always made me smile. I patiently waited for him to work up his courage, growing more and more fond as the time passed, watching jealously to see if the demeanor I interpreted as "attraction" was replayed for any other ladies. It was not.

One day he ventured to join me, casually, as if by accident seating himself beside me at table during mealtime, and pretended he was engrossed in a discussion two nearby ladies were having about the cuts of beef served for dinner. I spoke a few words to him and he responded in monosyllables, darting looks at me with love and terror in his eyes. His hand accidentally brushed mine and he froze, staring ahead of him, not knowing what to say or do. I found myself gently coaxing him into a conversation as if I were urging a small frightened animal to eat from my hand. He reluctantly turned to me, and our eyes met and held.

Well-versed in banter and small talk, I was surprised to find myself speaking to him from my heart in just a few minutes' time. I spoke of feelings, and long-secret dreams and he listened and nodded and offered a few of his own, growing ever more excited and passionate. Those around us slipped away as we fell into a discussion more intimate than one should expect between virtual strangers, and one more filled with hope, for we were both aware that we had found each other, and it was important. It just felt right, immediately, even in those first few minutes of conversation, much as if we had known each other all our lives.

He afterwards began to seek me out. Our initial conversation was resumed, and we explored each other's tastes, opinions and thoughts, and found them to be remarkably compatible. We moved past the courtly banter, never stopping there at all, and went directly to exchanges of a very personal nature. Yet our conversations did not have to be on a personal level to be intimate. We found that, even when we discussed the weather or the evening's entertainment, the people present would silently glide out of the room as if they felt they were intruding. I did not know why that was or how they knew, at least at those times when I happened to notice.

There is an aura that lovers project, and an aura surrounded the two of us. From the very beginning we looked as if we were "together" and we felt "together". We were a couple who clearly belonged to each other, as some couples do, so that even strangers had no doubt on first sight that we were meant to be mates.

We moved at the same speed, mentally, viewed things the same way just enough of the time to be harmonious without feeling boredom, and could spend extremely long periods of time together without irritation. There were no fights between us, and no arguing or silly lovers' games. We walked in step, in tune, in perfect rhythm. He made me a sweeter person, and a kind one, and a gentle one. I made him a stronger person, and a more self-assertive and confident one.

As I had been told, and as I had expected, I knew when I fell in love. There is no doubt, when it takes over. It is not a frantic, or an impatient, or a desperate thing. It is a very quiet, sure and steady thing. I was incomplete without Hal, and realizing that is how I came to be sure of my love for him. He was in my soul, and I was in his, and I discovered this within two weeks of our first meeting. In just that space of time, the two of us were speaking seriously of love, and discussing the future in terms of "we", and "us". We felt fused as if we had blended together, each into the other, where our hearts touched. I cannot describe it any more accurately than anyone who has been in love can describe it. Sometimes there is a key that fits the lock to heart, mind, body and soul, and Hal possessed it. That is all that can be said.

✠

It seems strange to think that this could be so, knowing as I do how bound I am to Henry.

"Why?" I ask. "Was it not real?" It certainly seemed so at the time. It seemed to me to be real.

The Voice explains to me that being bound to Henry does not diminish the importance of this newer, still-growing bond. Neither bond diminishes the other, for each soul has within it the capacity to love all other souls, and this love can take many forms. We all have a repertoire of possible marital pairings, each different and each important, for each comes with its own history and purpose. Hal's and mine was a love match, first and foremost, with two souls who were meant to spend their lives together if not as man and wife, than as something else; if not here and now, then in some other time and place. Choice drew us. We were bound more by this than by a Higher Law's insistence that we meet to resolve our conflicts and differences. By contrast, Henry and I are forced to it, loving or no.

And, yes, I am assured, it was real.

✠

I knew we would want to marry from the very start of the friendship, and looked forward to a lifetime as pleasing as any I could have imagined. I was floating with joy and anticipation. I had fallen in love with a man my parents would have chosen for me had they dared set their sights so high, and he was a man so tender I could feel my heart stretch and grow each day I was with him. He was attentive and caring, and was so proud he had won me that he paraded me around with a touching possessiveness, flushing with pleasure as people kindly and indulgently complimented his taste and good fortune with exaggerated praises for me. He shared his secrets and listened to mine. He ran to me with stories he just could not keep to himself, laughed when I made comical remarks, and blushed when I applauded his. In a short time he regained his humor around me and assailed me with one absurd observation after another, making the time spent in his presence a constant delight.

He was such a joy that I could not help but feel unworthy. Could he not have found a woman younger, or more beautiful, or from a more impressive bloodline? I dared not think about it, for I had grown to depend upon him for my very happiness. I was grateful and awestruck that I could be loved by a man such as he, and lit candles of thanks in the chapel. I had never felt so blessed, nor had my heart been so full.

Hal came to me when I was in the garden with several of my friends, took my hand and pressed it to his lips. From behind his back he produced a white rose, which he presented to me in a sweeping bow. Then he fell to one knee and proposed in front of all.

"I have consulted with your father, my dear lady. After a formidable amount of examination, we concluded that our pairing—yours and mine—might be somewhat acceptable to him. I have his permission to ask you," he said with mock pomposity. "And the weather is right for it, I dare say. One hopes never to kneel outdoors in a downpour."

I touched the rose to my cheek and tilted my head. I had been expecting this very scene, but had not known how Hal would bring it about. I only knew his approach would be unexpected. I giggled and touched the rose to my lips.

"Therefore, Mistress, will you take me as your husband? Will you endure my many, many faults till death—" and with a mischievous aside to the other ladies, who were clasping their hands to their chests in pleasure at his performance, he said in a loud booming voice, "Kindly remain silent about those faults, my ladies, until I have safely received her response and bound her to it!" Then he turned back to me and softly asked, "Wilt thou be my *very* beloved wife?"

One of the older ladies leaned toward me and hissed "Say yes, my lady." Others turned to each other giggling with excitement, pressed together like birds roosting, leaning forward to hear.

I grinned and turned to the other ladies. "Think you that this man is worthy of one such as myself?" The ladies covered their laughter with their hands and exchanged looks of merriment.

"My worthiness is *not* the issue, Mistress," Hal interjected quickly, his voice again raised in volume like an actor's. "I will not allow that to be considered in the discussion. The issue we are addressing concerns only whether or not you will *have* me. I forbid you to examine my worthiness until *after* the ceremony when it is too late to save yourself. Do I make myself clear?"

"What say you, my ladies?" I asked, shooting Hal a playful look. "Shall I accept him on those conditions?"

They giggled and nodded.

I turned back to Hal. "I will happily be your wife, and love you until death and beyond," I said for all to hear. Then softly, reaching out to take his hand: "Thee and thy many, many faults." I smiled. "They are part of *thee*, and I love them as well."

I spoke the truth. I did love his faults. It was Hal's faults that I came to miss the most, for they made him so human and so vulnerable and so in *need* of me. I felt protective toward him, and determined he should never know hurt nor harm. When he was gone, unable to act out my feelings of tenderness, I felt much as a mother would toward a child wrested away from her care. Helpless. Worried. Anguished on his behalf . . . and anguished over my own loss.

I erupted into tears at the memory of his hesitations and fears of rejection. I churned with sorrow over the impatience I felt when he refused to join the hunt with the rest of us and acted as if a mere fox could suffer pain as intensely as a man. I knew him to be weak in that way, and cowardly when it came to inflicting pain or viewing blood. I cried in shame for embarrassment I once felt when he shied away from confrontation. I would happily suffer those moments for an eternity. All gone. "My love, my love . . . "

I sobbed over Hal's well-intentioned efforts, which sometimes went awry, and wept at the memory of his thoughtful, bewildered, apologetic face fixed on mine while I laughed at a mess he had made of one thing or another. I sometimes scoffed at his fears and chided him. The memory of this later brought me pain, for it had not been intended as criticism. I loved him however he came down to the depths, as they say, of my soul. I prayed that he knew this.

In fact, he did.

Between us there was peace and commitment. Our lives should have been happy, harmonious and long. As it happened, and with intervention by Henry, they were not.

We had agreed to wait before venturing into physical intimacy, for we were both dutiful to God and our families, and both thought we had our lives to spend together. Part of my cautiousness traced back to the rapes, of which Hal knew (against my sister's firm advice to me) in more detail than I had ever told another soul except Mary. For that reason, he did not press. In later years I would marvel over his concerned acceptance of my claims of rape, and how gently he treated me out of fear he might frighten me. He never questioned my honesty, nor did he judge me or exert any pressure upon me lest he drive me away.

We limited our physical contact to kisses and hand holding, and warm hours with me held upon his lap. We sometimes sat in that way not speaking, yet we were intensely aware of each other, listening with our hearts, waiting and wanting with ever-increasing impatience. We had no need for words at such times. We had no need of anything but the Holy ceremony that would allow us to finally fuse our bodies as we had our souls. The ceremony could not come soon enough. We were tense with the need for it.

It had seemed at the time that we had something to wait for, and good reason to wait. It is a wistful regret, but it is also my deepest relief that we postponed our coupling. Had we been together, Henry might have beheaded Hal beside me. I could not endure the thought that I was responsible for his death too, as I was for my brother George's, and Mark Smeaton's and the others. I could not endure the thought.

Then again, Henry was suspicious of Hal from the beginning, despite my assurances that we were chaste. When Henry searched for men who might love his wife, he had no further to look than Hal, and he knew this, yet he merely questioned him, then passed him over and went on with his search. Henry could easily have concocted a story that would have placed him in my bedchamber, both before and after our marriage, but he did not. It could be that it was only Hal's endearing nature that saved him from the block. It would take a demon or a fiend to murder him, regardless of the mental state and motives of the murderer. Henry evidently found one line even he could not cross, so Hal lived on, unthreatened, yet closer to guilt than any man but one on the planet.

Chapter 2

Marriages were of as much interest to the King as they were to the participants and their families. They were less a partnership between a man and a woman than they were a means of creating alliances between powerful families. Since the distribution of power was of critical concern to the country's political welfare, approval was required before a marriage could take place.

For reasons of politics, Hal was betrothed when he was a child. It was an arrangement rather loosely made, and one that had been broken when Cardinal Wolsey, reassessing its virtue, stepped in to forbid it some years past. Talk of this arrangement had recently been resurrected, but no handfasting ceremony had officially betrothed Hal to this woman, and Wolsey's position had vacillated. The political situation was changing, and he had not firmly decided whether to proceed with this pairing or select another. He confessed his leanings were still against it.

Hal and I speculated that, under these circumstances, our marriage would be approved. In a private conversation with Wolsey, Hal had determined that there were no serious impediments to our marriage, and Wolsey had no immediate objections except to say he had not yet studied the issue in depth. He had however, distractedly, unofficially led Hal to believe that there would be no problems.

Then he moved on to issues of more immediate importance than Lord Henry Percy and Anne Boleyn, and dismissed the conversation from his thoughts.

On the basis of this (and as a result of some exaggeration on Hal's part that Wolsey was "wholehearted") Hal had obtained my father's consent, and conditional permission from his own parents.

Hal and I were young, and we had hopes. Hal counted on the good favor of Wolsey, whom he directly served. Both of us counted on the information Hal had obtained from Wolsey, so we proceeded with our plans to marry. We did this out of confidence, or more accurately, we moved ahead with blind and impetuous refusal to accept the possibility that anything might occur to prevent the marriage, simply because we wanted so badly to marry.

Once we had obtained approval from both sets of parents, we were privately betrothed with my family witnessing the vows. We exchanged rings in a simple handfasting ceremony, and wore them on our right ring fingers. They would be moved to the left hand in the actual wedding ceremony.

The ceremony was not officiated by a priest because it did not have to be in order to be binding. However, it might have been conducted by a priest, and should have been, and could have been had we only gone to the trouble to get one. This oversight cost us our marriage because it could never be proved that the handfasting ever took place. Henry could not even prove it years later, after he wanted very badly to prove it in order to invalidate our marriage. Had we gotten a priest, the betrothal would have been too binding for Henry to overthrow. He would have had to let us marry.

Sometimes decisions haunt you. Our lives turned upon that one decision: We had the opportunity, and yet we did not call upon a priest.

After the ceremony, I gave a token to Hal, which he pinned to his hat, as men do when they are betrothed. He did this with quips and a comical flourish, but his eyes were shining with love for me, and the token was to become one of his cherished treasures. The memory of his eyes became one of mine.

I took short periodic leaves from court to make preparations for the wedding from our London house. Hal stayed with us, when he was able, and traveled back and forth bringing gossip and presents. Among other things, he gave me a pearl and garnet pendant as a gift from his mother and, as his own engagement gift, a gold ring shaped as a love knot. Both of these had to be given away in time, for Henry knew their origin. I was left with precious little to keep as a remembrance.

My family made arrangements for a feast to celebrate and publicly announce the engagement. Hard work and continual spats had gone into the creation of a guest list we revised a dozen times. Dress makers and cloth merchants flowed into and out of our house while I stood and suffered hour upon hour of fittings for my bridal wardrobe and gown. In the meantime, Hal and I traveled to his parents' home, taking rides across their acreage, considering possible sites for a house of our own and consulting with architects over layouts and designs. They were happy, busy months.

As required, we officially applied for the King's approval of our marriage, and barely thought of this again, for we could see no reason he might to prevent it since Wolsey had not. We had no expectation of problems. Plans continued to be made. An artist was scheduled to come in three months to paint a wedding portrait. My mother had begun to list the game and libations needed for the wedding feast, and was making arrangements at Hever Chapel for the ceremony. She and Father met privately with Hal's parents to discuss and agree upon my dowry. The meeting was clearly a success—Hal and I both agreed it had been a success—and the outcome pleased us. Both sets of parents gave their blessings, with Hal's parents stating they could not but bless a union that promised their son such joy.

Decisions were now being finalized, and I was indecisively selecting the color of the flowers for my garland of roses. I had a weakness for bright things, and wanted a garland of every color, but my mother warned against such gaudy indulgences. I had to settle upon one. I anguished over details. Was the blue trim on my gown too bright? I loved red or yellow roses best, but would they be too colorful against the blue? Would pink roses be childish and make me too sallow? Should I change the color of the love knot on my gown?

If it were sewn in dark green I could carry yellow flowers . . . but the blue gave me such joy! It was the color Hal preferred.

As the day grew closer, my ability to decide upon anything grew weaker and I began to lean more and more on the words and advice of others. I suffered from lapses of memory and often grew confused and bewildered over minor things. I burst into tears one day, frustrated over having stared at a woman I had known for years, unable to think of her name.

"It will only get worse," Emma reassured me, patting my hand. "Thou wilt not regain full use of thy faculties until the day is past. 'Tis God's kind way of ensuring that His children go through with the sacrament of marriage. Were they in full control of their minds before the day, surely none would see it to its conclusion."

"God's efforts are wasted then," I answered. "I can assure thee I would see this through to a conclusion, even *with* a mind. Had I no limbs to walk to him, I would crawl."

"Aye," Emma said fondly and gently. "Thou hast found a man, not to walk, but to run to. I envy thee thy fortune."

Hal and I saw each other daily during those times when he was in London. Still chaste, we found it ever more difficult to wait, and were intensely eager to move past the wedding and into the marriage.

The day came when the King would give his approval. His decision would be relayed to Hal by Cardinal Wolsey while I awaited confirmation back in Kent, where my family had gone for a short rest. Hal promised to come to me immediately when he returned from his interview with Wolsey—a long day's ride or more on horseback—yet he still had not arrived by afternoon of the following day. I began to feel concern for his welfare. There was something terribly wrong, I knew, and while I did not sense that Hal was hurt, I could not pinpoint the reason for my dread. I worried in broad generalities. I had been feeling this uneasiness since early the previous day, so while Hal's delay was chilling, it was not altogether unexpected, based on the warnings I had received in my heart. I sent servants to ask along the road if Hal was spotted or found injured, then spent a sleepless night imagining all manner of horrors that might have befallen him.

A violent storm had moved in. I stood with my forehead pressed against the window, staring into the darkness through the rivulets, waiting for bursts of lightening to illuminate a drive empty of all but mud. I stood there for most of the night.

Hal finally arrived the day following, well past sunset, soaked and pale. When he was ushered in from the courtyard and into the kitchen by the servant, he looked as if he had been crying. I raced into the room to meet him, but he avoided my eyes. Frightened, I felt him for injury and pressed him for an explanation while he stood silent and distraught. Before he could explain—perhaps to postpone explanation—my mother ordered a servant to lead him to inner chambers where he could change into dry clothing and lose his chill before a fire.

He took his time, then when he emerged, he begged my parents to excuse us and requested that we not be disturbed under any circumstances. He led me upstairs to a quiet room where he ordered the servants away and barred the door.

My parents waited below with anxiety. They had taken a huge risk in supporting a marriage not yet endorsed by the King, and had done so on the basis of my word and Hal's. The blame, and the King's displeasure, would be pointed squarely at them. Consequently, they were severely frightened by Hal's demeanor and what it could mean for all of our futures. They sat in near darkness, waiting and not speaking for the duration of my discussion with Hal.

All servants were quietly ordered away from the second floor, and these scuttled about with feigned purpose in order to be at hand when we came down. A few raced to the servants quarters to sound a hissed warning that something was awry. Faces were peering from behind every corner, and more servants were visible or within reach than would be called upon for a banquet. There was a sense of dread in the household.

Our request was denied. Hal had spent many hours alone before coming to me, preparing himself for this unforeseen change in our plans and our lives, preparing his speech to me. Prior to that he had gone to his parents to request their assistance, and was alarmed to discover that they were in agreement with the King. Furthermore, they reminded him of his obligation to them, and to the family whose daughter was truly his betrothed.

Hal had not even *had* a "betrothed", aside from myself, until this day! Wolsey, himself, had raised the objections that had earlier ended that match, but was now changing his position and forcing it! Hal's parents were forcing it as well. And all of them were oddly ignoring the fact that a handfasting ceremony had bound us, and that we were, in fact, truly married (or as good as!) in the eyes of God and the Church. They did all this just that suddenly. Queerly. Just like that, and for no discernible reason.

He had no choice, Hal's father stated bluntly. Mistress Anne was not what they had in mind for him, and he was to marry immediately lest he show signs of defiance and do something insubmissive and rash.

My parents hurriedly leaped to a position of self-preservation. They made quick—*and conspicuous*—show of their own disapproval of the marriage. They publicly criticized me, and made deferential, placating apologies to the King for their daughter's headstrong disobedience to their wishes. They served me up for carving on a platter with a sprig of parsley and an apple in my mouth, leaving me publicly shamed and without familial support.

They had not shown signs of disapproval before. The mere suggestion that they should have found fault with Hal would have brought tears of laughter to my eyes. Hal was a plum indeed, and my parents could not contain their glee.

Hal had met this woman, his "betrothed", a few times over the years. He had always found her repellent. She was too portly for his tastes, and too tall. She cackled and insulted. She moved with lightening speed from mincing modesty to shocking vulgarity in her demeanor and comments. She blinked uncomprehendingly at Hal's witty observations, then flew into wheezing fits of hysteria over cheap and ribald quips of her own that caused Hal to blush with discomfort and shame. He had found her to be abrasive and offensive, and had on several occasions seen her eyes follow, not the men, but the women with looks of lust.

She clearly found Hal to be less than a desirable partner, and made no attempt to hide it. As for Hal, he would eagerly give her any chambermaid as a wedding gift rather than join her in the marriage bed and in one sense was relieved. She would never seek him out. He felt he simply could not do it with her, even drunk or threatened. Not even to produce an heir.

And so he came to me, ashen-faced with swollen eyes. He had an advantage over me, having spent his hours alone adjusting to these changes and regaining his composure. I, on the other hand, had to react to communication of the King's decision with Hal present, and no forewarning.

"Wolsey denied our request," he said. "We cannot marry."

I stared at him for a very, very long spell and did not speak, feeling blood drain out of me, not knowing where it might be going, and not caring if it ever returned to sustain me again. As his words echoed and taunted me, Hal tried to fill the silence with descriptions of his conversation with Wolsey. He grew more and more unnerved by my stare, for my face had no expression and I did not blink. I fixed my eyes upon his and looked at him. I did not twitch a muscle. I might have been a corpse.

"Anne?" He whispered finally, reaching over to touch my hand. I pulled it away from him in an angry motion. "Didst thou not hear me? Art thou not feeling well? Please speak to me."

I answered "No," in a whisper of my own. In shock, I whispered "No" over and over, then exploded into hysteria, pulling at my hair, tearing off my headpiece and hurling it, pounding my fists on the table and then against Hal's chest screaming "*NOoooo!*" Hal grabbed my hands and held them. He pressed them to his lips.

"I will *always love* thee!" I wailed, looking at Hal accusingly as if he were to blame. I twisted my wrists in an attempt to free them from his grasp; there was a table that still badly needed pounding and fists that wanted to bleed. "I cannot be parted from thee—I can*not*!"

I stamped my foot in a gesture that would have made the servants race to make things right and proper once again, had they any power to assist. I flailed at Hal and furiously pulled away from him when he reached over to hold and comfort me, pummelling him to make him keep his distance. I whirled, and knocked over everything that stood upright, shocking both Hal and myself with my strength. I babbled incomprehensibly, screaming "NO, I *canno-ot!*" in the midst of it. It was just as it had been when I was a child. I had more emotion than I had room for. I had no place to put the pain.

Hal stood and watched me with helpless hands at his side, an expression of terror and shock in his eyes. I was not the distraught woman he had thought to encounter this night. I was a demon unleashed from Hell.

I did not feel I could survive this. One half of me had just been amputated, the half that contained my heart. Having expended my energy in a fit far more wrenching than any I had ever had in childhood, I felt faint, and sank to my knees on the floor where I doubled over and sobbed. Hal picked me up, as I was now too weak to fight him, and carried me to a chair where he sat and rocked me. I pressed my face into his shoulder and wept. He stroked my hair, humming and shooshing and whispering to me as if I were a child. It was the last time he held me on his lap.

In time I calmed down and attempted to view the matter in a rational way.

"There must be something we can do," I offered hopefully, wiping my nose and eyes. "We will ask again. We will plead with the King. There is something."

"I am to be married just as soon as the arrangements can be made," Henry said softly, looking away, then back at me. "Arrangements are already in progress." He did not speak of the dread he felt in facing this.

"We must appeal to him immediately. We *must.*"

"My parents agree with him," Hal said gently.

"And thou wouldst obey them?" I asked, knowing the answer. Hal would never bring pain to his parents. He was as dutiful as I was. I understood duty. It was the one argument I could not argue against.

"Thy father's line," he began, then fretted that it might sound like a reproach and hurt me. He cleared his throat, paused, then shook his head in anger and exasperation. "You are not '*suitable*',"

Hal hissed, pressing his face into the back of my neck. "And I was told the King has someone else in mind for you, though you know it not." I could feel dampness where his face pressed. It was his tears.

For a split second, and for no reason, I thought back to the evening when I had flirted with the King, and I felt a cold chill. My eyes widened in terror that I had brought this down upon the two of us, then I dismissed the thought as vain. Gnawing at me in the back of my mind, however, were the looks of recognition I had seen in Henry's eyes of late. Should I believe that I was unsuitable for Hal? Technically I was, but pairings such as ours were quite common, and if convenient to the throne were most certainly considered "suitable". Had the argument been that the King preferred another sort of alliance for specific political reasons, I might have seen more sense in it. None of this rang true, unless I viewed it as a purposeful attempt by Henry to keep me unwed. Nothing else could have caused such rapid upheaval with such vague and conflicting rationale.

The man Henry said he "had in mind" for me would never appear at my door. No man but Henry ever would.

Nevertheless, I hated Wolsey as much as Henry, for his tongue had spoken the words. And as time went on and my love for Henry grew, I came to overlook that Henry even had a part in it and fully blamed Wolsey for my grief, much to his misfortune and my own shame.

I had a choice. Did I prefer to think of myself as not good enough for Hal? Or did I prefer to think that my stupid, playful indiscretions were the cause of this?

I far preferred to think my actions were not the cause. I would be disabused of that belief shortly when Henry would make his intentions clear, but while the wound was still raw, I had to believe that my bloodline was to blame, and not I. This was hard enough to bear. Again, I convulsed with sobs.

Hal looked at me, turned my face toward his with one finger, whispered "Shhh" and wiped my tears. "Shhh. It breaks my heart to watch thee weep," he murmured.

How could I cast loose a man so sweet? I could not lose Hal. I could no more give him up than I could give up food and drink. I could more easily give up food and drink, I thought.

Hal abruptly continued his original thought in a musing tone of voice. "Yet what *has* been found suitable—" He said it again to emphasize the word—"what has been found *suitable* for a man of my station is a bovine creature with a bad complexion and a bulbous nose. By my troth, that large round nose doth run," he added as a conspiratorial aside, his eyes deliberately widened to suggest innocuous, childlike sincerity. "Tis indeed a most remarkable nose contrived to excrete remarkable fluids."

He said this as if he were selling me that nose, trying to convince me of its value.

Do not jest about this, Hal, I thought. Do not make me laugh. I can never laugh again.

Still, a laugh escaped and nearly strangled me. Even now, I thought. Even in the midst of this, he can make me laugh. I nuzzled closer to him, and clung to his chest in grief.

At the sound of a laugh, he took heart and began to speak as if he were telling a story for my amusement.

"God help me on my wedding night." His hand made a gentle, caressing movement across my back. "I do foresee the need to install myself in my finest of all possible wine cellars for days before that night," he sniffed conversationally, "And quaff it dry."

I squirmed as the knife pierced ever closer to my heart.

"There are those who would envy me. I shall be belching upon the very finest and rarest of all possible libations—" He nodded at me briskly, with mock enthusiasm. "—which will then go on to nourish a rose bed as the very finest—and rarest—of warm summer rains. I shall make a special trip to the garden, to bestow my treasure upon the bonny blossoms."

He made a sweeping gesture with his hand and said softly, encouragingly, "Grow yon roses! Grow!" He turned to me, and explained himself in voice so controlled it contained not the faintest hint of irony. He made his voice sincere: "My betrothed once confessed she has a fondness for roses. I can only but give them the finest of care, now that they shall be hers as well."

I almost giggled at the thought of him weaving drunk, urinating on his carefully pruned and lovingly nurtured roses. The picture nearly pushed the rest of it out of my mind for just a moment. Then his words came back to me, and it was here that the knife found its mark. The mention of his wedding night caused my heart to palpitate with panic and despair. The words "my betrothed" hung in the air. "My betrothed" no longer referred to me, and the title was my holy right. I could not force my mind to accept. I erupted once more into frantic, violent tears.

Hal apologized profusely for upsetting me and sank into a despondent silence while I sobbed into his chest. A few moments passed, and he apologized for the disrespectful manner in which he had spoken to me about his betrothed, then sat silently once again. He spoke over my weeping a third time to apologize for talking in such a vulgar manner about such vulgar things as belching, and noses, and the watering of roses. He had no need to apologize for that. His vulgarity had been the only thing to bring a smile.

"She is my betrothed," Hal amended bluntly. "But *thou* art my beloved." He turned away from me and pressed his fingers to his eyelids.

Defiance began to surface. I would not lose him. I would *not.* My tears stopped and my face grew cold. Stiff with determination, I twisted around and placed my hands on either side of Hal's face drawing his lips to mine. He responded reluctantly, then gently pulled away. I wrapped my arms around his waist and turned my face up to his.

"Stay with me," I commanded. "*I* am thy true wife, and shall be in all but name henceforth, if thou wilt but stay." I fingered his shirt in an angry attempt to remove it.

Hal stiffened and gently pushed my hands away. "No, Anne," he whispered. "Please, no."

I had no use for my immortal soul without Hal and made a decision in that instant to risk it, in order to be his mistress. It seemed a small risk. God surely knew I was Hal's one true wife and would find no sin in this. He surely knew we were married—I wore Hal's ring. After our handfasting ceremony it must be the other woman who committed sin.

Stopping for a moment, I held up my hands for Hal to see, not even hesitating, my deformity in full view. I was thinking that Hal had never even blinked at my hand and often kissed and stroked it. That was one of the things I had always needed most from him. I pulled the ring off my right hand and fumbling, placed it on my left.

"There," I said. "It is done. Before God, I am thy wife unto death."

Hal shook his head and looked toward the ceiling. "Anne . . . no."

Determined, I reached into my bodice and pulled at one of my breasts so that the nipple peeked over the low neckline of the dress. I tugged at and pulled down the shoulder of my dress to free the breast so it was fully exposed. I took Hal's hand with both of mine and softly placed it on my bosom. Hal stared as if hypnotized and let his hand rest there. I held firm, so he was forced to feel my heart beat. For a few moments he closed his eyes and counted his breaths, then suddenly he shook himself awake and pulled away as if he were touching something hot. I reached for his hand once more and slowly drew it back. Hal closed his eyes again and breathed. He allowed his fingers to tentatively explore on their own.

I stretched up, pressed my lips to his, and felt him stir. I took my hand away from his, yet his hand remained where it was, gently cupping and massaging the breast he had never before touched or seen. I whispered "I love thee," between long hard kisses. Hal put his arms around me, and pulled me to him, kissing my lips and then my eyes, then moving downward and resting his opened mouth on the nipple of my breast. "I love thee too. Oh God, I love thee too," he whispered back. The words were muffled by my bosom.

"Be my husband, my sweet. Come, be my husband."

We both were weeping, now.

His breathing was hard and ragged. We were facing each other, touching each other in ways we never had before, urgently while time was left.

I found his waistband and pushed my hand within. He tilted his head back, his face contorted, with tears traveling in rivulets down his cheeks and onto my chest. Then I thrust my fingers down. I touched him and, eyes forced open with panic, he cried out.

Startled, I pulled my hand free.

My fingertips burned, remembering the touch.

Hal pushed me away and stood, straightening his clothing. He motioned to me to pull up my bodice. He did not assist me, nor did he come close to me.

"The command came from the King," he said in a deadened voice, shaking his head and himself into composure. "And my parents have threatened me. They have already taken this possibility into account." He enunciated the next two words very carefully and almost coldly: "We cannot."

I wondered what his parents had threatened but dared not ask because of the look in his eyes.

"We shall hide from thy parents. And the King will never know," I assured him, adding, "The king merely said we could not marry. He did not command us to keep apart. Besides, he does not punish persons for their lovemaking. What have we to fear from him?"

"There is much to be feared from my parents. I need not go into detail."

Hal grew silent and looked down.

We could not meet in stealth, Hal knew. He had thought it through. Primarily, he feared the consequences when we were caught (it was not a question of "if" for *Anne* was involved in it). I could not be relied upon to take only a small, secret portion of his time, no matter how frantically I promised it would be enough. I would want more and more, no matter what the danger, and I would have brushed aside any risks.

He knew we could arguably have escaped with one or two marital visits before detection. His fear though was of a pregnancy and a child he could never claim, and that possibility was to be feared each time—even the first time—we were together. Were I to become pregnant, there would be no question of paternity in anyone's mind, and such a pregnancy would be in direct defiance of the King's orders. Hal feared he would ruin me and be unable to step forward to salvage me, for not only would we be found out and punished, but he would be married and unable to rectify the situation. The "honorable" thing could not be done. He would be at fault, and helpless in the face of it while his dearest love volunteered for a life as his whore, and as unholy mother to his bastards. Hal knew I would do this, and he would not allow me to, for that would not even have been the worst of it.

He knew there was no point in explaining to me. My love was greedy, and cared not for logic. It cared not for safety, nor for sense. Partly because of my leanings toward indiscretion, he would not risk speaking of a plan aloud, nor even of devising one, although he had had some passing thoughts of Ireland or France. He discarded them, for in leaving, there would be damage left behind and two families that would suffer punishment. He had deduced quite accurately that a trap had been laid and there was no plan to serve us.

I only seemed to those outside to be the dominant partner. In truth, it was Hal who possessed the strength, and he was called upon to draw from it now.

I reached for his hand, pleadingly. He pulled it away and stepped backward, away from me, protectively hiding his hand behind his back. He knew the pain would last. He was opting for a lesser pain. He wanted not to weaken later and come back to me for more. He wanted not to know what it was he could not have, and, in this life, it was a wife.

I took a step toward him, and he jumped away, fearful that I might touch him and shake his resolve.

He tilted his chin up to prevent tears from spilling, and looked at me for just a second before looking away again.

"We will just need to make the best of it."

The pull was too strong for us. We were in pain " . . . of the writhing sort," Hal would one day muse aloud to a trusted manservant, draining his stout.

"*Please,*" I said calmly, knowing he could not abandon me.

"We cannot see each other again." He did not say that it had been forbidden; he did not want me to question him. Hal suspected the reason much as I did, but knew more than I the extent of Henry's determination.

Sadly, it made sense to Hal, that the King should desire his incomparable Anne. He was not angry; he was resigned and broken-hearted.

"Thou art taunting me," I laughed uncertainly. Surely he was only bargaining for the sake of his parents' threats and could be brought to reason. If he said "never", I could make it mean "sometimes". From there I could wheedle more frequent visits. "We shall meet in secret, surely? I shall make plans anon and meet thee."

Hal shook his head and turned to leave. He was not haggling price with me. He had rejected the sale.

It took a moment for my mind to register what my eyes were seeing. Hal was walking toward the door. My beloved one. My life. I screamed in panic then hugged myself. It had not been truly final until his back was turned to me.

"Do not *le-eave . . .* " I moaned, bending at the waist as if I had been stabbed. I jammed a fist into my mouth. I was dying. I was going to die.

He looked back at me with his mouth twisted, and his eyes burning. He started to say something, then stopped and raised his eyes to the ceiling.

"I cannot be with you!" He bellowed, slamming his fist against the wall.

I had never heard him shout so. I cowered in the face of it.

"Dost thou not under*stand*? Canst thou not see this is the *end* of it? Make the best of this as *I* am trying to do! Why dost thou make this so *difficult*?" He fell against the wall and stood there for a moment, then pulled himself upright, head lowered.

He appealed to me more softly with tears streaming down his cheeks.

"I cannot bear this. I did not mean to speak to thee in this way. I am sorry. I need to go now. I need to . . . to forget. I need for thee to let me go."

"Forget . . . " I echoed in a whisper. My whole body began to shake, and my teeth to chatter. My eyes suddenly lost their focus, and I drifted into a kind of stupor. I looked around me. Hal had chosen the sewing room to tell me. My half-finished bridal gown was crumpled on the floor where I had hurled it in my fit, cream-colored wool with love knots of that lovely blue—Hal's blue—and shimmering cloth of gold sewn to the skirt. It swirled through tears.

I thought of the garland of roses. "White," I decided in that instant, in a split second of insane denial. "I shall have white."

"In a few years we will both think things were for the best. Meanwhile, I want us to not see each other again. I could not endure it, nor couldst thou." Again, he did not mention that he had been forbidden to ever speak to me and had come to Hever in secret, and in defiance.

I looked at him stupidly with a slack jaw and parted lips. I shook my head almost imperceptibly, and hugged myself to stop the chattering. I could not make out his words.

Hal seemed to waver. He saw tears that needed wiping, and a shaking girl who required attention and a warm lap. Bracing himself against these things, he turned away again.

For just a moment, I seemed to lose my mind from pain and shock. I saw Hal's back and felt a scream welling up inside me. How could he have allowed this to happen to us? Why had he done nothing to stop it? How could he leave me so? He could not do so, if he had truly loved me. Did he not love me? Surely he must not! The agony of this truth erupted within me.

"May God *damn* thee to eternal Hell, Henry Percy!" I shrieked. I had never called him Henry. I wanted God to make no mistakes when He gathered up the damned and pitched them into Hell. "May Satan take thy miserable soul! Wilt thou never have a backbone? Be a man, sirrah, and be thou brave instead! Must thou ruin both our lives with thy sniveling cowardice? Is the fear of reprisal so much greater than the love? If so, I was deceived, and *hate* thee for it!"

My eyes were wild with fury and contempt. My hair was a clawed, disheveled mess. I could not take back the words once spoken, but in a sense they alone were giving me some peace. They were a wedge that was making it possible for him to leave, and for me to let him go.

Hal winced and sent me a look of betrayal and of hurt. Then, with sudden self-possession, he gave a small droll smile and called over his shoulder, "My dearest love, my bravery surely knows no bounds, for I am standing up to *thee*. I wouldst that thou were only Satan and his armies, for I fear facing them less than I feared coming to thee this night."

Then he stopped and looked back at me with sad and tired eyes. "I do love thee, Anne . . . " He said it again softly as if to himself: "I do love thee. I cannot stop it." Then, almost shyly, in obvious discomfort, Hal said, "I could not bear it, were thou to love another."

"I can never love another," I answered softly. "Thou knowest my heart. I vow to thee, I never shall."

We exchanged small smiles, then wiped our eyes.

In a stronger voice Hal made the simplest of apologies. "I am sorry," he said with the corners of his mouth twisted down and tears welling up in his eyes.

He stood and waited for me to respond, or for something to occur that would allow him to leave me.

"I wish thee happiness, Hal," I choked through tears. I gave him that. He deserved that. I stood and looked at him, still chewing my knuckles, still hugging myself with one arm.

Hal nodded and left for a roadhouse for the night rather than prolong the parting by remaining at Hever. We would not speak again except in the most formal of circumstances, and then only briefly. In time my heart would hardly break at all at the sight of him. For the duration of my life, we would both be careful to ensure our eyes never met.

Chapter 3

Hal's marriage, as expected, would be miserable and loveless. His wife did not understand, as most people did, that Hal was to be gently kept, so she bullied and criticized and publicly humiliated him. In a short time his spirit began to buckle. He could not endure confrontation or discord, and was living in the midst of it with no hope of escape. He faded into a quiet state of wasted years, nursing very real stomach ailments and complaining of other, imagined disorders of the body which then were manifested into real illness, with ready assistance from excessive drink. His health would decline sharply, and he would die young, just months after I would die.

Until then, his humor grew more caustic, and his view of the world grew less naive and less forgiving. He developed a talent for biting sarcasm he was hitherto unknown to have. His tongue became cruelly sharp with unkind wit, and the butt of his humor was marriage. He developed a deep long-lasting distaste for the institution, and will retain his strong feelings toward it, even when we next meet.

Our problems are not over in our having paid our debts this life. I will greatly fear marriage and he will deeply hate it when we meet again. Our challenge will be to love so well that we can overcome this and continue the business we started together.

In the years subsequent to the end of our courtship, Hal followed my progress closely, devoting long stretches of time to self-pity when I fell in love with Henry. He had somehow counted upon me to ward off the King—and every other man—forever, and was the only one not surprised that I held out as long as I did when Henry first pursued me. He drank for two days when word reached him that Henry and I had finally consummated our relationship, and drank for another two when word of my pregnancy was made public.

He did not drink on the day of my execution. He simply sat in the dark and stared. His thoughts revolved around my final accusations before he left me, and of how our lives would be had he acted differently.

He blamed himself for my death, overlooking that he had left me to prevent his parents from taking steps to bankrupt and ruin my family under clandestine pressure from the King. The plan had to do with the wording of a contract my father had once signed, that Henry was going to produce if I continued to see Hal. Hal's father served the King and felt he had no choice. He would be the one to enforce the damaging clause. If he disobeyed, or if I were found in Hal's bed, the King would retaliate.

Hal was publicly told only that he would be disinherited if he married me, but the real threat had been described to him in private, and he had followed his conscience by leaving me. His fear was not of his father's anger toward himself, but of the damage he could bring to me and to everyone in both families. He saw abandoning me as an act of love and indeed, it truly was.

When Henry began calling shortly afterward, my feelings toward him, not even knowing the full extent of his meddling, were murderous. He was offering himself to me after killing everything that mattered in my heart. His attentions came about so soon afterward that I could not help but understand the reason approval of my marriage was denied. He was expecting me to be grateful, and was bewildered by my coldness and refusal to accept him.

"Manipulative," the others said of me.

It matters not what any of them said. It matters not.

Publicly, it was announced that I was now being sent away from court for my rash behavior. My fury at this statement could not be measured, for in addition to the injury, I was to be further shamed before the court and held up to it as a fool.

In truth, I had gone to Queen Katherine when I was able. I had been stunned and hysterical for days, bedridden for the most part, and spoon-fed by servants I mostly waved away. I finally roused myself from my weeping long enough to request of her more time to weep and stare and stay in bed. I reported to Katherine and begged her leave for an undetermined period of time.

"A personal matter," I explained. The queen knew what that matter was, as did everyone at court, and in her eyes was a glimmer of compassion I would see little of, elsewhere.

Disgrace, like ill-fortune, carries with it a stench, and elicits more self-satisfied, triumphant glee than empathy. Of all the persons I knew from court, Katherine was the one who offered me empathy.

That one look from Katherine, and my heartfelt gratitude, cost Henry eight years of courtship to win me. I had Katherine's permission to stay away as long as necessary, and was henceforth indebted to her for her kindness.

Queen Katherine's eyes had followed Hal and me on many occasions, misty, pleased and nostalgic.

"Love makes Mistress Anne very pretty," she had once said in proprietary fashion. She had occasionally smiled in our direction, and had remarked in flattering terms about the other to each of us. We pleased her, yet she was aware of our bloodlines and their disparity.

She was not behind this, nor was she in concurrence with the decision. The queen had not influenced the King to nullify our betrothal, even with my sister only recently tossed from Henry's bed. I knew this then, and now.

Henry walked in as I was leaving Katherine's sitting room, and accepted my stiff curtsey with a slight twitch around his lips. He watched me leave. He could not know what fearsome invectives I was silently flinging toward him, nor did it occur to him that I might be angered, or that my pain and Hal's might be more than a superficial, passing disappointment. He presumed I had agreed to marry solely in order to better myself, and was pleased with himself for having found a way to proffer a far better bargain, he thought, than Hal. He did not agonize over the ethical points inherent in his actions, having rationalized them away. His path was clear, and that was all that mattered. He would arrive at Hever on Tuesday fortnight, and would summon me.

The mystery is not why I waited so long to welcome Henry's advances. The mystery is how I ever came to welcome them at all. I have no answer except to explain that the love was already there, dormant and waiting, and had been there since beyond memory.

I also never fully knew in life what Henry had done to Hal and to me.

Henry could have waited one lifetime more. He should have left me with Hal and stayed with his wife. I most bitterly reflect upon this at times.

But at such times I venture into nonsense. Had I not suffered then, it would have been later. Now that debt is paid and that lesson is learned, and it is behind me.

And with my Elizabeth, Britain got a fine strong queen.

Life most assuredly goes on.

PART 4

Bait

1523—1530

Chapter 1

I was alone, abed, when word came. It was well past noon, and I had not yet risen, nor had I any intention of rising. I was lost in my thoughts, and lacked any interest in diversions or healthy pursuits. I fully intended to grow old and to die in my bed, and rarely left it. So, settled in and waiting as I was for the end of my life, I found the interruption and the information relayed to me both jarring and unwelcome.

A servant hurried into the room and advised me that the King would be calling in two days. Mother had ordered her to help me select a suitable gown for the occasion, she said, and even as she spoke of this, she was already poking through the garments in the wardrobe while I angrily sat up and watched her.

"There is no need," I snapped. "I will not be coming down. Go."

"Your lady mother doth insist," she answered, hesitating. Deciding to obey my mother rather than me, she turned back to the gowns. Another servant swept in to assist her and the two of them discussed between themselves which gown was most becoming, and which headpiece should be worn with it. A third servant ran to my bedside and began, against my will and with harsh objections flung at her, to pull my nightgown over my head. I twisted to get away and hurled myself face down upon the bed.

"I will have thee flogged!" I shouted, bursting into tears,

pounding my fists.

Mother walked in upon the scene and coldly ordered me to behave.

"I shall not see him," I answered softly, defiant, not quite meeting her eyes. "He hath no business with me. It is Father he comes for."

"His Highness has expressly requested thy presence at the audience. Thou wilt obey." She waved the servants over and had them fit me with a gown. The three servant women pulled me from the bed and stood me upright, stuffing my arms and head into the outfit, while I let out muffled sounds of outrage and Mother watched. I wrestled through the fitting with tearful protestations, snapping at the servants for pinching me when they examined the fabric for stains and wear.

"I know what business His Highness needs to discuss with me," I shot toward my mother. "'Tis the same business he had with Mary. I will have none of it."

My mother responded by walking up to me and slapping my face.

"Thou hast not grown too large for the whip," she hissed.

He came.

The servants had spent the morning pressing cold cloths to my face in order that I might appear presentable before the King. Mother repeatedly threatened me against more tears lest I undo their work and spoil my features, and walked in often to see that she was being obeyed. My stays were fastened, my gown was brushed, and my hair and headpiece were arranged.

My mood was foul, but I was ordered to work my mouth into a smile, and so I did. The smile had not reached my eyes when I glided down the stairs, through the hallway, and into the study where Henry and my father awaited me.

I gave a deep, respectful curtsey, and sought a chair at an awkward angle from Henry, where he could observe me only by twisting his head. It was a carefully calculated gesture that could not be technically viewed as defiant, since women were expected to remain silently in the background. However, both Henry and my father were immediately cognizant of the distance I had chosen to place between them and myself. My father in particular was outraged, although he could not speak of this before the King.

I could determine from the way in which my father sat and smiled at me that I would be facing the gentle whip before the day was over. He did not know how else to deal with me. Heretofore my misconduct had always been the result of mischief or over-excitement; Father had never once before confronted mutinous insubordination.

This meeting was an opportunity for Father to negotiate for a better position at court—every audience with the King was a possible stepping stone to more titles and wealth—and his position was particularly fortunate in that he had me as bait. His intention was to dangle me temptingly with one hand while he begged with his other. My failure to cooperate in this ambitious endeavor threatened Father with a lesser position, or no position at all, and such a threat was not to be withstood.

"Aye me," I thought and crossed my hands at the wrist in my lap. I pressed my mouth into an insipid smile, and tried to appear as if I had no thoughts and was somewhat dim, as women were expected to be. I looked out the window at a robin and awaited further instruction.

Henry twisted around to face me while continuing his conversation with my father, and found the position uncomfortable. He sighed impatiently. He rose his hand in the air.

Seeing the movement from the corner of my eye, I looked sharply in his direction, and quickly lowered my eyes.

"Sir Thomas, please invite Mistress Anne to join our discourse. She shall sit here." He waved to the empty chair next to him.

Father nodded and stood, turning toward me. With a frozen smile and a controlled movement of his eyes, he ordered me to rise and approach him, then took my arm and helped me into the chair beside Henry. I settled my skirts while they resumed their conversation, which I was not, after all, invited to join.

A few moments passed. My father was looking increasingly smug, I noticed, convinced he had just persuaded the King to present him with a coveted appointment.

Then, seemingly startled by a sudden thought, Henry appeared as if he just this instant remembered something important. With feigned urgency, he sent my father out with a cryptic message for one of the royal servants. It was a message that could only be delivered in person, Henry said, and Father was to return with a response.

Neither Father nor I had any doubt that he would not find the servant in question.

Father left unwillingly with resurfacing anxiety about the appointment. (He would get it, and more. Henry simply had no patience for Father's tactics, with Mistress Anne in the room.) He feared what I might say to the King without a parent's cold stare to remind me of my duty, and made every effort to locate the servant he had been sent to find. He was nursing a small hope that the message was real so he could finish the business of delivery, then return to the task of chaperone and wheedler of wealth.

He unhappily discovered there was no such person in the service of the King. This did not, however, surprise him. He dared not reenter the room and resume his discussion with Henry after receiving this intelligence, for it clearly indicated he was unwelcome and had been ordered to leave. He waited in his sitting room and fretted, periodically dispatching servants to quietly observe and report to him. He had had the foresight to send one in just as he had left us, fearing the worst, and that servant made a quiet but annoying attempt to hover nearby without being noticed.

Once he had succeeded in removing my father from the conversation, Henry turned his attention toward me.

"Your presence has been missed, these long weeks," he said with interest that appeared only polite and negligible. I would discover later that Henry had a remarkable capacity for hiding his feelings when he chose to, and his seeming indifference was evidence of this self-control.

Two weeks was not an overly long spell. I was also in disgrace and officially awaiting his approval of my return (unofficially I was at Katherine's kind command), so the conversation was a pretense. I had no patience with pretense under the circumstances. I wished him far away from me and, perhaps, engulfed by flames.

I responded with a weak smile. "Thank you, Your Highness. I have been unwell."

"Nothing serious, we trust?"

I gave him a long, quizzical look and raised one eyebrow. "I cannot say, Your Grace. If Your Grace might first kindly condescend to define the word 'serious' within the context of the question so that I understand the meaning, I might form a reply." I smiled at him and dipped my head in a slight bow.

The servant cocked her head at my words, then slipped within my view to fix upon me a long, hard stare of exasperated warning as she passed. She floated out of my sight, and busied herself with some ornaments behind me, still carefully within earshot.

Taken aback for a moment by a remark and demeanor that could be construed as impertinent, Henry's eyes began to twinkle. He was remembering our meeting at the dance and was charmed instead of angered.

"Forgive us. Your health is not in danger? That is what we meant."

"I am in no danger."

"We are pleased."

"Your Highness is most gracious to be concerned." I dipped my head again.

Henry caught the hint of irony in my slight emphasis of the word "concerned", and cleared his throat. I flashed him a sweet smile. He smiled back, slightly confused, sensing insult but taken in by the smile. He cleared his throat a second time, and attempted another topic, one in which we had a common interest.

"We were pleased by your performance in the music room, shortly before your departure. You sang a song that has haunted us since. A song about birds, was it not?"

"I know a song about birds, Your Highness. Yes."

"Who was the author of the piece?"

"I composed it myself, Your Highness. A friend wrote the words."

"We would have you sing it for us now." He smiled and waited expectantly.

It would have pleased me to strangle him. It was a melody I had written for one of Hal's poems. What would happen now, I knew, was that Henry would assume ownership of the piece and have his musicians learn and perform it. They would all change parts of it to suit their tastes, replace the words, and the song would no longer be mine. It would no longer be Hal's. It would belong to the court.

I had the lingering servant bring me my lute, and I unhappily fingered the strings. I had not played for days and the weather had been damp, so the instrument was out of tune. I took an overlong while to put it to rights again, then plucked the strings softly, as if hoping Henry could not hear. It was a happy song and I did not feel up to singing it in the quick, playful, lilting tones that had captured Henry's attention back at court. I did not feel I could. I played it in a lower key than I normally would, and made the song sad. I hoped he would think I mis-remembered which song, dislike my delivery, and leave it alone.

Part of the way into the song I became lost, as I often did. I had no control over my muses; they came unbidden and they chose to visit me at this moment with Henry in the room. He was no longer of any concern to me. My eyes became unfocused and I was transformed into a conduit, drawing music from some source outside of me, pulling the notes into my heart and then pushing them out through my fingers and throat. I felt familiar shivers all throughout, and tears rose in my eyes. Music affected me most profoundly.

Sadness suited the melody, even more than did joy. It suited the feelings in my heart. What had started out as a jig was now becoming a ballad, and I knew in my soul it was beautiful. I grew more and more absorbed and sang it, not once, but twice so I could impress upon myself exactly how the song should sound. I barely remembered Henry, so deep was my concentration. I was again dedicating the song to Hal only this time it was not with happiness. I felt Hal in my heart and thought of that more than I thought of the music. I let the melody seek me out.

I finished the piece a third time and stopped to listen to some notes in my head. No, not my head. The new notes came, indeed, from my heart, for no real music is written with the mind. The song wanted minor keys. I hummed them and transferred them to the lute, then replayed the chords quickly, stopping, humming, replaying. Excited, I began the song again, incorporating the changes.

Henry did not stop me. He was a musician himself and knew precisely what was happening. He fully understood, and sometimes spent his free hours in the music room watching other musicians work through this very process. It fascinated him and made his heart ache at the same time to be in the midst of us, for he felt that he could locate the portal to the source of the music himself, and learn to do what we did, if he just watched with enough sincerity. He took no offense to my lack of attention toward him. He leaned forward slightly, listening with concentration nearly as deep as my own. He sometimes nodded but he was not smiling. His mouth was slackened and his eyes were unseeing.

"Aye! Yes!" I cried, after successfully playing it through. The melody had given me a signal that it was finished and my mind drifted back into the room with Henry. Melodies, I had found, seemed to create themselves without my conscious involvement and they always knew when they were complete (unlike painting, which for me always cried for one more, possibly disastrous, stroke of a brush). With an instrument in my hand and my mind tuned to that source outside of me, I became possessed. I could go for hours without food or drink, unaware that my bladder was full or that my leg had fallen asleep. It was as if I had two minds: one that lived within my body, and one that lived without. The mind that dwelt outside of me and within the music gave pleasure to others as it did to myself, inflicting goose bumps and involuntary tears on many who heard me.

Even the worst of my enemies could not deny me that.

When I snapped out of myself, I could not remember the steps I had taken to create a song. It happened to me again with this one, and I remembered every note but had no recollection of why I had chosen one note over another, or how long it had taken me to do it. Watching now, it appears as though the effort took me over an hour. It was an overlong time for a king to sit and patiently wait, yet he said nothing and showed no sign of irritation.

This was not the song I had begun. It was a new one. I knew it was special, as if I had given birth to a favorite child.

Beaming with pleasure I turned to Henry and gave a deep satisfied sigh. "I think I shall keep it this way," I said almost to myself, turning back to the lute and caressing it. "It is much improved." It was a conversation not unlike one we might have had in the music room.

Henry said nothing, but was staring at me with an odd expression, head cocked like a child's. He would not turn his eyes from my face, and they held an expression I had seen before. It was like seeing Hal's face again. It was a respectful, probing look of wonderment.

This was the moment he fell in love with me. This was the precise moment when the game became real.

His voice, when he spoke, would sound soft, I knew.

"Did it please Your Grace?" I asked, concerned. I remembered that the performance had been for Henry's benefit, not my own. I came back to myself ashamed and a little frightened. The song that he had requested was not the song I had offered. It occurred to me that I might have angered him, for I had not consulted with him before changing it, nor had I asked permission before playing it through several times.

What time had passed? I knew not, except my body told me I had a cramp from immobility that would not be there had the time been short. I had boldly and rudely indulged myself with him sitting there, and the realization of this made my face burn.

"I apologize, Your Highness. I forgot myself. I am most humbly sorry."

"What do you call it?" he asked. His voice had not returned to normal. His eyes still had a distant look.

"The Turtle Doves, sire." It was what Hal and I had called ourselves.

I shook my head, dissatisfied. This was a different song in need of a different name. It needed new words. I wished that Hal could read my heart and send them.

"I hath not named it," I corrected myself. "It is new, and Your Grace was the first to hear it." I smiled. "It was given life, in fact, as you sat and listened. I daresay your presence may have been the impetus, Your Grace." The last statement was pure flattery. One flatters a king. I would admit, however, he had played a part in creating the grief that gave birth to the song.

"We will request it again, just as you sang it today, upon your return to court." He smiled. "Until then we fear we shall be humming it daily. It catches itself upon the heart, somehow."

"Then it *did* please you?" I pressed eagerly, anxious for him to reassure me that he liked it. In the atmosphere of the music room, which we were recreating for a moment, the question was not forward, nor out of place. The music room leant an aura of near-equality to the players, among whom Henry was but one.

Aye, me, but we were *not* in the music room, I thought. How dare I be so presumptuous? How could I be so familiar with my king? Servants had come and gone this long while, and I knew they came to watch, and left with intent to tell. I would hear about my behavior, loudly, before the day was through.

I would be punished with good reason. I felt the fingers of embarrassment grasp themselves around my throat and felt a tightening in my chest. In entertaining my sovereign, I had behaved monstrously. I knew better than to behave in this manner toward my king. What had possessed me?

He responded in a gentle, deferential tone, "It pleased us very much. We can think of no song we have ever liked more."

"Would you have me play another?" I hoped to redeem myself by being more agreeable.

"No," Henry quickly answered. "Upon hearing another melody we would lose that one. We prefer to continue to hear it in our mind for a while. If you would play anything at all, please let it be that song, again. Once more for us now, just as you did before."

I played it again, and then another time at his request. I was now polishing my delivery. Henry nodded and listened with closed eyes. He had no better expression of admiration for a piece. I knew this.

But his behavior became odd, and it frightened me.

When the song was complete and my fingers stopped, Henry shook himself back, then stood and abruptly left the room looking distracted and distant, speaking few words to me and barely glancing in my direction. He sent word to his party to prepare for departure, then climbed the stairs to his room.

I did not know what to make of it, but knew it could only bode ill for me.

When the time came, I went to the castle gate to bid my farewells. While Henry was preparing to mount his steed, I spoke briefly to a servant, and Henry turned sharply upon hearing my voice. I curtseyed, and he stared at me with a look of bewilderment on his face as if he were attempting to place me, as in fact, he was. He had not the means to determine how though, for he could not remember past his own birth. He seemed slightly shaken, or shocked, or deep in serious thought. I did not know how to read him yet, and could not decide what his emotions were, nor could I determine what had affected him so profoundly since there had been nothing unusual in our conversation, except my neglect of him.

I thought: I have offended him. I hung my head, near tears.

I did not realize it was me who was affecting him, but that he was not offended.

"We have enjoyed this day," he said quietly and sincerely to me. My parents, also standing there, exchanged quick looks.

I bowed my head.

"We shall come again if it doth please you."

"Indeed, sire." I lifted my head and looked at him hopefully. He did not appear to be angered or displeased with me. Perhaps he would not complain to my father, who would be certain to punish me twice: once after Henry's departure, and later upon receiving the complaint.

Henry's eyes met mine, and I saw them flicker. I did not look down as I should have, nor did he turn away. He leaned forward, slightly, as if to study me more closely, and I, feeling weakened, looked back. The look lasted just a few moments, but I felt it in my heart. There was a man beneath the robes and jewels. I saw him in those seconds.

"Indeed, we shall." He hoisted himself onto his steed and rode away with his party following. I watched him leave thinking of how thrilled I would have been as a little girl to have this very scene played for me, and ambivalent as I was toward him, felt a small flutter in my stomach. I told no one of this, and retired to my room where my thoughts danced.

Over several weeks Henry would practice until he could play my song himself, and in one or two years' time and with some assistance from a poet, would write new words for my benefit. He, graciously, did not tamper with the melody. He would sing it to me in private beginning: "Alas my love you do me wrong to cast me off discourteously . . . " By the time the song was given back to me thus, I would view it less as a theft or an intrusion than as a gift, and I would love him for it. But as I first feared, the song would no longer be mine or Hal's. It came to be sung everywhere and the official credit for authorship was given to Henry. He called the song "Greensleeves" as a jest, referring to the scurrilous rumors that had spread about my morals (the term applied to women of low character) and insisted it be played at every gathering.

In the years to follow, it was never mentioned where the song began. Women, it was thought, could not compose music with such proficiency. It was not my place to disagree, nor to step forward and say the song was not composed by Henry. He had been present when it was created, helped select the words and had chosen the title and had brought it to the attention of the court, so his contribution warranted the recognition he received, he felt. Henry wanted very much to be respected as a musician, and was pleased that his name was associated with music people listened to with delight, rather than from duty. I allowed him that pleasure, for I loved him.

In subsequent years, as his reasoning grew faultier, he came to fully believe the song was his own. I was no longer there as a reminder, and those who knew any truths on any topics were not anxious to correct his self-deceptions.

He came again bringing his own instrument and, again, I sang for him. He played some songs of his own composition, which I politely learned from him, inwardly wincing. I played another of mine for him and, in the process, lost it as I had Greensleeves. This time I was careful to select a song I did not much like. I was also careful to restrain my muses and try not to lose myself in his presence, for one never knows what sort of song is forthcoming during its composition, or when it may want to be born.

Sometimes when he had tired of music, we would play word games, or dice, or chess or cards. It was in game playing that we uncovered the snapping, arguing banter we would be known for as a couple. I was not competitive and did not mind losing, but enjoyed pretending that I did, or that he was cheating or taking unfair advantage. Henry delighted in my "anger" at his successes, knowing I was merely teasing. He also took delight in *my* successes, applauding me with as much pleasure as if the triumph had been his own.

Over the ensuing weeks, I came to playfully insult him during the games, and to make comical threats that encouraged Henry to threaten me in return, although he could never insult me as I did him. There was always laughter in the room where we had set up to play. It was the laughter that softened my hatred toward Henry. I could never resist a man who was able to make me laugh, nor could I remain long angered. In the process of playing with this man, I found forgiveness where I had thought there would never be any found.

If the weather was fair, we would sometimes walk the grounds, or go riding, or hunting, or hawking, or sit beneath a tree and watch the clouds. He was good company, and as my heart began to heal, I grew to see more in him than I had previously. He allowed me more latitude than he did most others, so I could speak to him and tease him with a previously unheard of impunity. One could even say our discourse was intimate and relaxed.

In a very short time, Henry stopped using the royal "we" in private, and began addressing me as "thou." Such an unprecedented dismissal of decorum made me feel giddy with honor, power, and disbelief, just as it made me terrified and wary of his intentions. I dared not—I did not choose to—return this gesture for a much longer time, only after we became intimate and, of course (since it is never proper to address one's lover or spouse affectionately before witnesses) only in private.

My family disagreed on how I should proceed with the friendship. I was holding strong to my conviction that I should keep Henry at a distance as much as I could. My mother had come to see the sense of it as well, for there was more to be gained in the long term from a fortunate marriage than from a liaison with a king. Granted, the liaison would eventually, most likely result in a marriage arranged for me by Henry, but to whom? I could not face the thought of a lifetime spent with someone I disliked, or to an old and tottering widower. I had come too close to bliss, once, to compromise. I was determined to concentrate on a marriage of my own choosing, and Mother agreed. I was far too old to waste time.

My mother, as I said, was showing reservations whereas George and my father were growing impatient. They had the most to gain from an alliance with the King, and prodded me to press forward. The family fortune was in a low state at the moment. My gowns and my mother's were all carefully mended instead of replaced, and the Boleyn coffers were emptying. There was much the family could do with royal gifts.

However, when talk finally turned to marriage much later, the entire family stood against it, and respectfully suggested to the King that he reconsider. They pleaded with me, who had the power to dissuade Henry from anything but that. At the time, I would think they were spiteful and mean, conspiring to make me unhappy. I would later come to find they were attempting to protect me and, of course more importantly, themselves.

In short time the King rewarded Father with an enviable appointment at court, and enough riches to enable him to pay taxes on his new title. He bestowed upon George his own lucrative assignments. A ship called the Anne Boleyn was commissioned in partner to the Mary Boleyn, which Henry had had built previously. With no other alliance between Henry and me, these things alone had the effect of stirring up enmity toward me.

I had no say over which names the King might choose for his ships (I squeezed the bridge of my nose and let out a long sigh of dismay upon hearing of this one). As for members of my family, they were free to accept from Henry whatever he deigned to give. There would have been no stopping them from accepting it anyway—I had no power over their greed. I, however, stood firm and chaste and stubborn.

Henry had offered small gifts, and each time I had refused. On the third occasion of my turning down the king's generosity, my father threatened me with the ever-present (although now rarely used) whip. George shouted. My mother expressed disappointment with pursed lips and a dramatic sigh hoping I could walk away with something of value before the King moved on to someone else.

They all viewed Henry somewhat as a philanthropist tossing coins from his carriage, and were pushing me closer to the front of the crowd so that I might scoop them up before he moved on past us. They would eventually wear me down, and I would begin to accept tokens from Henry, reluctantly and resentfully. The shame I felt grew worse, for in taking from him I was no longer blameless. I knew I could not look Katherine in the eye from the moment I accepted his first one. I viewed it in my heart as tainted, and I felt myself tainted for having taken it.

Chapter 2

I often inquired after Katherine, and Henry assured me that she was well, and had requested word about my welfare and happiness. She was anxious for me to return, he said, and he pressed me to commit to a date, "so that we might not disappoint her when we return with word of you. You have always been a favorite of the queen," he said although I knew it was not true, and never had been. But like a child, I chose to believe what he said, and felt an even more fervent loyalty toward her, and an even more numbing shame.

I demurred for several months about my return to court and, growing impatient, Henry finally confessed that it was he who wanted me back. He asked me to be his mistress, sweetly, but with an air which implied that my succumbing was nothing less than what I owed him for the privilege of having been asked. It was, after all, a high honor to be chosen by a king.

I declined.

Henry grew red with hurt and anger, and left Hever in humiliation and bewilderment. He was determined that I should be punished by receiving no further visits or attention. I could, he decided, go to the devil.

He could, I decided, go to the devil as well. I meant it more than he.

My mother was not pleased, for I had angered him, but she could not dissuade me from my decision. Oddly, she did not press, nor did she threaten. She merely arranged for me to return to court. I was growing too strange, she thought, still weeping over Hal, and still clutching a once mislaid piece of his clothing to my heart as I slept. It had touched my mind, she feared. This was evidenced by the manner in which I conducted myself around the King, and in my lack of judgment in handling his admiration. I was scandalously rude, she thought. She was shocked by the vulgar way I behaved myself, laughing freely, teasing him, and taking unheard of liberties with his good nature. I would disgrace the family unless I recovered and returned to normal. I required the association of others, and the bustle and gossip of court to bring me back to myself, she believed.

Mother was fully well-intended. It was Father and George whose interest was of a more material nature. Their concern for my personal well-being was the lesser concern at the moment. Of even less concern to them were my wishes. My return to court was an issue of vital importance to them, and my feelings were to be set aside for the good of the family. I was, after all, only a female, and if I found myself in a useful position, I had an obligation to exploit it.

I did not want to go. I did not want to pass through corridors where I had strolled with Hal, or face the questions and the talk and the feigned sympathy over my shattered wedding plans. I wanted not to have to see the King frequently in territory that was his, rather than mine. I wanted not to have to face Katherine, who knew of his visits to Hever.

I begged Mother no. She insisted. I cried and threw a tantrum. She slapped me and spoke the word "duty" against which I had no power.

The request was written in her hand and sent by messenger to the Queen. We, all of us, awaited Katherine's response for weeks, each with a different sort of anxiety.

Chapter 3

My rejection had preyed upon Henry's mind and settled there, infiltrating his thoughts. He composed a letter to me confessing love he had dared not speak of before, describing pain of excessive proportions over his inability to win me as his own. Was there no hope that I might come to love him? he asked. As "unworthy" as he was, could I not find something in him that pleased me? Could I not give him any reason to hope?

When I read his dramatic proclamations, I laughed and rolled my eyes. If the letter was spared after I carelessly threw it on the floor, it was not me who saved it, for I walked over it and left it there.

I received another, a plea from Henry to see me. One may not refuse a visit from the King, so I welcomed him back. The span of time that passed from the moment he vowed I would see him no more until I was handed the missile begging for my company was four days.

He arrived two days after delivery of our invitation to visit. Henry meekly asked again if I would be his mistress and, again, I refused. The refusal was less surprising to him this time, and he did not leave in such a hurry preferring to uncover the reasons why I was turning him away.

"I serve my lady the Queen, Your Majesty. I serve your wife, and

I hope I do so with honor. I may not betray her trust in me."

"The queen has seen this before. It is to be expected." He was showing signs of impatience and irritation.

" Your Grace, my intent is to become a wife. *Your* wife I *can*not be—you *have* a wife whom it is my duty to serve and obey." I said this plaintively, hoping to appease him and yet make him understand. "Your mistress I *will* not be," I added, less gently.

He tried tempting me with jewels and land. I bristled back into my original anger. I looked at him with narrowed eyes and asked him to please never offer again. I would not risk Hell for jewels, I told him. I cared not much for jewels. As for land, we had enough. I could not be bribed, I told him softly and firmly, and would not be bought. (My brother George was advised of this conversation through a servant and confronted me later in a thundering bellow. He called me a mindless wench, and slammed his fist down before me with his face dangerously close to mine. Not only was I turning down the King, George roared, I would turn him against us with such rash statements as these! That land, *of which we had so much*, he screamed, could all be taken away in an instant! Had I not one ounce of sense at all? he asked. I had to wipe his spittle from my face as he shouted.)

Stripped to the root of the matter, Henry pleaded. He confessed love he said he had not the words to describe. Would I give him any hope at all to live upon?

No, I insisted. I respectfully could not.

During his next visit, he impatiently inquired as to my health, and asked when I would recover enough from my indisposition to return. He made no mention of Katherine or her need of me.

"My health is good," I bluntly replied.

"Then you are to return to us anon," he stated as fact.

"No," I answered. "'Tis still too soon."

Henry twitched with irritation and mentioned Hal indirectly in a manner that revealed he was uncomfortable with the topic.

"Surely a strong, healthy young lass might recover quickly from a minor disappointment. I do not understand thy persistence in nursing pain over a mere setback in thy plans." He amended the statement coyly: "There are better men to tempt thy heart."

Were he not a king, he might have winked.

I turned and gazed directly into his eyes. To do so was impertinent, even insolent, but I cared not.

"There are no other men to tempt my heart." Pausing too long, I added, "Your Highness."

Henry blew a soft "Phhtt" through his teeth and tossed his head. I could see that I had wounded him.

"I fear that despite your words of love, you do not understand it, Your Grace." It was a risky remark, uttered impulsively. I felt a shudder of apprehension, and wished I could take it back.

He shot a look to me quickly, and emotions passed across his eyes. I saw anger, and uncertainty, and a glimmer of what appeared to be hurt in a matter of seconds.

"I love *thee*. I know quite well what love is, my Anna," he answered impatiently.

"Then you know I cannot return yet."

"Phhtt. I feel a totally different sort of love for thee. It is *real*."

"And you know before God that my love for someone else was false." I did not form it as a question. I said it pleasantly, as a statement of fact, with no expression of any kind. It seemed to carry greater impact that way, for Henry found himself confused over the direction from which the arrow had come.

"No, I did not . . . I did not say . . . " he stammered.

"I can feel just as you can feel, Your Grace. I feel as you would, were you promised to me and then torn from my arms. I feel the same."

Henry thought for a moment, unmoving. His eyebrows were knotted above his nose, and his eyes looked startled. He then turned to me with a raw look.

"Hast thou felt much pain?" he asked gently. It had truly not occurred to him that his clever devising had made a victim of me. It had truly never occurred to him that I had been deeply hurt by his maneuverings. His concern was sincere. So, for the moment, was his self-reproach, but Henry was ever able to rationalize himself away from that emotion, and its impact was not long lasting.

I am certain he gave not a thought to Hal and the life he was now forced to lead.

Tears sprang to my eyes but I willed them away and met Henry's gaze again. He saw the tears come and disappear. Henry noticed everything.

"Yes Your Grace. I have felt pain," I said this slightly smiling, slightly narrowing my eyes, almost mockingly.

"I want thee not to feel pain," he said quietly. "I am sorry thou hast. Truly sorry." He looked confused and thoughtful and he looked sorry. He stared at his hands, then looked up quickly, crossed his arms over his chest and buried his hands under his armpits. "But thou wilt recover," he said reassuringly.

"Yes, sire."

"You *shall*," he repeated challengingly.

"As will *you*, Your Grace," I smiled, dipping my head.

Chapter 4

He began what he would continue for several years. He pressed, then he held back from pressing. He bribed and threatened. He begged and asked again, and again. I held firm. I teased him and made light of his efforts. I flattered to appease his wounded pride, then pulled back and coldly complained of head pains, begging leave to retire.

When he was not present, I made scathing comments about his motives and his character. I made him the butt of cruel humor among my most trusted friends. I acted out our conversations for their amusement. Perhaps most cruelly, I laughed at his songs.

It is difficult to describe the emotions I felt, being courted by a king. I was developing feelings for him that must be kept hidden, and so to hide them I laughed at him and teased. I wanted word to get back to Katherine and my sister Mary that I did not care for Henry, and that was the primary reason I was so cruel. The interpretation of my actions by those viewing them was far different though, not because of what I said and did, but because of the manner in which Henry was behaving. My actions were having an unintended opposite effect from the one I devised. It was presumed that their effect was intentional, and my crafty manipulations were premeditated.

Still, despite my protestations, I felt flattered to a remarkable degree. During the days of our courtship, Henry's attentions made me feel as if I were above the common sort. I generalized and believed that I must be quite unique and important in all things, which is not a comfortable thing to say about oneself in retrospect, and is impossible to view objectively when one is in the midst of feeling so. I had talent, intelligence and charm above the average, and these were heightened in my own mind when I saw the impact they had on Henry. I defy anyone else, however, to feel differently when faced with the same temptation of self-flattery. It is easy to feel flattered by emotions that powerful; it is impossible not to when the source of those emotions is a king.

Vanity often roots itself in insecurity. A lifetime of inferiority had prepared a fertile bed for vanity, and I was becoming a little full of myself. I would become more so in time. I would, in fact, become quite full indeed. That fullness would bring with it its own grief.

More strongly than I felt any other emotion, even that of self-aggrandizement, I felt shame and hurt and a desire to stop this. The dislike I was incurring, for the moment with little reason, tore at my heart. I did not regain most friendships, and so I felt betrayed and hurt and a failure at what I had been raised to do. I had been raised to please, and wanted nothing more than to succeed in pleasing. I wanted to make amends. When I failed in this, I reacted. I responded defiantly.

"So you are not pleased?" I might have asked. "Well, then let me please you even *less* so that you might know how petty and mean you are to complain of *this*!" Afterward, I would crumple with mortification that I could behave so.

Those feelings wore at my good nature and my good nature grew less good in time. The petulant child held tight to slights and insults, nurturing them and clinging to them for far longer than one should cling to hurt. That child liked to make people sorry they had wounded her, but the emotions behind the petulance were sincere. I liked them. I wanted to be liked in return and they would not like me. I was deeply wounded and knew not how to be wounded without dramatically reacting to the pain, or hiding it. I spent most of my days doing the one or the other. I wanted it all to end.

But still Henry kept coming to me.

Over the course of time, he became my friend and I grew to look forward to seeing him. My childhood infatuation was being resurrected by Henry's close presence, while Hal was retreating into a dull ache that erupted into sharp pain only at night. Henry's way was becoming more clear although I fought hard not to let him see this, and still fought against it in my heart. It was difficult not to let him see, for there were frequent moments when our eyes met. I could not deny there was a connection between us, and so I prayed. I did not want a king. And yet I did, if he were this one. In wanting, there is sin, and so I was torn.

What I saw in Henry's eyes could not be rationally explained, and so I often attributed it to imagination and passing infatuation. Other times I knew in my heart I was not imagining. I could not reason away the fear that Henry would draw me into him with those eyes and I would not have the power to say no.

I confessed these sinful thoughts, as ever, to the priest. My confessions vacillated. Sometimes I confessed pride for concocting a connection that did not exist between myself and a powerful man. Other times I confessed my temptation to give in to a love I knew to be true, yet sinful. I confessed more frequently as months passed, but nothing was resolved. The priest only suggested I pray, and so I did, sinking lower and lower into a chasm where I had no choice but to love and give in to Henry. I could not discuss this with anyone but the priest, so I never obtained more practical advice on what to do.

If God was giving me direction in response to my prayers, it was to lead me down the very path I was struggling to avoid. This bewildered me. Perhaps He did not hear me. I prayed more strenuously and waited for my heart to harden toward Henry, through God's grace. It did not harden. Instead, the love grew more tender, and moved me closer to my doom.

Our courtship took place over a period of eight years. It took years for the conflict within me to reach a crisis. For most of that time, I viewed Henry's interest in me as just a game with no lasting consequence.

In the earliest years, word had reached me that Henry was

interviewing potential wives. He had resolved to replace his Katherine in order to remarry and have a son. I knew I would shift into a position of limited importance the moment he narrowed his choices. Nothing could come of our relationship and so it must be trivial. This knowledge sustained me in the beginning. Perhaps, I reasoned, my heart was merely grasping at the first man available and using him as a replacement for my lost Hal.

Then sometimes, even as I pushed him away, my feelings toward Henry would surface, and I would feel terror that he might actually do my bidding, and leave. As much as I vehemently denied it, Henry was *mine*. He was my partner and my friend. The King of England listened to me and did my bidding, and it was a heady feeling to know this. I did not expect my power over Henry to be longlasting. I expected to lose it, so the prospect of relinquishing it did not overly concern me for a long while. I was merely borrowing it, and using it as much as I could while it was still mine to use.

The knowledge that nothing could come of our relationship proved less sustaining as time went on, and I grew more frightened and confused. Could I contentedly relinquish that power to another woman when I was truly faced with it? Could I so easily give up his love when it was time to step aside?

During that same course of time, Henry loved me with an adoration found only in the hearts of puppies and small children.

He would have been kinder to show more discretion. I would have preferred that he had. I knew the trouble he would bring me with his displays of infatuation, and I cringed at the thought of facing Katherine for, even blameless, I felt ashamed.

The thought of talk put my nerves on edge and made me fearful. In the very early months, before word had traveled, the king's obsessive love for me was a topic of amusement in the servants' quarters throughout the narrow confines of the neighborhood. There were bursts of laughter from the servants after Henry had safely departed from his visits, and I would suffer teasings from them all. He did not hide his admiration well. He could have, but he did not choose to because he fully, unwisely and selfishly wanted all to know.

It quickly spread from the servants to the conversations of the persons able to bring the news back to court, and soon was carried beyond. The Queen knew. The world knew and was aghast. The king was behaving like a schoolboy over an insignificant lady of the court, and a not very pretty one (although descriptions of me varied according to the speaker).

The murmuring—the rumbling—of distant gossip began to reach Hever through the servants who, during their trips to other manors, had initially played a part in spreading word. The Boleyn servants were now gathering the fruits of their own gossip from servants at other manors and were reporting what was being said. I was toying with the King in an effort to maintain his interest and to gain more wealth, it was widely known. The Boleyns were grasping upstarts who were using the King's weakness to their advantage.

I had not, as yet, accepted a thing from Henry when the first of these reports was passed along to me.

Katherine disapproved on moral grounds (as she did of most things in life), but was rising above the situation and ignoring it. I was no threat to her. I was of little importance, and was welcomed back to court in an attempt to emphasize this to me and to everyone else. Katherine realized too late that she had tragically miscalculated, but the end result was not of my doing. The mistake in accepting me back was hers, for I did not insinuate myself into court; I was opposed to it.

In her pride and her desire to put me in my place, Katherine did not understand that I was indeed a threat and that Henry's love for me was extraordinary. She could not, however, have known. I did not know myself.

I thought it was a game. I thought I could control it.

Chapter 5

Shortly after we received Katherine's notification that my return was requested, Henry sent word that my parents were to reside at the palace. This was an honor given only to the higher titles (one of which Henry had recently, conveniently, bestowed upon my father) and their families. Whereas I had previously lived in our London house near the palace, I was now to live in the palace itself, for my father's new role required it.

I knew it to be a trap.

I arrived in a finer carriage than the one in which I had left. Henry had had it sent to Hever to transport me back to London, and the ride was exceedingly comfortable. My parents would follow in similar style.

I was installed in my chambers by Emma, my maid servant, who was given a small room at the end of the corridor. These were larger quarters than most for ladies of my status, and amply furnished. When my trunks arrived later, my dresses were carefully wiped and put away by a half dozen servants. In the wardrobe were a number of new gowns sewn to my size. A tray of fresh and dried fruits sat temptingly on the table with a goblet and flask of wine. A round wooden bath was carried in and filled with warm water so I might wash away the dust. None of these things did I request.

"The Queen was kind to think of me," I wryly said to Emma.

The absurdity of the observation made Emma laugh. I giggled with her and stood still while she unlaced my gown.

"Hmmm," Emma answered playfully. "Tis true—thou *art* her favorite, Mistress. And hast grown ever more so by thine absence. Make haste! Go and thank her! I should like to see her expression when you do." Emma pulled the gown over my head and hung it carefully in the wardrobe. She turned back and began work on my stays, unlacing them as well.

I grew suddenly tired and serious. "I would that I could make the statement true. And that I could make the same statement false with regard to her husband."

Emma sighed while I grunted my way out of the whalebone girdle. I breathed deeply once I had been freed.

"What *are* thy charms, I wonder?" she asked musingly, helping me into the bath. "Hast thou ever wondered why?"

It was not intended as an insult, nor did I interpret it thus. Since our childhood together, Emma had always taken shameless liberties with me, addressing me in private as her equal rather than her mistress, treating me more as her cherished friend than as her social superior. I would never have asked her to do otherwise; her friendship weighed more than decorum (and if any were listening, she had sense enough to address me with respect). "Aye, I've wondered."

"Hast thou no feelings for him? It all seems quite strange to me."

Would it sound mad? I trusted Emma, even though I had kept my feelings for Henry to myself, this long while. "I have looked into his eyes and seen someone . . . wouldst thou know what I mean? He seems . . . familiar."

Emma nodded. "Aye." She gave me a steady look while an expression of understanding crossed her face. It was followed by a shadow of concern.

"I could not be so free with him except for that." I shook my head and laughed, blushing. She would think me mad indeed.

Emma did not probe. She looked at me. Then she quietly attended to sorting through my things before bedtime while I sat in the tub and washed myself.

I was embarrassed, thinking I had spoken like a mad woman. While I had spent many hours examining the phenomenon in private, the sensations were too odd to confess aloud. It was a recurring sensation of familiarity where none should be, as it had been with Hal. It was a deeper familiarity than we had earned in our time together and behind the eyes was someone who was not my sovereign. Henry was someone with whom I should be able to laugh and fight and play and, true to my peculiar sense of this, he encouraged and expected those things of me as he did with no one else. He was someone I should . . . *know*.

The affinity with Hal had been similarly odd, quick and strong, and Hal had responded to my confession with amazement for he had felt the same. In both cases, there was a connection that was almost electric, but the sensation within me felt differently.

How do I describe this? It had felt as if Hal and I moved side by side, while with Henry it felt as if he and I were facing each other—or perhaps facing off. With the one, I heard a soothing, beautiful ballad on a harp and was transported to a place of great joy and comfort. With the other I heard a joyous jig with tin whistles and drums, and I danced, feeling as I did a queer sense of coming home. In both melodies there was a deep passion, different in type, but the same in strength and meaning. I could not say which one I preferred. I loved them both.

I heard myself thinking the word "love" with regard to Henry. It was the first instant when I did. My body answered with a sharp rush of adrenaline and a prickly anxiety. My plan was not working as it should and I resolved to look no more into his eyes. I should not feel love.

Oddly, at that second, Emma had formulated her thoughts and encapsulated them in two words. She looked up and simply said: "Watch thyself."

"I want to go home, Emma," I responded. "I am fearful of the outcome of this."

"His interest is never long aimed toward any maid. He will tire of thee." It sounded as much a warning as a reassurance. Emma reached for an apple and handed it to me. Still soaking in the warm water, I took it and bit. "Eat," she advised. "Then sleep. Perhaps it can be viewed more cheerfully in the morning."

In the morning I reported to the Queen and discovered that it had, in fact, been she who had arranged for my rich accommodations. I was struck dumb by the fear of what it must mean, and struck so hard by the absurdity of my predicament that I nearly burst out in a laugh.

She was cloyingly pleasant toward me, welcoming me back with an effusive, yet cold-eyed greeting, and with excessive concern for my health and happiness. She referred to "my husband" rather than "the King" as she had always spoken of him in the past. She closely questioned me about the comfort of my quarters and often clapped her hands to send a servant scurrying to add to it "in order that I might please my husband, whose concern for your comfort must become my concern as well," she explained.

Emma concocted a list of preposterous requests for me, so that I might take advantage of this.

"Silken bedclothes," she said. "Thou must sleep nestled in silk lest thy complexion suffer. And it must be silk woven by a particular Mandarin tribe—name it as you wish—and a man servant to rub thy feet after a walk in the garden—no two, for one must rub thy shoulders. And thou must have a warm bath once a week, not just once a month—no, every day. NO! *Twice* per day, and the water must be *precisely* the warmth of child with a fever that is dangerous but not threatening, and thy clothes must be warmed to that temperature as well so that you suffer no chill in dressing."

"Anything else? Mustn't they twice daily dispatch envoys to find a feverish child and ensure the temperature is accurate? Thou dost plan poorly indeed, to forget."

"It tires me to work so hard for thee, thou thankless ogre," Emma sighed. "But I will give it more thought and tell thee anon what thou dost need, so that the queen might again honor thee with her service."

With each of Katherine's false pleasantries and overdone efforts to please me, I raised pleading eyes toward hers, then lowered them in shame. My demeanor became timid and submissive. I was ashamed and sorry for something I had not done, about which I dared not speak, and for which Katherine would not forgive me.

I was soon pushed to the outskirts of her inner circle. Those who had come with her from Spain closed in around her like veiled black birds and allowed me no nearer her than the farthest edge of the room. Katherine's orders were now relayed by them.

They were joined by some English ladies who had earned Katherine's trust in the years since her arrival. They all spoke Spanish in my presence, except when sharply addressing me directly, and were chillingly distant toward me. I was not invited to the inner sanctum of their daily lives, and was edged out of their society more and more as Henry's obsession grew greater and less discreet.

The young Princess Mary followed suit. Her eyes would only meet mine in a manner that was condescending and disdainful, and her remarks toward me were curt and contemptuous. Henry had been neglecting her of late, and was finding far more time for me than he was for his daughter. I was fond of the girl, and confess more pain from her treatment of me than her mother's. I tried placating her. I tried gently prodding her father to take more notice of her, but he brushed my hints aside.

The final insult took place at a dance when Henry had once again manipulated his position in the circle to be across from me. Unfortunately, I was standing next to the Princess Mary who held her arms out to her father, delighted, thinking he had made the effort in order to dance with her. I turned my back on both of them and curtsied to another man and took his hand instead, while Henry looked after me and the Princess Mary's face fell with understanding and hurt. Henry could be cruel in his single-mindedness. I burned with shame for him, and anger on his child's behalf.

From that moment on, Princess Mary made every concentrated effort to bait and insult me. I was never able to withstand insult in silence, and responded with hurt and fury while she moved more solidly behind her mother. As fond as I was of her, she said things to me I could not overlook. And so—and to the death—I would be her sworn enemy as well.

Meanwhile, Katherine persisted in her efforts to goad me into a reaction with her insincerity. Had she not been my queen, I might have slapped her. I was seared by Katherine's fire-hot "warmth" and frozen at the same time by the snaps and snubs of her ladies. There was no comfortable place for me. There was no safe place to hide.

Those who were not entirely within Katherine's confidence chose not to be within mine for sides had been drawn, and my side did not appear to have much hope for winning. I still retained good friends for, indeed, I had some. I had Emma. There were also my companions from the music room whose interest in me was not political. And there were a few men who would forever be loyal toward me for, somehow, they felt themselves to be in love with me and fully sympathized with the King. I was still receiving true kindness from some quarters, but the balance of my day was fraught with anxious discomfort over snubs and gossip.

I lived in shame and contrition for months, then could live that way no more. It was *she* whom I was protecting with my refusals of Henry's advances. My modesty was largely based on loyalty toward *her*. For how long must that loyalty be tested? For how long must I be apologetic for having done nothing to her? She did not fool me with her sweetness and I wondered: When would her forgiveness come? She, who went to chapel for hours each day, must certainly have heard that Jesus Christ spoke of forgiveness. Where, I wondered, was mine?

I grew resentful. Honor, like love, is *not* conditional. A vow of loyalty cannot be withdrawn, once uttered—not, at least, by someone such as myself who tried with full sincerity to live with honor. Because of my vows to Katherine, I owed my queen my loyalty, and I was bound by my honor to reject Henry for her sake, regardless of her treatment of me. However, I was not the saint I had once wished to become. My eyes gradually became more guarded and my glances less cowering.

Katherine enjoyed her small punishments, dispatching her ladies to do the mean-spirited work she really had in mind for me. I came to enjoy mine. I came to wear new gowns in her presence, gowns commissioned by the King and richly embroidered in gold, as well as the jewels he had awarded me. Noticing it immediately, Katherine became sweet as treacle, and her ladies more cruel. In response to this, I grew increasingly haughty and arrogant. My hand gestures grew more expressive to set off my new rings. Katherine's mouth grew beatific with false pleasure and feigned approval; I lifted my chin to expose a gold choker and smiled.

I would never have brought her harm. With all my other faults, I was not one inclined toward evil intent as I have been accused, nor toward evil acts. I was inclined, one might say, toward colorful retort. I did not take the "high road" as I might have. I shot arrows in response to being hit, and with Katherine this came to be a full time occupation. When the pain reached a certain level and my outrage exceeded my capacity for restraint, I could not resist fighting back, and did so until the ill feelings erupted into world scale enmity.

Finally, Katherine exposed her real self to me and only play-acted for the benefit of those outside her circle. The fight became ever-so-slightly more honest. I thought honesty might bring some relief and resolution, but the situation never improved. In fact, it steadily worsened. I had not counted on the depth of her hatred toward me.

I did not admit this to myself until far into the battle, for her approval was of utmost importance to me, but even had we not found reason for enmity, we were incompatible and should have disliked each other. Katherine was obsessed with God and purity and the condemnation of all who were not. She had no humor and no skills. She was inflexible, solemn and sanctimonious, preferring the company of Spaniards and viewing all others as foreigners, even in a country foreign to her. She dressed only in black, like a nun, and her Spanish ladies wore only black or other solemn colors. She and her company were tedious and dreary and self-contained and I found no pleasure or warmth in their presence. I thought of them all as yammering large black crows.

I, on the other hand, was vivacious and sociable. I was raised to be French, so I enjoyed engaging in flirtatious banter with men, and fussing over my appearance, two of the most grievous sins to the Spaniards who prized modesty and lack of adornment. I may as well have plied my trade in a roadhouse, they felt, for choosing gowns of yellow or blue or for wearing jewelry that was ornamental and not religious. They were even scandalized to learn my favorite color was vermilion, as if beauty should only come in shades of gray.

As for my conversations with the men . . . *well!* The women crossed themselves and pressed their lips and hissed in whispers. The married ones among them showed up in their beds because God willed women to subjugate themselves to their husbands' base desires. Aside from that, their society was solely with other women. Even mere conversation with a man was viewed as scandalous.

I would have been grateful for Katherine's exclusion of me had the repercussions not been so humiliating and so painful, and had I not cared quite so much.

Katherine no longer had the power to dismiss me from her service. She tried begging him and appealing to his higher nature, and found that Henry would not allow it. In fact, he even insisted (against the protests of both) that we sit (in intense and immeasurable discomfort) on either side of him, when playing cards. Hence we both were forced into the other's society, each now avoiding the other whenever possible, and hurling our small punishments like spears into the fray. The punishments grew larger as time passed, and at the height of our battling I hurled spears of the sort I would never have imagined myself capable of sending to anyone.

Katherine gathered her ranks about her and initiated fire from every direction, but never directly. She assigned people to fight her battles for her. She maintained her poise and an expression of wounded purity while giving cruel instructions phrased as "wishes" in gentle, wistful tones, delivered with sighs. She concocted and spread slanderous rumors while contriving to appear as though she were reluctant to divulge the information. She asked questions, listened carefully, then twisted my answers and had her party pass them along, quoting me out of context and rephrasing my statements in such a damning way that I could not deny having said things which, though benign, became abominable in the retelling.

Her faction would insult me and bait me, then gasp when I

responded in kind, as if words I spoke in my own defense were somehow more ghastly than their own unwarranted attacks. They would never mention what they had said to provoke me, or take responsibility for much of my angered speech. Instead, they would repeat my oaths without repeating their own, and whisper accusations of poisonings because I, outraged, vehemently wished "all Spaniards in the sea."

Katherine feigned disappointment in my "disloyalty" and "lack of character" (but never to me) and ever played the victim, all the while scheming to discredit me further and bring harm to me. She stirred up a whirlwind of ill-feelings and ill-will by "hesitantly" mentioning to people—for their own good, she assured them—that she had overheard me making vicious remarks about them, making certain that none within her circle of influence would vacillate toward loyalty to me.

I had never witnessed such a plethora of hypocrisy nor had my stomach ever churned as it did when, during this onslaught, I was forced to watch Katherine in chapel with her hands folded in solemn worship, her face raised and carefully arranged in an expression of innocent, long-suffering purity and endurance.

Had she more imagination, she might have timed her moments of prayer to coincide with the angle of the sun so she might always be seen in a shaft of light!

She played her subjects for fools and succeeded. They took her at face value, rallied to her defense and screamed to see me hanged, when who among them knew the souls of either of us and could judge? Her satisfaction in this was grim, but she derived pleasure from it, far more than she could and yet escape without punishment. Taking their cues from Katherine, her supporters aped her behavior and did as she did, earning ample rewards and praise from her at my expense.

Worst of all she—all of them—lied about me. They lied. I could never endure a liar.

There was no hope of reconciliation, and we came to hate each other with a hatred unbecoming to a lady and a queen. We were now mortal enemies. War had been declared, and would be fully fought until the death.

And as yet, when this war first became real—and for most of its duration—I had done nothing. Whatever I felt for him and whatever I wished, she could have Henry. I did not want him at this price.

However, I had no choice, for there was no price Henry would not pay to have me.

Chapter 6

Despite the attentions of the King, I was still free to speak to, and perhaps to flirt among, the men at court. I had no heart for it, having caught sight of Hal on rare occasions. The scar was torn open again, just as I had known it would be. Because of this, I flirted in the manner of one who knows with certainty that no man before her is, nor ever could be, her one true love. I had neither care nor concern for the men, and had no mercy.

I was being crushed from all sides, from Katherine, from Henry, from the ladies, and from the pull in my heart as I looked toward Hal's figure retreating down a corridor. I forced myself into cheerful spirits, and having done so, took little note of the impact I had on those around me except to sense that, somehow, I was drawing more notice than I had previously. It was partly due to Henry's partiality toward me, partly due to my being marriageable once again, but mostly due to the force of my character, which I now gave full rein, having not the strength in my heart to disguise it.

I was a woman all would see when she entered a room, with a voice and a laugh all could hear. Were I a gem, Henry said in the lyrics to a song he once wrote for me, I would be a ruby, full of blood and passion and sparkling red flames.

My mother queried often with tight lips: "Hast thou no shame at all?"

To which I would reply nothing, and retreat to my chambers where I lay awake in the dark.

There were many men who found themselves smitten with me as I pushed through this phase of my grief. Most admiration came from musicians and friends, but there were other men as well, and some of these forced attentions upon me that were not welcome. I had the unwitting misfortune to aim my charms full-force upon one man in particular, who was most decidedly the wrong one. These charms landed upon fertile soil where they grew into a weed most difficult to eradicate.

Sir Thomas Wyatt was the brother of a friend, and a man whom I had never viewed with interest, nor particularly liked. I was in fair form one night, flitting about from one man to the next and leaving them all staring after me when I came upon Sir Thomas. I dimpled at him, and feigned an interest in his stories, and laughed at his witty comments, and rewarded him with one of my mischievous sidelong glances during a dance. He was a married man. I felt such efforts would be safe with a married man, and learned soon enough to rein in my charm, for a wife was not a deterrent to Sir Thomas.

I quickly made attempts to discourage him, but he interpreted my discouragement as coyness, and persisted in wooing me.

Even though Henry was very publicly in love with me, Sir Thomas Wyatt began to make his intentions clear, not only to the court, but to Henry himself. The two of them faced off on my account more times than was necessary, since during that timeframe I wanted neither one. Their battles were pointless children's fights, arguments over which of them I most preferred while I attempted to escape the attentions of them both.

I often wondered why Henry did not merely squelch Sir Thomas. It is a mystery that can be explained in three words: They were men. The two of them met nose to nose over me as if they were equals, and not a king and his servant, because the issue, to Henry, had nothing to do with his power and his crown. His position, in fact, placed him at a disadvantage, for his objective was to prove himself intrinsically the better man. He needed to be chosen for himself alone, loved for himself alone, found attractive because of his personal charms, and desired for his skills as a lover. He needed to win me because I preferred what he was, not because he had ordered away all competition.

Henry envied Sir Thomas his youth, his handsome face and beautiful physique, as well as his reputation as a sought-after lover among the women at court. He secretly perceived from the eyes of a man (without regard for what a woman might prefer) that the younger Sir Thomas was more attractive to the ladies than he, and hence stood the better chance of winning me.

But surely Henry could prove himself more deserving of my love because surely he wanted my love more than did Sir Thomas. For this reason, he allowed the man to challenge him in competition, knowing he could win with one wave of his hand at any time, but never waving that hand because he wanted his triumph to be a pure one.

I should have guessed from this that he was truly in love with me: he allowed me to make the choice myself. In allowing this, he suffered unparalleled anxiety and self-doubt, for my sake.

Sir Thomas understood Henry and the terms of the skirmish, and faced him with a vain cheekiness he would not have dared under other circumstances. The two of them bragged and insulted like large bearded infants, with each of them claiming he wholly had my heart. Each of them lied himself yet believed the other, while I looked on amused and annoyed by turns. It was comical it its way (and in private I squealed with laughter), yet exasperating as well. For the duration of these joustings, I had nothing but disdain for either one.

Sir Thomas was a man full of himself: full of his charms and wit, full of his handsome face—and full of tales about his adulterous wife. It seemed in questionable taste for him to tell these tales publicly. He seemed intent upon amplifying his supposed humiliation, subsequently raising questions in my mind about the reason his wife found the need to warm another man's bed.

I answered those questions myself. I found Thomas Wyatt abhorrent, and presumed his wife was as cognizant as I. He made my flesh crawl, well and truly, and I grew cold and terse toward him. Yet still, he wrote poems for me (most described me as "fleeing") and fawned after me with a slavish devotion.

I sent friends into a room before I entered, and had them wave me in only if he were absent. It was a tedious way to live.

"I wouldst that thou could make him wear a bell and save me steps," grumbled Emma who was most often sent in ahead. "The tinkling sound would warn us which wing to avoid, much less which room. And if we heard it coming toward us, we could leap to our deaths from a window before he reached us. What say thee to that?"

"I do think the plan hath merit. Our epitaph might read, 'Here Lie Anne Boleyn And Her Useless Servant Emma, Most Cleverly Avoiding Sir Thomas Wyatt.' I am indeed inclined toward it."

"'Twould be better in rhyme."

This went on for a period of time, with no amount of discouragement seeming enough for Sir Thomas. The vulgar, braying ass could not endure the thought that Henry might have won, and so concocted a story that placed me in his bed. He told the slanderous tale as often as he had charged his wife with adultery, to his later reqret. He would pay for the lie with time spent in the Tower, and I would pay for the lie with my life.

Men who speak loudly about their "conquests" most assuredly have little to claim. Had he truly been my lover, Sir Thomas—or any man—would have exercised considerable discretion knowing the stakes. The fact that he did not, the fact that he bragged so loudly should have been reason enough to acquit him of the charge. Sir Thomas had to speak long and earnestly, perspiring freely, and be the fortunate beneficiary of a well-timed bribe from his family, before he won his freedom and his life.

It is hoped he also learned his lesson about telling tales.

Sir Thomas had a view of the scaffold from his cell in the Tower, and saw my execution. He wept to his heart when I died. I did not know, but that "braying ass" had been sincere. He had truly loved me.

I had so few friends at the time of my death. It is one of my regrets that I did not know sooner that Sir Thomas Wyatt would be one of them. I do think that, had I an opportunity to go back, I would be far kinder toward him . . .

PART 5

The Value of Children

Flanders

1101 AD

Chapter 1

I now see my favorite life. I am consumed with excitement, so pleased, in fact, that I do not immediately wonder why I should be shown these events. I enter into a pleasurable state of nostalgia and joy, re-experiencing the life as if I am there again, and in the process, my misery is quelled. I have not felt so at peace for a long, long time.

I see us traveling in the vicinity of Flanders in a caravan, making a noisy, gaudy procession through the countryside. There are long miles before us, and trees dominate the landscape on all sides, rustling and beautiful in autumn colors. We are on a road of sorts, a path, meandering along in our ribbons and costumes like bright splashes of color on a beautiful canvas. Even the carts are brightly painted in many colors, and the horses have ribbons, bells, and flowers tied to their harnesses.

The path winds through woodlands, and fields, and farmland, and is familiar to me, for I have traveled this road in this caravan since infancy. I see each portion of it at the same time of year, and think of this as the "autumn" stretch of road. I have never seen this countryside in any other season and can only imagine it in springtime. Spring occurs for us only in Holland, and summer is only spent in Belgium.

There is a saying among the adults that "there is no marriage in

Holland". I do not know what that means yet, but will learn in time that precautions are taken in the spring to not conceive a child that might be born in January. We have yet to have a January baby live its full first year. It is merely coincidence that none of the infants lived; their odds for surviving a winter birth are admittedly lower, but not insurmountable. We have become superstitious. We blame the cold, and the smoke from the fires, and think there is something about the bitterness of the month that must be the cause.

The village turns somber, when a woman expects her birthing to occur in January, and people grow especially kind to her. I think of this now, because one of our party is gamely placing the thought from her mind, convincing herself that she miscalculated—she is certain she will have the baby later. I watch her walking somewhat behind the rest of us, belly distended as she enters her 6th month of pregnancy. She has already lost three children, and never had one that survived.

Poor Genevieve. She will lose this one as well.

I am told I was a Holland baby, and that Henry was born in Belgium. We do not know our birthdays. Instead, we celebrate our annual arrival at the stretch of road where we were born, and count our age by the number of times we have passed it. I have passed through 13 times, and Henry counts 15.

When I was small, I believed we had to travel in order to find the seasons, and that we left our village to escape a perpetual winter and go where it was warm. It seemed strange to me, that we should choose to live for so long in a place where it was winter, since life was harsh during that season. Would it not be simpler to stay in Flanders? I always loved the colors of the leaves in Flanders. It would be my choice to live there. But there were more urgent concerns than what I preferred for myself.

"Can we live in Belgium?" I asked my parents when I was seven. My grandfather was old, and I was often concerned for him. The old only died in the village where I believed it was always winter, and winter routinely brought with it illness or death. By living where it was summer, I thought we could keep my grandfather alive. Flanders had too much of a nip in the air for his lungs, I reasoned. I would make the sacrifice for him.

"No," they told me, and were bewildered when I cried and would not be consoled. It had never occurred to them to explain the seasons to me, or the rhythm of life and death. These things they presumed to be self-evident. It was finally Henry who told me that seasons change of their own accord, and are not driven by the country we pass through. He discovered this when he was 10 and was forced to remain in the village throughout an entire year in order to tend to his pregnant mother, who was showing signs of distress at the time the caravan was packed to leave. He found that the seasons that occurred in the village after our departure were the same as those we had always encountered on our route. He found also that babies can die as easily in spring as in January.

He was given credit for having passed his birthplace, and he earned the extra year, even though he stayed behind.

There is a workhorse pulling a large wagon that is packed with supplies and covered with a bulging tarpaulin of thick, oiled cloth. Four small children sit up front with the driver, giggling and waving hand puppets at each other while the driver whistles and occasionally shouts encouragement to the horse. Often he turns and speaks to the puppets, which sends the children into shrieks of laughter and prompts the puppets to speak back in high-pitched childishly disguised voices.

A second wagon packed with more supplies follows behind. Genevieve occasionally rides with that driver when she tires, but the bumpy ride makes her uncomfortable. Generally she prefers to walk and, since she has walked her whole life day upon day upon day, the strain is not too much. Being pregnant on the road is only a minor inconvenience to the women in the troupe. They are built to withstand it. Those who are not stay behind.

Henry and I follow behind the slow-moving horses and wagons, along with a group of about 20 adults. Our entire group is still dressed for the acts and skits we performed earlier that afternoon in a town a few miles past. There was no point in hauling out the sacks of clothes and dressing properly with only a short distance to go. We each have only one change of clothing anyway. Wearing the appropriate one is far less important than arriving at our destination before nightfall—and there is also another town nearby. It serves us best to be costumed when we approach a town.

I am an acrobat, and cannot perform in my skirts, so I am wearing a pair of wide trousers that are gathered at the ankles, bright vermilion in color and embroidered with yellow flowers. With this I wear a green bodice over a yellow shirt. Henry is wearing a similar pair of trousers, blue with white stars like the night sky, and a vest of black with tassels of red. The others are also wearing brightly colored clothing: dancing skirts, or flowing capes and peaked feathered caps. The children are all dressed as little fairy nymphs, with reddened cheeks and gauzy wings.

There is no word for us, exactly. In time, in English, a word "circus" will be invented. However, a roughly equivalent term is used in our language, which is a pidgin combination of French, Flemish and Dutch. The term can also mean "gypsy" or "beggar" or "troubadour." In our case, we are a little of each.

We live upon the "charity" of the townsfolk, one could say, although we do not feel as if we are needy. Our benefactors certainly do not view us as pitiful. They welcome us wildly as we approach, spilling out by the dozen to greet us after their first spotters dash back to the village shouting, "They are coming!" We are one of their very few diversions, aside from holy feast days, so they excitedly line up along the road on either side and watch us as if we were a parade.

We become a parade for their benefit. Among us are jugglers, acrobats, fools, dancers and actors. Musicians perform, and dancers dance past the crowd. The little dogs flip backwards head over tail, again and again. Henry carries me on his shoulders so I can somersault to the ground, and the horses lift their heads and walk with a lighter step.

Our stage is any cleared area in the middle of any village, perhaps the steps of a great building, if there is one, or the area beside a church. We are not "acceptable" in a social sense, but are most certainly not driven out as the gypsies are. We are akin to beggars but are better loved, for we give pleasure in return for our pennies. We invariably draw entire villages out to see us, including the old, and the sick, and the lame who are often carried to the show. Work ceases for the duration of our visits, and smiles greet us wherever we go, so my perception of life thus far is that it is always a holiday, and that village people always smile and laugh as we do.

The townspeople do not begrudge us our coins or feel resentment in tossing them our way, though it seems at times we must cost them dearly. In return for their sacrifice, we put on skits, and play music, and sing ballads about the distant towns we have been through, and about people we have met. For a short time we bring them some color and music, and we make them forget. It is for this that they happily pay us.

When we are far from a town, the travelers we meet along the road smile, wave and shout to us. In response, there are always some in our party who will produce juggling balls to entertain them in passing. Sometimes Henry and I do shoulder stands and flips. Whenever we spot a figure in the distance, we prepare as if for a show, and often earn extra coins for our efforts, or fresh-killed game, or in Flanders, where the textile makers are, lengths of fabric we can use for costumes. It is certainly worth the effort to perform, although most of the group would gladly perform just for the applause (I am certainly one of these. Henry is perhaps the worst.).

We have a greater level of freedom and self-determination than most. We exist on the outskirts of "normal" society, so we are not constrained by its rules, and can decide upon our own direction and goals. The men tend toward unfurrowed brows and an ease of temperament, for they have not the burden of toil, nor of servitude.

The women tend to be less submissive, and more outspoken and headstrong than their village counterparts because they are not chained to hearths and gardens, and because the success of the troupe depends equally upon them and their skills. Everyone knows and accepts this, including their husbands who sometimes jump at their voices, unabashed and unashamed.

Such freedom is a gift, and such a gift is a blessing, although some who live on pennies and exist on society's fringes might view their lives as cursed. Like wealth and royalty and most other things, it can be experienced as either a heaven or a Hell.

It is a year during the Crusades. A fervor seems to have overtaken everyone. There are soldiers moving through the country to or from their Holy Quest, and textile workers hauling carts of cloth, and farm wagons sharing the road with us, all busy and purposeful. In addition to the usual travelers, we pass holy pilgrims on the road who threaten us with eternal damnation for our frivolity. We juggle for them and receive somber stares in return, as well as a barrage of shouted scripture and curses. They do not tempt us with their sincerity. None in our party leaves to fight the Infidel, and none of us except Katherine leaves to join the Holy Church as a servant of the Lord.

At this moment, though, Katherine has not even joined us. We will see her in two years, and she will not even stay an entire season with us. However, she will make an impression.

In my eagerness, my mind flits through a span of 51 years touching on one fond memory after another, but the focus is on the most meaningful of these. I am not allowed to flit about for long. I am returned to the scene I was initially shown and I know I will have to watch as it plays itself out.

An uneasiness fills me as I suddenly recognize the landscape. I know the significance of this particular stretch of road, and this time. I am not feeling discomfort over the event that will soon take place, but over the reason why I should have to see it. There can be no purpose to this except to cause me further anguish over what I feel I have lost.

I am forced to it, but do not really object for long. I want to reach into the memories, and stroke faces and hug these people just as they are now, on a road toward Antwerp. The children in the cart, God bless them. Two of them shall die of a fever three years hence. It will break our hearts, all of us. I stare at them now with an emotion akin to happy tears. They are precious, pretty little winged fairy nymphs, alive and laughing. I forget for a moment that they were very firmly alive in this past life. One of these children was my father, and the other my sister Mary. This knowledge does not dim my pleasure in seeing dappled sunlight on their hair as they wave their puppets in the air and speak for them. They are frozen in time, here in the Memories. I want to remain frozen with them.

But there is so much more to see and I am eager to see it.

I see Hal lumbering along, hiding within a hooded cape as much as he is able, even though the day is warm. He feels safer in his hood, and unseen, though he can hardly be missed, he is so large and ugly and fearsome. I see myself fall in step with him. I play a familiar tune on my recorder, and he responds by singing nonsense in a loud, booming voice, which he then switches to a falsetto trill. He makes me giggle and I can hardly hit the notes.

Emma and the Princess Mary have their heads together, as usual, whispering and laughing. The day will come when the three of us are close and inseparable friends, but as of yet I am too young to be welcomed as their equal. Even still, my later knowledge of them tells me that this particular pitch of laughter indicates they are discussing either Emma's husband, or Princess Mary's suitor. Princess Mary's eyes lose some of their amusement and dart uncertainly toward a young man who blushes and looks away. It is the suitor. Knowing her present fears from stories she will tell me later, I would like to say to her through time: "Be not so wary of his heart and his intentions. He will marry you." Looking again at his thick, long hair I could then wickedly add: "And he will lose it all!"

Emma has pulled away from Princess Mary and jumped up onto the cart to join the children's puppet show as a nasty witch. One of the children is hers. She pulls him onto her lap before producing a new puppet from her pouch. This one has green skin and a long hooked nose. It cackles and threatens evil magic and harm to the other puppets who scream in unison with feigned terror. The cart driver throws back his head and laughs.

Emma performs as a puppeteer with Hal, her brother. Hal and Emma were originally to follow arranged scripts for their performances, but found it too difficult to restrict themselves to the same lines again and again, when each day they thought of new ones. Now their performances are improvisations, each improvisation has a different theme, and each time they perform, the rest of us drop what we are doing to listen. They are perfectly paired for the task and perfectly suited to the job, for they convincingly become the puppets, and the puppets are more convincingly real with them than with anyone else.

And, of course, they are more comical. Both Emma and Hal have a way of knowing just what to say, and how to say it, and how many seconds to wait before speaking in any language. They are so in tune that they each know how the other will respond to a quip, even though each skit is new. They feed—and feed off—each other. Their audience laughs until tears form, shouting and stomping, and clapping louder for them than for any of the rest of us.

I am allowed to randomly view one of their performances and watch them, just for the pleasure of it. I marvel once again at how gifted and remarkable they both are.

Princess Mary is a dancer and musician, and Henry's sister, older by five years. She is a mild-tempered woman with a penchant for animals. She has with her three small dogs with ribbons around their necks. One of these is in her arms, and the other two nip at her feet and play. She has taught them tricks and shown them how to walk along a high strung rope, and to jump through hoops, and how to dance by whirling in circles on their hind legs.

She is a jolly woman, friendly and generous. I love her much, and pause for a moment in anger over the power and circumstances that will cause her character, as Henry's daughter, to shift so radically that she will one day be known as "Bloody Mary". I grieve over the events that will make her my enemy in the court of Henry VIII and I pray that, next time we meet, her soul will remember more of this than of what is to come, for the loss of her friendship is painful to me, and unfair.

I turn my attention toward Henry, tall and gangly with long blond hair that hangs in his eyes. I catch him in one of his moodier moments, and know his conversation thus far has consisted primarily of whinings and complaints. Now he is walking some distance behind Hal and me, off by himself again, tossing pebbles in my direction to get my attention. I ignore him until, frustrated, he purposely sharpens his aim and catches me on the elbow. At this, I turn and shout at him to stop. He scowls at me and falls even further behind the rest of us.

Henry lets a few minutes pass, then runs up and joins us. He still has nothing to offer in the way of cheerfulness or good humor I notice, no more than he has had for most of the afternoon. He tries to take my hand in order to lead me off. I impatiently pull it away from him. He provokes me with an insult, and I toss my head and glare at him. I am irked with him, this day. He was often an exasperating lad.

I will recover, and we will be off together soon, as we always are, bickering and inseparable. Until then, Henry is feeling lonely and excluded, and I feel that he deserves to. I have no reason to feel this way, other than that I am annoyed with his gloominess and tired of his moods for the moment. My annoyance never lasts and it is due to lift shortly, but for now, it pleases me to punish him.

I rejoin Hal who has wandered over to Emma and Princess Mary, and the four of us begin singing a round while Henry circles us, glowering, and kicks at clods of dirt in the road.

✠

Seeing Henry again, in this place, I feel my heart weep with longing for him. Then I stop myself, and remember that I do not wish for him at all. Is this not the same Henry I want never to see again? He will prove himself in time to be heartless, will he not? Worse than heartless. He is a killer and a monster, merely disguised in this setting as something benign.

I pity the young girl I see here, for she adores him and will spend her life with him, never suspecting the villain he truly is.

✠

We often insulted one another and fought, sometimes even coming to blows when we were small, yet Henry and I did not fight cruelly. I had only to grow serious for a moment, and Henry would instantly turn into my concerned and sympathetic confidant, probing to see what was wrong and what he might do to help. That part of him was never far from the surface and could always be called upon even in the midst of arguments so ferocious it might be thought we would never speak again. We, each of us, fought knowing this.

He was ever aware of me, conscious of my speech, and my reactions, and my feelings, even as he looked away and was engrossed in something else. From this attentiveness, he knew precisely how to wound me, and so he only very rarely wounded me and always grieved for it afterward. His tongue could be sharp, but I never knew him to turn me away when I was in need of him. If one of his barbs hit too close to my heart and tears rose in my eyes, he would hug me and abandon the fight.

He seemed to know that it was not manly to act toward me in this way, and never allowed anyone to see. In private though, he would listen and console me over something that worried me, never trivializing it or me, even when the problem was, in fact, trivial. He would meekly give in to me if I pouted, and wipe my tears if I cried. Our fights and squabbles had no impact on his loyalty or his sense of being my protector—it was his role in the relationship and I trusted this, and trusted him. He was a rare man, for all his faults, and a treasure.

✠

"You saw him as a treasure?" The Voice interjects, aware of the direction my thoughts have taken.

"I misperceived him," I answer, remembering that I am only playing a game with myself to momentarily quell the pain. "He was less a treasure than I thought, as this last life has proven. Or else grew to be something less than he once was."

"Could you not have misperceived again?"

"I think not," I snap in response.

I choose, at this time, to focus on Henry's faults. It unnerves me that I should have been caught feeling tender thoughts toward him, and would like to make my position quite clear . . . but clear to whom? To my mentor? Or to myself?

I have no use for him. He is self-absorbed, and has a poisonous, sometimes violent temper. He over-punishes people for fancied slights. He reacts childishly and selfishly, whatever the provocation. He is lazy and a procrastinator, and will do nothing without a preamble of nagging and a long string of excuses unless it is somehow to his personal benefit or provides him amusement. Yet when he wants something and is set upon it, he will pursue it stubbornly, insistently, without regard for the impact his actions have on anyone else, expecting everyone else to make sacrifices in order to accommodate him. His "truth" can, at times, be absurd, yet he will tenaciously defend that truth as a fool would.

That is the Henry I see here, and that is the Henry I most recently knew. I cannot imagine why I should feel so much more tenderly toward the one I find here except, perhaps, because I know that this Henry would have killed, or been killed, before allowing any harm to befall me. He would have never initiated the harm, even during one of his rages.

He could not control his anger. If I am to be truthful though, I must add that his fights were always honest ones, and his fury was never physical toward the children, or toward me. When he hurled something in anger, his otherwise perfect aim was always off, no matter what the provocation. I could face this man's fury with trust, and without fear.

That is how he set me up for the fatal blow, instilling trust in me. And that is the source of my pain now.

Betrayal of trust is, by far, the very cruelest sin of all.

✠

As Henry was always there for me, neither could I have turned from him. He had only to ask, and I was at his service. His needing me gave me the greatest pleasure, and I could never have declined or found excuses, no matter what he asked of me.

I will prove this once again within 24 hours.

Our main focus was the other, for each of us. It had always been this way, from the time my mother held me new in her arms. Henry had waved at me, sensing already in that small baby a great friend. He followed my mother and insisted on helping tend to me, and it was toward Henry that I went when I took my first step. We were always together, and our perception of the world was filtered through the other's perceptions from the beginning of that life till the end.

It was clear that Henry and I were destined to marry. We seemed always to have taken it for granted, for we had been raised together in the troupe, handily provided for each other, the only children surviving within a span of several years and hence each other's only friend. Our marriage was first spoken of by our respective parents as a wistful possibility, then as years passed, was treated as an event both factual and inevitable. Neither Henry nor I had any objection to it, except when we had somehow infuriated each other in a childish game.

"I would *never* marry *you*!" we sometimes shouted to each other in anger. I sometimes elaborated on the insult by declaring I would marry any drooling, toothless, dog-faced troll, before pledging my troth to the likes of Henry. Henry's standard response was to claim that, compared to me, he preferred an old hag with a crooked nose, or a leper with no nose at all.

We both knew however that we would be married. Had either of us found the other objectionable or fallen in love with another, the rejected one would have been well-wounded, for we belonged to each other and we knew this. Neither of us gave thought to any other sweethearts, for the road was there before us waiting, and we loved each other truly, and like family.

It is difficult to pinpoint when these plans shifted from wishful thinking to accepted fact. It is easier to pinpoint the circumstances that led to our becoming lovers, and the event that hastened our wedding. These circumstances take place just a few miles up the road, and one day later than the scene I view with such pleasure now.

Even in those times, a 13-year old girl was somewhat young to become a wife, and a 15-year old boy was not really ready to be her husband. We were still darting about the meadows chasing butterflies, and I was not yet even ripe for bearing children; I was a several months away from that. It was planned that I should be 15, and Henry 17, when we took our vows. Our parents felt that that would be an appropriate time for us to wed. They had not counted on their matchmaking to be quite so successful, and did not ever guess that we would not be able to wait that long. They saw no hint of this until it was too late.

Maturity hit Henry first. His beard grew early, a shocking black in contrast to his yellow hair, and his voice grew deep in a matter of days, it seemed. He was suddenly tall. He played with me as he always had, but grew sullen at times, and moody. He looked at me differently, sometimes surreptitiously staring at my chest where two modest bulges had appeared, sometimes pretending he had stumbled upon me by accident, when I indignantly shouted at him for peering at me from a distance as I lifted my skirts behind a tree. During tumbling practice, he would catch me as he was supposed to, but would often wait a few seconds before releasing me, always giving me a probing look as if I were supposed to understand what he wanted, or know about something he would not tell me. Sometimes he would willfully catch me wrong so that his hand might run over my chest. No one noticed any of this or we might have been separated into different troupes, with stern precautions taken during our winter layovers in the village for the next few years.

Children always grow faster than their parents' image of them.

I would scold Henry for his strange behavior and roll my eyes, and he would grow angry and dark for a time. Then he would return to himself again and we would rollick with each other in the tall grass as we always had, shouting and arguing, or would try to outdo each other with high flips, or would act out skits we had made up between ourselves. Often we would lay in companionable silence and watch the clouds. He sometimes took my hand at those times, and held it in his, or absently twirled one of my braids between his fingers.

Though I was to be a child in the true sense for months to come, my thoughts had begun to shift to the curve of Henry's body and the feel and smell of his skin. Just as he crept up to watch me when I slipped behind a tree, I did not avert my gaze when Henry performed that same business himself. I would scowl at him for catching me wrong at practice, but would secretly be pleased that he should want to touch me, and was sometimes disappointed if he did not try. I liked the few moments when I was lifted up in his hands, or close to him in a movement that called for him to hold me on his shoulders. We appeared to still be acting out our children's roles of competitive adversaries, so we had not yet drawn notice from our parents, but we were moving into new territory swiftly. The dam would not hold for two more years.

It started as a game we had played since early childhood. Henry would wrestle me down to the ground, shouting boasts of his own superiority that I would angrily challenge, pinned as I was beneath him. He would then make me agree to whatever he said or he would not let me up. If I held stubborn against him, he would tickle me into submission. I would always say what he wanted, eventually, and he would let me go. Then I would run away calling names and laughing at him, tormenting him from a distance, and he would chase me until we both tired of the game.

In a twinkling, things changed. He seemed to watch me more now, scowling should I turn and catch him at it. Then he would fly at me, grab me from behind and pull me down on top of him while I kicked and squealed. He would roll over until I was beneath him, and hold his face within inches of mine.

Instead of forcing me to admit my inferiority at tumbling or music and his own expertise in those skills as he always had, he now would be still, and would look at me in the eyes for a few long seconds before gruffly letting me go. He would raise himself from the ground, and reach down to help me up. Then he would speak to me gently and lead me back holding my hand, or would say nothing and wander off by himself waving at me to stay behind.

The wrestling episodes suddenly increased in frequency—he seemed always to be looking for an excuse to pin me to the ground—and the seconds we looked at each other grew longer. He would be close, pressing me down and looking at me, and I would fall into his eyes as if they were a place, not just two orbs of blue. His eyes held a very peculiar look, probing me. My own eyes would be locked in his, but I did not know why they should be. I did not know how Henry's eyes managed to control me as they did. Often we would lay there, just looking and saying nothing and at those times, I felt a queer sensation in my stomach.

Sometimes I responded by curling my lip and forcing myself to look away because I felt queerly and uncertain of him when he stared at me. I knew not who he was anymore. More frightening, I knew not who I was.

Sometimes I would simply look back, feeling weak.

I see Henry do it to me now, lightening quick. He pulls me away from Hal and Emma, and pushes me up against a tree. The caravan keeps moving and no one even glances toward us, for we have always stopped for horseplay. He is pressing against me, wordlessly, with a strange, intense look on his face.

"Stop it," I hiss. "You're hurting me. Let me go."

He does not speak, but looks at me in his strange way.

"Let me *go*!" I twist and squirm and cannot move from his grasp. I make a noise of frustrated anger and I glare at him.

His fingers are iron but his expression does not change. He says a strange thing to me in a musing, conversational tone of voice. His voice is at variance with his actions, which are controlling and forceful. He is taking advantage of his strength, and I cannot get away from him. He asks thoughtfully, pleasantly: "Do you think I am handsome?"

I curl my lip at him.

"Because I think you are very pretty." Then he releases me, and walks back toward the wagon.

"Yes!" I call after him.

He turns. "Yes what?"

"Yes, I think you are handsome." I blush. I look down at my feet.

He cocks his head and narrows his eyes, waiting for the rest. Handsome for a pig? Handsome for a frog? Handsome for a hairy, hump-backed, one-eyed ogre?

I say no more but poke my chin into the air, and turn away from him with mock disdain. I toss my hair. I watch him from the corner of my eye.

Henry turns away and walks toward the wagons, looking back at me once. When he does, I see that he is smiling to himself.

✠

I am now shown the day following: the day I did not want to see. I recognize everything, for in years to come we will privately count our passings through this stretch of road in the same manner as we do our birth sites. It is a wooded area, still, though the forest will grow thinner through the years as farms spread out to claim the land. The forest is off to our right as we head north, and to the left are fields of flax.

"May I look away?" I ask. There is more to come, and I would prefer to move on to something else.

The question is unanswered, and the scene does not even pause.

Forced to watch, I am forced to consider what Henry was. I do not want to compare him to the Henry I most recently knew because there is too much pain in that. I try to view the two Henrys as separate beings: I love one and hate the other. However, the one I loved grew into the one who betrayed me . . . They are both the same, I think, as the pain resurfaces.

But I do so love him, here. I will force myself to only think of that, and see if the pain lessens somewhat.

I find it not only lessens, but I am filled with joy. I try to sustain the sensation by forgetting all the rest and focusing on the love.

I can return to hating him in a little while, I reason. There is ample time for that later . . .

✠

Henry and I are finishing up our music practice in a meadow by the side of the road, and I am about to pull out my harp to practice on my own. The adults have set up camp but left the harp in the wagon, for it should not be set upon the damp ground. I am heading there to get it. Henry has things of his own that he should be doing, but he follows me doggedly, complaining of my performance at practice and criticizing me.

I glare at him and call him "Stupid". This prompts him to charge at me and pull me to the ground where I writhe and protest under the weight of him, while the horses quietly graze nearby. One of them knickers softly toward us and snorts a greeting, which both Henry and I ignore, for we are facing each other in a challenge of some sort, both stiff and ready, it appears, for a fight. Henry starts to say something, then stops and grabs hold of my eyes with his own and looks for a long moment. Then he ventures to softly run a finger down my cheek.

He moves his face down close to mine to kiss me. I grow suddenly fearful, and stiffen, and twist in his arms. I jerk away, and he pulls his head back, not surprised.

"Let me go," I say. "I have work to do." Henry holds me still, now tighter, pushing his weight down so I cannot move. He defiantly attempts another kiss, and in nervous fright, I giggle then spit at him and twist away, assisted in my escape by having startled him. He lets me go without resistance, and sits for a moment wiping the spittle from his cheek. He watches me with a hurt expression as I race away from him. He looks, I think, as though he might cry.

I almost run back to console him, but I cannot stop to worry about him at this moment. Everything is going to change, and I want it to stay the same a little longer. We are going to be completely different together from any way we have known before, and I know this, and there is little time left to cling to what we had been. I am making one final effort to be with him as I always had, knowing in that instant that it is already too late. It has been too late for some time. I would have known this if I had heeded the signals in his eyes, and the peculiar feeling in my own stomach.

Recovering, he leaps up and shouts my name with a curse. He chases me across the field and into the forest, furious, reaching down and hurling rocks toward me, issuing hot threats and shouts of insult and anger. I hoist my skirts up to my thighs, and run ahead of him in manic, desperate fury, squealing and laughing, darting quick looks behind me, thinking for just this moment that we can forever be children and remain as we were. Henry does not want to remain a child, and part of me wants to grow up and join him, but for just this one last time I resist and lead him in our final childish chase through the underbrush and deep into the woods.

I see something ahead. I stop in my tracks and hold my hand up to Henry to be silent. He quells his shallow anger, creeps up behind me, and looks in the direction I point, his eyes widening. He looks down at me quickly and blushes, then returns his eyes, hypnotized, to the scene before us. A woman is bent over, hugging the trunk of a tree, with her skirt raised up above her waist and the ends of it grasped in her fingers. Her back is arched and her wide rump is exposed and tilted up as she carefully spreads her legs more widely apart. A man with his breeches around his knees moves closer behind her.

My eyes are riveted.

"How did he make his thing point up like that?" I ask in a whisper.

Henry, the expert, explains, "It just does."

"How?"

"By itself. It just does."

"Any time you want? Like you could make a fist? You tell it 'Stand up' and it does?"

Henry thinks for a moment. "It stands up when you think of doing what he's doing. That is all. You just think about doing that, and voila, it stands up."

"I see," I say, but I do not really.

A year earlier I might have wondered why the woman didn't slap the man and run, but something within me has changed, and I feel weightless and breathless. I cannot move, nor can I avert my eyes. I feel a rush of pleasure as I watch. The pleasure I feel seems to increase when I think about being touched in the places he is touching her and, when I think of that, only Henry comes to mind as the one to touch me.

My eyes widen, and I lean forward.

"Mon dieu!" I say. "What is that he is doing to her now? Why would they do such a thing as that?"

"Shh. You talk too much," Henry answers. Behind me, his breath comes fast and shallow. I can tell without looking that he is breathing through his mouth.

We know these people. The man is a minstrel, and his wife is a dancer. They are now beginning to make the noises we had been taught to run from, as children. During forest walks we sometimes heard grunts, and cries, and moans, and had been told they came from angry forest spirits who would capture us if we did not run away. I had never before seen the source of the spirit noises, nor had I ever questioned it. I had always been too fearful of the consequences to investigate.

"Does this mean that forests are not really haunted?" I whisper to Henry, turning around to see his face. I feel very clever and mature for having deduced the truth on my own.

He says nothing and stares at me, coldly superior. He clicks his tongue at me, shoots me a look of amazed contempt and rolls his eyes.

How dare he? It was an honest question. Yet I now burn with embarrassment from Henry's reaction.

"I hate you so much!" I whisper. "You are so—"

"I said *sshh*," he hisses, and grabs my shoulders from behind. He wraps his arms around my chest in a protective gesture, as if the participants in the scene are dangerous, and pulls me backward a step or two. He leaves his arms where they are, and I do not pull away.

A moment or two passes, and we watch the couple, frozen within our own thoughts and sensations. I feel boneless, and melt into Henry, grateful that he is holding me upright. Arousal, I discover, is as contagious as a yawn. I do not know that arousal is what has taken hold of me. I feel a secret sensation I do not admit to Henry, but I now understand that the look I saw in his eyes was indication that he is feeling this too.

"We will have to do that ourselves, when we are married," Henry finally whispers to me. He picks up a braid and tickles my neck with the end of it, pressing his lips to the top of my head. He has not kissed me since we were tiny children, and never tried until today, yet it seems natural and appropriate. I like the way he is tickling my neck.

"Us?" I ask shocked. "You would do that to me?" I sound aghast but do not entirely feel so. I stare half-interested and half-terrified. I would not have admitted this to him, but I am more interested than frightened.

"I will have to. We will be married." Still standing behind me, he grasps me around the waist and hugs me tightly, touching his cheek to mine. Strange as it is for Henry to hold me like this, I still do not pull away. I lean back into him, and turn soft and pliable in his arms. I feel warm, held as I am against him. Safe.

"Did you know of this before?" I ask him while he rocks me back and forth. "Had you seen it done before to know?" I continue, babbling as I often did. "I did not know that it was even done at all. Who else does this? Are there others?"

"I've seen it," Henry answers. He does not mention where and why, though knowing Henry, I suspect he was often prowling the woods in search of it to watch, following the sounds that would lead him to it, and moving in stealth. I suspect he has been watching for quite some time. Had I any experience at all, I would soon know from the way he touches me, and where, that this is true, and that he has spent many hours thinking about it on his own. I would also know it has never been far from his thoughts when he has looked at me, of late.

"You have seen animals do it. Did you not know that we will do it ourselves one day when we marry?" His voice is even, and matter of fact—even nonchalant—as if to deflect attention from his hands, which have moved up to cup my breasts. I press back harder against him and think of nothing but his hands and how they make me feel.

"*I* knew," he continues in a boasting tone. "I have spoken in secret to the men. Men and women marry so they can do that with each other. They like it. See?"

He points to the couple. The woman is grunting, "Yes. Yes. Yes. Yes. Yes."

I have to presume that, if she were unhappy, she would be saying "No". It *is* somewhat of a convincing argument.

As an afterthought, Henry adds, "And you must do it if you are to have babies, which, of course, we shall have, you and I."

I ponder the prospect while watching.

A thought occurs to me. I would wonder about the woman and whether she was to have a baby, but would do this at a later time. More practical issues are of concern to me now.

"At least you are not large like he is," I state as fact, hoping for confirmation. "I have no place where something that size would fit. It would not work if you were large."

Henry says nothing for a moment, thinking. "It *always* works," he says, finally, with conviction.

I have not been spoken to on the subject myself, and assume he knows of this on some authority. He is older, and the man.

Still, I am not satisfied with his answer. I pull away and turn around to ask again, "*Are* you large?" adding, "I need to see. I want to see for myself." I not only want to see his size, I merely want to see, right now, and am considering it with some anticipation. I do not let on to Henry.

He backs away from me, and will not say. I reach over and loosen the tie of his breeches, and try to pull them down but, irritated and embarrassed, Henry shoves my hands away. He turns his back to me then slowly, hesitantly, slips his trousers down past his hips. He turns to me with his hands covering his groin, and a look of childlike pleading on his face. I know this look. I feel suddenly tender toward him and reach up to touch his face, looking into his eyes.

"I will not laugh," I whisper. "I just want to see."

Henry moves his hands away in a gesture both hopeful and embarrassed. Behind them is revealed a huge, angry erection.

I stare. This is not the benign organ I had seen passing water behind trees, nor is it the tiny mushroom I had seen on him in childhood before modesty forced us into separation. It is something alive, and vulgar, and grown. I gasp and stop myself just in time from covering my eyes. I am shocked. His manhood is shocking. He grew so without ever telling me. When I look at it, then up at the start of a black beard, I wonder where my friend has gone, and who this is that I am left with.

For a moment, I am dumbfounded, then I force myself to speak, and do so gently. I know how easily he is wounded, and I take advantage of this at times. Something within me warns that this is not the time.

"It is a very fine one," I say (just as if I had some basis for comparison), "but it would never fit. We could never do that." I gesture first toward Henry's organ and then toward the couple. I hug myself and make myself small while his organ points toward me, large and threatening. It seems not to belong with Henry's hesitant and apologetic face.

Henry looks befuddled, as if at a loss for conversation now that his breeches are around his ankles. He bends over to pull them up again, then stops and looks at me as if he were not being wholly polite, to put it away so soon.

"You can touch it though," Henry says affably, moving closer again. "Go on. I will let you touch it if you like."

That is very generous of him, I think. I am curious, and

appreciate the offer.

"Perhaps just once," I say, and finger it lightly. The skin is as soft as silk and I run my fingers over it to savor the texture. Henry's eyes grow sleepier and his head rolls back. He grabs my hands and presses them hard around himself. It is very peculiar, that Henry should want me to do this. I wonder if my parents have ever heard of people doing this. I make a mental note to ask my mother.

At his insistence, I obediently move my hands over him. He breathes and closes his eyes, and reaches gently for my neck, barely touching me. He fingers the hair at the nape of my neck, and it gives me a shiver of pleasure. He pulls at the ties of one braid, and then the other, and loosens them. He moves his fingers up through my hair, and leans over to kiss me. I tilt my chin up and let him, and am surprised because I like it. I kiss him back, and then I lose his lips, for they move away to cover my face and eyes with soft kisses. The arousal I felt in seeing the couple becomes my own, and the source of it, Henry.

I feel his organ in my hand and remember how he intends to use it. I pull back sharply.

"This will never fit inside of me." Terror and what I believe is common sense take over. "You will hurt me with it. When we are married, you have to promise me you will never do that to me. Yes?"

Henry is breathing hard. He answers me with stern superiority.

"I cannot promise I will not do it. It would be against nature and God's will to be married and not take you in that way, even if it hurts you." Henry found pleasure in saying such things. It was manly to hurt a woman. He finds less pleasure in the act of hurting than in saying he will hurt me. He merely likes thinking he could hurt me if he willed it, and in imagining others assume him capable of being rough.

"But you are too *big*!" I insist, near tears. They are not entirely tears of fear and protest. They are also born of confusion. This is something I had never been warned of, and I cannot decide for certain if I am, or am not, eager to learn more. I have moved away from "eager" to "not" for the moment.

I reach up and place my arms around his neck, and hold him hard. When I am afraid or worried, I tend to run to him for hugs and comfort, and I do so now, even though he is the source of my anxiety.

Henry cups my face in his hands, attempting a bargain and a compromise. "I can do it gently. If I were to do it slowly and softly would you object?" he asks solemnly. "You must let me do it, after all. You will be my wife, and you must."

Tears well up in my eyes. I have never been faced with such as this before. My inclination is to please him, yet I am afraid. Henry wipes the tears, then gently kisses each eye.

Nature, with some gradual, small coaxing from Henry, begins to take its course. The tears dry and are forgotten. The fears give way to something new. We are kissing and touching and breathing.

Henry speaks first.

"Perhaps we should test it first before we marry lest we make a terrible mistake. People who are married *must* do it, so . . . so if we cannot do it because we do not fit together, we cannot be married in the eyes of God. Everyone knows that. And if we are not married in the eyes of God, we risk damnation." Henry's expression is one of earnest, God-fearing, self-righteous good intent.

It is so like Henry. Had I eyes, I would roll them as I watch.

I nod, dumbly.

"I think we should test it so we do not waste any more time making plans if they should not be made, yes? It is important that we know soon, while we still have time to each find someone else we could marry . . . " He gulps and continues in a distracted whisper, " . . . without sin." He busies himself with the laces of my bodice. His fingers fumble.

I feel a moment of concern that Henry is considering abandoning me. He has never seriously spoken before of not marrying me. I never realized that our marriage would be conditional, and would take place only if my anatomy proved acceptable. I look at him with hurt and alarm in my eyes.

He sees the look and does not need explanation. He seems slightly ashamed of himself, although I do not know why he should be. He hurries to reassure me.

"And if it fits, then we shall marry as planned," he continues, reaching into my bodice. His fingers are cold. "Do you agree?"

"Yes," I whisper.

"In my opinion, we should make certain right now. While we are thinking of it. Before we forget." His fingers are making me gasp.

I nod again. I need for it to fit so that Henry will not marry someone else. I do not want to spend another instant worrying that it won't.

I would also like for him to test it for other reasons.

We pause, momentarily, as the two people finish their business, straighten their clothes, and pick their way out of the woods and back to the encampment. We are motionless and silent so they do not notice us, but Henry is nuzzling my neck and exploring the contents of my bodice, and I can barely keep still. I need to be pressed against him and held. I need for him to find me and touch me.

"Yes? Are you certain?" He has stopped, as if the full impact of what he is about to do has suddenly occurred to him. He is looking at me questioningly, hesitantly, with real love in his eyes. I have never seen love there before—not love like this—because he is guarded, and has always hidden his love under scowls. The look shoots an arrow into my heart, which leaps and responds with a rush of feelings I had not known I felt for him. I feel so much emotion I sense tears coming to the corners of my eyes.

He stops to touch my cheek. "Because I will not, if you do not want to." His voice is gentle, and he is in earnest.

"Yes." I whisper. "We have to know."

"It is important that we know," Henry agrees indecisively, rationalizing. He is suddenly hesitant.

The couple is gone. I can kiss Henry now, and so I do.

I am not often aware of how deeply I love him, but I know it with certainty now, and feel it coursing all through me, powerful and agonizing. I say to him solemnly: "I want it to fit."

Henry pulls my head to his chest in a tender hug. I hug him back.

I see expressions on his face that I missed at the time. For a few seconds, he appears to be feeling guilty triumph, then fear. Then suddenly his focus is solely on me and he knows what to do. He lets his body do what his heart feels. His heart feels love with the force of a myriad lifetimes.

✠

Love takes on a character that is almost physical, when viewed from here. I can reach out and nearly touch the love I see in Henry. It is an impressive, humbling love, and it is for me. I marvel: a soul is capable of feeling this for me. I would weep, if I were able. I cannot weep, but I can feel awe.

This force the two of us have created between us cannot be easily undone I suddenly see—or am I shown? The love is strong, and it is very old, and it is real, shared equally between us. It can withstand attack and erosion, and will regenerate itself no matter how it is despised or ill-used, for it has been sorely tested over many lifetimes.

I am made to flash upon the end of my last life, then am told the love is only bruised, not killed. I do not love alone, nor does he, and we have no power to change it. It almost exists separate from us, like a living thing that controls us, and over which we have no control.

"Do you remember how it felt?" I am gently asked. "It is still there. Do you remember the love?"

I jerk back from my reverie, defiant. I have been asked: "Do you remember?"

I remember indeed.

What I remember are my tears as I whispered "I love thee still." I remember the sensation of a dagger being thrust into my chest, then twisted, when he responded to me by coldly snapping, "*That* is *thy* misfortune." Then he ordered me to my death and let me die.

I remember *that.* I remember sitting in the Lieutenant's Lodgings in the Tower compound and sorting it through my head. I remember my efforts to confront the knowledge that everything I had once believed about him was untrue. He had never loved me. Still I could not fully believe that for, if I did, I would have to sacrifice one of the few things of value I had left. I would not give up that love, for whatever short time it had been true. I had sacrificed everything in my life to claim it. I had given up, or given away, virtually everything I had of worth. I would, in fact, give my life itself. I had to trust that, for a while at least, it had been real or all was lost and I had no pride at all.

I remember watching my husband slip away from me, moving on to other women. I wondered, if the love *had* been real, which of my failings lost it for me? Where within myself did I begin to point the blame, and where did it end? I began to feel as if I had no worth, if I could not even hold the love of a man who once loved me so well. I felt humbled and chastened, wondering who in heaven or on earth could want me, if Henry's deep love could turn to contempt? No one could, I reasoned. No one should. All England was right to scorn and revile me, for I had no worth at all.

At the moment when I knelt before my executioner, finally knowing with certainty that Henry would not stop the sword from severing my neck, I grew angry that I, who had done him no purposeful harm, should have been made to feel so unworthy by comparison to him, who let me die. I vowed I would never allow Henry to hurt me again. I would never again allow myself to feel love toward him, for he is evil, and my enemy. I had sacrificed everything for a wisp of cloud, a dream. More the fool was I, even more a fool than *ever* I swore I *never* would be!

Love? I once spoke aloud a vow to harden myself against him, then spoke it again within my heart, and I feel stubborn. I disbelieve the Voice for Henry does not love me. He said he did not, and behaved as if he hated me. I cannot be tricked in this manner.

I cannot be tricked, and I will not believe.

The Voice seems to sigh, and lets me watch as one thing leads to another in a forest long ago.

✠

I cry out, for I am a virgin, and the noise calls attention to us. It is not the normal cry of a "forest spirit", a warning to all who hear it that distance should be kept. It is unmistakably a cry of pain. My yelps draw two members of the troupe who had been searching for mushrooms nearby, and who push through the undergrowth out of concern that I am wounded.

We hence are discovered in that position: two flaxen-haired children mating like dogs, skirts up, breeches down, pressed together groin to groin.

It is a surprise for all concerned.

We are dragged by our ears back to the encampment, fiercely scolded and soundly flogged, then told we will be forced to marry when we reach the next church four days later. That suits us anyway. It seems good fortune that we should not wait another two years. We both agree after our second—and less painful—attempt that he fits me quite well indeed, that I am neither too small nor he too large, and that we should marry after all. Married, we will be free to indulge in this new kind of play without frowns and scoldings any time we like, and we like it very much.

We like it a mere hour after the flogging, in fact, ignoring warnings to keep apart until the wedding. We both pretend we are answering a call of nature, which in fact we are. We signal each other with whistles, then meet and resume the interrupted act. Nothing we had ever experienced compares to completion of that act.

We stumble out of the woods, disheveled and disoriented, holding hands. We are seen, and had been heard but this time we were not stopped, and now, not even scolded. A conference of parents has ascertained that there is no way they can keep us apart, for they have neither locks nor doors to hold us in. They cannot tie us down, for we need to walk with the rest of them. They have no access to a chastity belt until we reach the town, and no means of controlling us except through guilt and heavenly threats, for to flog us again would be to spoil us for the next show.

Our parents soon realize there are no words they can say even to cause us guilt. Nothing has an impact on our behavior. They can do nothing at all except wait grim-faced and angry for the church spire to appear in the distance ahead of us, and to quicken the pace of the troupe in its direction.

Our parents blame themselves, though they are not to blame. This has nothing whatever to do with them, and what they have or have not taught us.

I am a lovely young bride, and Henry a handsome young groom, in our hastily borrowed, ill-fitted wedding clothes. We receive a special dispensation at the request of our desperate parents, and are not forced to wait three weeks for Banns to be announced. A priest steps forth within minutes of our arrival at the church and, upon hearing that rapidity is of the utmost importance, hears our confessions, assigns heavy penance, then gives a stern Mass and fierce looks to us both without wasting more than half an hour in the process. When he asks if anyone among us has any objections, my father shouts "No! Get on with it, sir!" and the priest finishes up the ceremony with words spoken so fast they run together.

And so we are wed, firmly and forever, till death us do part.

The troupe ever drew attention to itself, and not surprisingly its appearance at the church attracts the notice of people in the village, who gather around outside to watch us come out. The entire village comes to the feast we hold afterwards in a meadow, all strangers attracted by the music and the merriment, and the joy of celebrating the good fortune of the newly married. They bring mead and stout and food, and leave coins for us with their wishes for our happiness, knowing us not at all. Their kind wishes will all be amply realized, and we will live as happy a life as anyone ever hoped for us.

✠

Life was brutal for most who lived in those times. However, I did not know it was brutal when I was part of it. I ate and I slept and found comfort in the warmth of a rough blanket, or a pile of hay on cold nights. I found joy in my husband and the people who surrounded me. I found happiness in the birthing and raising of children. I found pleasure in my recorder, and harp, and lyre, and the applause of an audience, and the coins that were thrown to me. I had a strong, healthy body. It was a good life.

I sift a life's worth of memories and images through my fingers, and caress each one. There is no need to pry my eyes open to watch. I am home. I linger on reminiscences, referring back to them at times, and I forget how sour things turned in the lifetime just past. I want to stay here in this life and, in the absence of that, want to keep remembering, as if memories can erase what is to come afterward.

It is not a coincidence that in Flanders I do not miss wealth, and

I do not long for power. It is not by chance that my happiest life is one that places me far from either. There are more important things, and I see them here. Now that I have a basis for comparison, I will know what to pray for and strive for, when I return again.

✠

Each spring we start out from our village five days west of Antwerp, travel north to Holland then down toward Brussels, over through Flanders then up toward Antwerp again. The life is lived on a winding road through miles of forestland, thinly peppered throughout with knots of cleared space where farms or villages have grown. Through the span of my life, the forests grow thinner then, after my time, disappear altogether as if they never were. I would in time, as the child Anne enroute to the court of Margaret of Austria, travel a portion of that same road again and find it markedly changed beyond all recognition. I would have no sense of having been there before at all.

There are three troupes in all, each numbering in members between 20 and 30. The other two troupes move in other directions, one traveling west toward the North Sea, and the other moving further into Holland and remaining there. We each cover a circle of about 100 miles, visiting about 10 to 12 towns along the way.

We travel with the troupe we are born to. People who were not born to a troupe choose according to their language skills, or in the direction, or with the group that most suits their tastes.

Our troupe has the strongest skills in French but we cover territory where each of the languages is prominent, and some like Hal and Emma, are completely fluent in all of them. The other two troupes speak primarily Flemish or Dutch, though we all know each of the languages to some degree, for we all converge again in winter.

Each year we follow the same road, departing only occasionally from our route. We are not hunted by road thieves who prey upon the wealthy, so our travel goes safely and our nights are spent soundly. The pace is leisurely because we are not expected, and we have no obligation to arrive. We find our audience along the way and in the towns we visit, or else we do not. We perform whenever there are people present, and spend the rest of our days traveling for five to eight hours in one direction, slowing on occasion while the men prowl with their bows in search of game. We stop and set up camp while the men move into the forest, if there is one, with traps to catch food for the morrow, or to gather whatever they can to supplement the evening meal. If we are entering an unwooded stretch of road with little game to kill along the way, we barter in the last town before it, and carry our meals with us.

Our expenses are limited to road tolls and fabric, musical instruments, boots, paint and wagon repairs. We sleep when the sun sets. When it rains we continue until the mud stops the horses, then take shelter in our tents, or in hovels we have built and placed at strategic distances over many years. Sometimes we beg for a night's stay at farms we pass.

During the winter, we live in huts like village folk, although our village is deep within a forest, and is populated only by our own kind. Its population is thin during the warmer months, swelling to over one hundred during the winter when the troupes return. There are some who live in the village year round because they are too old, lame, or ill to travel anymore. Some are pregnant women with a history of difficult births or stillborn babies, who want not to risk the strain of travel. Some are merely tired of travel, and choose to stay in one place. Among these, there are some who have taught themselves skills like farming, animal husbandry, spinning and weaving, curative herbs and smithing, so we go to a place with all the trappings of a real village.

We even have a small church, presided over by a monk who once entertained a dream of living as we do. He justifies himself by calling us "lost souls" and in need of him, but he knows how to juggle, and he eagerly plays a reed flute whenever we gather to practice our music. He issues mild penance, when we confess our sins, and views us all with a tolerance and understanding uncharacteristic of most men of the cloth in those times.

The people there are not like village people. All who live there can perform some feat for an audience, and most days are spent working on new acts or new songs. It is a fairy tale place, with much laughter and dancing. It is an open-minded place where much is accepted, and much is overlooked. People like Hal, who would not find love elsewhere, are embraced and important. We welcome all.

I look forward to going to our village, just as I look forward to leaving in the spring and sleeping on the ground. It is my home, and does not seem strange to me. Other villages seem strange, where folk walk about with tired and drawn faces most times, toiling for naught but short lives filled with more toil. They seem only to smile when we perform for them, and our stays with them are always short. I have grown up enough now to have learned that their lives are not the holiday that mine is. I have heard the stories from new members who escaped that life. I was shocked and dismayed by the discovery, and more determined than before to be good at what I do for the sake of all those who smile when I do it.

In the troupe and the village there are many whom I will meet again. Katherine has recently joined us. Hal and Emma, of course, are among us. Seven familiar souls from the music room at the court of Henry VIII are here. Two of Henry's court jesters are here in this place, including my darling soon-to-be born son Peter who will return as my own dearest fool. I see Sir Thomas Wyatt. Princess Mary. Servants. Ambassadors. Henry's court will be partly recreated from those who surround me in this place, and among them are some who will one day be my enemies. Most, however, are destined (or doomed) to retain their affection for me, for it is from this life that I draw my most loyal and passionate allies.

At the moment, we are all one in purpose. Despite squabbles, personal irritations and personal preferences, we have strong ties and strong loyalty toward one another.

All of us but Katherine.

Chapter 2

The next scene I am shown is two years after the wedding. It is another autumn, and again we are heading toward Antwerp and home, but at this moment have stopped to rest. The jugglers practice while Henry and the other actors rehearse their lines a short distance away. I play upon my flute with three other musicians, and Emma plays chase with the children.

We rest frequently for my sake, for I am heavily with child. The going is slow, and we must make it to our village before winter sets in. We have fallen behind even the loose schedule we keep, and are shortening our stops along the route.

None of the children traveling with us is mine, as yet. I am carrying my first, a son, who will be born in two weeks' time under a tree with Princess Mary and Emma attending the birth.

I am now 15 years old, and Henry is 17. Our parents have chosen to remain in the village, and no longer travel with us. We are hoping and praying that we safely arrive to present them with a living grandchild, whose existence was not evident when we started out in the spring.

We are too young to seriously consider that Henry might return alone, as some husbands have before him. Still, as the birth draws nearer, Henry has grown more reflective and more solicitous toward me, and there are traces of fear in his eyes. He awakened screaming on two occasions this past week, startling everyone. Most in the encampment then stayed tensely awake and prayed for him as much as for me. He will shriek in the night several times more, while we await the birth.

We do not have the same relationship we had as children. Our roles changed the instant we knew each other as man and wife, that day in the woods. We still bicker and argue, but we are each here only for the other, and know this now. We sleep together in our tent with our limbs entwined, stripped of clothing so we might feel each other's skin, sometimes giving in to the temptation to couple in the encampment despite the fact that, out of consideration for others, it simply is not done. We do it with hands over each other's mouth, furtively, silently wrestling, swallowing the sounds. And we do it facing each other, each moving into that place in the other's eyes where we meet and rise above ourselves. It somehow makes the act more potent for us, and harder to be silent.

After the birth of this first child, though, we will be forced into the woods again, for the children will sleep with us when they are small, and there will always be small ones. We will even find moments when we are certain of privacy and can hang our clothing on a bush. This is a scandalous and sinful way to perform the marital act, for God is watching, but we do it anyway, praying He will momentarily avert His eyes and quell His displeasure, for we truly mean no harm and we cannot help the wanting.

✠

"Do you remember?" I am asked. "It was the same again for you last time in the beginning, was it not? In the form it took for the two of you, it was more than bodies needing bodies. It was a soul needing one particular other soul, and needing it truly. It was not false."

I say nothing. I think nothing. Had I teeth, I might gnash them.

✠

The birth scene appears, and I watch with anticipation. He is coming! It is pure pleasure to see my son as an infant once again.

I will try and birth the baby at a distance so that Henry cannot hear my screams, but he will hear them, and will sit upon the ground with his head in his hands, sobbing. The others will attempt to drown out my noises by singing and pounding drums. In addition, Henry will be numbed by Sir Thomas Wyatt, his best male friend, who will pour strong spirits down his throat to stop his weeping and his fears that I will die. With astute and affectionate foresight, Sir Thomas procured a jug in the last village to force upon Henry, who will vomit and lose consciousness, to everyone's relief. He will discover only in the morning that he still has a family, and that all is well.

He will pretend to me that he had drunk solely in celebration, and was worried not at all.

It will be an easy birth and a beautiful, healthy babe who will survive and reach his manhood, then have children of his own. Few children survived. The ones we carried with us amounted to less than one third of the children actually conceived by the women in the troupe within the last five years, and even these will not all grow to adulthood. I am blessed in that I can look back upon this birth with joy.

We camp for a week until I am ready to walk. I pad the baby with rags, tie him to my chest with a shawl, and sing him lullabies as I follow the carts down the road. The others in the troupe hear me, and Emma joins me softly, singing a harmony. Another joins in, an octave lower, and a fourth adds a high trill, like a bird. Still another pulls out her flute and plays along.

Hearing this, the men cannot resist it themselves and they add their voices, vying with each other to be heard over the din, out-performing one another, throwing their arms about for theatrical emphasis. The air is filled with loud, shouting voices that are bellowing words intended to be soft and sweet for a baby's ears. It makes me laugh, and I shout the words as well. The baby himself seems to enjoy the clamor, and stares about himself contentedly. Henry boasts and struts, singing more loudly than all the rest, occasionally pausing to kiss his wife, and gently stroke his baby's head.

✠

"And he loved your babies," the Voice interrupts. "All of them. You never saw a man grieve the way he did over the three who died."

The three that died were little girls, not boys. He cared not whether he had boys or girls then. It was all the same to him.

"He loved your little Elizabeth, did he not?"

"Stop!" I order fiercely, defensively. "Stop this!"

The Voice recedes, sending me a signal that it has made its point.

Henry loved Elizabeth more than I. I never loved her at all. I never could.

✠

We immediately name the baby Peter, after the saint. I choose the stronger-sounding Germanic version over the softer "Pierre" out of preference, not even waiting to be certain he lives through the winter before declaring it to all. We take the risk that he will live, and call him by his name, investing more love in him than is prudent, trusting that he will not die and that we will not suffer a larger pain for having given him an identity too soon.

Still nearly children ourselves, we play with him as if he were a doll, and he grows, smiling and affectionate. He is handed juggling balls at the age of three, and sits behind a harp at the age of five. I teach him leaps and somersaults during those short periods when I am not pregnant. Henry teaches him how to remember lines and make his voice large so that all can hear it. Emma teaches him to sing notes and rounds, and Hal teaches him to deliver funny lines and to make faces, and then uses him as a comic foil in many of the acts. Other children follow and are equally loved and trained.

I will bear Henry 14 children in all, one or two years apart, and of these fully 11 will survive. It will be a lifetime full of blessings. It will be necessary for us to build a third cart, and buy a third horse, and then a fourth, just to hold the swelling population of small children within the troupe. We will shelter them in three more makeshift tents, and in the village we will need to build a larger hut to house them. Henry will purchase some hunting falcons, for we will need them to find enough food to feed them all as the daily catch with traps and arrows alone will come to be too lean. The children will all perform early in cunning little costumes and will bring in coins and loud applause, for even the smallest few of them will flip and leap through hoops when they are only two or three years past learning to walk.

Henry and I are deeply in love but do not ever notice this, since we have never experienced life without each other. We have never in our lives said "I love you" and we never will, for love, we know, is not the point of marriage. We live from day to day being gentle toward each other, fretting and fussing over one another, aching and impatient to couple when we are prevented from doing so on days when it rains too hard for the woods or is too cold, but we do not know that it is love. We think it is simply "marriage" and we conclude that marriage is good.

When I grow old, I will retire with Henry to the village where our parents await us now, and our children will continue the tradition, following their children in the cart, singing songs and juggling.

Henry will discover upon my death the depth of his emotion, and he will die himself within months, as I would have had he gone first. For now, there is no other life, and no other possible mate for either of us, and we accept this without question or examination. We will never know any lovers but each other, and will never even wonder what another would be like.

Well, Henry will wonder about Katherine, but in this life he will never know.

Others grew up in the troupe in the backs of carts as we did, traveling as these new children do while the parents walked behind. There are new members however, who joined us out of a desire to perform, as a risky escape from serfdom or personal trouble, or to follow spouses met in tiny villages where we had camped.

Katherine is still new to the troupe, having joined us in Holland. She is finding it difficult to adjust. Even though she seemingly knew in advance she would not care for the life, she chose her husband from among the actors who travel with us. We speculate, finding her all the more fascinating in that she will not tell why she chose him, or why she left a comfortable life for one that displeases her.

The theory among the women is that she selected her husband for his beauty. Although most of the unmarried women with us have tried to win his attentions, none was successful, presumably because all except Katherine were pale and wanting, compared to his splendid self. The women view Katherine as an icon of sorts, for she has beauty and has won the man most coveted by the others.

Among the men it is said she had troubles with her family, and sought a fast escape. Her husband just happened to appear at the right time, they say. They do not appreciate, most of them, the power of a man's appearance, and they look for other reasons why a beautiful woman might choose a man. Each of them thinks that Katherine would have preferred him had he found her first, or were he eligible to sweep her away. This number includes Henry. Henry is smitten with Katherine.

Katherine's husband will not say what her motives were in choosing him, nor does he much care since it appears that his plans to leave the road and live in her large house have fallen through. He simply avoids her company as much as he is able.

To Katherine, this life is difficult, the costumes garish, and the travel a grueling displeasure. She does not understand our need to move from town to town, and is scandalized over the manner in which we all perform our marital duties and the abandon with which those duties are performed. She has no empathy for the excitement we feel as we stand before an audience, or for our pleasure when a crowd erupts into applause. She seems embarrassed when townspeople look at her traveling with us. Still, she will not go home.

She is tall and graceful, with yellow hair the sun has bleached to almost white. She frets over the freckles that have sprouted on her face, but these give her much charm, and the men tend to be solicitous toward her, for she is lovely to see. She follows a husband who is indifferent toward her, and she keeps to herself, but has recently learned to say lines in the skits. Her increased involvement does not soften her feelings toward the life.

Soon she will run away and take refuge in a convent, telling tales of us as if we were all wild heathens who had captured her and held her against her will.

She is, as ever, Katherine.

I have attempted a friendship with Katherine. She is lonely and out of place, bewildered by the colorful personalities that surround her. She prefers silence to music, and solitary meditation to the society of loud, attention-hungry performers. She sees us all as inferior to her because she grew up in a house with servants, and was even taught to read and write.

She never warms toward me, for I am younger, and am entirely too boisterous and loud for her. I would like to be her friend, but do not know how to coax her into intimacy. We were born into different classes and have nothing whatever in common.

I am in awe of her fine mannerisms and her refined speech. I emulate her, causing Henry to double over with laughter, which leaves me in tears he quickly runs to wipe. I tell Henry in tedious detail all the little I have learned about her, then press him for details on what it is she says when they speak. He listens with interest when I tell him what I know, and pretends he is not eager to tell me what she has said to him.

She seems to have a tolerance for Henry, who can draw upon his acting skills to behave much like the people in Katherine's social class. They have long conversations at times, and exclude me, but I do not mind because Henry is mine and would not leave me. I have no fear of Katherine. I can see she wants none of these men and the life they would offer her. She already has a man like that, and is not pleased. Instead, I am grateful that I am married to someone who might come back to me with gossip about her, and tell me all he has learned.

Henry struts and preens, so flattered is he by her mild attention toward him. I bask in the reflected glow.

When the truth comes out, it is a scandal. It is not truth about Katherine that we learn. Her life to us will always be a mystery, though here, I find the speculation of the men was true. Her father forced himself upon her, and she left. She chose a man who was not physical in his attentions toward her, as most men were, and who offered her a ready escape.

Katherine finds that her husband prefers to be with men. She was never really married to him at all, in the true sense. We did not know this. It will be a walk through the woods with Princess Mary, and their discovery of him acting upon his preference, that will make Katherine run away and blame us all.

There is a convent 14 miles behind us that she noted on our travels. She has gone there, and will remain for the rest of her life. She will become a nun, and eventually the Abbess. She is better suited to that life, than to this one.

We never find out where she went, and never hear word of her again.

I discuss her situation with Hal, only days after the discovery is made. Princess Mary will not speak of what she saw, and makes the sign of the cross each time she is asked. Katherine is gone as quickly and as mysteriously as she came, as is her husband and the musician he was found with.

I do not understand what happened, exactly, and Henry will not explain it to me, so I turn to Hal for the truth. I know the men have been discussing it quietly among themselves. Hal is one of the few men who might be coerced into talking.

The questions I am asking embarrass him, and he does not explain to me in more detail than Henry had. I linger, hoping for more information, but I get none, so I move the conversation to other topics in hopes of tricking Hal into speaking later on.

Hal, it seems, is not easily tricked. He can, however, be made to blush on command if I even hint toward our original conversation so, out of compassion, I abandon it. Still, the time passes quickly, and I find myself staying because I do not want to leave. Hal does not encourage me to go.

I nurse the baby while Hal recites some lyrics he has written for the minstrels. I clap my hands and laugh. They are full of wit. He asks me to play a song for him on my lyre, and I do while he holds Peter for me and listens, smiling.

I have known Hal for most of my life but have never been alone with him because he is older and a man. I now find I would even prefer his company to a number of the women's, and I sit with him, contentedly chatting about things I never confessed to Henry—or the women—before. Hal listens, and responds in a way most men would not. I feel full, somehow, talking to him. I feel complete and calm.

He is not like most men, which perhaps accounts for the manner in which he responds to me. He was born with a cleft palate, a "hare lip", and is ugly even with a beard to disguise the torn and gaping upper lip. He cannot speak clearly, for the roof of his mouth is not fully developed. Understandably, he is shy of meeting those outside our circle, unless he is performing.

Hal has dealt with his disfigurement by learning to be funny, and has succeeded in turning revulsion into laughter: people laugh *with* him rather than *at* him. He amplifies his speech impediment during the puppet shows, and he makes wildly frightening faces, and tells jokes while he juggles. He acts as well, so he can wear a mask and play the fool or the villain.

He is a gentle soul now. He was once less so, and his face is one of the prices he is paying for a cruel past. He is loved, but not as a lover; no woman will have him. This is painful to him, for he has sweet, romantic imaginings, and an enormous amount of love to give. He writes beautiful love ballads which he, until just recently, passed along to Katherine's husband to sing. The women would listen misty-eyed with longing—but would have sneered or laughed, had they seen the man who wrote the words.

Hal's compensation is laughter from his audience, and affection from those with whom he travels, but it is not quite enough. He will confess to me one day that he is lonely. He will confess nearly everything to me, in time. Beginning with that one conversation, Hal becomes my special friend.

He gives Henry no concern for, fond though Henry is of him, he views Hal as not quite a man, and therefore not a threat. He looks, after all, like a gargoyle or a monster.

Henry does not treat Hal as I would like. There is always a touch of dismissive condescension in his attitude, as if there were no soul behind the hideous face. I try to shame him, but Henry does not change.

Hal often wanders over to our hut in the winter, or settles in front of our fire on the road while I cook. He touches my heart with his kindness and shyness, and he amuses me with his wit and his poems. He composes most of the ballads the minstrels sing, turning his acute observations into riotously funny lyrics that he brings to me first. I am his best audience. We talk for long periods of time, and through the years will become as close as family and love each other as dearly.

Although I do not know this as I face him, we have a history together. He was twice my spouse, and once my twin, and has long been involved with me in some respect or another. He is still a part of me now. I often wonder why I should feel so strongly toward him, and think it is merely compassion. His face makes me sad for him.

But it is more than that. I do not love him out of pity. There is a real intimacy between us, and the reason for it is that we have unknowingly perpetuated one past identity as identical twins, easily the most emotionally intimate of all relationships. We find early that we can read each other's feelings, as twins do. We are comfortable together. We think alike, and we fall together in a rhythm and a harmony that cannot be purposefully designed.

Hal very soon becomes dependent upon me, and likes having me near, just to talk. He seems to need me as my children do, and there is enough room in my heart for him. I would have had room for him, no matter what the circumstances.

I do not know that he pretends I am his wife, and my children his. It is his livelihood and his destiny to be laughed at. He faces this with philosophical good humor, but in his dreams he is handsome, and I am not repulsed. This is the one secret he does not divulge to me.

It is in our next life that a far stronger passion will erupt between us, and we will marry, this time out of choice rather than at the arrangement of our families, as was the case two times before. Hal will indeed be handsome, and I will be powerfully attracted by his beauty, just as he once wished. Henry will be our child. We will not have long, and it will not be long enough for us. During the dark days of the first wave of the plague, Hal will be the first of us to succumb, then I will follow. The incompleteness of the pairing will strengthen our resolve, and we will be impatient to be together again. We will return as lovers.

Henry will choose to separate us in order to reclaim me.

But I have told that part of the story.

✠

Henry and I are both hot tempered, and amused by verbal battling. We have sniped at each other since infancy, and cannot quite break the habit. Henry likes to throw things in order to make a point, reveling in the theatrics of an argument, and I like to prick holes in his masculine pomposity. We shout and bicker, in jest most times, usually providing diversion and amusement to those who surround us. We often dissolve into laughter, for our arguments tend to be absurd rather than heartfelt, and are intended to sharpen wits rather than to wound. We call each other "old woman" and "old man" before we reach the age of twenty, and parry incessantly. We are a loud family, and the children are equally sassy and high spirited. A few of them have Henry's temper. I am often pulling them apart, cleaning bloody noses and wrapping sprained fists, Henry's among them.

I love them all so much.

Chapter 3

The scenes shift once more, and I now see a stretch of road and a time that makes me want to turn away. I feel a bittersweet pang of longing and loss, for the scene makes me remember one of the few truly painful episodes in that entire life. It lasts a fleeting second. We are in Belgium and I awaken, dizzy and sick as the sun rises. I leap up and race to a tree, where I double over and vomit. I have already had three children, and I know what this means. A quick calculation and the knowledge that Henry and I were not prudent sends a hard arrow of fear into me. I conceived in Holland.

It is just cold, I tell myself. We can dress the baby against it. It is just smoke from the fire. We will keep it out of his tiny lungs. We will buy a cow for milk and butter, a goat to feed my smallest boy, and a sheep for meat so I do not go hungry and lose my milk for the infant.

In preparation for this, I am hoarding coins, and have refused Henry's pleadings that I sew him a new shirt. We cannot afford the cloth. I agreed to share the cow with Emma to defray the cost, and refused every nonessential expenditure, but I still cannot risk being a penny short. I mend Henry's old shirt instead.

I cannot grapple with the concept of disease, which always seems to spread among the children in the wintertime, so I do not dwell upon it. Had I thought about that, I would have been terrified for my three older ones as well. The youngest of these was only just born in Belgium the year before, and is still at risk. I decide to strap this newest child to my chest as if we were traveling, only tucked beneath my kirtle and wrap. I will keep it close to me, and always warm. I will not worry and I will not fret.

I will wrap the other baby as snuggly as I can, and hold him close to me through much of the day. The oldest two will be kept indoors, and placed before the fire. My chores will remain undone, or Henry can do them for me while I tend to the smallest ones. The fire will be kept burning clean, and the chimney cleared to prevent a back draft of smoke. I will follow my mother's advice to keep a cauldron of water on the flames when I am not cooking, so the air does not get dry.

I pray at every church along the way, and keep a holy relic tied to a string around my neck.

We arrive in the village, and are welcomed with the usual fanfare. The obvious advancement of a pregnancy causes some glances, but the women make cheerful comments to me and knit little garments that they give to me with tender looks. I hug my little ones, and hold up the tiny dresses to show them, but I do not tell them there will be another child, and I do not choose a name.

Henry has stayed close to my side since the morning I awakened ill. He is cheerful and does not speak of his fears, but as soon as we arrive in the village, he begins plastering the sides of the hut with straw and mud to keep out the chill. He does this, uncharacteristically, without my having to prompt him to it. He overfills our sleeping palate with hay, and takes our small savings to pay a weaver for some extra woolen blankets. He borrows a goat from Father Martin, with promises to return it in the spring. He comes back with Emma and a fine cow that will stay in a barn not far from us when it gets cold. He ties a fat sheep to a long rope, and lets it wander near the hut.

I suspect he stole the sheep.

I feel the pains in mid-January during a blizzard. Henry takes the children to another hut, and stays with them there. His mother and my own arrive and bustle about while I writhe on the palate and moan. The day passes, and the baby does not come. I pace back and forth across the room and, when it is time, I squat on the birthing stool and push.

The difficulty of the birth is a surprise to us all, for I have never had such a problem before. When she comes, finally, she is red and beautiful, and on an impulse, I name her immediately and call her Gabrielle, after the angel Gabriel. I do so as an act of faith in God, not even waiting until she is wiped clean before saying the name. My mother and Henry's turn and stare at me, and I look back, stubborn. This child will have a name, and she will be loved.

She lives. She stays strapped under my bodice, and the two of us pass through our days wrapped in a blanket, only coming out of it long enough to change her rags. The careful precautions Henry and I took, and the prayers we said in our own hearts, rewarded us with a smiling little girl who is cutting teeth at the time the caravan is packed to leave. She grows, and learns to crawl in Belgium, and toddles her first step in Flanders, far earlier than we expected.

We fuss over her and spoil her because we did not expect to keep her this long. We expected a fever or the croup to take her away during the winter, and feel blessed and grateful that she escaped. She is our only girl, and a beauty.

Henry often holds her up and talks to her about the young men he will have to shoo away when she is older. He carries her on his shoulders, leaving the other children to me. He makes her little toys, and holds her on his lap. She is her Papa's little pet and favors him, and in return, he worships her. The boys have to settle for the time he can spare them when Gabrielle does not claim his attention, and they have to share that time three ways.

Henry would have denied it, as he loved all his children fervently, but all who saw him knew he was soft and silly with his little girls, and at the heart of it, preferred them to the boys.

The irony of this does not escape me.

I am not shown the accident when Gabrielle was two. I am spared that. I try not to remember her climbing up on a boulder and onto a wagon while I chased the boys who had wandered too far during a short stop while we rested the horses. I did not see her until it was too late, and it was Henry's scream that brought it to my attention. She stood up on the platform where the driver and the children sit, reached down to touch the horse and fell. Startled, the horse began to rear—

I blot it out. I am allowed to blot it out.

Henry sits in the road and cradles her, kissing her and sobbing. I hurl myself onto both of them, and moan and keen. I pull up fistfuls of dirt, and grass, and leaves, and I throw them into my hair.

My baby girl. My baby girl. There was nothing Henry and I could do, the two of us. The boys scream for me in terror, but I am of no use to them now, and Emma leads them away.

I am pulled away by Princess Mary, who holds me while I grab my stomach and retch. She tells me to calm down, that I could have the baby too soon, but her words cannot be heeded for I cannot be calm. I am shaking, numb and disbelieving, reeling from the magnitude of what just happened. When a child dies of a fever, you can attribute it to God's will, but what of this? Tired horses. A wagon stopped too close to a boulder. Three boys playing too far from the troupe. A father whose back was turned for just one moment, and two dozen people all stopping behind a tree, sitting down and resting their eyes or looking in another direction. None of these things in and of itself could take the blame, but a change in any one of them would have saved my baby's life.

Our camp is hurriedly set up for the night, and I am made to lie still with three women watching over me. Henry never comes to me that night. He has his own private grief.

Henry sits for a very long time, rocking Gabrielle. She covers him with her blood, which cakes and dries a sickening brown. He buries his face in her stomach and weeps, tears and blood streaking his cheeks while the little girl lies there and grows stiff in his arms. The others let him remain as he is, while two men quickly build a tiny coffin, and three others dig a hole to bury her. Yet another constructs a cross on which Princess Mary paints bright flowers. None of us knows how to write her name upon the cross, or where to find a priest to bless the grave.

It haunted me to my death, the little unblessed grave that contained my baby girl.

Henry is still in the road in the morning, sitting with his child.

We bury her, and cover the grave with wild flowers, then move on, slowly, numbly, with heavy steps.

As I walk away, I feel panic rise within me. I am leaving behind a child. She is supposed to be in my arms–she only just *was* in my arms. It was only just a minute ago, a dream ago. If I close my eyes, I can still hear her, and smell her and feel her.

I keep turning around to look, and when the grave is first out of sight, I run back again to catch sight of it one last time. I cannot reason the fear away, even knowing she is beyond my care. There is a terrible pain of separation as if she will come to harm, or feel fear and cold and loneliness without me; as if it is my duty to stay with her and stand guard over her; as if I am a bad mother to leave her. She is just a baby girl. She is just a little thing. We cannot leave her alone like this.

Henry takes my hand to lead me away, and in his eyes I see the same uncertainty and fear.

Four weeks later, and miles away, I have another baby, another girl. She is the image of Gabrielle.

It takes Henry and me a long while to recover, if one can be said to ever recover from the death of a child. The little relief we came by after the safe delivery of another baby and months of traveling is lost when we return to the village with the news. We have to relive the grief again, in sharing it with all of those who did not know before.

Each year, we now count the passings of Gabrielle's grave, and stop for a day to spend time with her, and to repaint the flowers on her cross.

✠

"Your prayers were answered," the Voice says. "Every word addressed to God, and every action taken on her behalf, was an answered prayer."

"She did not stay," I respond. When I was first shown the scenes at the end of that life, I responded the same way. I still feel an old sense of confused betrayal as if God did not hear me and did not care about my pain.

"But she did stay, for far longer than was intended. She was never intended to stay with you at all."

"It might have been better if she had been taken immediately, before we had time to love her," I muse.

"Would it?"

"No, no," I say, and I mean it. I could not give back the time I had with her. It meant far too much to me.

"Death was not the end of her, after all. Death is just a passing, only painful to the ones we leave behind. Your Gabrielle, as you know, was fine."

I know this. I simply like the reassurance. It calms me. Sensing as much, the Voice continues.

"Sometimes an illness or an early death is simply a challenge, or a time of growth. The child chooses parents who will help her through it, and the parents make the sacrifice out of love. It is not a punishment. It is simply a turn in the road to push them all forward.

"Then, there are children who choose to die in order to open their parents' eyes to their purpose. Some people are chosen to work toward seeing that others do not suffer in the way their child suffered. Life's greatest good often flows from loss."

I sense it coming, and so it does. I listen, bracing myself, agonized, defensive . . . And in my case?

And in *my* case—

"Sometimes it is a lesson. From pain comes wisdom, growth and compassion. From loss you learn the value of what you have, and you learn which things have value. It is hoped you will carry such lessons with you."

"I knew the value of Gabrielle, and of all my children. There was no need for such a lesson." I am fully defensive, now.

"There was not?" the Voice pointedly asks.

My thoughts turn to Elizabeth and I am silenced.

✠

I have yet another baby girl. Then two more, then three boys, and a girl, and another boy, and my last, a girl. Two more of the babies will die, one from an illness, and the other at the age of four months, for no reason at all while she slept. I will die myself, each time, and Henry will be equally inconsolable. There is no pain on earth comparable to the loss of a child, and there is no cure for it, even braced for it as you are, when you live in a time when children frequently die.

Still, we have so very many babies that live. We know of no others who escape with such good fortune as we. We have such good fortune with our children.

We have equally good fortune with our grandchildren. They number 17 at the time of my death.

✠

"And it did not matter to him that you had grown thick from bearing children, or that your hair grew thin and gray."

No, it did not matter to Henry. I will give him that. "As long as you can still play the harp," he used to say, "I will keep you." He loved music as much as he loved us. Yet when my hands grew stiff and I could no longer play, it did not matter to him.

I wonder, for what purpose is this being done to me?

✠

Eventually, my time was used up. I grew old, fell victim to a lung ailment aggravated by the cold, and died during a winter layover when my children were there surrounding me. Even my death was well-timed, and the illness that preceded it, short.

I want to go back and see more, but I am pulled away. I have seen enough, I am told. I was shown this life to remind me of what Henry is, and what he means to me, lest I become too absorbed in the circumstances of our last meeting.

"Do you remember him?" I am asked. "Do you *remember him*?"

Yes. I remember.

I am almost softened, and I feel as strong a pull toward him as I always had, but there is still too much anger.

As if in a flash, I see him taking my hands and twirling me round and round until the centrifugal force causes us to fly in opposite directions while our small children laugh, and clap their hands, and twirl themselves around as well.

Why this image? At the time it occurred, I did not even take note of it enough to form a memory I could draw upon later in that life. It was just a moment in one of our days, yet now I am viewing it as a distillation of that entire life.

And then I know. An outside force stronger than our grasp on each other has pulled us apart. It is not the life in Flanders to which the image refers. It is the most recent one.

Power had a devastating effect on Henry. He will henceforth avoid it as I have vowed to do. I see from examination of this life the scope of the devastation; the Henry I knew as king is not the Henry of the caravan.

For the first time, I feel grief for him. He fell so far, and I was unable to stop him or protect him from himself.

The image returns, and we twirl again, laughing. I see tangible forces pulling us apart, a corruption of the heart from Henry's position in the world as king, then a corruption of the mind from his disease. I see damage done to me as the result of rapes, and I see the effect that damage had on our marriage. I see my own vanity and weakness and an inability to quell my fears that caused me to speak too sharply and drive him away. I see the force of our notoriety as another influence. Had we been allowed our privacy and the tolerance of those who surrounded us, we might have lived as happily as we had once before.

However, even the absence of meddling and ill-intent could not erase the sickness that ravaged Henry.

Henry, I am told, had the "pox" or syphilis. His condition was far advanced and its destruction had spread to his brain where it twisted his thoughts and changed him. His symptoms of madness went unnoticed, for these included delusions of grandeur which, in a king, go undetected–even when the king in question imagines himself as equal to God. Such imaginings in an ordinary man would have drawn comment and he would have been stopped, but Henry appeared lucid till the end, and hence was allowed to indulge his whims to a frightening degree, reasoning poorly, destroying as he went.

I would have succumbed as well, and would have continued to suffer failed pregnancies as I could not bear healthy children with

Henry. I was only allowed the one, Elizabeth, who was born before the disease had spread within me.

Henry saw or would have seen this one-child or no-child or ill-child pattern with any woman, blaming her when the root of it lie with him. As the disease progressed, he believed we should suffer death or expulsion because of it.

He would believe many should suffer death or expulsion, just because they crossed him and he willed it.

The Voice says: "Do not judge him. That should be left to God. What you need to do is forgive him. Try and find it within your heart."

If Henry was not in control, was I then just another delusional whim?

His love was as real as he proclaimed, I am assured. It was not delusional.

"Then why did he hate me so in the end?"

"You must pose your question to his disease," I am gently answered.

This knowledge does not soothe, it rather irritates. I fear and detest him, and cannot forgive him even with an infusion of softening memories and the knowledge that he was not fully in control. I am too caught up in the momentum of my anger, and would prefer not to taint it with understanding. I resist a voice that asks me to reconsider.

"He was ill," it says again. "He deserves your forgiveness."

"And if he were not ill, I would not have to forgive?"

"You would have to forgive, even then. You see? Your task is not as difficult as it seems."

Even still, I refuse to forgive, knowing I will have to change my heart or pay a price.

PART 6

Dreams and Awakening

1533

Chapter 1

I had an insatiable appetite for apples. The season was past, but there was still a supply of apples in the storerooms, and so I was left a tray of them each day. I ate them all by evening, touching little else, and asked for more. Even after they grew pithy from age as the winter progressed, I asked for more. As I depleted the supply of apples, Henry gave instructions that they should be rationed to all others to ensure I had enough. By February they were gone, even the pithiest among them and I was left to settle for dried ones. These carried me through until the earliest apples could be harvested in summer.

By then I was sated, and could not stomach them at all. I waved the trays away, and could not even touch apple tarts or drink sweet apple cider. The thought of apples made me queasy and ill. I never developed a taste for them again.

My appetite for Henry also waned as the pregnancy progressed. Even seeing me in my bloated state, Henry was anxious to hold me and did it gently, reverently. I did not respond to him as I once had.

He teased me in a wheedling tone saying: "Dost thou not love me? I miss hearing thee cry out." He snuggled up against me and nuzzled my ear hoping to trigger the violent passion he had come to expect. The baby kicked him and he smiled. Henry could wait, for his son would come soon and, with his birth, would return Anne to her passion. There were two wondrous things in store, and Henry could patiently wait, he said.

I did not know where the passion had gone. It went away one day, and did not return. Henry came to me each night and lifted my gown, and murmured his love to me. I wanted only to sleep. Still I would go through the motions and, truthfully, I liked it, once it had progressed. I just no longer had the pressing need for Henry that I had in the beginning, nor did my body whip into a frenzy of lust at the feel and the closeness of him.

In the early days I would have started to breathe harder in anticipation as I lay in bed waiting, just seeing him approach me from across the room. He still responded that way to me, even as I waddled toward him after a visit to the chamber pot with my swollen belly, thick ankles and bloated face. He did not care how I looked; I was his Anne. He patted the bed beside him, his organ at attention and in need of me while inwardly I groaned, but not from pleasure. I was so tired. I was always tired. Our lovemaking had become an activity I had to endure in order to be allowed to sleep.

I did not love him any less. If anything, I felt more toward him, and continued to feel a stronger love each day, as his baby grew inside of me. I could not fathom why I should love him so intensely, and yet not want him to touch me.

"Thou art *pregnant*, my dear," Emma had laughed, rolling her eyes. "Thou art so formidably pregnant that I suffer pain just imagining thee spreading thy limbs for the old villain. He hath done his work. He might leave thee to thy rest."

There had been a soreness in my groin for a while, but it had passed. I had begun pulling away from Henry when the cancre appeared, for I felt a sharp pain when he touched me there. I attributed it to a particularly long lovemaking session, and begged him to allow me to heal. Emma had raised her eyebrows with concern, and questioned me about it when I once complained to her, laughing, that Henry, in his enthusiasm, had torn away the skin and left a sore. She kept pressing, asking if I had seen such a sore on Henry. Embarrassed and defensive, knowing what she implied, I ordered her away.

"I am not diseased," I snapped. "The king is not diseased. Now go."

Taken aback by my tone, Emma left the room without a word. She was too good a friend to take it to heart, or to dissolve into tears. She let the subject drop.

I healed, but my thoughts had gone down strange paths in the interim. I could not consider that I may have the pox as Emma had intimated. Yet I dreamt of it on occasion, and awoke in a sweat. I told no one of this, and never expressed my fears even to Emma. Since the sore had gone away, I saw no reason to bother the court physician. I did not want a man to examine me down there, and he could do nothing to stop my worries anyway. I rather thought he might increase them with a diagnosis, and I preferred not knowing to being certain. I did not tell Henry about my dreams, but when he came to me, I thought of them, and wondered if indeed he was diseased. Even with the damage done, I saw him differently, and saw our lovemaking as a threat to me.

There are many strange dreams and fears that come with pregnancy. The fears of the pox would pass and be replaced by other, more pressing fears. Would the child be male? Would he live? Would I survive the birth?

I kept my rosary in a pouch at my waist—or rather, that area at the center of my torso that had once been a waist. I pulled it out, and slipped each day into the chapel to pray that my child might be a son. I found my favorites among the winged cherubs that peeked out from the walls, and fixed my eyes upon them. I asked, for at least an hour each day, that my child might look like one of those, praying to my very soul that I be carrying within me a strong male child with an angel's face and fat soft curls. Most important was the gender of the child, but I had a strong desire to present Henry with something beautiful. I wanted to please him, and make him happy that he had chosen me. I wanted a child that would tell the world that God had blessed this union despite the way it had begun. I also wanted God's reassurance for myself, for even now, I still had doubts.

As sometimes happens, I felt that God had heard my prayers. I knew this from the warmth that spread throughout me each time I knelt and prayed.

I told Henry that I had felt the glow one feels when prayers are about to be answered. He beamed at me and patted my belly. They were his prayers as well.

I dreamt of a sweet little boy one night. He was about two years old and had bare feet, unkempt yellow hair and blue eyes. Oddly, he wore brightly colored old-fashioned peasant clothing yet, in the dream, it did not seem strange to me that he should be either barefoot, or dressed in peasant garb instead of gold and velvet. He was laughing, running in a field chasing butterflies. He turned and called me "Maman" then ran up to me and hugged my knees. I reached down and lifted him up and turned to Henry, who did not look like Henry at all, and said, "He looks just like you," in French. A hoard of children followed him, boy after boy after boy, of all sizes, smiling, clamoring "Maman, come see!" Then the dream vanished with a kick from the baby. I awoke, still remembering the tiny voice that called me "Mama" in French, placed my hands on my belly thinking "I know now who thou art, little one. Thou art beautiful."

My mood was calmer after the dream. I told Henry about it in the morning, and he listened as if the dream was prophetic. We both preferred to believe it was, and so we did. We believed it would come true.

The calmness did not stay for long.

I had mood swings. I whipped from hysterical laughter to tears in an instant. I grew ever more petulant in my demands, and found fault with everything. I slipped into bouts of self-pity, for my sleep was fitful and, as badly as I needed to sleep, I could not seem to do it successfully. I was up frequently in the night to visit the chamber pot, or else found myself in a restful doze only to be kicked awake again. I twisted through the night, and stared at the darkness, then dragged myself out of bed in the morning when the baby would finally settle down to rest.

"Why couldst thou not have slept during the night?" I often muttered to my belly in irritation. The weariness made me ill tempered and short. Everyone stepped quietly around me, for there was no way of predicting how I might react to anything.

I complained to Henry incessantly, tossing reproaches that he accepted with a mixture of patience and exasperation. He would leave and attempt to right these imagined wrongs with a touching sincerity, yet still I would find fault with his efforts. He often shouted with frustration as I nagged and listed my grievances, then would see me shifting in my chair to get comfortable, or note my reddened eyes, and soften toward me.

I shot blame at everyone around me, amplified minor things and shouted. Servants were at fault because there was not enough of something, or there was too much. Tasks were performed too late, or before I was ready for them to be done. Visitors were ill-timed, no matter when they came. Nothing was scheduled properly, or rescheduled, or scheduled again so that it suited me. Food made me ill, and I blamed the cook. Smells turned me queasy and I demanded the source of them be removed—next time before the odor reached my nose. I sometimes wept because I was so miserable, and because no one read my mind to remove irritants before I was aware of them. In the absence of actual sufferings, I invented some so that I might have a means through which to vent my general discomfort.

Pregnancy did not suit my temperament.

Emma drew Henry aside and begged for him to be patient. It was not her place to do this and, while Henry took her pleadings to heart, I was furious when I heard of them. How dare she view me as a demanding child? How dare she imply my complaints were ill-founded, and that my mood was off? I had good reason to complain, I thought. Everyone was conspiring to see that these months were a misery for me. None of them understood. And now Emma was whispering to my husband about me as if I were something to be endured, rather than a woman who truly required special attentions she did not receive.

Another part of me was ashamed of my behavior, but this part I hid, even from myself.

In an effort to improve my outlook, I hosted gatherings on an almost daily basis. Wine flowed, cards were dealt, dice was thrown, laughter was loud and shrill, and often ladies and gentlemen indulged in behavior never allowed in front of the former queen.

They downed the wine until they were tipsy, vulgar and coarse in their actions and their speech. I did not mind, as Katherine would have. I saw no harm or insult in bawdiness and found it rather amusing.

These gatherings created a diversion, but I could not stomach wine in my condition, and could only wistfully watch while the others carried on. Often my outlook was more soured than improved, particularly since the behavior of the attendees, while essentially harmless, brought scandal to my name. But on some occasions, the laughter allowed me to take leave of my misery, and at such times, I could even laugh with the others.

Sometimes I had a good night's sleep. Not often, but sometimes. On the days following a real rest, my mood rose and I was far easier to live with.

During those months I made enemies among the people who surrounded me, for I could instantly become a churlish, demanding witch, as trying as a spoiled child, but less appealing. A part of me knew this. Another part of me took advantage of my position, and screamed its dissatisfaction with the people whose misfortune it was to serve me. That part of me could not stop—I could not stop it though I tried. With each effort at being more amenable, I would find in the midst of it some small trifle that seemed to me to warrant an exception: "In this case I *must* be churlish for anyone of good reasoning could *see* . . . " And so I passed the long months, accumulating ill-feelings from everyone, at every level within the court.

I tried to recover my sense of duty and my restraint, but with such discipline comes the need for release. I did not even have the release of my music as my belly grew. I had no place to set my lute with the mountain of infant resting upon my thighs as I sat, and attempts had just led to frustration. There were still my harp and the virginals, but in my peevishness I wanted only the lute. On top of this, I was locked in the present and could not see past the irritations of the moment. I would always be this uncomfortable. The baby would never be born. I could not abide the suspense of not knowing its sex. I would never sleep well again.

Then suddenly, pretending to me that he did not want to disturb my rest, Henry took to sleeping in other chambers. It was clear to me that he did not sleep alone. It was known to all that he had found someone else to comfort him, and it was evident this was a source of spiteful amusement to everyone.

I challenged Henry about his mistress and he snapped at me, drawing comparisons between Katherine and myself. For the first time, I was found wanting. It was my duty to avert my eyes, he said irritably. It was his right to bed whomever he chose. Katherine had never mentioned his transgressions, nor complained of them, and he suggested I follow her lead and be a "modest goodly wife."

"Katherine never *loved* thee as *I* do!" I sobbed.

Henry did not respond to that. He turned his back to me.

Then I recovered and snapped, "Did *God* give thee the right to bed other than thy wife? Didst thou speak it in thy wedding vows?" To which vows did I refer, I wondered, suddenly hearing the words? His vows to Katherine, or his vows to me?

He turned on me in fury, demanding me to tell him how I dared speak to him in that manner, after all he had done to make me his wife. And for what? For this? I burst into tears. It took me quite some time to compose myself. Once I did, I erupted into tears again.

"I love thee so much," I sobbed. "My heart is breaking over thee." The knowledge that he had come to be my husband through a lack of concern for previous wedding vows did not console me. I was learning and understanding too late that a man who leaves his wife for another woman is just as apt to leave the other woman for yet another. I had believed it could not happen to me.

After the first of these conversations, Henry comforted me and paid me more heed than he had as of late, but did not discard his mistress. Nor could I think of other than her. She was always in my thoughts.

I could not endure Henry's betrayal. I howled like a wolf caught in a trap and turned on my servants. Not only was I by nature excitable, but I was living in a constant state of defensiveness and Henry, my only safe haven, was slipping away. It all came out in words like: "Look at what you have done! You are a stupid fool.

Leave my sight at once!" Bad words. Ill-chosen words aimed toward underlings who did the best they could for me. I cringe upon hearing them. I writhe with discomfort and shame.

Only Emma took my side when others would whisper complaints of me. It was a hard chore to place upon her. It did not earn her love among the others, but she had mine. She always will.

And suddenly Emma was gone, married and moved away.

"Do not leave," I had told her in a small voice. "I beg thee."

"I shall not be far, and I shall be a wife. 'Tis certainly past time for me to be a wife, dost thou not agree? My teeth are longer than my fingers, I am so old."

I was now alone to face these people with no one as intermediary. I had three attacks of nerves on my first day without her, and even feared leaving my room.

Chapter 2

I had been secretly married to Henry almost the instant my pregnancy was known to us. As soon as it was feasible, I was crowned Queen of England. I was in a position no safer, and was no more loved by the people surrounding me, than I had been when I was still Henry's whore.

I could see, and Henry could see, that respect for me was a pretense. The crowds still shouted and spat. Henry could no more stop them than I could. Immediately following my coronation, as we moved down the Thames in splendid ceremony, I saw that masses of people did not even remove their hats as I passed. It seemed to me that they lined the river for no reason other than to show me they would not remove their hats.

If I was not safe beside Henry within the palace walls, if I went alone to visit friends, I was perilously close to danger. On one occasion, crowds of women had chased and accosted me, surrounding a house I was visiting, forcing me to flee out the back. I was no further from danger within the palace, for enemies constantly surrounded me. And Henry's love was slipping from me, if he could bring himself to take another woman to his bed.

✠

The pregnancy ended, finally, as all pregnancies must. The birth was in September.

When I felt the pains, Henry and I grew frantic with anticipation. "He is coming," he whispered to me, and I giggled nervously awaiting our son's arrival. The midwife forced Henry out of the room, and he waited elsewhere while I groaned through the labor, giggling and babbling with excitement between pains until they grew so intense I could only barely endure them, and could no longer speak. I screamed.

There was a head with no hair, but the scalp had a fine red down. This was reported to me while I panted and pushed. "His father's hair," someone said. I pushed again and heard him cry.

"Yes?" I asked weakly. Women pressed around the midwife blocking the child from my view.

"Push!" A woman ordered, pressing down on my belly. Another woman ran to my side to wipe my brow. I pushed again to expel the afterbirth, still not seeing or knowing. I could hear him cry, but in the bustle to help me finish the birth, no one stopped to say, "It is a prince."

"Tell the King," someone whispered, and a servant raced out of the room. The mood had turned somber, and the babe was silently held out to me.

It was a girl. They wiped her clean, and wrapped her in a warmed cloth while I lay there and watched, unspeaking.

"A wee lass," the midwife said with false brightness. "A fine, healthy, bonny lass for Your Majesty." I still said nothing. She moved toward me with the infant and placed it at my breast. "A fine little princess," she continued coaxingly, placatingly. "A *fine* one."

After handing me the baby, she stepped backwards quickly with a tightness around her lips and a glimmer of fear in her eyes, as if she felt I might blame her.

I stared at the infant, uncomprehending and stunned. I had never seen such an ugly, shriveled little babe. I spread her legs apart, and looked again to be certain there was no mistake. I held her for a moment and touched her cheek, waiting to feel love and tenderness, but there was none. I felt instead that my child, the one I had been so certain was within me, had been stolen, and this changeling left in his place. Instead of a beautiful gift from God, there she lay: a punishment and a reproach.

"Let me sleep now," I said, and allowed a woman take the baby to her wet nurse. I rolled over and closed my eyes while the servants gathered up the linen and whisked away the bloody mess I had made.

I heard the bells toll in the tower. The tolling was a signal indicating the birth and sex of the child. All of London would be stopping to listen now, and would hear from the number of chimes that it was a girl, not a boy, and that Henry's whore had failed him. Many would be most gladdened by the knowledge. My moment of triumph had now become theirs.

Henry swept into the room and sat at the edge of my bed. I looked at him, frightened, and waited for the judgment.

"She is a fine one," he said, patting my leg. "Soon we will try again and have our son."

Did I imagine it? Or were his eyes disappointed and distant?

I did not know what I was to do. I reached out my arms to him, and he held me. I did not cry until he left, and then I sobbed myself to sleep.

Throughout the pregnancy Henry had reassured me that, if it were a girl, we would simply have baby after baby until our son was born. Throughout the pregnancy I had believed any child was good enough, for he loved me and took pains to reassure me.

Those reassurances were given with the unspoken expectation that I succeed the first time. It was only now that I realized he had been fooling himself, as well as me. The sex of the child was of critical importance, and Henry's patience had boundaries. He had already spent that patience on Katherine, who had reached the end of her childbearing years without a son, and for this he had set her aside. Henry was seeing a repeat of this in me, after just one birth. The question foremost in my mind was: How many more chances would he give me?

Before her birth, I had intended to feed my child at my own breast, even though Henry had, on more than one occasion, strictly forbidden me to do it. I now no longer had the will to defy him, and was grateful for his objections. My breasts filled with milk, to bursting. They were sore and inflamed and grown hard as rocks, dribbling milk until my gown was saturated.

I needed the baby to suckle me—my body told me so, and perhaps I should have listened. An angry part of me did not want to share my milk with that child, nor had Henry's objections softened over time. The latter was my excuse. The former was the reason why I never held Elizabeth to my breast.

Henry did not visit me as often as I thought he might have. He spared me just a quarter hour a day while I recovered, and I could not complain of this. The failing had been mine.

Why had God betrayed me? I had prayed so hard, with a faith so strong I knew He had heard me and would respond. I had felt it.

✠

The betrayal still has the sharp edge of a knife.

"Sometimes prayers are not immediately answered," the Voice interjects gently. "That does not mean they are not heard."

There was an imprint of painted cherubs on my soul and it would one day be manifested in the births of fine sons with beautiful faces, and shining soft curls. God just had not said that my prayers would be answered in a later life, and that their father would not be Henry.

"Then of what use will they be if they come too late?"

"They will be of whatever use you can find in your children," the Voice answers, amused. "You will one day have children who are the answer to a prayer. That is all."

"And if I had not prayed, I would never have sons?"

"You receive what you have earned. Had you asked for something else with the same amount of faith, that would have been your reward instead."

"Reward? But I did not earn reward as a mother to Elizabeth. I rather failed at it."

I feel compassion coming from the Voice, and a gentleness I do not expect.

"Be more patient with yourself. They will come when you have earned beautiful angels. It is just up ahead."

"But I needed them then," I respond, not satisfied.

"It was not intended that you have a son. It never was. You have always known that."

Indeed I had. We all enter life with a broad sketch of our purpose. There are some things that are predetermined—they form a skeletal structure around which we build the rest with free will. Sometimes we can change them through prayer, or by exercising a determination to learn our lessons and repay before the time has come for punishment; prayer, mind and will have great power. Sometimes we lose rewards through wrong acts.

There are times when we cannot change the plan for, sometimes, what we think we want in life is at variance with what we truly know we need. While the story of my life seemed on the face of it to be a random combination of events, and the sex of my child a random accident, I had memories of the plan for it. It was known to me even before my time in Flanders, and preparations had been made for it throughout several of the preceding lives.

It had started with the birth of a female infant, long ago, whom I had left on a hillside because I had wanted a boy. It was something often done, and was almost to be expected, when one had already given birth, as I had, to several females.

I still retained a decided preference for male children—and even male animals—that I would need to overcome. As a result of this preference, my treatment of daughters typically was overly harsh or neglectful. The consequence of this was that I had had a string of painful losses similar to the ones in Flanders, for I would not learn.

Not all of Anne's life was predetermined. Most was not. It was only intended that I endure accusation and severe punishment for sexual misconduct, whether I chose to misconduct myself or not. The intent was for me to pay for my hardness toward other women. Then I was to be tested again with the birth of an unwanted female. The rest of it was designed daily, as the life unfolded.

I, of course, did not know of any "plan" as I prayed in the chapel. My fervent prayers were not ignored, nor had they been answered with a "no". They had simply been set aside for another time.

More important than whether or not God had answered my prayers precisely now, and with precisely what I wanted was this:

Elizabeth was neither my punishment, nor was she a reproach. She was my child.

I churn with regret. I might have set aside my own disappointment and thought of her. I might have allowed myself to fall in love with her. In doing this, I would have quelled the fears and the nightmares. I would have been able to hold my temperament in check, for my focus would have been on someone other than myself. Henry might have found me far easier to endure than a shrew of a wife he could never make happy. Had I succeeded thus, my challenges would have been concentrated mainly on the opposition I received at court and, throughout it all, I would still have had Henry as an ally. He would have even reconciled himself to leaving no male heir behind.

There are lives that would have been saved.

I failed again.

"It is not that simple," the Voice insists. "There was still Henry's illness and your own. It would not have ended happily, no matter how you altered your life by feeling differently toward Elizabeth. Deal with what you know, and do not speculate."

Chapter 3

I did not return to myself after the birth. I was wary and frightened, and sank into a melancholy the midwife insisted was common after the birth of a child. My irritability increased with the fear, the defensiveness and the sadness. Had Elizabeth been male, my safety would have been assured, but now I was in a position as uncomfortable as Katherine's had been. My position was worse. And within me was the knowledge that, once again, I had failed to please.

Of greatest concern to me was my apprehension that Henry would cease to love me. I daily feared losing him. That fear caused me to watch him and fret when he glanced at other women, which he had subtly begun to do, even in my presence. His patience with me was shorter than it had been in the past, and his shouts of "Good God, woman!" now had tinges of irritation and displeasure rather than amusement. He now went about his business with less interest in pulling me into it, and responded to my reproachful complaints without his former quick desire to please me. It seemed rather that he would do anything to silence me. And I could not be silenced. Fear edged into my voice and made me sharp. I could not stop.

Anxiety reached a high level within me and manifested itself in symptoms that did not make me more endearing to Henry, or to anyone else. Having developed the habit of shrewish-ness during pregnancy, and still passing one sleepless night after another, I grew used to being difficult and did not even notice that I was. I was too consumed by worry and terror to have much energy left for pleasantries, or for concern toward anyone else. Neither did I make any effort to change; I had other things on my mind and no one dared to scold me or remind me to behave myself. Only Katherine and her supporters made public comments about my behavior. I discounted these for we were at war. Aside from them, I had moved to a position above the reproach of everyone but Henry.

There are some who grow more silent with fear. There are people who curl up within themselves and swallow it. I was not one of those. My temperament did not allow for silence. Almost every emotion and every thought needed to be expressed in some manner, and I could not hold my tongue, for fear made it wag. I did not express my fear by simply saying, "I am fearful," or by shuddering and weeping. I expressed it as anger or haughtiness so that no one would see how vulnerable I was and attack me.

I used words that caused fear in others. That never made me feel strong, but my instincts told me that I could only be safe by driving away those who threatened my safety. And there was no one I thought of as truly "safe". All I had with which to defend myself was my ability to rise above others and misuse my power. From my perspective, I was climbing up to the highest branches of a tree while the water rose about me.

I was too consumed to notice that I was pecking upon my underlings like a chicken in a barnyard. That was dangerous enough. More dangerous was the way in which I turned my fear onto Henry by counting the minutes he spent with me, or the seconds his eyes followed a woman as she passed. I could not stop myself from commenting, in part to solicit his reassurances. As time passed, his reassurances came less often, and my comments grew more reproachful and more frequent. I could not be reassured. He in turn felt less inclined to reassure me.

He was set upon having a son. He forgot his irritations at night and still came to me, but he was more determined than he had been in the past. He came to me with concentrated intent, and obvious purpose. In response to this, I stiffened in fear, knowing now why

Katherine had prayed aloud during their lovemaking, and wanting to do the same. Henry sensed the change in me, and answered my daytime reproaches with his own at night: he performed the act then left the room without a word, and went to sleep elsewhere.

I lay awake long afterward and stared.

I began having dreams about France. I thought I had placed it behind me, but still I had vivid dreams about being cornered in the corridor, and pulled into an empty room by my attacker. The dreams always placed us in a church for some reason and, in these dreams, he was dressed in a long black cape, a large, pale, flaccid, thick-lipped man with narrowed eyes that darted about in search of me. I grew small in the dreams, even smaller than I had been in life when he first took me. I would run and hide beneath a church pew where he would always find me, and I would scream myself awake. So unsafe was I in the dream, I could not even find shelter in the house of God.

In place of insatiable passion, I now had no desire for Henry at all. In fact, I quite recoiled from him.

I tried not to let him see this, for I needed to become pregnant again. Yet I feared becoming pregnant, for I might give birth to another female. He had married me solely so that I might give him a son, and I had already failed in this. To do so again was unthinkable, and yet I had no control over this kind of failure, past or future. I needed somehow to gain control, but could not. Was it preferable to not be pregnant, or to present him with another daughter? I had no answer to that and felt as if I was choosing between death from a sword and death from poison. I would in the end, of course, leave it up to God, the very God who had already betrayed me.

My passion would have returned when my body went back to normal, had I not been so plagued. I loved Henry deeply. However, I was frightened after Elizabeth was born. I had no one to tell, and nowhere to run. The fears had taken hold of me and had spawned bad dreams that came with greater frequency until I was again a girl, feeling all the terror of being forced.

I now could not stomach our lovemaking. Too much was tied to it. It nearly made me ill.

It was in this that my attacker lay the groundwork for my

sentence of death. He wounded my mind as much as my body, and it was only the bodily wounds that healed. The scars inside my head were larger than the faint one on my neck, and they resurfaced when I faced the strain of having had a daughter rather than a son. Deep inside me, repressed for years by my determination to move past it, that man still waited for me with his knife at my throat. When Henry touched me, I saw that man and remembered, and relived, and felt the same revulsion again.

Why, after so many years? Why was it stronger in these years than it had been earlier on? I did not understand. It made no sense to me. It would make even less sense to Henry, who wanted only that I get on with it and return to being the way I once was. He did not want to discuss rapes he did not believe had really taken place, or examine the effects those rapes had had on me.

Henry would send me away for this. He would send me away and replace me with someone else. I knew it. The thought of it caused me even greater anxiety. Worry quelled my desire even further.

Henry could not help but dwell on what might be causing my lack of passion toward him. He was in constant fear that he could not perform like other men. He had gotten so from Katherine's coldness. Now he had a second wife who seemed to find him as unappealing as the first had.

He began to "confess" to his advisors that he could not perform the marital act because I had bewitched him and rendered him impotent. Henry had difficulty performing the love act when he did not feel he was desired, so in a sense his words held truth. I was, in fact, the source of his impotence. He did not explain in full, however, when he made this accusation. So ashamed was he that he preferred being viewed as a man who could not bed his wife, rather than admit that his wife would not have him.

Had I done anything but shy away from his advances, I might have lived. Had I merely had a succession of daughters or miscarriages, I would have been divorced instead. My death was a punishment for frigidity more than for any other thing.

It tore at Henry's heart.

He was a very proud man.

"Wouldst thou deign to have me?" he coolly asked me one night from just inside the doorway as I lay propped among the cushions. I had complained of head pains or monthly cramps for days. For a week prior to that I had used other excuses. I was pushing him into the arms of his mistress, and I knew this and was frantic with jealousy and fear, but I could not change how I felt about his coming to me.

No, I thought. Please no.

"As you do wish, my lord," I had answered, with no expression.

"I care little either way," he snapped at me. His eyes were wounded. "Soon, I shall not care at all."

My feelings instantly warmed toward him when I saw his eyes. I did not ever want to wound him and felt a rush of love, and shame, and regret.

"Henry," I had said holding out my arms. "Come to me." I felt deep remorse toward him. I did not even remotely deserve him. Why was I doing this to him? I must stop. I could push aside my distaste once and for all if I willed it strongly enough. It was a weakness I had to overcome.

This was my husband. This was my life's greatest love. He had done so much for me, and I should not bring such grief to him. I kept my arms outstretched, while he thought for a moment.

"I would not keep thee from thy rest," he said with narrowed eyes and a tinge of sarcasm.

I read accurately that he was hurt and in fear of rejection.

"Come to me," I said softly. I leaned forward toward him, stretching my arms. "Please."

Henry hesitated, then softened and casually walked over to me as if he were doing so by coincidence rather than design. He sat at the edge of my bed and looked at me with an expression of indifferent disdain.

Then his face crumpled and he buried it in my lap. He began to shake, and to twist at my gown with his fists like a small boy. I heard a muffled sob.

"Sshhh, my sweetest," I whispered. "I do so love thee."

"Dost thou?" He asked looking up.

"With all my heart and my soul," I answered. "Nothing will ever change that, Rex." I stroked his hair.

"Thou hast become cold to me." He said it accusingly, plaintively, like a child.

How do you explain fears and dreams and wounds to a man? He would scoff and tell me to simply not heed them. I had tried not heeding them, and yet they haunted me still. He would scorn me for that, and think they were an excuse rather than a reason, or that I was weak, or looking for attention.

"I have dreams . . . That is all. They make me fearful."

"Of me? How couldst thou ever fear me? I could never harm thee."

That statement gave me faith that perhaps all was not as hopeless as I thought. Perhaps he was not planning to wound me after all, by discarding me for someone else and, perhaps his love for me had not changed. With this small reassurance, I felt safer. All I really needed was to feel safe, and not feeling so was the cause of all that plagued me.

I cupped his face in my hands and kissed him and felt the passion stir within me again.

"I do not fear thee. I have bad dreams that taint my thoughts. They haunt me." I slipped my hand down to unloosen his codpiece and began to breathe more heavily. I nuzzled his ear and grew limp when he reached for me. "I will try harder not to have them," I whispered.

"What kind of dreams?" Henry asked distractedly. He sighed when I reached inside and found him. He did not await an answer. "Oh Anna," he whispered. "Oh my love."

He came again the next night and the next, and stayed, and for that short time our passion was as it had been in the beginning. I did so love the man. I did so love him. If I could only purge myself of demons . . .

Then I had another dream. In this one I was raped again, and gave birth to a hideously monstrous child. It had the face of the man who had taken me in France, and claws instead of hands. It was handed to me and I held it, then it reached out its claws and cut my neck. I screamed.

I screamed myself awake, and sat up in bed hysterical. Yet I was not quite awake. I was a child again and back in France. When Henry sat up in bed and grabbed hold of me to calm me, I struck him and screamed louder, for the dream continued and, in it, my attacker had come back for me.

"Anna—please. Thou hast had a bad dream!"

I wrestled away from him and stood up, clutching my nightgown at the chest with my fist.

"Touch me and I will kill you," I hissed in French, and was suddenly entirely awake.

I blinked, disoriented. "Rex?" I asked. I wondered why I was standing so.

"Thou hast had a bad dream," Henry repeated, more calmly. He let silence fall for a moment. It was not a comfortable silence. Then he spoke.

"Thou didst just say to me that thou wouldst kill me, were I to touch thee." His voice was strained beneath the calm.

I stared at him, and slowly shook my head. I could not see to read his expression, but his eyes shone in the moon's reflection. They did not blink.

"Wouldst thou *indeed* kill me were I to touch thee? Wouldst thou in*deed*?" His voice had taken the slippery tones he used when confronting someone who had defied him, someone he could crush. His tone of voice rose and fell unnaturally along a musical scale. There was a studied cheerfulness to the words, and a conscious effort to carefully enunciate each one that I recognized as ominous. He had never once before directed that tone toward me.

My words even in sleep, we both knew, were treasonous.

"I was speaking to *him*." I was shivering and my voice shook. "I was not speaking to thee—if in fact I spoke at all! I remember not, except for having said that in my dream."

"To whom didst thou speak, if not to me?" He looked around himself dramatically, and waved his hand. "I see no one else."

"The man who forced himself on me when I was young."

"Was that thy dream just now?" His voice still carried the ominous inflections, softly encouraging the cornered animal to move closer and allow Henry to strike. He thought I lied about the rapes, and thus was lying when I said I dreamed them. He believed, much as the women in the French court had believed, that rape was merely seduction and a weakness of the victim. He did not accept my stories as truth and viewed them as an insult to his good nature and his intelligence. Knowing this, I had stopped speaking of the topic very early on.

"Aye. It was most . . . horrifying. It was not you to whom I spoke, Your Grace. I beg your forgiveness for having spoken out of turn." I had not phrased my words so formally for several years when addressing him in private, but his voice demanded it. "I am most humbly sorry."

He still stared. "Come back to bed," he ordered. His voice had not warmed toward me.

"Yes my lord," I said. Feeling both terror and embarrassment, I slipped into bed. I pulled myself into the fetal position with my back to Henry, and when he edged closer to me, I pulled away. He tried again, and again I moved from him. I just could not be touched, even knowing how unwise it was to spurn him.

Henry lay there and thought for a moment, then rose and left me to spend the rest of the night elsewhere.

"Do not leave me, Rex. Please—" I whispered to him as he stood. He continued toward the door as if he had not heard.

He did not return the following night.

Chapter 4

I visited Elizabeth on occasion. In the beginning, I explained that holding her and being near to her somehow had the effect of causing my breasts to become engorged. I would sacrifice my visits in order to hasten the drying of my milk, I said, and so saw her very rarely for weeks. When my milk finally dried, I ventured in to visit her.

She had not grown more beautiful with time, nor had she grown to be more male. I held her and waited to love her. I did not love her with that visit, nor with the next one or the next, so I concentrated instead on the details of her existence, speaking to the nurses about her feedings and the schedule she kept.

It was all the concern I could offer her.

In return, she did not cling to me or need me. The focus of her adoration was the wet nurse, not her mother. When she cried, I could not comfort her at all, and had to turn her over to Sarah, who would hold her to her breast and let her suckle while I watched.

I knew nothing of infants at all, and did not feel myself fit to be a mother. The women entrusted with Elizabeth seemed so much more adept than I in making her happy and keeping her well. I felt a sinking sensation each time I paid a visit, for I was neither loved nor needed by my child. This was, in fact, the way I was raised, and what I had been taught was proper, but something inside of me suggested that perhaps Sarah's role was the one to be envied. I resolved to earn back the love it is a mother's right to know, and yet each day I found reasons not to go to my daughter. Petty reasons.

Then, Henry ordered Elizabeth moved to another location, away from us for a good portion of the time, removing any possibility that I might come to know her and grow fond.

Had Elizabeth been a boy, I would not have had the dreams and the fears. I would still have a husband who nightly raced to my side—and I would have welcomed him. Things would have been very different, and I blamed the baby for that. I did not hate Elizabeth; I did not feel enough toward her to hate. I merely did not like her much, for she was the cause of all my grief.

I thought of this as I watched her look up at me from her cushions, cooing and kicking and punching the air with her fists, a princess, but motherless except for a servant named Sarah. Then I turned and left the room and, except for high level plans one must make for a child of royalty, I gave her not another thought until next time.

It was, of course, my loss more than hers. She had others to take my place, whereas I never had another child that lived.

When she was near at hand, Henry found more time than I for visits to the nursery. He fussed, and spoke to her, and held her. He found in her more beauty than I could see, and more worth. Knowing what questions to ask, he grilled the nurses about bowel movements, and her progress at smiling or rolling over. He asked about the foods Sarah ate that might have turned her milk and caused Elizabeth a colic. He took strict note of Sarah's diet, and had her eat the best the cooks could prepare, eliminating onions and other items he had heard could give a baby gas. He reported all this to me, and I listened dazed and uninvolved in it. There was much in the care of an infant that I did not know, and it seemed to me to be overwhelming, all taking place in a land foreign to me.

✠

"And yet, I am amply skilled at motherhood. I truly am."

"You never gave yourself a chance."

I sink into numb anguish and regret, seeing the baby and now finding her to be sweet and beautiful. How could I not have responded to the sweetness of the child? I remember another little girl whom I loved, but only had for a very short time. I wish to pass along to Elizabeth the feelings I once felt toward other children, but it is too late. I am gone, having made it her fate to be motherless for the entire span of her life.

I find one small grain of comfort. As Elizabeth grew, there were kind souls who took pains to tell her how proud I had been of her, and how dear she was to me. They described the joy I felt whenever she came to me, and how I could not bear for her to leave my sight.

For once, I do not cringe when I see my story distorted. God bless them for giving her that. God bless them.

Can I love her from here? I force love out of me in her direction. I push it on her. I love her. I *love* her. Can she feel it? Does she know? Would she condescend to love me back? In shame I think "no" and let the love flicker for an instant, then stubbornness takes hold, and I love more furiously. I need nothing in return from her. I will love her no matter what she thinks of me, or how fiercely she condemns me.

Still living, grown old but still alive, Elizabeth feels it, and begins to cry in deep hard sobs, not knowing what has caused her to do so. She has only the faintest recollections of a mother, and has been taught the woman was a villain. Even still, she has spent her life loyal to my memory, a gift I did not earn and for which she received nothing in return. She thinks of that mother now and cries, and I force the love on her still. Something is broken inside of her and somehow my efforts help her just a little.

I have earned a punishment in my neglect of her. I receive affirmation rather than words from the Voice.

A child is not a prize, nor had for some purpose other than to love it. It does not matter what form the child takes in its gender, its appearance, or the state of its health. It is a part of the life force that is God, and is a blessing. I do not place conditions on the outcome by saying it must look a certain way, or possess a certain skill, or be of one sex versus another. It is placed with me so that I might nurture, guide and teach it—and learn from it. It is not given to me so that I might find it lacking, or blame it for all that goes wrong, or abuse it, or abandon or neglect it.

Each child entrusts itself to its caretakers in a form wholly helpless, and depends upon those caretakers for unconditional love, the right of every human child. If I betray that trust, my reward may be an all-encompassing hunger for a child and the inability to have one, or receiving a child only to lose it.

I think I already know what my punishment is. A scream rises within me. I will lose another child.

The deaths of three little girls had been preparation for Elizabeth. I had every reason to value a female child because I had painfully lost three of them. I was given the chance, and when tested, I failed for selfish reasons.

"You did not abuse her, nor did you abandon her. You took great pains to assure her future as your own looked more bleak. You were not a fiend toward her. You merely forgot she had worth in her own right, and focused all the blame for your fate upon her."

"And so?"

"And so you will know how it is to be devalued for having been born what you are."

"Will I lose another child?" It is a terror that I will always carry with me.

"Perhaps not. It is up to you."

"I will not lose another child. I will do anything to prevent it. I will sacrifice anything."

"Remember that you said that."

I am silenced with fear. I hear a warning in the words.

The skeletal structure of my next life plan has already been set forth. The design in this plan is that I learn self-effacing service. Lessons in duty and discipline will continue. There will also be corrective punishment: I will be on the receiving end of tongues as sharp as my own, and I will not have the freedom to protest or respond. Lastly, because I failed a test with Elizabeth, I will now face that same test again under even more difficult circumstances.

In the Orient is a land called Cathay, or "China". There is an ancient tradition called Astrology, which is commonly thought among the Chinese to portend a person's future and determine his worth. Within this discipline it is said that a female child who is born during the Year of the Horse is not marriageable, or rather, cannot find a husband except among those who cannot find acceptable wives. Worse is the fate of the female infant with the misfortune to be born in the Year of the Fire Horse, which occurs every 60 years. Large numbers of these female infants are put to death, for they will not find anyone to marry them at any price, and a woman's value is based solely upon her ability to marry well. If they live, they are destined for hard servitude and a lifetime of societal contempt.

We are all subject to the rules and beliefs of any society we select and, in Cathay, the horoscope is one of the most important defining factors of a person's life. It will stay with him throughout life like a birthmark, and will influence the way he is treated, and so influence the entire span of his life.

In this realm, horoscopes are treated as valid in the sense that they are self-fulfilling. If, within a society, a child is deemed unmarriageable because of her time of birth, she is unmarriageable because it has been declared that she would be, and will suffer for it. All who believe in Astrology and act upon their beliefs make its influence real. Because of this, Astrology is considered here to be as important as the physical situation in the life plan of a person destined for birth within such a society. In preparation for arrival in Cathay, the horoscope is carefully plotted in advance down to the moment of birth so that it is in concurrence with the life plan. That which is the soul's destiny, that which is not determined or influenced by society's interpretation of the birth time, will take place—or not take place—regardless of the position of the stars and what they predict.

The plan is that I will be born in Cathay in the Year of the Horse. My position in the family will be as unwelcome daughter to a couple with several other daughters, but no sons. My physical surroundings will be reasonably comfortable by comparison to many, and my appearance will be satisfactory. However, I will not be male. I will be held accountable for this, and for the trouble I bring my family as they attempt to marry me off. A husband will finally be found for me and in my 24th year, the Year of the Fire Horse, I will give birth to a female.

Beyond that, I may write the story as I choose.

"Remember that there are times when that which appears to be a virtue can be a burden to you. You have learned duty, and will learn it to an even greater degree. However, you must be wary of it, and decide to whom you must be most dutiful. Duty, more than any other thing, will have the potential to betray you.

"Remember, also, that there are times when that which might seem to be a grave fault is actually your greatest asset. You are willful, defiant and stubborn. Where you are going, females who possess those qualities are more than unacceptable—they are contemptible, and seen as an abomination. You will learn to subdue your will to such a degree that it might be thought you have no strength at all. However, it is your will that you must call upon, and your ability to defy others, and your refusal to give in, for it is only these three things that might save you from wrong choices. You are equipped for what you are going to face. You can succeed."

I do not want to think of all that now. I do not wish to dwell on the future yet.

PART 7

Remember Me When You Do Pray...

1534-1536

Chapter 1

There were several palaces where Henry, or Elizabeth, or I—or we—stayed from time to time. Our main residence was Hampton Court, built at great expense by Cardinal Wolsey until Henry saw it and fancied it for himself. At Henry's subsequent hinting, Wolsey was forced to offer it to the king as a gift (having little choice but to relinquish it). The king accepted it guiltlessly and graciously, added some improvements, and moved his court from the sprawling Whitehall Palace to Wolsey's former home. Meanwhile, Cardinal Wolsey went elsewhere, a poorer man.

The palace boasted hot and cold running water, an elaborate sewer system that removed substantial waste deposited by substantial numbers of palace occupants, and a wing of kitchens where hundreds upon hundreds of kitchen servants prepared food for several hundred people at a sitting. It was the finest, most inventive and most modern dwelling any king had ever inhabited.

Within the palace were rooms that had ceilings painted to resemble the night sky, dark blue with a myriad white stars. Large gilded cherubs peaked out from every arched beam and every corner of the chapel, fairly cluttering the ceiling and walls. The rooms were massively high, and elaborate stained glass panels that displayed my initials and Henry's (and sometimes Cardinal Wolsey's, poor man) went from ceiling to floor. There were tapestries larger and more richly detailed than any to be found elsewhere hanging upon each wall, and paintings, and the finer examples of my own handwork.

The feasts laid at table boasted peacocks (skinned, then prepared, then replaced within their feathered skins and served), truffles, game, and every gently-seasoned rare delicacy the cooks could prepare for the royal family and the upper nobility. Any dish the royalty or higher nobility waved away untouched was offered to the lower nobility, who would otherwise eat simpler fare such as meat pies. Anything sampled and rejected by either group was distributed to the poor, who daily lined up outside the castle gates for scraps.

I sometimes tasted food and rejected it solely because it pleased me to share with the poor outside, particularly on those days when I had passed them and seen their faces. I even viewed it as a form of religious fasting, to pass over and share a dish I loved in order to eat a dish less pleasing. On the day of my coronation I, rather giddy with excitement and anxious to give thanks, took one bite each from 23 separate dishes, then waved each one of them off to the crowd at the gate while everyone watched, disapproving and aghast. At court, it was considered improper, selfish, spiteful and boorish to share with the poor, rather than with the privileged and well-fed.

Hampton Court's bricks–hundreds of thousands of them–were painted in checkerboard red and black. The walls that enclosed the lavish gardens were painted white with red crosses (this was Henry's solution to the irritating and persistent problem of courtiers who insisted upon urinating there - they would not dare relieve themselves upon a wall that displayed the Holy Cross). Gargoyles and statues shone in bright yellow or blue.

Overlooking the courtyard on a wall near our apartments, Henry had installed a huge monstrosity of an astronomical clock that could, it was said, be read from a mile away, were it not enclosed by walls. It was, along with everything else at Hampton Court, intimidating, stunning, excessive, magnificent and fantastic.

Colorful flags and banners flapped in the wind above the courtyard, where scores and hundreds of people merged and converged as they moved to perform their daily business. The courtyard sometimes held a population larger than many a village, and was filled with liveried footman, pages and servants, entertainers, color bearers, soldiers, foreign dignitaries, carriages, horses . . . It made one dizzy to look out a window at them all and watch. Of course, when I was in the midst of them, the scene was entirely changed. They all ceased their activity and stood at attention, or with knees bent and heads lowered–every one–and let me pass.

I felt that Hampton Court was a huge, cold, unwelcoming place, and one I did not much favor for all its color and finery. Forced to live within its walls, I made the best of it, and passed my days.

Chapter 2

During the summer, we always went on progress throughout the country, packing up ourselves and our entourage, then touring England to reassure those who resided outside of London that the King was in good health and concerned about their welfare. It was at such times that we moved between the various palaces and viewed our holdings.

I had always looked forward to this festive season. I loved to travel, and I enjoyed the excitement and change of scenery. I most loved the opportunity it afforded me to give directly to the English subjects by passing out alms, or sewing clothing and distributing it among the poor.

I sent messengers on ahead of us to gather up a list of the families most in need. When we arrived, I then gave them the shirts my ladies and I had made, and money or livestock, or I arranged for medical care–whatever was needed. I was invigorated whenever we were on the road, for it was the season when I was busiest, felt most useful, and was most at home.

Now, however, the prospect of our summer progress brought me no pleasure. Henry had plans to go without me. It was for my own good, he insisted. It was out of concern for me, he said.

It was 1534, and I was pregnant again. Henry had stopped coming to me, so a quick calculation was all I needed to place conception around the time of my nightmare, and the birth around late summer.

Henry was not as solicitous toward me as he had been the time before. Knowing now that my temperament in pregnancy was foul, he spent a large portion of his time away from me. Since I had daughters rather than sons, his interest in me was spent.

Word got back to me that he was lecherous in his pursuit of other women while I awaited the birth of his child. There was no shared pleasure and expectation. No longer did he show more than superficial concern for my welfare, and when he did, it was only for the benefit of an audience. He showed no concern in private and he placed no buffer between me and shocks I might suffer, either physically or emotionally. This time, I was pregnant alone, bristling with resentment and struck mindless with fear.

As my belly grew larger, I carried on long conversations with God in the gilded chapel, gazing up at the clutter of sweet winged cherubs, eyes wide, lips pressed, fingers white from gripping rosary beads.

Emma was gone, replaced by other ladies who could not ever hope to replace her. I had never been so lonely in my life.

I had no Emma with me, but I had my fool. He alone could cheer me into good temper. Easily wounded and prickly with distrust, I allowed only my fool the privilege of chiding and abusing me as, before him, I had allowed only Emma. He was the only person upon the earth, besides Emma, whom I knew with certainty loved me. I had removed even my own family from that small list.

We spent our days together, and I took my fool with me wherever I went. There were several instances when we ventured outside the palace gates by carriage, and crowds screamed their insults. Each time, he screamed right back in my defense, making a mockery of them by aping them, and pointing his finger, and twisting his face into horrible contortions.

Then he would turn to me and say "But you know, all they say about you is true, Your Majesty." He would pause then continue: "You did eat ham this day, just as these goodly people insist." I would laugh nervously at his nonsense if I were able. When I was not, when I was in tears or white from panic, he would hold my hand tightly and pat it while the shouts rang out: "Nan Bullen be damned!"

"Nan Bullen had ham!" he cried to drown them out until the carriage rolled past the angry crowd and its threats.

I never knew he held my hand, for he only did so at critical times when the shouts drove me to near hysteria. It was a shocking breech of propriety for a commoner–and a man–to touch a queen. It was an act that could even be construed as treasonous, and considering Henry's state of mind, could have meant death. My fool was well aware of this. He did not seek reward in comforting me. Yet a fool's seemingly small, unnoticed act of defying convention and precept to hold a terrified woman's hand looms large, in this realm. It was a compassionate act of selfless courage, and he will be amply repaid, I am assured.

This pregnancy ended with the early birth of a stillborn male child we named "Henry" and placed in the crypt. The nursery preparations were hastily removed and nothing further was said about them, or about my poor dead child for whom, it seemed, only I grieved.

Henry's lips grew more taut.

I grew more shrill as I plummeted into an abyss of misery and fear. I could not hold back the fear, nor could I keep it from dominating my thoughts. When I was fearful, I could not stop my tongue. I lashed at everyone. I aimed carefully restrained reproaches at Henry, spewing louder reproaches into the ears of others. In private I chewed the cuticles from my fingers, and lapsed into long moments of absent staring.

My eyelid uncontrollably twitched.

Was I turning into Katherine? I now understood her as no one else on earth could understand. I did not hate her less, but I knew, as no one else did, what Katherine had prayed, and why.

Chapter 3

There were two means through which an English subject might guarantee the hastening of his death: treason or heresy.

Treason consisted of any act actually committed against the Crown, any act that might be construed as disloyal or threatening toward the Crown, and any act that might either provoke Henry to rage, rational or otherwise, or incite him in a moment of abstract displeasure or whimsical pique.

Heresy, on the other hand, consisted of any thought or deed suggesting God was something or someone other than that which Henry decreed Him to be. Heretics were typically burned at the stake; this was considered apt punishment for wrong thoughts or ideas inconvenient to the Crown.

Parliament had earlier passed the Act of Succession, which declared Princess Mary a bastard, and my own children Henry's successors. All England was now being called upon to declare fealty, and to swear an oath. Few refused: to refuse was treason and the punishment for treason was death. My Elizabeth was now the heir to Henry's throne, and England was forced to swallow this. It was forced to swear it swallowed willingly, and with pleasure.

Then, since the Pope would not acknowledge Henry's marriage to me, or children born of our union, Henry had declared a new church, and assumed a role equivalent to "pope" within it. I even helped him with this, by locating literature that supported his position and handing it off to him to use in his arguments. In other words, it was I who fueled his flame. I was there behind him, encouraging him and showing joy when his efforts succeeded. It was I who had done all this.

It was I who, after these efforts had succeeded, felt the icy cold rush of second thoughts and of doubt. Not Henry.

So, Henry solved our problems with a wave of his magical, regal wand. With a wave of that wand, he dismissed the Pope, took his place as the highest representative in the Church of England and (in his mind) took his rightful seat at the right hand of God.

According to the rules of Henry's church, our marriage was legal and Elizabeth was legitimate. Henry's God (one must assume a different God from the one we knew before, since His opinions were so changed) viewed our marriage as valid and blessed. Those who thought otherwise must die.

To escape condemnation, the populace was therefore made to swear twice, first declaring loyalty to Anne Boleyn and the Princess Elizabeth, and then to Henry as Supreme Head of the Church of England. All were also forced to deny the Roman Catholic Pope in Rome.

In terror, people swore their oaths to save their lives. In one breath the people of England were spitting out the words "Little Whore" and "Great Whore" and in their next, were declaring their undying loyalty to Elizabeth and to me. I did not question which of the oaths was the more sincere. Nor did Henry. He had long since abandoned all hope of persuading our subjects to love me. He was forcing their love–a love he himself no longer thought he felt–out of stubborn perverseness. He angrily, tenaciously, insistently promoted my cause throughout the country, even though he scarcely looked at me anymore and responded to me with irritation when I spoke.

Faced with the anger of England, I once had begged Henry, "Make it stop!"

Now, by God, he would. He would make it stop. And he would make me watch.

The butchering began.

Words declared against Elizabeth and me were now whispered, not shouted. Public, and even private displays of disloyalty toward us could send a man to prison, or even to his death. Some people took advantage of this as neighbor turned against neighbor, reporting treasonous speeches by those whom they disliked or wished to be rid of. The accused were then sentenced and dragged away to prison with neither proof, nor interest in proving within the courts, which churned out guilty verdicts one behind another.

Four monks, criminals for having worn priestly robes and hence shown loyalty to the Roman Catholic Church, were disemboweled and their heads paraded, rotting on sticks, through the streets of London. More clerics and cardinals were rounded up and slaughtered, and their severed hands and feet were nailed to the city gates.

Had Henry lost his reason? No one dared question him lest treason be their crime and death their just reward, so Henry moved along, unchecked.

There was a fine line between heresy and treason, once Henry became both Church and Crown. In fact, one accusation was quite as good as the other. It hardly mattered *why* you were dead, precisely. The important thing was this: If you were dead, you most likely were dead because of me.

I did not have the influence I once did, and could not reason Henry away from the murderings. I grew drawn and gray as they continued. I could not even mourn because I could not feel; to feel meant I would have to lose my mind from responsibility, guilt and grief. Some self-preserving reflex numbed me through the months of slaughter. I watched it all unfold with detachment, as if from a large distance, and viewed it as if it happened because of someone other than myself.

For a time, throughout the bloodiest days, Henry seemed to need me again, and during that time he set aside his latest mistress. The guilt and the sorrow were beginning to fester within him.

Then, his fear grew even larger still, for the sky had burst open and the rains would not cease. Henry heard it said by many that God was taking His vengeance against him and, in his heart, he suspected it might be true. Rain pummeled against the palace walls, and washed away the roads, and brought the river Thames to the point of flooding. Cracks of thunder and bolts of lightening hurled across the sky in judgment and reproach, making Henry silent, pale and jittery. He spent a significant portion of his day knelt in prayer. He installed himself at my side through night and day, as if only I could offer him protection. I seemed the only one who could comfort him, during the storms.

I reassured Henry that he did the right thing. My critics might ask themselves what they would say, when asked by *that* king under *those* circumstances if he was right to kill. One does not argue with the man who wields the knife and who shows no mercy or restraint. Even I could bite my tongue when faced with that, or lie.

Furthermore, the killings were being done for my sake and for the sake of my child. If I protested, Henry was enraged and screamed that I was an ingrate and a peasant, and could instantly be flung back into the mud from which I had sprung. Such words bit me and stung because I had come to believe them to be true, and so I took measures to appease him in whatever ways I could. For the first time since I met him, I was frightened enough of Henry to become his quiet helpmate.

I aged years during those months, standing at his side as he grew ever more insane.

Meanwhile, in light of what they saw unfolding around them, our subjects searched their hearts and souls, reevaluated their religious faith, and made the decision that Henry's God was the one they much preferred to worship.

Just that quickly, the population of Britain gave up its faith and accepted a new one. With naught but an oath, they let the old God die, and welcomed Henry's.

I say, "They let the old God die," but mean this more symbolically than literally. Henry did not outwardly change the Church except to change the structure of its hierarchy, remove Rome's influence, and rename the pope "Bishop of Rome". Priests still said Mass as they always had, and the Scriptures remained intact. But thoughts churned and whirled about in my head that perhaps we—both Henry and I—had gone too far.

I could still sympathize with Henry's desire to rid himself of people who committed treason (by my definition, not Henry's). As aghast as I was at the frightening speed of conviction and the injustice in many instances, I was quite as willing as he was to be rid of people who physically threatened my life and my child's, and I fervently wished these people as dead as they wished me.

Try as I might, however, I could not quite grasp the reason why we must kill a person for his religious beliefs. There must be some sense behind it, for it had always been done, but I could not follow the logic. I had known Jews in my life, and they were no more evil than Christians. They were, in fact, about the same in their evilness and goodness. I would not think of killing one of them. The same was true for heretical Lutherans, and now, the Catholics. I could find no compelling reason why any of them must die and had not, as yet, had a reason explained to me in terms I could fully understand. If the issue were one of goodness versus evil, I would need to see more proof on either side. If, on the other hand, it was an issue of punishing sincere good intentions and simple interpretation of the Scriptures, I had to protest.

I knew there was a movement within England to reform the Church and to promote the various Protestant religions. To them, Henry's and my actions were welcome and long overdue.

Pitted against this movement were the traditional Catholics who were driven to the point of war, and would war, and would, in years to come and with Princess Mary at the forefront, ruthlessly kill in defense of their religion, just as Henry was now killing in defense of his.

Each one of these people–on both sides–believed that only he and his kind were privy to the Truth because of a larger wisdom and mental sobriety only accorded to those who thought as they did. Each one of them was certain God loved only him and his kind, and would cast the rest into oblivion, or flames.

Each prayed to the same God to strike the other dead; the same God, for there is only one.

Caught in the middle, still worshipping and thinking of myself as a Catholic but having been thrust by circumstance into the very odd role of "patron saint" of Protestants, I was forced to think more deeply than most of the other participants in the bloody drama.

I did not presume Protestantism was wrong. New ideas were fascinating to me, and I fully respected and even encouraged them. However, neither did I feel "Protestant", myself. I was a Catholic as certainly as I breathed. I just did not feel strongly *against* Protestants and was now forced to become one to secure my child's future.

I wondered: How do I choose? I had no choice, being Henry's wife. I could not turn back now. I had brought Henry to this point and, having done so, I had to follow his lead. I had no open options left to me, yet still I viewed this as a situation that called for careful thought.

And so I weighed the issues.

I was in desperate need of my God through these dark days of doubt and fear, and it was in the midst of them that I found myself questioning His very existence. I began to think thoughts, terrible ones that had never crossed my mind before. Had I spoken these thoughts aloud, I surely would have been burned at the stake myself as a heretic.

I saw that each faction thought God existed only within a circle it had drawn to enclose itself. Each believer believed that to step outside his own circle was to hurl himself out of God's reach and beyond His concern. Each believer believed that the reality of God could neither be greater than his own marred and human perceptions, nor could it reach out to embrace the other side.

All of them believed their own understanding and beliefs were All Truth, and that settled it. They each had made God just as small as they were, and just as they left no room for mercy or respect, they left no room for logic or for thought.

I did not believe, as they believed, that such circles and borders were supposed to separate the children of God from each other. Did God really forsake one circle for another? I did not believe so, nor did I believe those separations were of God's choosing. I did not even fully believe it mattered *how* one worshipped God, or how one defined God.

A small question grew larger within me. I wondered if perhaps God did not care what we called Him, or how we described Him to ourselves, or how we chose to worship Him. Did the image we fixed our faith upon, our specific rituals and sacraments, and the particular words we said in prayer have such power that they counted more than what we felt within our hearts, or what we did? I did not think so. I crossed myself whenever this question taunted me.

Was my assumption correct? Or were the others—those others with their bloody circles—the ones in possession of the greater wisdom?

Was I, after all, becoming ensnared within a circle that did not contain God? By *their* definition, by *everyone's* definition, someone *had* to be without God. The mystery was, which circle? Each one pointed to all the others and said, "You."

Someone must be wrong. No one thought it was he.

In weighing thus, I came to the frightening and disturbing realization that none of us could make our beliefs real by believing, no matter how intensely we believed, or how certain were that our viewpoint was true. Were we able to do so, I wryly thought, Zeus would still preside over all of us, for the ancient Greeks would have made him real, through believing.

It does not fall to Truth to find us; it falls to each of us to think and search and seek it out. Truth, after all, does not ask for our permission or require our concurrence. It simply is. With or without us.

So what is true about God if we can manipulate and change Him just so a king might marry his whore? What is real and what is false? I did not know. God would not say.

I would go to Hell for this, if for nothing else. I knew it. I would burn in place of all the misfortune-struck souls who trusted Henry to be right about God for, if he was wrong, it was not their sin. It was mine. It was my thinking and speculation that prodded Henry to give lengthy consideration to a church other than the Roman one. It was in order to marry me that he abandoned his faith. It was I who was the impetus.

It was *I* who believed the Protestant circle we were about to enter and embrace was not outside of God's long reach and, as yet, I had no proof that I was correct. I therefore had no right to take unwilling others with me.

What was I to do? I made my decision, firmly, by not deciding at all.

I could not bring back the old God, for Henry had declared Him dead. I could only do this: I could only try to see that no one—no heretic of any kind—would lose his life in England for his religious beliefs while I still drew breath. I could not view any religion as a crime or its believers as dangerous. There was too much doubt and too much upheaval, too many conflicting views, and too many contradictions for certainty about what and who was God.

As queen I had, from the first, defended heretical writings. I had routinely obtained censored works and read them voraciously, quieted Henry's objections, and even pointed out the logic and validity of some of the ideas they presented. I thought these authors brave and sincere and felt they should be heard, or at least not condemned and persecuted.

I had seen to it that Henry made it legal, finally, for common folk to own Bibles rather than be wholly dependent upon the clergy to intercede for them with God. I even persuaded him to allow the Bible to be translated into English so more people could be reached with God's Word.

Throughout, I had persuaded Henry against hangings, and firmly seen to it that no heretic was ever burned at the stake during my tenure as queen. I must again defend the lives of those who wrote, or who spoke, or who believed. This would no longer be easy to do, for my influence had grown weak and my power was greatly diminished.

The clerics and the cardinals had slipped past me to their deaths. For that I grieved, and for them I built my resolve. Henry might be God's spokesman, but I was still his queen and I could try to stay his hand in this. God had not made it clear to me whose beliefs were false, and so I would see to it that all were viewed with tolerance, at least as far as my power would reach.

I would let God sort them out. Better He than I. Better He than

Henry.

It was far easier for me to persuade my husband to slow imprisonment and killing for heresy than for treason. Henry was the greatest heretic of them all in ousting Rome, and could not condemn without inviting condemnation. Even his convoluted logic shrank in defeat against that (though he would find new rationale after my death, and the burnings would resume). In this, at least, my will prevailed for a time.

And once again I did not earn Hell at all. I find that, in the midst of this mental and emotional turmoil, I chose correctly in deciding to protect and defend rather than draw circles and condemn. In so choosing, I unwittingly earned my greatest reward.

Chapter 4

Henry's next step was to commence a long campaign to pillage and strip the monasteries. Through Henry's swift change in Gods, the gold and riches formerly claimed by the Church became ours.

Greed. It was greed. Holy Father forgive me, I could not restrain the greed around me. I even had to feign pleasure and accept these riches as gifts to me—blood riches that made my stomach queasy with sorrow and shame.

I had had no real fondness for priests since my childhood in France, but still felt toward them a habitual level of respect. I felt enough respect to wonder: Had we become such petty road thieves that we now could steal from them? Had we, in a palace like Hampton Court, a real need for more riches, while the priests and nuns were now forced to beg? Furthermore, the poor that these priests and nuns had once cared for no longer had them to turn to in their hunger, and in fact, now begged beside them.

As the riches poured in, I distributed a vast fortune in the name of "charity" to offset them, but could only touch a few of the hungry, after all, in the time I still had left.

The rains stopped, and Henry's confidence swelled again. No longer fearful of God, he left my bed once again, and found another.

Henry had married two opposites, first a modest, quiet wife, and then an outspoken, assertive one. He now sought a wife who was different from either Katherine or myself, and he found her in Jane Seymour whose singular noteworthy quality—and what made her noticeably different from Katherine and me—was her remarkable stupidity.

Secondly, the difference lie in her seeming inability to remain upright and clothed, when in the presence of a man. I suppose her dim-wittedness contributed in part to her lack of balance in the bedroom; she toppled backward easily and indiscriminately, whereas a woman of wit and sense might have shown better taste and more restraint.

Neither did she *once* restrain herself with loyalty or duty. I should have thought that my own thankless efforts to spare Katherine during those early years might have been rewarded with even a *feigned* attempt by Jane to discourage Henry. However, that was not to be. Jane had no honor, and no integrity. She had no power against her ambition, and no scruples. Her solemn vows to serve me loyally caused her no anguish of conscience at all, when afforded an opportunity to overthrow me.

She was not even pretty. She was pale and pasty-faced, with a thick neck and no chin. If I had been a ruby, then *this* one was stained glass. That Henry should want her after me was an insult.

England sought to overthrow its Whore Queen, and cared little for the purity of her replacement. Purity, it seems, was never the point even as they had screamed "Whore!" with such fury, for they embraced Jane Seymour who had bedded most of the court, and chose to overlook her indiscretions so long as she ousted Queen Anne.

These past indiscretions did not even matter to Henry. He had chosen Jane for her wide child-bearing hips (though I found out here, they failed her in the end, and she died soon after giving birth to the son Henry wanted so badly) and for her family's reputation for whelping litters and legions of dim-witted, pasty-faced infants.

✠

I await a scolding and a reminder that my thoughts are uncharitable and cruel, but my mentor is withholding comment.

"Did you not hear what I just thought about Jane and the dim-witted infants? Did you not hear me loathing and despising her?" I am defiantly braced for sharp words, and would rather hear them a hundred-fold, than make my thoughts more charitable.

The Voice says only this, and says it gently: "I only heard you weeping in despair."

✠

Katherine could not have been any happier than I was at Henry's choice. I cared little for Katherine's happiness, as intent as I was upon hurting her, but years of enmity had bound us into a form of twisted alliance (in fact, when she came to die, I would be shocked to find I felt a deep grief). I wondered at times what she thought, and would have valued a short truce wherein we could discuss the current happenings together.

I was losing my edge in the battle with Katherine. Her attacks were becoming far crueler than my own, for she still had her focus and her clever supporters, whereas my mind had now been pulled elsewhere. I no longer had Emma to coach me in my wickedness. I no longer had Henry to lean on, nor did I have his love, so my words and threats rang hollow and were better left unsaid. However I said them anyway, as I was typically wont to do, and let them ring hollow as they would. And now, with word of Jane Seymour, I would quite possibly have to withdraw from the fight with Katherine altogether. There was a woman I hated far more.

I could not abide Jane. I took to pinching and shaking her, and slapping her witless face. At least Katherine had been a worthy opponent. Katherine had been one for whom I had to plan and hone my insults and attacks—and these had to involve some artistry and imagination in order to have effect. Jane could only understand a simple boxing of the ears, but even that gave me some pleasure. It was satisfying at times, to box the harlot's ears.

Ye gods! Why had they never called *her* a whore? Why could she warm dozens of beds without criticism? Why was I, whose only partners were a rapist and my husband, enduring attacks more rightly owed to Jane?

More importantly, how could Henry love her? *Did* he love her?

Or, did he simply claim to out of spite? How could a man who had always required thoughtful discourse and the mental stimulation of an intelligent woman abide the company of Jane, who was more aptly viewed as a *pet* than as a lover? She could not even read or write, except to copy letters written for her by someone else. She could only write her name, and unskillfully at that!

Had Henry ever really loved me?

Chapter 5

I did not fully realize it, and it would not have pleased *her* to know this, but Katherine was the one person saving me from abandonment. Henry could not claim his marriage to me invalid as long as she lived or the end of his marriage to me would, through political pressure from Spain and Katherine's followers, mean resuming his marriage to her. This, of course, was out of the question. He wanted to marry Jane. He would need to rid himself of both Katherine and me in order to do this.

Most terrifying to me were the circumstances of Katherine's death, for indeed she died, writhing and vomiting, in agonizing pain. Since I was not made aware of the details of her cancer, I assumed she had been poisoned . . . by Henry? He certainly was not displeased to hear word of her passing.

He was now rid of one.

I saw this only in retrospect. My fool, however, clearly saw it all as it was happening. He took bites of my food before handing it off to me, not trusting anyone. In the beginning, I humored him and thought he was silly to be concerned on my behalf, for Henry, I told him, could never harm me.

"Of course not, Your Majesty," he quickly replied with a strained and guarded look. "The king deeply honors Your Majesty. However, there are others who may wish Your Majesty harm, and it is from these that the threat comes."

He was so solemn as he said this. His words held no humor at all as they should, and it was his jarring absence of humor that shook me into vigilance.

I would soon learn I was suspected of being Katherine's murderer. I was roundly accused of plotting to poison everyone– there were even persons who would die after me, whom it was said succumbed to slow poison administered by "the she-devil, Anne Boleyn while yet she lived". My fool had heard the rumors and did what he could to protect me from retaliatory actions from that camp. He suspected Henry might be planning mischief as well, but could do nothing about that, except fret.

It was at this time that Henry first asked if I would renounce Elizabeth's claim to the throne. My reaction to this was to swallow down the bile of outrage. It was a disgrace and a shame for reasons that went beyond his lack of loyalty to his children, for had he not treated Princess Mary the same? I felt it was right that *I* should hate Princess Mary, for she continually snubbed and insulted me, and furthermore was a threat to me and my child. But Henry's cold treatment of her had, at times, given me pause to reflect— even as I, in hurt or in anger, had pushed and goaded him to do it.

What infuriated me more than that was how frivolously Henry could destroy lives. For what reason had he caused those people to die, if not in defense of Elizabeth's right to be queen? Were their lives all so cheap that Henry could simply say: "I changed my mind"? I would that he could bring them all back as easily as he had just now made their deaths so meaningless with his request. Were he able to do this and give them back their lives, I would happily renounce my rights and my daughter's. However, as it stood, I could not. I never could. I would die myself before doing so, and I told him as much, and I did not back down.

Furthermore, I would never allow a child of mine to step aside and make room for a child of Jane Seymour's. I had lost virtually everything when I married Henry, and in return had gained nothing that still remained, or that I still valued from my marriage, except the knowledge that my child would be a queen. I would not relinquish it to the likes of Jane.

Henry would have to do what his conscience dictated. I would not give in to this. Not ever. Not even if it meant divorce.

That was what I feared: divorce. I never, ever feared for my life–truly I did not–even as I stood and smelled the corpses rotting.

Henry was preparing to move me out as he had moved Katherine out. I did not have supporters as Katherine had had, and my outlook became hopeless. Even my family was leaping like rats from a ship. All my loved ones, the same ones who had haunted me ceaselessly throughout my marriage with hands held out for gifts and favors, were seeking shelter elsewhere by disassociating themselves from me.

There was seemingly no end to the humiliation. Henry ordered me away to the palace in Greenwich, even though I was pregnant once again and could be carrying a male child, a legal heir to the British throne.

Surely, I thought, the timing was such that this pregnancy was God's kind intervention. Surely He was answering my prayers and would give me a son. When that occurred, I told myself, I would be called back to London, and Henry would love me again.

I comforted myself in this manner, but it was an unrealistic hope, that this child could reunite us. The pregnancy had come about in violent fashion, and without love. Henry raped me, in hatred and in spite, because it suited him to frighten and punish me for all the times I told him "no".

I am certain he had other reasons: my tongue, the naggings, the dead male heir, the healthy daughter, the greedy, grasping in-laws, and years filled with curses for me from his subjects and his court. Every whispered warning and unheeded bit of advice from his counsel was coming to the fore of his consciousness and mocking him. And so, it was only right that he make a mockery of me and my love for him.

One night when Jane was presumably indisposed and Henry had time to mull over all the grief I had caused him, he made his way into my chambers. Then, he wordlessly grabbed me and hurled me onto the bed, pressed me face down while he held my arms and tore at my clothes. He raped me, and left me there, weeping.

I tried to believe afterwards that his actions were prompted by passion, even though he had shown no gentleness and spoke no words of love. I sometimes pretended such as this to myself, all the while knowing the truth in my heart.

When I could face that truth, I wondered: Does Henry now understand that a woman can be forced? Then I realized, "No." I was his wife whom the law said he could abuse as he wished. The rape taught Henry nothing about himself, or about me. He viewed me coldly, and had barely spoken to me since.

Then, one day when Henry was away, word reached me that he had fallen from his horse and was dead. This declaration was uttered prematurely, or perhaps the message was purposeful and malicious; I was surrounded by people who took pleasure in causing me upset and distress.

With Henry dead, I would be drawn and quartered by the crowds, I thought. I could not survive a day.

I also felt sorrow for my lost husband, and despair that we had parted on bad terms before his death. I shared this only with my fool. I trusted no one else with the shame I felt in still loving the man (though all knew, and made me the object of their sniggering contempt).

I had a fit of nervous hysteria. Soon afterward, I lost the child, which was said to be male and severely deformed. In truth, I could not determine myself either its gender, or the state of the infant's overall development. I trusted what I was told by persons who were not my friends.

Henry was not dead at all, but had suffered a head wound from which he was thought to fully recover. By now, however, the child was lost. I had no hope of conceiving another, convinced as I was that Henry no longer even cared enough to rape me.

I did not know this then, but he was not recovered, nor would Henry ever recover from the head wound. There was damage to one sector of the brain from the fall, and this weakness gave his illness full rein there. He now had only a tenuous hold on his own mind.

He seemed at times a different person, though how, exactly, I could not say. He had, more and more over time, given the impression of a dual character, and I had long been aware of this "second" Henry. What I was viewing now was simply all of the second Henry, and none of the first. The person I now saw was the one whom I did not much like. When I appealed to my husband, however, I spoke to the first Henry as if he could somehow still hear me, not understanding why he did not, and not knowing where he had gone.

Henry was understandably upset by the aborted birth. He was curt and said only that God obviously did not want him to have a son. Then he turned and left me without further word or concern.

To others, after he left me, he publicly mentioned that the child could not be his, since it was deformed.

Chapter 6

After I miscarried, Henry began to orchestrate a conspiracy involving the family of Jane Seymour, Jane Seymour herself, my underlings and officers, members of my own extended family, and members of the court. This would ultimately result in my death. I, of course, could not know this then. My suspicions were only that he was plotting a divorce.

With increased confidence from having finally gained his ear with regard to Anne Boleyn, Henry's counsel now spoke more loudly, and with stronger conviction against me. Added to their voices were the voices of those they recruited. There was no end to the line of people prepared to discredit me. Some of these I had never met, nor seen.

One by one, these people stood before Henry (at his invitation), and denounced me as a whore and an adulteress. Others did the same, without provocation or encouragement. Even people whom I barely knew provided shocking reports of a very personal nature. Some of these fabricated stories out of spite towards me; others believed what they were told and were repeating tales as though they themselves were witnesses. These strangers and near-strangers were caught up in the momentum of the movement to overthrow me, and were anxious to be treated with the same consideration as the others.

They had proof. Had I not once dropped my handkerchief? Such an act was clearly one of seduction and proved I was a flirt.

And they had names. In response to the accusations, Henry called for the arrest of several people, all of whom I was said to have bedded, including my own brother George.

Henry nodded in seeming pain at learning the "truth" about the wife who had so betrayed him, and rewarded my accusers who lined up their friends for more rewards.

I was taken away to the Tower of London, in broad daylight rather than in the dignity of darkness, and locked away to await my trial. I was alone, now. I had no fool, no Emma, no husband, no friend.

I had no family. My father . . . my own father made public declarations against me in a vain attempt to hold onto his influence, and perhaps his life. My mother was silent and, I presumed, felt the same.

"Let her die," my father said.

He said to let me die. Could my heart break any more than it already had?

"It is too good for me," I said, when I arrived and looked around me. My prison was the very house in which I had stayed while awaiting my coronation which, ironically, had led me to another form of imprisonment, as queen.

"Jesu, have mercy on me." I fell to my knees and began to cry.

In the carriage on my way to this place, I had heard someone taunting me with a child's chant. Or perhaps they were not taunting. I heard taunts in everything. Now, within my large and well-appointed prison I thought of that song, for I could not expel it from my head: "Ring around the rosy, pocket full of posies, ashes, ashes, we all fall down!" I whispered it, kneeling, rocking myself, tears streaming down my cheeks, chuckling softly. There was a certain irony in this.

"Mr. Kingston, shall I die without justice?" I asked, looking up.

In response, the man said: "The poorest subject the king hath, hath justice."

His face increased the absurdity of the remark by being as sincere and as devoid of irony as Hal's might have been had he been saying those same words in jest. I thought to myself, "Well done!" and nearly applauded as I would have done, had he been one of the jesters. I found Henry's "justice", and this man's suggestion that it was "just" very humorous indeed. So I burst into a laugh.

But having shown amusement, I did not stop. I erupted into hysterical laughter, like a hyena . . . like some wild, crazed, filthy lunatic who wandered the streets and ate rats and bit dogs. It was the crack in my mind that I had feared. The laughter was the crack that let the demons in.

And so I laughed for minutes or perhaps hours, then through the entire day or a lifetime–I knew not which–quite mad, having completely lost my grip on my mind, falling down a well more terrifying than the one that leads to Hell. Or, perhaps it was the same one, for I lived in Hell while I outwardly laughed. I had no control over myself while the laughs convulsed me. It was hysteria that went to incalculable lengths beyond my normal tantrums and dangled me over a chasm where even God would not venture to save me.

There was no God amid the laughter. There was no hope, and I had no mind. I had only an icy, gripping, all-encompassing terror and a total loss of self-control.

"So this is what it means to be insane," I thought at one point, overseeing myself from a distance. "It hurts."

But there was nowhere to run to escape it. It followed me.

With great effort, I struggled to regain my mind and escape the fear. And then, shaken, I felt my self-control return, and I was calmer. I slept.

When I awoke, I had a greater fear than death. It was that death would not come soon enough to spare me a return to madness.

Periodically the laughter did threaten me, and with it returned my struggle against lunacy. In the end, I would win, and would be able to stand at my trial, then walk with a degree of solemn dignity through the crowd to face my executioner. It would be a triumph of stubborn willfulness, that I could shake the madness long enough to die.

The treason commission convened in late April. I stood before the jurists, most stone-faced and hardened against me, spoke the truth, and was called a liar.

I learned from the commission that I had indulged in lascivious acts for years, cavorted with my own brother as if I were his wife (and perhaps with my sister as well) and had arrogantly made my poor husband a hapless cuckold such as had never before been seen in England or beyond.

I heard it said that Mark Smeaton, a young man from the music room, confessed to being my lover. It was known by all that he confessed under torture; no one cared about the reason he confessed. He would die for it.

My brother George would die for it as well. And others . . . others of us would die. We would die, you know. All of us.

We would die.

Henry had not even waited for the trial to disband my household and dismiss my servants. He knew before any verdict was reached that I would have no further need of them.

So, there was never a hope of fair sentencing or release. Each judge, 26 in all, had a task to do, and it was to please the king and see that I was sentenced to die. Each participant's task was to make the accusations seem plausible before those judges by drawing in young men who were handsome enough to be convincing temptation for a lecherous queen. Their task was to loosely link persons to the story who were inconvenient to the king in some way, or expendable, and to condemn them to death.

But having arranged for all that, Henry's job was still not complete. Even in this, even when there was clearly no need for further harm, he chose to twist the knife. Included among the judges was Hal, forced to join their number as both a judge and a witness.

Hal sat among the other judges hearing me speak but not hearing, jaundiced and ill, trapped and tortured, avoiding my eyes, mostly staring at his hands and not looking up at all.

Very few of these judges and trial participants warred within themselves about the injustice. Most who did felt powerless to stop it, or were too cowardly or uninterested to protest on behalf of anyone at all, much less someone such as me, whom they did not much like. Their feelings, so prejudiced against me, in fact, were all the justification they needed to forego justice.

Still there was a very small brave handful of men who, infuriated, spoke up about the manner in which the trial was being conducted, but these were silenced.

King Henry's justice moved onward as his whim and will decreed.

Lord Henry Percy was called to testify about his association with the whore, Anne Boleyn, then was released to take his place again within the jury.

Sir Thomas Wyatt was imprisoned for his false confessions and bragging, still loving me, yet still earning from me only feelings of contempt. He sat in his cell and wrote poetry for me until his family's bribes freed him. Only now do I grieve for him, and for my own unkindness.

Interviews and questioning continued until Henry and his team had accumulated stories enough to sentence everyone who needed to die for His Majesty's convenience.

At the announcement of the verdict my childhood nurse, who had come to support me, rose up and screamed. Hal collapsed and had to be carried from the courtroom. He died not so very long afterward.

I held my head high and pretended I had been acquitted. I would not give them the satisfaction of seeing me crumple. I would walk out as a queen, and as mother to a queen. For the moment, I still had that.

I was returned to my prison to await my death. These lodgings were far better than I deserved, considering the others accused were locked in small tower cells because of me. My concern was mostly for them, for they were not deserving of the punishment, as I was. After all, it was *I* who had loved a married man (I harkened back to that large sin to explain my circumstances). I prayed for God to take the others to His bosom, prayed they would forgive me, and prepared for the passing of my own soul into either darkness or light, I knew not which.

The house was large and I had freedom of movement within it, although I was followed everywhere by people I viewed as shadows and ghosts. None of these was a friend–quite the opposite–and all of them wished me dead. I wandered the rooms, watched coldly by all in attendance. I was more fearful than I had ever been in my life and spent my days in prayer and preparation for my death. I wrote a letter to Henry. I played my lute. I wrote a poem about death that my chaplain later turned into a song. I stayed in my bed, and stared up at a window or wept. My melancholy was so deep that even sunlight, on days when I was allowed access to the grounds, could not penetrate my grim hopelessness.

At times I was allowed friendly visitors. These were so welcome and such a relief that I developed high spirits and made light of my situation. I called myself "Queen Lackhead" or "Anna Sans Tête", then laughed despite—or perhaps because of—their stares of consternation, shock, and horror. Afterwards, when they left, I sank quietly away into fear, despair and loneliness.

My family stayed away, intent upon making my father's cold words sound sincere, fearful that Henry would imprison and behead them along with George if they stepped into the light to side with me.

Emma did not come. Probably they would not admit her, or perhaps she could not travel, for she was nearing the birth of a child she would name Anne.

My fool was allowed entrance, for whatever reason, but he wept and this unnerved me and brought me too close to tears myself, so I sent him away. I watched him slip through the door at my command, away from me, then walked to the window where I stared after him as he disappeared down the path, pressing my fingertips, forehead and nose to the glass.

Chapter 7

Between a man and his wife, there is a basic, minimum level of trust. Accurately or in error, a woman trusts that her spouse will do more to keep her alive than to hasten her death, even if that spouse cannot abide her character.

Even if neither spouse has ever loved, each is beholden to the other as a result of marriage vows. They each owe the other the reasonable assurance that murder is neither planned, nor desired. And if spouses have ever loved one another, as surely Henry and I loved, their hearts are tied together by a little thread. Neither spouse can cut that thread without suffering internal damage, just as neither spouse could kill without inwardly bleeding to death from the other's wound.

This, and God's Commandments, are what keep endlessly sniping couples from doing each other grave damage. This is what I trusted. Consequently, I had been very slow to learn the true nature of Henry's plan for me.

There were times before my sentencing when I spoke the words: "I fear the King might kill me" to obtain someone's reassurance that he would not. However, I could not wholly grasp, even as I spoke those words aloud–even as I knelt and waited to die–that my husband wished me dead and would not halt the execution.

Over the weeks of my imprisonment, the understanding came to me but was frequently replaced by other thoughts. It was a test, I sometimes hoped. "He is trying to prove me, and once he is certain my heart is true, will come to save me." I convinced myself that I needed only to make him understand that I had not betrayed him. When that happened, he would shudder over what he had almost done to me, and pray for my forgiveness.

Even at those times when I fully understood that the charges against me were real and not a dream, and that the verdict would hold, I never, *ever* doubted that Henry truly believed I had betrayed him and that he was doing this in anger. I was able to sustain myself by believing Henry earnestly sought the truth in my trial, but that my defense was insufficient to persuade him. Since I never committed the act of adultery, even in thought, the problem was in the words. I must convince him! I thought. I must find the right words! When I did, all would be well, or at least, I would be alive.

I fell back on Basic Marital Trust to sustain me, and never once thought that Henry might have fabricated the charges in order to rid himself of me. I sometimes ventured to experiment with the thought, then recoiled in horror. It was more than I was capable of absorbing, and so I rejected it. (Even here, the full knowledge is only doled out to me in measured doses. I know, but only from the corner of my eye.)

On occasion, when I was able, I carefully sorted the facts in my head and painfully considered that Henry was an evil man who had never loved me. His pursuit of me had, truly, only been a game designed to amuse him. He could never otherwise allow me to die. It was only during the last few seconds of my life that I fully succumbed to this conclusion, and by that time I would allow the entrance of no other thoughts. I would allow no forgiveness whatsoever.

While I was struggling with that, I was also attempting to understand the crime for which I was to die, and for which I would be known throughout all time: I would forever after be the queen who had bedded her brother.

I cannot describe the sensation of crawling horror one feels when accusations of depravity and sexual misconduct are spread hither and yon about oneself and then are confirmed by court of law. The embarrassment and shame—and the certain knowledge that I could say absolutely nothing and be believed—gave me such heightened anxiety I periodically, truly, lost my mind.

The thought of dying was nothing compared to living through this. I wanted no eyes staring. I wanted nothing more than to hide and be seen by no one again. I wanted great distance from the shouts and the humiliation; I wanted succor and safety and warmth again, as I had had from my nurse in infancy.

I wanted to be anyone but myself. I wanted fervently to be anyone at all, and would willingly have paid any price.

Had I not once dreamt of being a nun? In my imagination, I replayed my life in my mind, but the fork in the road never appeared. There was no rape, and no reason to discard my dream. There was no reason to marry, and therefore no reason for a man to find me lacking and abandon me. And so I lived in quiet solitude and prayer, never once recognized by strangers, nor ever addressed with scorn or contempt.

In my mind, I also erased the fork in the road that kept me from Hal Percy. I was now his grateful wife . . .

Chapter 8

They killed the others, five of them, first. In preparation for this, they came and fetched me, then installed me in the Bell Tower overlooking the scaffold, and forced me to watch. Henry was very clever: In this manner, I might die six times, instead of only once.

My one hope, that Mark Smeaton would tell the truth in his final speech and declare that he was never my lover, died with Mark. He said a few hurried, thoughtless words then let the lie live on. He allowed me to die without truth.

Throughout the days preceding my execution, they built my own scaffold outside my window, overlooking pretty East Smithfield Green. It was there for me to see and ponder, and the noise of the hammering was there to rob me of all rest during night or day. As I would die without friends, without family, without dignity, without justice and without truth, so would I also die without sleep.

At least I would die by the sword, and not burned at the stake. Henry took a long while to reach that decision and, in the end, found a shred of compassion for me. He even honored my request for a French executioner who used a sword and not an axe. (Perhaps he did this to impress his virtue upon Jane Seymour, who was already preparing to wed him. Henry could thus show her that he was a "kindly" man . . .)

My chaplain sat up with me the entire night while the

hammering and pounding shook the walls.

"My poor lamb," he said to me as I rested my cheek upon his knee. He stroked my hair. "My poor, poor lamb."

It hardly mattered who touched me now, or stroked my hair, because I was no longer a queen. Our marriage had been annulled two days earlier, so Henry could now rest easily and content for, having stripped me of all the rest, he would have me die without my marriage and without my crown, and without the certainty that Elizabeth would ever be a queen. There was nothing left for him to take from me. Henry's work was finally complete.

Well done, my love. Well done.

Then the sun rose and the day came for me, a sunny day in the height of spring, in May, my favorite month. This date was a silent anniversary I had passed through my entire life, never knowing it to be the eventual day of my death, but knowing now.

One can think preparation is sufficient until the moment arrives and it is tested. I had been frantic for the day to come, not knowing how long my mental reserves would hold. I had experienced near-collapse when the executioner was delayed in his travels and the execution was postponed. Now, my jailers faced me and said it was time. I was not, in fact, prepared. I wanted to run, and I wanted to fight them. But where would I go? Who would hide and protect me?

Then I thought, "What reason have I to remain alive?" and willingly submitted myself to them.

We walked in a solemn line to the scaffold.

I stood and looked over the people in the crowd, some of whom were tearful but most of whom were there to cheerfully watch and comment.

I spoke to them all in a final speech. The entire time I spoke, I awaited the shout: "Halt!" I awaited rescue by Henry, and watched for running foot soldiers from the corner of my eye. Henry's voice and his army never rose against my murder, though I waited.

I exchanged my headdress for a white cap, then turned to my ladies who were weeping. I told them I was humbly sorry for having been harsh toward them at times and meant it sincerely, then asked them to remember me in their prayers. I gave my waiting woman my prayer book in which I had inscribed: "Remember me when you do pray that hope doth lead from day to day." She thanked me, then succumbed to sobs.

I said my own prayers for them. It was their responsibility to recover my severed head and prepare my body for entombment when all was done. My poor waiting woman was squeamish, God bless her, and would no doubt grow ill from it, I knew. I felt embarrassed and ashamed that I would be in such as state as to make my ladies ill, and hoped they would forgive me for it.

Finally time ran out, and no Henry appeared. My death and his abandonment of me were both absolute. Forgiveness for this betrayal was now sealed away from me by a heavy metal door that slammed shut within my heart like the door to a prison cell. Forgiveness was firmly on the other side.

And now, stomach fluids rose and fell in my throat. I was to face the final moment of my life. The moment was real, and it had come.

Holy Father . . . *Afraid!*

A swell of panic convulsed me and I felt the madness creeping toward me again. The only cure for it was death and so, in the end, I welcomed death as my salvation.

My executioner stood waiting, sword waiting, block waiting . . . crowd . . . waiting. It was my duty not to disappoint, nor to make them wait.

I looked into the faces one last time, searching eyes for pity and grief. I saw some, and took comfort. I felt just slightly less alone.

I knelt before my executioner and was blindfolded. All was black. I pressed my eyes closed and prayed while the remarks and catcalls hushed to deathly silence, unearthly still.

In the midst of this, I heard a bird sing then heard its wings flap as it flew away. Would the crowd be watching it now? Forgetting me? I pretended this was so.

I resolved to follow the bird to a better place, away from here. We would leave this earth together, the bird and I, and would never, ever look behind us.

My last living thought, as it happened, was a cheerful one. In my mind, I called out to the bird to wait for me and, in my mind, it did.

It circled back—one friend after all—to carry me on its wings to God. I might lose my life, I promised myself, but I was neither crushed nor truly broken. Like a bird, I was merely poised for flight.

"Where is my sword?" the executioner shouted. As he swung it into position to strike, the air whipped against my skin. I could feel it.

"To Jesus Christ I commend my soul; Lord Jesu receive my soul–"

PART 8

Choice and Circumstance

Egypt, 2437BC

Chapter 1

I am making flour, grinding barley between two large, smooth stones, while the two little ones play with pebbles on the dirt floor. I occasionally stop to go and pry these same pebbles out of the younger child's mouth, scolding her. My thoughts wander no further than the narrow boundaries of my life and, in the midst of this, I am shocked to attention by running footsteps and shouts outside my dwelling. Startled, I look up to see a small figure in the doorway, a boy of about 10. He bursts in and screams that my husband has fallen, and is being carried back from the construction site. I leap to my feet and run into the street, terrified.

I can see a stranger in the distance, pushing through the merchants and villagers. He carries my husband across his shoulders, arms dangling and useless, eyes closed.

There is still hope. Perhaps my husband has merely had the air knocked out of him and will recover. Perhaps if a bone is broken, it will not set crooked. I squint, trying to force my eyes to see farther and to diagnose the injuries.

He looks as if he might be dead, I think. If he is dead I might still marry. There are certainly those who would keep me; I could easily find another man. A worse fate would be impairment. Even if his injury keeps him in bed for a time, we will suffer. If he is permanently crippled, he cannot work, I cannot remarry, and I cannot eat or feed my children.

After considering the possibilities, I select the one that suits me best, and softly plead to the gods that he is dead.

Perhaps we will not go hungry. Perhaps we will not all die as a result of this.

I stand in the street, absently caressing the heads of the little ones who toddled after me, and watch the man approach with my husband. The smaller girl pulls at my tunic, and says her word for milk. I lift her up and press her to my breast where she suckles, as oblivious to these events as I am oblivious to her. The older girl clings to my leg and sucks her thumb, whining softly about something I do not bother to take note of.

I know the older girl. It is Mother. I know the younger girl. It is Katherine.

Furthermore, I know my husband. He is Sir Thomas Wyatt from the court of Henry VIII, the passionate, persistent suitor whom I rejected. He is not as fond of me here, in fact, he thinks of me as only barely human. I am his woman, nothing more. He beds me, and eats what I feed him, and beats me when his mood is foul. I carry bruises, for his mood is not often good. He also beats the children: tiny girls aged one and two who know more of how to cower than to hug.

Aye, but that is what men do to their women to keep them in line. They all do. I am grateful he has not sold the babies or me into slavery. He has not yet gotten that tired of us.

The man who is carrying my husband catches my eye, but says nothing. I motion him into our dwelling, and he stands, waiting for me to show him where my husband will go.

My husband's bed is a low cot made of leather straps that are interwoven and strung across a wooden frame. It has a half-circle wooden neck rest that protrudes, like a wishbone, from the head of it.

I think he might do better if he lies flat, so I spread my reed mat upon the floor. If my husband were conscious, he would protest the insult of being laid upon a woman's bed, but I do not bother for his concerns. At the moment, his concerns are not *my* concerns, for he is near death.

The man sets my husband down, not altogether gently, nods at me, then pulls out a pouch and gives me a small, polished lapis figure of the god Horus. He suggests I trade it for some food, then leaves while I stand there motionless, still in shock, clutching the figure in my fingers. Tears spring to my eyes at his kindness, and I race out to the street to shout thanks toward his retreating figure, but he quickly disappears into the crowd, and I do not know if he has heard.

I turn back, uncertain, and examine my husband's injuries. I discover the broken bone is in his shoulder, and I wince. This does not bode well for us. He has an enormous lump on his head with a trickle of blood running from it, and this I wipe clean, not suspecting that the greater damage was done here, rather than to the shoulder. The babies study him and touch him gingerly, unafraid when he is like this, but hesitant nonetheless.

I do not know what to do.

I go out again into the street, call aside a boy, and plead for him to find someone to help me. I cannot pay, I tell him. He gives me a contemptuous look and disappears.

I try again, and then again, weeping now, but all brush me aside. They do not like my husband, and view that as good reason to push his wife away. Finally an old woman agrees to come, and enters our home with darting looks as if she is searching for something to steal. I send her away with a curse, and she curses back at me and spits.

It is up to me, and I do not know what to do.

Chapter 2

Whatever it was that I did, it was wrong. My husband healed crookedly with a protruding bone, and one useless arm. The pupil in his right eye became large and strange-looking because the blow to his head had been severe, even though the skull appeared intact. My efforts to clean the external wound did nothing to heal him internally.

Now, some time later, he seems normal on the surface, but can no longer control his temper even to the degree he had before. He still has one good arm with which to hit us, and a club to extend his reach, but he cannot perform his usual work, or any other kind of work that he is willing to do. The children and I live in terror and suffer in hunger, for he demands what few scraps I am able to find.

I take to nursing the older girl again, though she had been weaned. I suckle both children and beg on the streets for food for myself so that my milk will not dry up. I sometimes eat and sometimes do not. I have to be careful to spare a little of whatever I receive for my husband lest he grow discontented and violent, but I sometimes gobble crusts and scraps before returning home, then tell him there was none. He never believes me, and often draws blood when he beats me, but at least my hunger is sometimes quelled for a time.

I still have milk, but as I had feared, it begins to dry. I am concerned for the babies who are not growing as they should. They are very, very small, and somewhat listless. Their hair does not shine. I am afraid they will die.

I have been shown the next scene many times before. I am forced to view it again with each passing, for I have never been able to reconcile it in my heart and have often chosen badly as a result of it. It might have been a passage into understanding, but it was not, so I am left to watch it again. Perhaps this time, with this last passing, I learned.

I feel that this time, I have. I see it differently, now.

The girls need bread and fruit. I cannot continue to feed them through to adulthood on breast milk—can the milk even last another week? Still, I hesitate to use the lapis figurine. I will not part with it. I view it as a good luck charm, and a reminder of someone's kindness. It has greater value to me than the little I would receive in exchange for it, so I continue to beg, keeping the figurine close to me in a small pouch tied under my tunic. I will carry it with me for the rest of my life: a small blue beacon, hidden in a leather pouch beneath my skirt.

Once again I hold out my hand. A man stops and looks me over, then laughs and grabs my breast. My stomach chooses that instant to growl, and in the desperateness of my situation, I do not pull away. Instead, I ask: "What will you give me?"

He takes a scarab ring from his finger and holds it up.

"Yes," I say. I reach for the ring, and grab it. I already sense that you take payment first.

I know of a place where we can go. There is an area hidden behind a clump of palm trees, in an alley that has no traffic. I take him there, and spread palms upon the ground. I look around me, terrified that I will be seen or that my husband will find us, but no one passes.

I close my eyes tight, and think of food.

When he is finished, he stands up and leaves me there without another word. I start to weep with shame over what I have done, but I have the ring and I know that we will all eat well for a while. I stand up and dust myself off, wipe my eyes, then run to the market and exchange the ring for food, enough for a week.

My husband does not ask where the food comes from. In truth, he does not care.

When the food runs out, I find another man with another small treasure. This time I do not cry, afterwards. This time I do not wait for the food to run out before finding a third man. I leave at night when my family is asleep, and prowl the streets for soldiers. My husband does not know what I am doing, nor can I tell him.

I meet other women who are doing what I do, and they are kind to me. There is a sisterhood of sorts between the street whores who know they cannot count upon men, are scorned by women, and have only each other for support and solace. They teach me what to do and what to avoid and warn me to carry a dagger. They show me how to walk and how to look at a man to draw him over, and they describe certain acts that I must be willing to perform without revealing any revulsion or disgust. They give me advice in handling the drunken ones and the mean ones, and name certain men that I must never, ever go with at all, no matter what they offer.

I learn from these women that I can earn more if I ply my trade in the Valley of the Kings. It takes courage to go there, and I wrestle with mine for a long while before seriously considering the journey.

I have long heard about it. It is a village of tomb robbers and criminals who are not averse to also earning riches from prostitution. Over time, an area around this village grew into a notorious brothel with row upon row of tents that teem with teetering, drunken soldiers and wandering workmen. It is dangerous, the street whores say, and the women there are hardened and cruel. The very worst men I have seen on the streets are what I can expect to find in the Valley: drunken brutes, gangs of thieves, military misfits, and social pariahs . . .

There is construction going on in the Valley, as the pharaoh has commissioned a new pyramid. The women go where men are most apt to be found and, during any massive construction, there are always scores of men nearby who are anxious for entertainment.

For my entire life, there has been ongoing building, men who build, and women who follow them. The brothels seem as enduring as the structures that loom above them, and certainly as enduring as the thieves who plunder them. The Valley is a place where campfires burn until morning, where music is played, and women dance while fights break out around them. It bursts with life after sundown. The free men linger with their wages after the slaves have been led away at day's end, and the rougher elements all find their way there. They pour vat after vat of fermented drink, and rut like animals among the women who are there to service them.

My father threatened me with the place when I was growing. It was, he said, where they send useless daughters. Now I am faced with going there of my own volition. I have no remaining family, and no other place offers me escape from my husband.

I am terrified but I go, and I bring the children with me. It is a long walk, and takes two days. I struggle with one child strapped to my back, and the other led for short distances by the hand until she cries to be carried. At night we sleep in a doorway, and we stop to beg for food along the way. For the final leg of the journey, we ride on a donkey whose driver I pay with my body. My husband does not know why we have left, or if we will ever return. I slipped away while he slept.

When we arrive, it is nearing dusk and, shy and timid, I look about me. I feel out of place. I am a matron with two small children, primly watching from the periphery.

I am not a whore. I am not like these people. Surely they can see this. Surely no one suspects I have done this before. I will only stay until I earn enough money to live another way.

There are shouts already coming from a knot of men who are placing bets on a game of Senet. The players hurl the casting sticks, and their audience erupts into either triumph or frustration at the resulting throw, depending upon which player they have bet. The women are primping themselves and gossiping for a short time before nightfall when the workmen leave their shifts and their own day begins. Caravans of donkeys are arriving with water, food and drink, and urns are carried into tents while the drivers scream and haggle with a woman over price. Huge shiny-black Nubian guards wander back and forth with whips held and ready, weaving in and out of the growing crowd. Torches are lit, and a fire is built in the pit as the sun sinks. Men appear from nowhere, growing louder and louder as the first vat of drink is emptied. Someone has begun to bang a drum, and three women climb onto a low platform where they dance suggestively.

I find a woman who will let me use a tent for a price. I pay her in advance, then settle the children inside and stand in front of the tent to wait. It does not take long, and I have a customer whom I invite inside.

As we slip through the entrance of the tent, the children softly stir on the mat. Katherine opens her eyes and smiles at me before going back to sleep.

I cannot work in front of my babies. I had not given any thought to that before.

I tell the customer to wait, and I go back outside where I see a whore standing in front of the tent next to mine.

I ask if she knows of a place where children might be kept. She eyes me suspiciously and tosses her hair. I look at her closely and cannot immediately pinpoint what it is about her appearance that disturbs me, but I press on with my request. I have no time to search for someone else.

"Please," I say. "They are babies. I have someone waiting for me, and he will pay me enough to feed them, if he doesn't grow angry and walk off."

"Leave them with me until you finish," the whore says grudgingly. "I expect a slow night anyway."

At the sound of the voice, I stare. It is a deep voice, a man's voice. I realize this is not a woman, as I had first thought. I blush. He is merely dressed as a woman with kohl-painted eyes and earrings of gold. I have never encountered a man like this before, although I had heard that they exist.

It is Henry.

I cannot stop to think about what he does in his tent, or whether I should look for someone else. I have a customer and no time. As for Henry, he has offered to help me on an impulse, uncertain of why he should be generous to me, speaking the words without thought, regretting them as soon as he hears them spoken. We say nothing else about the agreement, and go through with it despite our misgivings.

I race back and grab both sleeping children at once. I hand Katherine to Henry, who holds her as if he has held little children before. He holds her as a mother would. I follow him into his tent with the larger child, and we lay them down side by side on his mat. I decide it is safe to leave them with him. I can see he will not molest them, for he is a fancy man, not a true one, and he holds Katherine gently, and with sureness I have never seen in a man. He will take care of them, and I know this. Had I any initial inclination to feel contempt toward him, those feelings are buried under gratitude.

I smile at him and whisper my thanks, then run back to my customer who is growing impatient.

When the customer leaves, I return to Henry's tent and find him inside of it, squatting beside the mat, watching the girls with a soft, wistful look on his face. He pushes Katherine's hair back with his finger, then starts upon seeing me. He quickly covers his gentle expression, and rises.

"You may leave them a little longer, if it suits you. But next time you will need to find another place for them so that I can work as well." He walks toward the entrance of the tent with mincing hips, opens the flap and peers out. He turns back to me. "I can find you a small tent we can set up behind these. We can take turns watching the children when we aren't busy. And when we both are, I have a friend who can stand guard."

I am speechless. My inclination is to recoil from him, or even to curse him, but I am alone and afraid, and have already received glares from the other women who neither appreciate, nor do they admire my modesty and moral superiority. Plus, there is need. I have children, and I need someone's help.

The gods sometimes send strange soldiers to protect us.

He is about the sort of soldier I might expect. I sigh.

"I will see to it tomorrow," he continues.

The offer is selfish. He is one of those who feels he should have been born a woman, and has always dreamt of having a child as a woman would. Now, given an opportunity he never expected, he intends to steal secret moments when he can hold the girls and stroke them, and sing to them. He raised his younger sisters until he was driven from his home by his father when his taste for men became evident. Fathers drive out or kill sons such as he, and Henry left under threat of death. He misses those children, and misses having a child to tend.

He has considered the situation and views it as good fortune. He hides from me the excitement he feels, for if he shows me any, I might remove the children out of spite. He expects me to do this anyway, and thinks he is buying only a very short respite from his loneliness.

"Why would you do this for me?" I ask. It is not typical of people to do good for one another, particularly strangers. "What is it you want in return?" I ask with narrowed eyes.

He rolls his eyes and gives a dramatic shrug. "I may run out of kohl and have to borrow some from you." He pats his hair, and sighs as if he is bored.

"I will happily give it to you," I say solemnly, meaning more than I say.

Chapter 3

After a few months, I fall into the life as if I have known no other. I meet all the other women who work as I do, and develop relationships with them of both friendship and enmity.

We have differences, and we reconcile them like whores, arguing with shrieks and scratching nails, reasoning with fistfuls of each other's hair. Our disagreements are debated in the dust while other whores watch and cheer, and laughing men place bets on who is stronger.

In addition to the animosity between the women, there are stabbings and poisonings of brutal customers, and valuables stolen. In return, customers have been known to kill women on occasion, sometimes for good reason, sometimes over something trivial, sometimes over something that had nothing to do with the whore. It is easy to kill a whore—her life is worthless. She leaves the world unmourned, and a man cannot be faulted for beating one into the grave if he has had a bad day. Henry is particularly at risk because of what he is, and is sometimes bloodied and beaten for the amusement of a crowd. It is always I who helps him up and cares for him after they leave him on the ground. He is my friend, and I have only a few of those.

There is little of the sisterhood I found on the streets. The whores brag, and criticize each other, and think of ways to attract more men than the others on their row, steal each others' customers, and tell vicious lies about each other to the both the whores and the men who use them.

It is not to my advantage to act as though I feel I am better than the others in the Valley. It is not wise, I find, to compound this insult by having too much success in finding customers. The cruelty is then turned upon me, and is vengeful.

By accident, I have learned a trick. There is a gland in the vicinity of the nose that excretes a sex hormone, and I have somehow learned to activate the gland at will. It has an immediate effect and is as potent as a drug, when sensed by a healthy male. I am aware that I am controlling my attractiveness to men, but do not know exactly how or why, and am unable to teach the trick to others or explain. It is not, I know, entirely my appearance or the feminine skills I learned on the streets. It has something to do with the way I "think", for when I think a certain way, I have greater success in luring customers.

I remembered this trick as Anne, not knowing I remembered. It accounted for much of the irrational appeal I had for so many men and, partly, for Henry's insanely persistent pursuit of me. It was the main reason I was ever described as "beautiful" by anyone.

Having learned, and not even knowing that I am doing so, I activate the gland each time I am on the job. As a result, I always have customers, and there are women who are furious with me for it. Competition is stiff in the Valley, so I am pulled into the dust and clawed several times, saved on those occasions by Henry, who has all the strength of a man and no patience with women. They get the full force of his fist before he carries me away and tends to me. His consistent loyalty in the face of my attacks, and the impact of his blows, eventually send a signal to the others that I should be left alone. Those who were most envious attempt to make friends with me as a means of coaxing me into passing along the overflow of customers to them, and perhaps divulging my secrets. Thus, I get by more or less safely throughout the years after surviving the initiation during my first few months.

In that jealous environment, free from the servitude of my marriage, I develop a mean tongue and, if I grow to dislike another whore, I use it against her with little constraint. In particular is one who has a disfigurement that, even had I liked her, I would have found comical. I often scoff at her with shouts that she is a misfit, and should find work at something that does not require beauty. Each time she passes, I laugh at her, for she has a hand that looks so silly! It has six fingers. She spits at me, and I shriek at her then convulse into laughter again.

"It is all in good fun!" I shout. "You need to learn what is funny!"

I make a few friends among the other whores. My sister Mary is one of these, as is Emma. These two in particular are good-humored and philosophical about the life, comparing that which they have to that which they left. They find the life to be satisfactory. They are not slaves, nor are they bound to brutal men. If they are beaten, Emma reasons, they at least have something of value to show for it afterwards. They are free, and independent, and they have money of their own. They have friends. They have good times.

"Things can be worse," Mary notes cheerfully. She was enslaved as a child, and forced into service by the age of eight. She has known no other work than this since then and, when she was lost by her master in a wager, she went with a shrug to the man who won her until he abandoned her. She then came here and was still tasting freedom. She liked it.

Emma cares little for the opinions of the righteous.

"It is an honest life, is it not?" She insists. She shrugs away arguments to the contrary. "I willingly offer a service for a price, and men willingly pay. They are not forced to come to me, and I am not forced to entertain them. I do not steal from them. They get the service they pay for, then I send them back to their wives."

She likes the men, and she likes the women she works with. She likes the money, and the presents, and the storytelling by the fires. She feels no anguish over any loss of respect. She does not care for the kinds of people who would not have her anyway, and dislikes their company. She prefers the laughing soldiers and the unruly townsmen.

As for me, it hurts me to be there, and I never quite think of myself as one of them. I feel as if I am better than they, for I once had a husband and a home, and could once hold up my head and move through the streets of a town without suffering glares of contempt and blows from hurled stones. I want to be a wife again, but can never return or my husband would kill me for having left. I have forgotten the hunger and the beatings and have told myself stories about the life I left until I believe it was happy and comfortable. I believe I was evil for leaving, and imagine my husband weeping with pain over my abandonment, or starving because he no longer has me to find him food. Our dwelling grows larger and larger in my mind, and my status in the community is inflated. I berate myself inwardly, and sow seeds of shame and unworthiness that will long haunt me.

I am different from Emma and Mary because I feel that I have fallen, whereas they both accept the life as the best they are able to do under the circumstances. I am hiding the reality from myself, and they are not. The consequence of this is that the experience damages me.

Some of my customers have peculiar tastes and unusual requests. There are some who wish to dress like Henry, and some who prefer several of us at once and have the money to pay. Some like me to whip them, and some of them like to turn their mean natures and their brutality upon me.

One of these is a man who repeatedly comes to see me. He is vulgar and mean and disliked by most men, but is most especially disliked by the whores who notice with relief that I have become his preference. I do not mind so very much. He has not hit me or insulted me as he did the other women, and he always pays without argument. As for his idiosyncrasies, they are no stranger than some of the others, and I do not care, as long as he pays me.

He is a soldier and a captain, with a penchant for rape and warfare. He lingers most fondly on stories of his rapings, as these greatly entertain him. He describes the attacks in detail before turning his attention to me. It is his ritual, when he visits a whore, and the stories stimulate his desire. He likes to tear off my robes before taking me. Then, he throws me down and ravages me as if this were a rape as well and not a business transaction with me consenting. He insists that I resist him and scream, and so I do, for that is why he is paying me.

He has burned and killed, in his travels. Doing so excites him. He likes to see people quail before him, weakened and begging. It proves he is stronger. Cruelty is an art, he claims. It takes imagination and finesse, not just strength, although he has more strength than most, does he not? He describes, for my approval and admiration, the imaginative methods he has used to kill or dismember prisoners. No one can torture like he, for no one is quite so manly as he is. Do I not agree? Is he not the most manly of the men who come to see me?

I agree, enthusiastically. If I do not, he might beat me.

In time Hal (for that is who it is) asks me questions about myself. I speak to him in short sentences but, with some encouragement, I begin to tell him more. There is not much to tell, yet he still tries to draw me out, and then questions me about my girls. He sometimes brings them little gifts. I cannot fathom why he would be interested in my children, except as replacements for me when they grow older. Still, he has never offered me money for them, and there are many, many other men who do. Even when they begin business on their own, he still treats them as little children and comes to me.

I accept the fact that he comes with regularity for years, following his same rituals, but I cannot imagine why he would be interested in what I have to say–I have little to contribute, and my observations interest none of the other men. I ask him why, and he says he has grown fond of me. I ask him why that should be, and he shrugs.

I have never had a customer grow fond of me before. I begin to view him in a more positive light, and open up to him, then even come to think of him as almost a friend. Thus, we fall into a pattern of companionship that continues up until his death: I, holding my hand out for coins, then screaming for help and writhing upon the mat while he "rapes" me.

Hal brings a harp to me and tells me he likes to hear music. He demands that I learn so that I might play for him. I learn because he pays me, and it is my job to do as he asks.

"He is not such a bad sort," I tell Mary.

"Hmmph," she answers spitting. "He will be a good sort only after his bones are gnawed by wild dogs."

In a sense, what she says is exactly true.

I pluck the strings and can get no sound from the instrument that reminds me of music. Emma shows me a melody, a droning non-melody favored by the people in those times. I play it and practice, singing along in a droning voice. Doing this, I feel calmed, somehow. When I play for Hal, I am so proud of myself that he smiles, amused. I continue to play for his approval, and I learn more. I have no inherent ability at all, for this is the first I have attempted it, but the pleasure it seems to bring Hal increases my own pleasure in playing. I then play it for other men, and grow to enjoy their approval as well. They are drunk, most of them, and do not notice that I have no skill, but I am encouraged nevertheless.

The act of learning to play a roughly-made harp in the Valley of the Kings leaves an indelible impression upon me. I take pains from then on to select situations in successive lifetimes where I might learn more about music. My love for it grows to passion, and then obsession. Time passes, and I become good. More time goes past, and I am among the best. Now, when I enter a body, it is clear from the outset that I have unusual skill, displayed in early childhood as the ability to pick up nearly any instrument, and play by ear upon my first introduction to it.

None of us is born knowing without having learned.

Hal is eventually knifed and killed and, oddly, I miss his visits though I do not care enough to mourn him. Yet I still play his harp and think of him at times.

Through the years, Henry becomes my best friend, and then, a part of my family. I soon learn to shrug away discomfort at his strange appearance, and to be indifferent toward his customers and their requests.

Early on, we set up housekeeping together with his lover, and we pool our funds to make a home for the girls. Henry cares for them both with a touching gentleness, and I do not walk in when I see him rocking them or he will push them away and storm out, ashamed.

His lover stands guard over the children's tent at night, and fetches them water when they awaken and cry for it. I know him. He is Bessie Blount, one of Henry's mistresses during my last life. He is not entirely jealous of me, but is nonetheless possessive of Henry, and resents his affection for my family. Still we manage to be friends until he takes off with a soldier, and leaves Henry to me.

Henry is distraught and tearful at his parting. Out of loneliness, he settles in next to me on my mat and holds me as he sleeps, "Just until I recover," he promises. But a habit is formed and he never finds his way back to his own tent and his own mat.

"It is lonely there," he explains. "There is no harm done," he continues. "Do you want me to leave?" he asks frightened.

"No, you can stay," I tell him. There is no harm done—he is right about that—and I have grown used to it.

We are as married as two people can be, except that we couple with anyone but each other. Sometimes we fight. He takes offense at the smallest provocation, and overreacts with childish rages, and I have no patience. Sometimes I feel Henry's fist, and sometimes he feels mine. We shriek at each other, and wrestle on the ground screaming, insulting, pulling at each other's hair, slamming each other's heads into the dust. We have bloodied each other's faces and lost a week's income on more than one occasion, waiting for the swelling to go down before standing outside our tents again. Despite this, he does not leave, and I do not send him away, nor do I leave myself. Henry never finds another lover. The focus of his life is our odd little family, even as he stands with his back toward me, turning only to spit in the direction of my tent.

Chapter 4

There are potions the women take to prevent pregnancy, and others we take to terminate pregnancy if the first potions fail. These are actually quite effective, and the rare pregnancy one of the women may endure has usually been pre-planned. I do not plan one. The children I have are burden enough, and this is no life for a child.

The girls grow in a tent, raised by a community of whores, surrounded by the worst of mankind in the shadow of pyramids. They have two mothers, one of whom is a man, for Henry has grown close to them and loves them as much as I do. They never see their father again.

When the oldest is nearly a young woman, we set her up in her own tent. She has grown up in the life and has developed a toughness of character that is completely necessary under those circumstances. She does not tell me if she likes the work or hates it. At 12 she is a hardened whore, tight-lipped, saying nothing of her feelings, giving nothing of herself to any of the men who come, except that for which they pay in advance. She gives nothing of herself to anyone. She learns early how to handle her customers, and is remarkably good at hurling out the bad ones, even as a little slip of a girl. She has a tongue that shames and blisters. She has strong nails and carries a knife. I do not worry about her.

By the time she is 15, she has been servicing one particular man for three years, and he comes to her every night. She does not mention this to me or to Henry, but we recognize him as a familiar face in the Valley, and a familiar one in the vicinity of her tent. He is Father. He has fallen in love with her and is willing to pay for the privilege of seeing her, though she does not admit to anyone that she long ago stopped taking his money. He spends what time he can with her and, when she is working, joins the crowds at the campfires for stories, songs and fights. He returns throughout the evening as often as she will allow him. The time she allows him grows longer and more frequent.

When she is 16, they both disappear.

As we suspected then, and as I have long since known, they ran off to be married. They then lived together for the rest of that life raising children I never knew of or saw. She took pains to be respectable and she succeeded, learning all the things a chaste wife should know, doing all the things a chaste wife should do.

Perfection in all things did not include admitting she had a mother who was a whore, and so she discarded me. She never came back, nor did she inquire after me or offer assistance when I grew too old to work and died destitute and a beggar. She suffered punishment for that later, but it hardly matters to me. Even then, I was relieved and happy for her.

She became the most chaste, and the most proper of all possible wives, and retained throughout time and successive lives a pressing need to bury a past she could not remember. She strove for society's approval and for perfection in her every action, and she demanded it of her offspring. She also retained the hardness she had come by as a child who gave sex for money to drunken, brutal men. She did not resort to cruelty toward anyone; she merely internalized her shame and obsessively strove to keep up appearances. Her hardness covered, as it often does, a tender, loving soul afraid to show any weakness.

I do not fear her any longer as a mother I could not please. I now see her as a child who never lost her fears, and I feel a sweet protectiveness toward her. It is a freeing sensation. I do love her. I do love her.

Katherine also sets up shop and seems to accept the life, though there is a conflict about it in her, as there is in me. She feels she was born for better than this, and dreams of riches, and life in a town where she is not forced to service men. She rightfully blames me for having seen to it that she could never have those things. No man comes to take her, as one did her sister, and she dies young, without having ever forgiven me.

She still has not.

✠

Later, Katherine responded to that life in much the same way that I did, by enshrouding herself in a veil of denial, respectability and condemnation. Over time, she made many of the same mistakes I made, for the same reasons. She has a fate similar to Anne's to look forward to, in some future time. She has been slower to ready herself, but one day it will come.

It does not please me to know this. Neither does it please me to learn of Henry's fate after a lifetime as king. We all create our own misery.

I have learned that Henry has already returned to inhabit another physical body, without me. He is in Russia where he will lose his family, his home, his property and substantial riches to ransacking soldiers, much as he took land and treasures from the monasteries in England after declaring himself the head of his own church.

A plan has already been put in place for still more lessons when he returns again. His next experience will be in West Africa, where he will be sold by his family into slavery to European merchants who will take him to a country referred to as "new" (although we have both been there before, long ago). He will arrive and find a wife, then will be sold and taken away from her. He will find another woman, and be sold away again. He will have poor luck in keeping wives for some time to come.

As part of the plan, he will be charged with the crime of rape, and tried before a judge and a jury as biased against him as the trial he held for me was biased. He will be hung, and hanging beside him will be others I remember from my own trial, also lynched for crimes they will not commit.

I wonder: What would Henry's murderers think if they knew they were hanging a king? It is a fanciful thought, but one that amuses me. I am not as amused as I think I might have been in life, had I been reassured at the block that Henry is destined for the noose.

All this will seemingly be for no reason other than the whims of people who do not like skin that is black. It will be another strange fancy of another strange society, that skin color determines worth.

My thoughts wander, here, to what I have learned about life. I recite these conclusions to myself, looking toward the Voice for validation, and then guidance.

In every society, I know, there are class structures of some kind, and most take this further. Each society–each group within each society–chooses something with which to assign inferiority. In China it is the time of birth and the size of feet. In Europe it is the Jews; in England, the Irish. Among the powerful, it is the powerless; among the rich, it is the poor; among the men, it is the women. In this "new" country, that will also be true.

In reverse, there is often a vehement hatred by an oppressed group toward the ones it sees as representatives of oppression. The oppressed view their own feelings of contempt as nobler than the contempt they receive, and more justified. They view their own hatred as right and pure. They nurture it, and bequeath it to their children, and sometimes see to it that it is carried on for generations.

Neither side sees the humanity in the other. Both sides are equally wrong in this.

To what purpose is such hatred generated? Even if it is seemingly justified, it heals no one. If its object does not understand, or does not personally deserve a punishment, it is an injustice and a crime. To what end is such punishment served, except to bring it back upon oneself? What is the cure for it but forgiveness?

Can a beheaded wife understand that the hatred she feels toward her husband exceeds the hatred he earned with his fractured mind and muddled judgment? Would she have been called upon to forgive him, even had his mind been sound? These are the questions placed before me, and I toy with them.

What I am thinking now, with this passing, is that I cannot be vain about my goodness and virtue, or smug that another has been entrapped by weakness to which I am not at the moment susceptible. My virtue can be taken from me.

I cannot applaud another's punishment, however amply justified, or assume the role of judge and administer punishment in vengeance. When I encounter those who are paying for grievous sins, I must show compassion and mercy, and not compound their suffering for, truly, it is my own. We are all on the same path.

"You are learning," the Voice says softly, like music. "I am proud."

The same is true in reverse. Virtue is learned–or is it earned? Upon close examination, it appears to me to come at a dear price and be quite hard-won. It is truly something to admire.

I think now of Hal, who once preferred soldiering and used it, not to defend, but as a convenient excuse to destroy. He killed and raped for pleasure, without thought for his victims or the pain he inflicted.

When his punishments came due, Hal endured the manifestations of his cruelty by repeatedly suffering physical weakness, deprivation and emotional isolation. He found himself repeatedly on the receiving end of barbaric or emotional cruelty as vicious as his own. The anguish was the same. The blood now drawn was his, in equal measure to the blood he once drew.

We learn compassion from pain, and thus did Hal. In time, it transformed his desire to harm others into a desire to nurture, protect and appease. His taste for blood was transformed into revulsion—even a fear of it. Along the way, he developed humor and kindness, and earned the love and deep affection of his peers.

He also earned a future far more pleasant than his past, and I am very pleased to know this, because I love him.

Chapter 5

"Shall we cover it again?" the Voice asks.

I say nothing. I have heard it all before, many times. I go over it within myself without assistance: a poem I have memorized by rote.

Now, however, I hear the meaning behind the words.

A part of me always clung to the myth that I could live among whores as a whore, but not be of their kind, not really. *I* was in the Valley as a result of tragic circumstances, whereas the other women were there by choice. It mattered not what tragedies had brought them there, for tragedy was always behind it and every one of the women had been driven there by desperate circumstances and suffering. Yet, I felt my own tragedy was more tragic than theirs, my degradation more demeaning, my reasons more honorable and my fall from a greater height. I felt that they "dirtied" me by association.

In the past, I focused on the discord and the arguments and the thievery, or on the scorn I received from respectable society and the contempt with which I was viewed by most of my peers and customers. I bristled with indignation and defensiveness when faced with the scenes. I was bitterly resentful of the circumstances that forced me into that life, felt hatred toward my husband for driving me into the streets, and responded with fury to the suggestion that I should feel kindly and sympathetic toward the women in the Valley.

I even rejected the suggestion that I was, in fact, really one of them.

There is none of that now. With this viewing, I am philosophical. My husband eventually learned I had value, but then had to value me only from a distance, all the while enduring my derision and disgust. There is no point in holding onto anger toward him. He is not the same, for he has grown.

As for the women in the Valley, I peered at them through self-centeredness and self-pity. I saw their experiences as less painful than mine, and viewed them as less victimized than I was because I was not wise enough to draw a fair comparison, nor fair enough to respect their pain.

At the same time, I demanded respect for mine. I now see their humiliation, and understand what they felt and why they were there, and know that most of them were as unhappy and as victimized as I was. I now know that my pain is *not* more sacred, my suffering is *not* more noble, and the injustice I endure is *not* more ill-deserved than someone else's.

I see, and I know that people were cruel and spiteful and hateful at times, but so was I. I now see, and now know they simply had not learned, as I had not learned, to cherish one another.

That is the only lesson we all are meant to learn: to cherish each other. It is the one that takes us down a road so long the end seems out of reach.

And finally, I must take this lesson and expound upon it. It is, in its way, like a child who stops believing in fairies but still believes in trolls, if I learn a narrow lesson then reject it in a broader scope. Can I expand what I have learned to include other inclinations toward unfairness or injustice, and eradicate those within myself as well? Can I see that it is not just this one type of person toward whom I must feel empathy, but all types? And can I be moved to assist and show patience, rather than to pass judgment? In time I will see it and live it, for I must. If I do not, I will be forced to learn tolerance again and again by passing through life as the very thing I now ridicule, despise, or most condemn.

"Do you see how they have changed? You can still recognize them and they are still struggling, but can you see? They are trying as hard as you."

What I see suddenly amuses me. I look around and see one person after another, all of them. *All* of them! They were, *all of them*, fine ladies, or courtiers, or royalty in this past life. The entire Valley, it seems, was transported, en mass, to Henry's court.

I feel a giggle rising. The Voice joins me and between us we send out barrages of laughter, pealing like musical notes into the space that surrounds me.

I would give anything to solemnly ask Katherine her opinion of these scenes. I saw a number of her ladies there, where they most certainly did not conduct themselves with the propriety Katherine demanded at court. I can envision her squirming with denial and distaste. Oh! I could never have designed such a punishment for her, when we were at war!

I would give anything to face Henry with the intelligence that he, a vain and womanizing king, was once a half-man who dressed in women's clothing.

And then, I would like to go back to the Valley and point out to the men who beat and bloodied Henry that they would one day cower in the face of his displeasure. They would bow before him, and do virtually anything to gain his good graces and keep their lives.

Were I alive, I would most assuredly be hiccuping now, and that thought makes me convulse with even more merriment.

I have not wanted to laugh with such abandon since I came here, and it heals me. I have always loved irony, and life, it seems, is designed around it. One just never knows who one is meeting in life, where they have been, or where they are going.

Epilogue

China, 1666

As a child of the Horse, with unbound feet, I was sold in marriage to a man who worked the fields. I worked beside him, stooped over, with infants strapped to my back until my spine grew curved from the constant weight and I could no longer walk completely upright at all. Year upon year, from before dawn till well after dusk, I toiled. My world was narrow, and within its confines there was no music, and little laughter.

I had enough to eat, and several sons. However, I did not even live long enough to earn the honor of being "the" mother-in-law, for my own outlived me and I was her servant until my death. So were the wives of my sons, though, as is custom, they should have served me.

My husband was the youngest son of seven and, as his wife, I had to answer to the elder brothers and all of their wives. In addition to them, I had to serve my husband's mother, who had given birth only to sons. Birthing seven sons and no daughters was clear evidence of her superiority. As a result, she felt honor was her due, and she showed no kindness.

Her kindness, what little she had, decreased in incremental portions toward family members of lesser importance. It was bequeathed, in small measure, toward her older sons' wives (whom she treated as well as she was capable of treating anyone), then was meagerly meted out to the wives of the younger sons. It was completely withheld from me, substituted with vengeance as repayment for my having been born to a better family than she. I did not come from peasants; I became one when I married her son.

My mother did not bind my feet in infancy, as she had my sisters, knowing from my horoscope that I could only find a husband who would want me as a worker of the fields. When the time came to find a husband for me, my father bartered for the best, then settled for a man who would take me. It was the fate my parents had known I was destined for all along.

Being the only daughter who could walk without assistance, I performed household chores with our servant from my earliest years. I was ordered about by my beautiful, crippled sisters who patronizingly told me they "envied" me my huge, ugly feet, for I did not know the pain and discomfort of being bound. They soaked their twisted feet, and had me change the rags that bound them, pretending that they would exchange places with me in order to know how it was to run. It was shallow kindness, and the contempt beneath it was not well hidden; my feet were clear evidence of my inferiority.

My sisters found well-situated husbands early, and moved away to large houses. They were each assisted down fine hallways by devoted servants who held their elbows as they took beautiful, mincing baby steps on feet that were a perfect three inches long. They all had sons. One even had a son in the year of the Fire Horse, a most propitious time for the birth of a male. There was much feasting and celebration over the birth.

I, of course, did not attend.

During that same year, I had a pregnancy myself, my first. I worked the fields until the pain grew too difficult to bear. I begged leave of my husband, and walked beyond the fields to a stand of trees where I squatted and gave birth without a sound, placing a stick between my teeth and biting down, so as not to disturb my husband as he worked.

I had been told by my mother-in-law to not return home with a female.

I caught her shoulders in my hands as she squirmed out between my legs, biting the stick and pushing my bare foot into a sharp rock to shift the pain away lest any cries bring irritation to my husband, who was still planting. She wailed while, exhausted, I sat down and leaned back against the tree. I stretched her across my lap and sawed through her cord with the sharp edge of a painted bone I wore on a string around my neck. There was no need for me to do this. I had an obligation to kill her, and it hardly mattered if she was cut loose from the afterbirth before I did the deed. I reasoned that I was too tired to kill her now, and would hold her to keep her quiet while I rested for a time. This would be easier if she was unattached.

My husband wanted nothing to do with the birthing, and would not come looking. He could not protest that I dampened the edge of my shirt in a nearby stream to clean her, or that I held her to my chest with her head pressed close under my chin and my arms wrapped tenderly around her. I was stealing this guilty time with my child before returning her to the spirits.

Her wailing stopped and we both slept.

When I awoke, the sun was higher in the sky. I would have to show myself to my husband, and apologize that I could not present him with a child.

My poor child was exhausted from the effort it had taken her to come to me, and still slept. Her mouth made soft sucking motions and her tiny belly moved up and down with each breath. She was warm and soft, and possessed, it seemed to me, of extraordinary beauty. She took in a deep breath and gave out a little sigh, and at the sound, tears sprang to my eyes. I studied her ear, the most perfect ear I had ever seen, and ran my finger over it, staring at it with pride and wonder.

I felt her hair, soft as goose down, then pressed my nose to it and smelled. She smelled sweet. She had the smell given by nature to all infants as a safeguard against mothers who might not be inclined to care for them, as I was not inclined (or rather, as I was forbidden to do). It triggers something in the human brain, and stirs something in the heart. It is a smell to make a mother drunk with instinct, and it filled my nostrils, saturating my brain. I pulled my face away, and took gulps of air to clear my head.

I had to leave her now. I placed her upon the ground and squatted beside her. It was my duty to smother her, or drown her. I had done this any number of times in my imagination, preparing myself for just this contingency, bracing myself for an infant that was female. I had worked carefully to harden the part of my heart that would want to let her live, and had deliberately turned that part of me cold. In my mind, it was easy: she died quickly and I could walk away satisfied that I had performed my duty to my family. In my imagination, she was merely a lump of tenuous life, not a person, and no feelings welled up inside of me to complicate the scene.

But in reality, she woke and cried.

I could not let her cry. I would hold her for just one more moment and smother her afterwards, I decided. I picked her up, and held her to my breast where her tiny, beautiful mouth rested and suckled contentedly like a little animal's. I had no milk yet, having just given birth, and I gave nothing to her at all, yet she seemed to feel that I had. I wished she did not trust me so much, and ran my finger down her cheek. I wished I at least had milk for her.

I softly sang a funeral dirge to her, as a good-bye. She opened her eyes, yawned, then went back to sleep.

I could easily kill her now, I thought. She would feel no pain. She would feel a greater pain in being allowed to live as a child of the Fire Horse. Deciding to do it now, I quickly moved to set her back upon the ground, but as I did, her tiny arms shuddered and threw themselves outward. It was as if she were afraid to fall. In that single, small, reflexive, self-preserving motion, she broke my heart.

With uncharacteristic determination, I picked her up again and rocked her, then lowered her and propped her against me on the ground so my hands were free. I tore the bottom of my shirt into rags and stuffed them between my legs to catch the blood. I pulled on my trousers with one hand, cradled her head with the other, then fashioned a sling out of my undershirt and tied her to my chest. I returned slowly, and in pain, to the fields where my husband looked up approvingly, seeing the child, knowing it could only be male, if I were carrying it back with me.

"A son!" He said approvingly.

I said nothing and looked down.

"You would not dare bring me a daughter, yes?" He chuckled at the absurdity of the thought.

I glanced at him for just a split second with a stubborn jaw, then looked down again. My shoulders were stiff, and my hands were clenched.

"Let me see the infant." He reached for her.

Head down, I stepped backward and did not offer her to him. Then, seeing my husband was furious with my insolence, I stepped again to protect myself.

He leaned toward me, and swiftly struck me across the face. I lifted my head slowly, and stared straight into his eyes with an expression so enraged and so defiant he was taken aback. His eyes flickered, much as they did when his mother shouted. Then, remembering I was his wife, his anger grew twofold. He struck me again. Rather than face him with my head lowered as I always did, I stared back at him, unblinking, and raised myself to my full height. He lifted his fist again to frighten me. I still stared without flinching, without noticing the fist or the pain from his blows.

He nervously turned his eyes away from mine before I had yet to blink. He hesitantly lowered his arm.

"It is a girl," I said calmly, studying him with more wild threat in my eyes than I knew. "She will not marry well, of course, but I will need her to help me with the chores. If you wish, she will be mine alone." I would sort out the task of caring for her as an outcast of the family at a later time.

"Leave her," my husband ordered.

I caught his eye and stared. "And next time, I will have a son for you," I continued as if he had not spoken.

"Did you hear me, wife? I said *leave* her!" He was outraged and a little frightened. I had never challenged him before.

"I would now like to show you your little daughter, Husband."

He turned away. "I do not want to see it."

"She would like to see *you*. She has your mouth, and your esteemed mother's eyes." I did not coax or placate. I spoke the words pleasantly, without expression, staring intently at him with eyes of fire that burned a hole into his thoughts, and disturbed his assuredness.

He stood and did not move.

I pulled the baby out of the sling and held her out to my husband who looked at her grudgingly then looked away again.

"She has your honored mother's eyes," I repeated, bowing my

head. "See?"

"I will not see."

"See?" I insisted. "Your honored mother's eyes." I pushed the baby in front of his face, close enough for him to smell her. His nose twitched. "I could not leave a baby with the eyes of my esteemed mother-in-law."

My husband peered down reluctantly, studied her and shook his head. "Her eyes are my eyes," he said. "And my nose as well." He looked at her with more interest and a little triumph. "I see nothing of you, in her. She is the image of me."

"I could not leave an infant who was the image of you, my honored husband," I said humbly, bowing my head.

We arrived at the house together, and I knelt before my mother-in-law to present the infant. I was quaking inside. I did not know what to expect from her fury. She could cast me out, or burden me with tasks that would kill me, or simply speak to me with more derision than she already did. Perhaps it would be the last . . . perhaps she would feel mercy toward the child if she saw it.

The rest of the family stood around us, watching. Some viewed me with amusement; all viewed me with contempt.

"I beg you humbly for forgiveness," I said with my forehead touching the floor. "It is a daughter."

The woman stared, and said nothing.

I waited.

"Take the child away," she said finally. There was no mercy in her voice, or in her eyes.

"It will be no trouble, my esteemed mother," my husband said. "It will be trained to do the chores." He hung his head, then knelt beside me on the floor.

"Why is the child not dead?" My mother-in-law snapped. "You have a duty to obey me. You will take it out and leave it for the wolves."

It did not occur to anyone to be appalled at the suggestion. They looked at me sternly, in agreement, more inured to the killing of female infants than they were to a woman's flagrant disrespect toward her mother-in-law. Vacillating and weak, my husband swiftly moved into their camp where it was safer, and looked over at me with an expression that mirrored their disapproval, even as he knelt in supposed supplication for the same reason as I.

I was alone in this fight.

"I will leave as well," I said softly to myself. There were gasps from those close enough to hear, then laughter, and my words were repeated more loudly so my mother-in-law could share in the joke.

"You cannot," she chortled. "Where would you go, an ugly, useless, clumsy, big-footed field girl? Who would have you? You could not even sell yourself, except to blind fishermen, and even they can do better than you."

I said nothing.

"Take the child away."

I stood and bent over in a deep bow and took my daughter out, presumably to leave her to die. However, I kept walking. I was shocked and frightened by the intensity of my determination. It was unlike me to question my elders, or to be defiant in the face of their commands. I did not know where the willfulness came from, or what would become of me as a result of it. I was ashamed of myself, but could do nothing except walk away from all of them, carrying an infant with no life to look forward to anyway.

I made a walking stick of a fallen branch, and leaned on it heavily. It was not easy walking, having given birth only hours before. Had I been more respected, or perhaps more loved, another might have volunteered to spare me the pain of this chore and do it for me. However, the killing of my child was my task alone. I thought it a fortunate burden, as I walked toward the sparing of her life.

It was not hard for my husband to catch up to me. When an hour had passed and I still did not return, he went looking for me. He took a false turn or two, allowing me to press on farther than I otherwise might have, but he easily covered the distance when he spotted me on the road. He said nothing, when he reached me.

I looked at him, and continued to walk.

"Stop!" He shouted, finally.

I narrowed my eyes at him.

"We must," he said.

"I cannot," I answered.

"We must obey."

"I will not," I said.

"You are my wife!" he screamed. Spittle shot from his mouth, and onto my face.

"Not as of this instant," I whispered, staring down. I glanced up at him for just long enough to catch his eye and give him a look that was both dangerous, and oddly, inappropriately, commanding and powerful. Then I hung my head again.

He stared at me with disbelief and flew into a rage.

"This is what I get for taking pity on you! No one else would marry you, and this is why! *This! This* is why a Horse woman cannot—and should not—be chosen as a mate. You are too headstrong for a woman." He muttered, "Horses always are. And this girl would be even worse. This girl would be uncontrollable." This was the very first indication that I might be headstrong. This was the very first incident that even suggested so. I was meek and dutiful, always. From birth, any tendency toward independent thought or disrespect had been carefully, methodically and purposely eradicated from my nature.

"Then you are well-rid of us," I snapped. "You are now free to find yourself a better wife and to father a better child," My tone of voice threw my husband into a state of frightened confusion, and he blanched.

I did not mention that he had tried for a better pairing, before settling for me. As the youngest son of a large peasant family, he had no expectation of inheritance or fortune, nor could any wife of his expect more than I received. There were no women queued up to replace me. There had been none queued up before my parents offered me. I was the best that he could do.

"I command you." His words trembled unsteadily.

"She is mine."

"*You* are *mine*—and you will do as I say!"

"I bid you good-bye," I responded, and continued to walk.

He grabbed my walking stick and struck me with it until I fell, bleeding. He kicked me. The infant howled on the ground, for she had torn loose from her sling and was hurt, how badly I did not know, but the cries seemed to indicate that it was serious. My husband aimed his foot at her, then hesitated, and kicked me again, full force in the stomach. I crawled to my knees and vomited from the impact, heard the baby cry, and wept myself. Anger surged through me, and my determination to help her grew to a panic.

I felt a rush of blood between my legs. Had he broken something within me?

I tried to move toward the infant, but I was too weak, and the kick to the stomach had taken away my breath. I attempted it again, forcing myself. I would do this. I would fight him. She was just out of reach, and her cries sounded odd. What could it mean, that they sounded this way? I had to hold her and see. I stretched my arm toward her with no thought but to make it longer.

My husband placed his foot upon my arm to stop me. He pushed his weight down hard enough so that I cried out in protest.

A sense of resignation suddenly overcame me, and I collapsed.

Was it worth all this? Was it worth it? In one instant, I threw away my resolve, and decided it was not. I was exhausted, in pain, and the effort was proving to be futile. It was easier to obey. I could not force my husband. I had no power to win against his mother. I had no strength left to fight. Furthermore, the infant was damaged–I could tell as much from her cries. She might not even live. Did it really matter that she live? The fleeting thought "It is only a female" passed through my mind, and decided me. The defiance that had overtaken me earlier retreated behind a veil of obedience, and I shut my eyes with shame for having challenged my husband and defied his mother: I was not being dutiful.

"Take her," I whispered. A string of vomit hung from my lip. I broke it with my hand and wiped my mouth. "Take her away."

I lay there in the dust, staring at the sky, while my husband roughly picked up the infant and walked some distance away from the road, where he left her on the ground. He did not even take the time to smother her. She screamed in shrill wails, and each one of them tore at my heart. My fingernails dug into the palms of my hands until they bled, but I did not feel any pain.

My husband returned to me, and pulled me to my feet. He held me up, for I was weak and wobbling, and waved to a lone ox cart that was passing at that moment to ask the driver for a ride.

We bumped along the road toward home. I stared at the countryside, crossed my legs to stop the blood, and pressed my arms against my breasts, which were suddenly hard and full and dripping milk. I was numb, feeling no pain in my loins at all, but could still hear the cries though they were far behind me now and, in truth, had stopped.

New York, 1814-1867

I wanted no more of husbands and marriage. The thought of it made panic rise within me, and any threat of it made me churn with nausea. I chose a body that would not appeal to men, and as a further safeguard, selected one that would ensure my preference would be other women instead, although within the constraints of that society, I would neither act upon that preference, nor understand or acknowledge it. I would not be enticed by urges that had brought me such grief in the past, and would not be tempted by any man. I hid safely behind a wall no man could scale.

I was born the middle child of a family of nine in a place called New York. My father was a renowned composer and violinist, and each of us was trained on a different instrument from our earliest days. I was assigned the piano at the age of three, propped up on books with my feet dangling, and I took to it as I had never taken to another instrument before. It had such a glorious sound! I grew to have a love for it that transcended that of any instrument I'd ever played, and delighted my parents with a talent they had never seen before in any child, except my elder brother who exceeded even me on the violin.

We had nightly concerts in the parlor, playing compositions by my father and many of our own, and as I grew, my ability was recognized as exceptional. Still, I had a brother even more gifted, and this piqued me to try harder than I might have otherwise, even motivated as I was to learn every single thing I could about music. My father exploited my talent and that of my brother by having us play for audiences, but neither of us minded. It was what we loved to do. There were nights when my brother's performance was a little weak and my own was spectacular, and it was these nights that I lived for, and thought of long afterward.

I adored my family. They were among the intellectuals of the time, led by a brilliant man, my father, and a mother who could charm the winter into spring with her warmth and kind heart. We were raised to think and to question, to appreciate art in all of its forms, and to respect ideas. Our library was filled with books we were all encouraged to read and discuss, and because of my father's fame, I met an endless variety of people who would argue into the night about religion and philosophy and politics. Even as small children, we were allowed to sit on the floor and listen and participate, and through the years I absorbed it all, chewing on ideas and expounding upon them internally, thinking at length about conversations that were forbidden to most women of that age.

They came from all over the world, it seemed, to visit my father, and my exposure to these people opened my eyes to viewpoints I would never have known of otherwise. These experiences colored my opinions until my thoughts began leaning toward the eccentric, although I would only have behaved and spoken in a way that was precisely as expected. I grew to have respect for philosophies others in my time considered laughable or threatening, and had an unquenchable thirst for more of them.

I developed an insatiable appetite for mental stimulation, and craved association with people who were different from me because I felt I had less to learn from people too like myself. I yearned for conversations with immigrants, and slaves, prostitutes and beggars–anyone at all who might have an interesting or poignant story that would introduce to me another kind of world. I wished I were a man so that I might travel and have adventures. However, I was afraid to reveal my inclinations for fear that I might be scorned for my curiosity, or thought of as odd. Instead, I read everything I could find, and escaped with my mind.

On the face of it, I was just exactly what a woman of my era was expected to be. Underneath, I supported causes only the courageous could fight, but I did not have the courage to join in. I might have done some good but for that, backing causes that ranged from allowing married women to teach in the school, to taking part, as I had heard the Quakers did, in assisting runaway slaves on their journey to Canada. I daydreamed myself into heroic roles, but did nothing.

In particular, I had a hatred for injustice. Most of what I saw of brutality and pain was from the windows of my enclosed carriage, and I could have easily ignored it and dismissed it from my thoughts had I chosen, instead of craning my neck to see more. I saw immigrants living in terrible slums, working for pennies. I saw the poor taken away in chains because they could not pay their debts. I saw children whose bones were brittle and bent from poor diet and no sunlight, working in factories, carrying crates too large for a man.

On one occasion, I saw several freed Southern Negroes lynched for rapes an undercurrent of rumor suggested a gang of white thugs had committed. Concerned, I questioned the wife of the police commissioner who told me the police knew who had actually committed the crimes, but wanted to rid the streets of "darkies". The world, it seemed, preferred rapists to black men. She assumed I was in concurrence with this hideous, unspeakable crime against the innocent, and smiled a little as she told me. I said nothing to suggest I was not. I had never felt such self-loathing as I did on that day.

I went to this public lynching to offer my silent prayers and support for the men, since it appeared there was nothing at all to be done to save them. I knew that very few people cared whether the men lived or died, and that some did not ever consider, nor were they burdened by the thought, that these "creatures" were actually men with feelings and souls.

As for myself, I had an inexplicable compulsive need to make certain those men saw one face that showed grief, when their eyes scanned the crowd. I had to lie to my family in order to cover up my plans, and had to go alone, but I was adamant about being there no matter how silly my whim, or macabre that whim was. And so, I was there, gripping my smelling salts to be certain I remained conscious through to the end, pushing as close to the front of the crowd as I was able.

The haunted look in my red-rimmed, saucer-round eyes caught the eyes of one man, a particularly proud-looking Negro, as someone slipped the noose around his neck. He nodded to me without lowering his eyes, which under other circumstances would have earned him a lashing. Had his hands not been tied behind him, and had he been wearing one, he would have tipped his hat.

I touched my gloved hands to my mouth to cover a gasp as the platform was kicked from beneath him, and he hung.

For years that scene reappeared in dreams to trouble me. Most troubling were the nightmares that placed me on the scaffold, where it was I who wore the noose. Those Negro men always stood in judgment against me for my silence.

I seethed inwardly over that incident and many others, grieving over all injustice, over all cruelty. However, I could not move a finger against any of it. I was afraid to not be liked. It was so comfortable, to be as loved and accepted as I was. I would do nothing to jeopardize that.

There were many who would have appreciated my support. There were many people who stood alone and fought for things I too believed in, while I averted my eyes and stayed silent. I betrayed these people, and myself, by publicly taking popular stances that diverged from my convictions, just to incur approval from those who listened when I spoke.

I envied courage more than any other virtue, and wondered how one gained possession of it, for I was certain there was no courage at all within me.

✠

As a respectable woman, born to a high social strata, I led a very sheltered life. I could not travel any distances without the company of a brother, and spent most of my time studying or visiting friends, or performing charitable works throughout the town.

There was no mischief in me, or disrespect, or dishonesty. I was a good daughter, a good sister, a good neighbor, a good friend and a good aunt. I took great pains to do nothing to disappoint anyone. I could not force my own wishes onto others, was thoughtlessly ordered about by my siblings, and felt guilty if I did not volunteer for every chore or do twice the work of any of the others. There were many who took advantage of me, but I accepted this, for mostly they treated me with kindness.

I had a reasonably contented life except for one thing: I wanted a child of my own with desperation so intense I could not even describe it. I spent many hours doing volunteer work that would place me near children, working with the school and the orphan home, or caring for children when their mothers were ill. In place of children in my home, I kept animals, as many as I could find and of any species: rabbits, dogs, cats, horses, ducks, squirrels and wild things I found that needed care. I stepped over insects rather than kill them, caught them in my home and set them free in the yard, speaking to them as I let them go. I mothered everything, my siblings and their offspring, my parents, my neighbors, and even the plants in the garden, and the furniture in the house.

I watched my sisters and my friends marry, one after another, but felt no temptation to follow them, except to envy them the children they bore, and to wish I had one of my own. I had daydreams of a baby girl, although a boy would suit me as well. It did not matter as long as it was a child.

My mother fretted about finding me a husband, for I was short and squat and large boned, given to excessive weight, and had a face that was mannish. I took after my Russian father, whereas my sisters favored my willowy Scottish mother. I had never had a suitor, and my mother thought this brought me grief. I reassured her often that I wanted no marriage and preferred to spend my life caring for her and my father. It did not pain me, I insisted, to remain the "maiden aunt". I was not lonely with a large, ever-growing family close by. My father had enough inherited wealth so that I could be assured of an income throughout my life and would never need to live with a sibling or a niece as the recipient of charity when I grew old. Only the prospect of being a burden to my family might have prompted me to consider marriage.

I had thought of all that, when I selected my place in this life. I chose to see that nothing about my circumstances would ever force me to wed.

My entire family was close, but it was toward Emma, my younger sister, that I directed most of my devotion. We shared a room and all of our thoughts, and throughout childhood, could always be found together, Emma doing mischief and me fretting that she would be caught and punished.

When Emma married, I was ecstatic. More than any of the others, I knew that her children would seem closest to being mine. It took her many years, but finally when all hope was lost and she, scandalously, was old enough to have had grandchildren, she got pregnant.

For months I fussed over her and visited her daily, cooking and cleaning while she rested or sat with her giant belly, and gossiped and watched me. We talked endlessly about names and plans for the baby and, as the birth approached, my anticipation kept me awake in the night. I knitted tiny sweaters, and embroidered little dresses to calm myself, and babbled to my mother every detail of the conversations Emma and I had had earlier that day, repeating them oftentimes until my mother rolled her eyes and laughed.

I was at her side when Emma gave birth. I was the first to hold the baby, whom I cradled in my arms, pretending it was mine. I was so enraptured that it took me a moment to notice the doctor's sweating brow and frightened eyes, and to allow his frantic motions to register, while he bent over Emma and desperately tried to save her life.

"She was too old to try for a baby," he muttered, as if the fault lie with Emma, and not God's will or the doctor's own impotence when faced with inevitable death.

Then, she slipped away without ever having held her little daughter.

The doctor took the baby from my arms to show it to Emma's husband, and to tell him that his wife was dead. I remained in the bedroom with Emma, sobbing, tenderly smoothing her hair and patting her hand, stunned, shaken, wondering how I could continue to live without my beloved sister. I had never known such shock, grief and loss before.

Emma's husband was stricken with terror at the thought of raising his child alone. He was an older man, unused to children, and he looked at his daughter in bewilderment.

"I cannot. I would not know how," he whispered plaintively with tears welling in his eyes as the doctor held the baby out to him. He recoiled, even from touching the infant, and the doctor did not insist.

"You can hire a woman," the doctor suggested. "I know of one. Or you can leave it with family."

Hearing this from where I sat, I rose and joined them.

"I'll take the baby," I offered. "No one could love her as much as I do."

Emma's husband nodded in gratitude and relief, then hesitantly walked into his wife's room to say good-bye.

In that manner, in a way I would never, ever have wished—a cruel and twisted answer to a prayer—I finally became a mother.

I named the baby Margaret Ann, for it was the name Emma had selected for a girl before she died. I called her Maggie. I had always wanted a baby girl as I had never wanted any other thing in life, and insisted against my parents' wishes that she call me "Mama".

I could not put her down, when she was an infant. I held her, and covered her with kisses, and changed her dresses and hair ribbons several times each day. I held her in my lap when I played piano, marveling and cooing over her cleverness when she pounded the keys with her fists. I twirled her hair into the neatest ringlets, sewed her the fattest ruffles, made her the most cunning bonnets, and sang nursery rhymes until my voice was hoarse. I prepared her food myself, not trusting the cook. I could not bear the thought of her being cold and lonely in the night, and had no husband to object, so I slept with my arms around her as if she were a doll I took to bed.

She did not grow spoiled, as my mother had warned, for I was strict with her and consistent in my expectations. ("You have a gift for it," my mother admitted.) She grew to be open and sweet, kissing me impulsively and saying "I love you, Mama," conversationally each time the thought occurred to her throughout the day. She helped with simple chores from the time she was able to walk. She shared her toys, and rarely fought with other children or cried. She never had a nightmare in her entire life. I was proud in having somehow seen to it that she was happy, for she clearly was a happy child. I would not have been as proud if she were my very own, and was perhaps more proud, knowing a child that was truly mine would never be so lovely to see as Maggie.

Still, she was "a pistol", in the words of my father. Maggie was

Emma all over again, mischievous, playful and comical, always getting into trouble and always finding trouble where I would never expect her to find it.

She had an imaginary friend who was always responsible for her naughtiness. She sawed away at her cello with a look of grim importance, but kept stolen sweets hidden in her apron, and tucked them into her cheek whenever my back was turned. She carried on lengthy conversations with puppets she'd hold in either hand. She loved to dance and twirl about like "a gypsy princess", she said. She made up stories about the circus, to which she planned to run away when she grew up. She liked gaudy, whimsical things, and sometimes decorated the family dogs with ribbons, bells, and flowers. She taught two of them to jump through hoops, had them flip backwards, head over tail, and put on shows for us in the yard. I once caught her standing on a tree stump, trying to make the smallest dog walk along a clothesline.

Maggie dressed up in clothes from the attic, wore quaint old-fashioned hats she found there in the dust, and play-acted with her cousins when she wasn't racing the dogs and chasing the ducks around the yard, or climbing trees.

She made me laugh.

She called me one day from the top of the attic stairs, "Come see Mama! Come look at me!" and I called back that I was busy, and that she would have to wait.

Impatient to show me, dressed in a long satin ball gown and a pair of dainty ladies' dancing slippers that were too large for her, she tried to maneuver the stairs, tripped on her skirt and fell. Her neck snapped and she died, instantly.

We buried her beside her mother in the churchyard, and the light of my life flickered out.

Chicago, 1947-1970

"I am not ready," I say.

"Then just walk away."

"Not yet," I plead.

"Now," says Henry. "Please."

"It is still too soon," I insist.

He says: "Please. It will be different. I am different."

A thought like a moan consumes me. No. No.

But he is calling me.

Then there is silence, and I have a short time to decide. I look upon him squalling in his new mother's arms, and hesitate.

They are all converging: Hal, Emma, Henry, Katherine, Mother, Father, Mary, George, Elizabeth, the court, the music room. They are all arriving, or will arrive, or have arrived one by one in different places, with different stations in life, with different plans to meet at different times. I am included in many of these plans, if I choose.

I wait, perhaps a little longer than I otherwise might have, then I select a situation.

I will walk away from Henry, I have decided. I have not come here for him.

And so I am born. I shriek with colic.

And then I grow, and Henry grows.

We've returned to join the others. We've chosen an interesting time when there are airplanes, and automobiles, and telephones. There is also television, and shows we sometimes watch simultaneously not knowing, of course, that the other is. We watch The Mickey Mouse Club, and Howdie Doody, and I Love Lucy, and Make Room for Daddy. We study American Bandstand (me for the dance steps and the clothes, and Henry for the burgeoning breasts), see a President shot in Dallas, and watch the first man to walk on the moon. We both can sing the advertising jingle for Lincoln Carpets. We both eat Cheerios for breakfast and have the radio as a backdrop to our lives (I prefer classical music and softer, melodic rock and roll whereas he prefers hard rock). We join the Cub Scouts and the Girl Scouts at the appropriate times, dress up in costume and go door to door for candy on Halloween, and have, on two occasions, passed each other in crowds.

When the world begins changing in earnest, when 1967, 1968, 1969, 1970 come, youth is taking sides for or against social conformity and the war in Vietnam. We are unofficially called upon to choose a side ourselves. Henry and I are both riveted by news coverage of the Woodstock Festival, and are drawn to the counter culture–the "hippies"–that flooded upstate New York to attend. The whimsical outfits, the communal living, and life on the periphery of society is a homecoming for us in a way, but neither of us knows why that should be or, if asked, would describe it quite that way.

Mostly, I'm attracted to the idealism and the activism. People everywhere are standing up, fighting for this and fighting against that, holding demonstrations and sit-ins, marching, picketing and changing things that need to be changed.

I don't like the aimlessness, though, and the lack of purpose inherent within some factions of this new movement. I don't like the promiscuity or the drugs. Still I'm drawn to it all because it represents something that I have a yearning for, but can't quite put my finger on.

Henry is completely at home with all of it. He appreciates the fact that women are now so easy to come by, and so compliant.

As for the drugs, he's there at the forefront, experimenting with them all. In addition to this, he has an alcohol dependency that will reveal itself in time. He is now controlled by his addictions in much the same way as he was once controlling, and is usually intoxicated to some degree from one substance or another. He is in that state when I walk into a party where he's standing, leaning against a wall.

Had either one of us not gone to that party, we would have crossed paths in some other way.

He sees me and stares. He experiences the impact of an adrenaline rush he attributes to very good hashish, and is suddenly fully cognizant with all of his senses on alert. He pulls a pair of mirrored sunglasses out of his jacket pocket and puts them on, even though it's nighttime. He thinks I won't notice him watching me that way.

Knowing (even with the sunglasses) that he's staring, not knowing the impact I'm having on him, used to being stared at and expecting it, I notice him but have no desire to meet him. My internal alarm is going off. There is something about him that makes me uneasy, almost as if I sense he's dangerous. But that's not quite it. I don't know what it is. It might only be that I can't see his eyes behind those awful sunglasses.

I flirt with the knot of men that surrounds me (I always have a knot of men), but I'm not with any of them, nor does it appear that any of them are making much progress with me.

I fill my paper cup from the spigot of a beer keg and sip one glass, but I pass the marijuana cigarette to the person next to me, holding it out at arm's length. I ignore the lines of cocaine on the coffee table, and watch without interest as people inhale them up their noses through tubes made from rolled-up dollar bills.

I talk with my friends (these include Valerie, whom I do not know is really Emma). The people I'm with pass pills among themselves, but none of them leans over to ask me if I would like any.

The man sees all this and makes mental notes.

He continues to stare, rebuffs some friends who wander over to chat and brushes off the overtures of two women, but makes no effort to speak to me. He's immobilized with fear. He has started to walk over to me a hundred times and can't. Almost two hours pass without him leaving his place against the wall, even to get another beer.

Finally, he can't wait a minute longer, and walks down the hall.

I notice that he's left for the moment, and I see him enter the bathroom. Sensing the act is faintly, purposely malicious toward him—and enjoying it—I yawn, get up from the floor where I've been sitting cross-legged, say a few rushed good-byes and go home.

✠

I have no idea that he has been on the phone describing me, asking everyone who I am and where he can find me again. He knows my name, now. He's become obsessed with finding me and is single-minded in his pursuit. He prowls the usual hangouts, driving from place to place with someone who says he knows Valerie's roommate (but not where she lives), ringing doorbells, crashing parties and waiting in coffee houses, scanning crowds, watching doors, asking questions, speculating on who my friends are, and where they might be found.

"She's a stuck-up bitch, man," his exasperated companion tells him, again. "She thinks she's too good for everyone. And, she's got a mean mouth on her. Seriously. Don't give her the satisfaction of cutting you down. *I* wouldn't."

He steers the car onto a side street, and cranes his neck to read the house numbers. They're looking for a party—or to at least be told where one is. They're looking for me. They think they'll try an apartment that someone earlier today said is Valerie's.

Henry now knows that she's my best friend.

"Did you hear what she said to Eddie?" He exchanges looks with his girlfriend who makes a face as if she's heard the story before. He turns around to Henry who is impassively looking out the window in the back seat. "When he tried to put the moves on her, she asked him if he was doing cocaine, right? Because she said an ego like his 'does not occur in nature'." He says it in a high mincing voice. He interrupts himself to ask rhetorically: "Who *talks* like that, huh?" He continues: "So then she says to him, '*There*fore, I conclude that you must be artificially ego-enhanced.' *Ego*-enhanced. Snooty bitch. Like her point was: who the hell did Eddie think he was, to ask her out?"

He does not mention to Henry that I once turned him down too, nor does he tell Henry what I said to him to send him scurrying away. Instead, he mimics me by tossing his head with his nose in the air, and flipping his hair over his shoulders. He mutters, "*There*fore I con*clude*! *THEREFORE* myew-myew-myew-myew-myew-I'm-a-snooty-little-bitch . . . "

Henry snorts and hoots and slaps his thigh. He can just see the look on Eddie's cocky face. Eddie definitely had it coming, but the story increases his terror of me. This isn't the first one he's heard. I'm leaving them strewn behind me, and word is getting around.

"He probably had his hand down her shirt, knowing Eddie. He's a slob." Henry is still chuckling. "He was probably also doing cocaine. So did it shut him up?"

"Nothing shuts Eddie up," the girlfriend remarks. "That came close, though. Hee hee."

"Well, I don't like her," the friend tells Henry (and his own pride) indignantly. "I don't even *care* how hot she is."

He realizes what he just said. "I don't *personally* think she's hot," he says to his girlfriend. "I *personally* prefer brunettes, like you."

"Nice catch," she answers ominously, staring at him. Then she addresses them both: "Would somebody please tell me what the big deal is about this girl? Seriously. She's okay, but she's not *that* pretty. She just has every guy in the world *thinking* that she is for some reason." Then she mutters, "Men are such morons. Honest to God."

"She's a goddess," Henry says. The statement does not invite discussion or rebuttal. Then he leans over and whispers in sing-song, "*You're* just *jeal*-ous . . . " She reaches back and whacks him over the head with her purse. He ducks and laughs.

Her boyfriend chooses to ignore the question. He can think of no response that won't get him into trouble. He pulls the car in front of a fire hydrant and parks (it doesn't matter because he doesn't pay parking tickets anyway). He turns around to Henry irritably.

I'm getting sick of being your damn chauffeur. Get your car fixed. Okay?"

Henry rolls his eyes and salutes with his middle finger.

The party was weeks ago. Now, on this night, I'm sprawled on the couch, barefoot, with my hair tied up in a messy knot. I'm waiting for Valerie to take her turn at chess while, in the background, the stereo plays *Abbey Road* by the Beatles.

The doorbell buzzes. Valerie hops to her feet and ushers in an acquaintance of her roommate, who has left for the evening. We know him by name and by sight from parties. His girlfriend smiles—we know her slightly too. It's unusual that they should have come here, but not altogether surprising. Weekends in our town are always spent dropping in on anyone we know with his or her own apartment, ringing doorbells, looking for parties. Our entire crowd mills around in this manner.

"Just looking around for something to do," he says. "Is anything going on tonight that you know about? Any parties?"

Valerie shakes her head and waves them through the door, grateful. They have just spared us the hassle of going out and actively searching for something to do. That would have required putting on shoes.

"Come in for some wine," she says.

Following behind them is the young man I saw at that party. His name, we learn, is Michael. There's nothing unusual in his expression when his eyes fall on me, except that he looks away as if I'm of no concern to him.

They all settle in on the few pieces of cast-off furniture Valerie can offer them, or sit cross-legged on the floor. One of them lights a joint.

I go to the stereo to select some music while they smoke without me. Michael offers me a hit, and I shake my head and turn back to flipping through the record albums looking for something to play. Michael doesn't ask why I don't smoke pot, but he kind of likes it for some reason. He kind of thinks he would probably scold me if I said 'yes'.

"Stones!" Michael calls out. I'm about to place a record on the turntable, but hesitate and put it back in its jacket. I find an album by the Rolling Stones and play it one time, for him.

Even though Valerie has a boyfriend and isn't interested in Michael (at least as far as I can tell), she appears to be flirting, and looks flattered when he flirts back. I'm not interested in him either, really, but the flirting bothers me. I say to myself that I'm angry with Valerie on behalf of her boyfriend who is working tonight. Beneath that, though, it's more personal. It's as though Michael is supposed to notice *me*, and the fact that he doesn't is vaguely insulting. Wasn't it *me* he stared at all night, that time?

Where's *mine*? I think to myself. Nowhere, evidently. He ignores me.

I aim toward Michael a number of off-handed remarks that I

consider witty. There is no change in his expression. When I speak to him directly, his responses are polite and reserved.

With Valerie he's completely goofy. The two of them are now talking to each other with sock puppets in Warner Brothers cartoon voices. Earlier, they had been singing "I Am The Walrus" with chop sticks up their noses.

I don't know what to make of this. Men never ignore me.

I decide I want Michael to ask me for a date so I can turn him down. I'd enjoy that because he needs to be taken down a notch, I think. I have nothing in particular I can point to to support this except, perhaps, that he's paying me no attention, but there it is. I'd like to punish him for that. At least I think that's what it is. There is no other explanation for this compulsion I have to make him want me desperately so I can reject him.

"You're such a bitch with men," Valerie remarks when I confide in her in the kitchen. The marijuana is gone, and everyone is hungry. We scrounge for something edible to serve, finding only peanut butter and stale potato chips.

She doesn't care, really, if I'm a bitch or if I'm not. If that's the way I came, it's fine with her. But I do have my moments, usually around men, and Valerie feels it's worthy of note at times. I don't take offense when she periodically reminds me.

"And a vain one. He likes *me*. In fact, I might just pounce him. I think he's cute."

"I am *not* a bitch."

"Honey, I love you, but *you* are a *bitch*."

"I am *not*. I'm just misunderstood, that's all." My "that's all" trails off into a pouting lower lip.

"Aren't we all."

She dumps the potato chips into a cracked bowl while I repeatedly slam an ice tray on the counter. She then commences a fruitless search through the cabinets for glasses that are clean. She can't find any primarily because she hasn't washed a dish in days, perhaps weeks, and her roommate hasn't washed them either. Valerie keeps reaching into higher cabinets, patting the shelves and feeling around for something she might have missed. She hoists herself up onto the counter, nudges the mess aside with her bare foot, stands there with her head brushing the ceiling and conducts a final, futile inspection of the dusty, uppermost shelves.

"Be brave, men," she says as she jumps down. "We'll just have to wash them."

I look with revulsion at the pile of dirty dishes in the sink.

"Ew. Not me. Too gross." I put the ice tray back in the freezer, grab the bowl of potato chips and carry it into the living room. "Nice try though," I call over my shoulder.

"Another fine vintage from the makers of Ipecac. Bottoms up. No pun intended." Valerie, underage, passes out bottles of 89 cent apple wine from her illegally-procured soda-pop wine stash as if they were party favors. "No glasses," she adds.

"No problem," says Michael, accepting his wine with very charming mock hauteur. "I prefer to suck this particular brand from the bottle." He uncaps his, and takes a long swig.

Valerie settles in on the rug beside him and gives him her biggest dimpled smile.

I don't know why that irritates me.

Michael asks how old I am, phrasing his question so we'll think he's more interested in obtaining facts about Valerie, and is merely asking me as a polite afterthought. I truthfully tell him my age.

I'm six years younger than he is. His eyes flicker just a little, and he scratches his chin. Jail bait. Shit. He's thinking that I'm the very same age as the little uniformed girls at the Catholic High School, and that I could be one of them. He imagines me in a plaid uniform and saddle shoes, and comes up with a few ribald comments he plans to make later, when he is among his male friends.

Then he shudders at the thought of giggling girl conversations. There are midnight curfews. He can't bring me into a bar. There is always the threat of being charged with statutory rape. Of course, he is *so* looking forward to meeting the parents, God help him. ("Yes sir. Your fresh-faced teenaged daughter will be perfectly safe with me—I only intend to ravage and seduce her at the very first opportunity. School sir? Finished, sir. Yes, sir. I *am* too old for your daughter, sir. Job sir? Sort of. I'm a musician, sir. I'm in a band. No, sir. We haven't actually been paid yet. *Real* job? I won't cut my hair as a matter of principle so, of course, no one will hire me for a *real* job and there's no point in looking. But if one were to reach out and grab me, I'd probably show up for work, unless I had a hangover. Army sir? Why no, sir. I happened to duck the draft a few years ago by showing up for my physical totally wasted on LSD. It's a hallucenogenic, sir. So I was exhibiting signs of schizoid behavior at the time of my interview—which was pretty darn lucky for *me*, don't you agree, sir? They threw me out and referred me to a shrink. Hell no I won't go! There's a war on, you know, and someone has to stay home to take care of the women. Old joke, sir. Ha ha. Yes sir. Yes *sir*. I see the door, sir. Goodbye, sir.") And he couldn't even take me to Summerfest in Milwaukee for fear of getting stopped for a traffic violation, then being jailed for crossing state lines with a minor. This all runs through his mind in a continuous loop fought down by two words: "I want."

He nervously taps his fingers on the table in time with his thoughts: She's the one. I know it. God help me. I'm sunk. Oh shit.

I only want to sleep with her, he reminds himself. I probably wouldn't even call her again. It's just sexual attraction gone a little haywire. That's all. It'll pass.

But he sees my profile and notices a tendril of hair curling over my cheek, and he feels a tug in his chest. He wants to brush the curl over my ear. He has never been this stirred before.

She's incredibly beautiful, he thinks. That's all it is. I turn in his direction and catch him looking at me. He looks away with an expression of boredom and disdain. *God*, I hate that! I run my hand over my hair, fretting suddenly, because he doesn't like me or think I'm pretty. I'm even thinking that I *wouldn't* turn him down, if he were to ask me out. He wouldn't do that, though, I remind myself. He likes Valerie.

Those two are having a little too much fun together, I think. Two couples, and me. I'm always the odd one. I bristle suddenly, because I'm being left out, and because Valerie is being just a little too charming for someone who has a boyfriend.

I'm angry with Michael, suddenly, because he seems to be taken in by it all.

I don't understand why he doesn't notice me.

I can't tell that he has spent the entire evening watching me from the corner of his eye, and that he's being charming for my benefit, not Valerie's. I don't suspect that he's spent weeks trying to find me, and that the visit this evening was solely to see if I might be here. I have no suspicion that he doesn't have the courage to ask me for a date, and doesn't mind that my hair is a mess.

I run to the bathroom to tuck in some tendrils and to quickly apply some mascara and blusher I find in the medicine cabinet.

He notices that I've done this. He notices everything. It strikes him as a positive sign, but he can't make himself speak to me directly, or even look at me. He finishes off his bottle of wine, then uncaps another. ("Look everyone!" Valerie observes. "He can even walk without falling. He exhibits virtually no evidence of intoxication at all. Very manly of you, Michael, my friend. You're a very manly man. *More* than a man, in fact." She waves her bottle and solemnly taps her chest and gives him a mischievous flash of her eyes. "A *prince*! A *princely* man!" That said, and with a coquettish smile, Valerie coaxes Michael into supplying her with next week's wine stash. Michael, helpless in the face of flattery, however coersive or contrived, darts out to the corner liquor store and comes back with several bottles of the more "upscale" $1.19 wine to impress me.)

He waits for nerve to hit him, postponing his move just a little longer, and then a little more.

The evening passes. It's now late, and he still has barely acknowledged me.

Valerie can have him, I decide. I have to go home.

He sees me walk into the kitchen to get a drink of water. It's now. It has to be now. It's getting close to midnight, and I've said I have to leave. He's gripped by a growing sense of helpless urgency. He can't screw this up.

He follows me and stops in the doorway.

He doesn't seem at all terrified of me as he stands there filling the doorway, blocking my exit. There isn't the smallest of hints that his stomach has sunk to his knees and then rebounded into his throat. He has a remarkable ability to hide his feelings when he chooses to.

I smile at him politely, and he approaches a step, but he doesn't say anything. His eyes catch mine and hold them.

I can't look away.

All of my defenses are now on alert. I don't like this. I don't like his eyes and the way they grab *my* eyes. It's worse than feeling undressed. I feel violated and threatened. He's gotten into my "space", so to speak, and I feel panicky, as if I'm suffocating. I pull my eyes away, and yawn to cover up my nervousness.

The spell is broken.

"So, Kiddo, how've you been?" Michael asks pleasantly. He tilts his head and raises an eyebrow.

"Since the living room, a minute ago?" This is marginally better than silence, but I'd still rather be somewhere else.

He shrugs. "Since that party. Since whenever. Just making polite conversation is all. Just being conversational . . . " He hears himself and winces.

He's between the door and me. I don't know how to get past him and out of here, and I'm sorry I wished he would like me. I didn't mean it. He's large. He's old. He does that thing with his eyes. I've changed my mind. I need to go away now because my throat is closing. I'm afraid.

I'm so much braver in theory.

"In that case, I've been wonderfully well, thank you." I dip my head politely. "And you?" I keep looking at the doorway, then at him.

"Good," he says, nodding. "I've been good."

"Good. That's good. That you've been . . . you know . . . *good,* and everything . . ."

"Yeah."

"Yeah . . . " We're both nodding helplessly and looking around the kitchen for a topic of conversation. None seems to present itself.

I look at my watch. "Scintillating though this conversation *is*, I really have to go—"

"Where does a bubble-headed teenager learn a two dollar word like 'scintillating'?"

He moves a step closer to me.

"I'm literate. I read."

I move a step backward, away from him. I've just backed into the sink and knocked into a pan. The sound startles me so I jump, but I quickly recover.

"Besides, that word's only worth a dollar. I've got much better words than that." Whenever I'm frightened I get defensive and antagonistic, and I can feel "attitude" creeping into my voice, now: "I also take exception to being referred to as bubble-headed."

I point my finger threateningly, as if a finger could save me from this large man.

He grabs my finger as if to intercept it, but he doesn't let go. He runs his thumb lightly along the side of it, up and down.

What was that game in there with Valerie? When did he decide it was *me* that he liked?

What do I do now?

I feel a little nauseated. My heart is pounding; I can hear it in my ears. My eyelid begins to twitch.

"Why aren't you snapping gum like every other bubble-headed teenager, instead of reading books and playing chess?" His voice is low, a purr, a caress. He's aiming those eyes again. I look down, then up and over his shoulder to avoid his eyes and to shake the panic.

My defenses have me prepared to insult him, or to argue with anything he says until he clears away from that door so I can leave.

"I can snap when I want to. I can even snap and read at the same time." I can hear the hard edge in my voice. "I happen to be a multi-talented individual. With a little extra effort, I expect to be able to read, snap gum and tap dance." I turn my eyes back to him, narrow them, and yank my finger away.

Why do I do this? Why do I freeze up and antagonize people? The smallest threat of potential (not even *probable*) intimacy sends me screaming. Even when I like a guy, I can't stop my mouth. It's as if there's something in me that's determined to drive men away.

Any other girl would have been able to stay calm, bat her eyelashes (or do whatever it is that *normal* girls do at a time like this) and let him hold her hand. Not me. My heart sinks. There's something wrong with me. I look up at Michael, and I know it's true. I can't do this right. I can flirt, and I can summon men with just a look and juggle a dozen of them all at once, but I can't handle one, alone. I never can. I always have excuses like, "it's just *this* guy who's wrong for me", or "it's just *this* situation that's scary", but really, I've never been able to do it, not even once.

He hates me. I know he really must. Even if he doesn't now, he *would* hate me eventually. Sooner or later, he would figure out that I'm not as good as other girls and leave me for somebody else. It's safest to never get involved in the first place.

"Not very impressive, really, unless you can twirl plates at the same time. Can you twirl plates?"

"Nope. But I can *hurl* them. Do you want to see?" I reach for a plate in the sink, and pretend to aim it at him. Involuntarily, I smile at him and relax just a little. All of a sudden, this isn't a serious pursuit, and he isn't as scary. It's play.

Michael ducks his head, pretending to dodge the plate. "I have a feeling that you have the potential to be an exceptionally talented plate hurler," he says brightly, "but it's not good enough. You really ought to consider giving the whole thing up."

"I *won't*," I retort with narrowed eyes. "It's my *dream*." I stick my chin in the air defiantly.

Then I break into a giggle.

Grinning, Michael is thoroughly charmed. Some guys like women with blond hair or pouting lips. He, however, is fatally attracted to women who sass him back. He has no idea why that is.

Silently, without resistance, soul-searching or question, and without making me aware that he is doing so, he simply relinquishes himself to me. He is in my hands now, but I don't suspect this, even a little.

He wonders if he should cut his hair and look for a job. He'll need to, if he expects to buy me dinner and birthday presents, and take me to concerts. *Please* don't let her turn me down, he thinks. *Please*.

I don't know how to interpret that funny smile, or the look on his face. I decide he must be really drunk.

He thinks: Her eyes. He's never seen eyes that could do that to him. He wants to sink into them. He wants me to look into his eyes again, but I won't.

He likes a challenge.

"You'll never find a person who can crack gum and also appear to be intelligent," he warns me. "In fact, gum cracking is an automatic 20 point deduction from your IQ. Don't ever do it around me. I hate it."

"So if I snap my gum three times, I'll be as smart as you?" *Stop it*! Why do I *do* this? I bite my lower lip.

He throws back his head, and he laughs.

"You really *are* a bitch," he says approvingly, admiringly. "But I was warned in advance."

"Who called me a bitch?"

"Everyone calls you a bitch. They say your name, and then they say 'the bitch'. Everyone." His eyes are twinkling.

"You lie," I say, but I know he's telling the truth. My shoulders slump a little, and I pull myself into a pose I believe is cool, cocky and defiant. It only succeeds in making me look younger and more vulnerable.

Damn, she's cute, he thinks. Damn.

I'm feeling very nervous and edgy again. I stiffen and narrow my eyes at him. He obviously doesn't like me, seeing as he thinks I'm a bitch, but he won't move away from that door so I can remove my bitchy self from this room. It would be impolite to scream and run past him, but I give it a moment's consideration.

"A pretty bitch can get anything she wants." Michael says. More softly he asks, "Did you know that?"

"Then I want a million bucks," I shoot back.

He sighs dramatically. "If I had it, it would be yours, my dear lady." He bows at the waist with a flourish, then reaches for my hand, which he smoothly, gently presses to his lips. "That, and much more. I kid you not."

"Actually, that's okay. I think I'd probably rather have a driver's license anyway."

He stops short, exasperated and incredulous.

"*What?* You can't even *drive,* for chrissake?" He's not sure he's ready for a 17-year old. He thought he was years past this sort of inconvenience. His car needs $400 worth of work and I live 20 miles away from him. He'd expected *me* to provide transportation. He will *not* pick me up and transport me on the bus. He does not take public transportation under any circumstances. What a *pain* this all is.

"We don't have a car," I answer.

God help him. The hair has to go. He needs a job.

She hasn't said yes, he reminds himself.

His parents have a car: a '64 Chevy station wagon. It's completely uncool. It will have to do until he can hustle the money to fix his own, or get a paycheck. He has weighed being "cool" against not seeing me at all or insulting me with public transportation, and has opted for the Chevy. Earlier in the evening, he would have guessed that it was more important to be "cool". But things change.

"I'll just have to teach you," he says.

"Where have I heard *that* before?" I ask. "You wouldn't have the nerve. You'd never survive it." I roll my eyes.

Suddenly, impulsively, he kisses me while my eyes are rolling, bobbing his head toward me sharply as if he thinks I might dart away. I might very well have done that, had he not taken me so thoroughly by surprise. I feel myself starting to sink into him with a sense of almost joyous relief, while the irrational, frightened part of me screams *"No!"*

✠

And so it goes, I am thinking from this over-level. There we are again, but how can I allow it? I have so much anger, still, and I cannot be certain I am able to set it aside. I can make things worse than they are, not better, and pull both of us down with my fury and resentment. Then, there is his temper. Has it improved? Or will he turn on me again?

This is unwise. It is too soon.

Furthermore, there is the trauma. I am correct in suspecting that there is something wrong with me. My trust was broken, and my fear is too strong to be reasoned away. It needs to be loved away, but I do not ever allow anyone near enough to do that. I cannot. I cannot risk further harm.

Can I handle his problems? Can he handle mine? I do not think so. I do not know if either of us has anything to spare the other.

I have fulfilled my obligation to him. I have appeared, and we have met. I owe him nothing more than the decision that I am ready to return to him—or I am not. I am now free to leave and to never see him again in this life.

In this moment, my final moment of unburdened choice, I should have the power to edge away from him, and to walk out without a backward glance. I just need to back away and walk out. *Now!* I say to myself: *Run!* It is what I had planned to do. It is, in fact, what I had already done before he hunted me down and cornered me.

But I stay.

✠

As terrified as I am, I don't pull away. I don't leave. I let him kiss me, and when he asks me for my phone number, nuzzling my ear, I find a pen on the kitchen counter, and a paper napkin, and I obediently write it down.

The internal alarm is going off again. It's telling me to run away, but it won't say why I should. I suspect I know the reason. I know instinctively that this one will want to stay. I don't allow any of them to stay—I can't. Maintaining a relationship with a man is the one thing I cannot do well, or perhaps, cannot do at all. Even at 17, I already suspect this. I'm more afraid of boys—of men—than other girls my age, and I don't know why that is, or what I can do to fix it.

Perversely, I hand him my phone number anyway with rising anxiety, a fluttering stomach, and a sense of resignation. I know with absolute certainty that he will call and that I have initiated something that will not be completed for years, if ever. I have somehow signed on for a tour of duty in the simple act of handing this man a paper napkin.

Or, perhaps I've sold myself to the devil. Was that napkin a contract? Is this man the devil? I've read too many books, I think. I have too vivid an imagination, I know, because I look into his eyes again, and have a sudden flash of peculiar imagery that, like the devil himself, this stranger came tonight to claim my soul.

APPENDIX

ANNE BOLEYN'S FINAL SPEECH

East Smithfield (Tower) Green
May 19, 1536

"Good Christian people, I am come hither to die, according to law, and therefore I will speak nothing against it. I come here only to die, and thus to yield myself humbly to the will of the King, my lord. And if, in life, I did ever offend the King's Grace, surely with my death, I do now atone. I come hither to accuse no man, nor to speak anything of that whereof I am accused, as I know full well that aught I say in my defense doth not appertain to you. I pray and beseech you all, good friends, to pray for the life of the King, my sovereign lord and yours, who is one of the best princes on the face of the earth, who has always treated me so well that better could not be, wherefore I submit to death with good will, humbly asking pardon of the world. If any person will meddle with my cause, I require them to judge the best. Thus, I take my leave of the world, and of you, and I heartily desire you all to pray for me."

INFORMATION SOURCES/ HISTORICAL DISCREPANCIES

- Folklore has always given Anne six fingers. There isn't much evidence to support this legend, or to suggest that she really had a huge "wen" on her neck. All her biographies concluded that she probably did not have either one but there is no solid proof either way.

- There is no proof of the order in which the Boleyn (or "Bullen") siblings were born. Various references each prefer a different birth order, and no two agree. The most supportable and convincing evidence, noted in "Anne Boleyn" by E. W. Ives, favored a birth order of Mary, then Anne, then George. (There were two additional Boleyn infants who died.) This book also favors a birth year of 1501 (versus 1507), a date that is further supported by an example of Anne's handwriting in 1514 (shown in "The Rise and Fall of Anne Boleyn" by Retha M. Warnicke). The handwriting sample is unmistakably that of a young adult because it has small, tightly controlled and evenly formed letters. A child of seven, no matter how intelligent, would only have the mechanical ability to write in a large, uneven scrawl.

- There was a rumor (unverified) that Anne Boleyn was raped by one of her father's officers at Hever when she was seven (I placed the rape in France instead, to make the situation more traumatic for her). Only

Alison Weir even mentions this in passing, but she then dismisses the rumor as untrue. There has never been any hard evidence, even in the midst of rampant speculation and very close scrutiny, that Anne was ever intimate with anyone but her husband. Despite this, considering the times, premarital chastity was highly improbable. What is known about Anne is that she a) was not a virgin when she married (only Karen Lindsey suggested she was), b) conceived immediately after commencing relations with Henry, and, c) was regularly pregnant thereafter. Her obvious fertility would not have allowed for much illicit premarital sex leaving the child molestation theory still open to explain her lost virginity, particularly for a work of fiction. The two men she was most likely to have been with, Lord Henry Percy and Sir Thomas Wyatt, both survived the accusations and the interrogation prior to her execution for adultery. Whether this is because they were innocent or useful to the Crown is unknown.

- Anne Boleyn was not listed as a passenger on the ship that carried Mary Tudor and her entourage to France. "Mistress" Boleyn was. There are three possible explanations. One is that "Mistress" pertained to the older Boleyn sibling, while the younger sister was insignificant and not worthy of mention on the ship's passenger list. Another was that it was simply an oversight. The last was that Anne went directly from the Netherlands (where she had been living) to France by land. This last explanation is most plausible. However, I preferred the first explanations after seeing the size of Anne's bedroom at Hever Castle, and because I had reason to want to make her arrival in France a bleak one.

- Anne Boleyn's love affair with Lord Henry Percy is recorded as having been kept secret, whereas in *"Threads"*, it was more or less carried out in public. In addition, their "goodbye" meeting is entirely fictitious (unless something of the kind was done in secret, as in the story). The king did not allow them to say goodbye, in fact, Alison Weir mentions that Anne's parents locked her in her room to prevent her from trying to contact Percy, as she was frantic to do. I let them say goodbye primarily to develop Hal's character and to explore the effect King Henry's decision had on the couple. Percy did send a note to Anne begging her to never love anyone else, and history suggests she gamely made the effort, as Henry soon found out. *How* soon is another matter open to conjecture. Some references suggest that he did not openly pursue Anne for as long as one to four years after her betrothal to Percy was broken. Others mention that they had had a courtly flirtation for years, and that it may have grown serious from Henry's perspective even as he kept Anne's sister Mary as his mistress. However, exact dates are unknown.

- According to Karen Lindsey, only one person suggested that the betrothal of Percy and Anne Boleyn was broken at Henry's command rather than Wolsey's (as noted by the official version). However, that one person was a close and trusted servant of Wolsey, and a reliable source. Lindsey states it would have been in keeping with Henry's personality to take measures to shift the blame to Wolsey in order to deflect Anne's resulting anger.

- Other information is speculative, and *could* be true, but probably isn't. According to legend, Henry VIII wrote the song, "Greensleeves". However, some Encyclopedia sources place the date of the song's composition somewhere in the 17th century, perhaps 100 years after he died. Other references claim it was first printed in 1580 by Richard Jones, who specialized in ballad printing. Some sources point out that the song contains elements that were not popular until later in the 16th century, about the time of the first printing and years after the death of Henry VIII. Either way, it was noted that Henry VIII, while being a most enthusiastic musician, primarily made small changes to existing songs, then claimed them as his own. Most of his own songs sound very much alike (and nothing at all like Greensleeves), and he is not viewed historically as someone who had the talent to write a song of that caliber. Historical references suggest that Anne Boleyn, by all accounts, *did* have that kind of talent. I wanted to make the strong point that Anne lost everything, even credit for her talent and creativity, when she married Henry VIII. I do not know-or presume-that she wrote Greensleeves.

- To the best of my knowledge, none of Anne's songs survive, except for one, "O Death, Rock Me Asleep", with music written by her chaplain after her death. However, the source of both the lyrics and the music is in question. It is only known that the poem was found in the Tower immediately after Anne's death, and that it was later put to music.

- Anne had a fourth pregnancy I didn't mention in the book, resulting in another stillbirth.

- There are some theories about the health of Henry VIII. One was that he had scurvy because of his notoriously meat-heavy diet. Another is that he, his siblings and his offspring, suffered from diabetes. Still another was that he suffered from syphilis. His body was last exhumed in 1812 before any conclusive tests were available. However, there was an epidemic of syphilis in Europe during the 1500's, and the symptoms of syphilis listed by The New Complete Medical and Health Encyclopedia (published by Lexicon) somewhat match the health ailments Henry VIII experienced in his lifetime. In particular, the changes in his personality and mental state from the start to the end of his reign make syphilis possible. Katherine of Aragon, his first wife, was known to have suffered from a "mysterious female ailment" that might possibly have been related to infection. In addition, infants born to infected mothers can be stillborn, die shortly after birth, or suffer health ailments that can lead to death years later. Henry VIII admittedly had some trouble fathering viable infants, and produced children with all of the aforementioned results. Syphilis is one possible cause. However, there is also nothing to prevent someone from suffering from two or more of these ailments at once, and nothing more substantial than speculation to support any theory at the present time.

- According to Eric W. Ives, her executioner was so taken by Anne that he was shaken, and found it difficult to proceed with the execution. In order to distract her, he shouted, “Where is my sword?” just before killing her so that Anne could die thinking she had a few seconds more to live.

Additional information and resources about the Tudors are available at www.nellgavin.com.

BIBLIOGRAPHY

"*The Six Wives of Henry VIII*" by Alison Weir
"*Anne Boleyn*" by Eric W. Ives
"*Mistress Anne*" by Carolly Erickson
"*Divorced, Beheaded, Survived* by Karen Lindsey
The Rise and Fall of Anne Boleyn" by Retha M. Warnicke
"*Everyday Life in Renaissance Times*" by E. R. Chamberlin
"*The Royal Palaces of Tudor England: Architecture and Court Life 1460-1547*" by Simon Thurley
"*The New Complete Medical and Health Encyclopedia*" published by Lexicon

THE AUTHOR

Nell Gavin lives with her husband and two children in Texas. The older of her children created the original artwork that Nell enhanced for the cover of this book. It was inspired, he said, by a dream.

Printed in the United States
22305LVS00002B/181-195

9 780741 409164